Bradley Bay

by

Ana P. Corman

ISBN: 0-75965-092-6

This book is printed on acid free paper.

1stBooks – rev. 09/28/01

To my Catherine:

I thank you,

For strengthening my lions courage.
For inspiring my scarecrows brain.
And for being the flame in this tin womans heart.

I dedicate this book to you.

For all the dreams you have nurtured from my cocoon.
For all the butterflies you have set free from my imagination.
And for all the wishes you have made come true.

*I also dedicate this book to all my spinal
cord-injured patients that taught me the
true meaning of patience, perseverance and hope.*

*I want to thank my editor, Geneviève Duboscq, for all the
professional direction she gave me that helped add dimension
and depth to my story like I never imagined. She helped me to
gather the proper tools for my writer's toolbox that allowed me
to grow with my characters. I thank her for helping me to shape
my dreams into the novel you hold in your hands.*

⚙ 1

Sierra punched in her four-digit security code then pushed through the large double doors labeled Neurosurgical Intensive Care Unit. She was just about to step into the staff lounge when she saw the flurry of activity in room number five. The night nurse flipped through several pages of admission orders and blew a strand of hair away from her face in frustration. She stood up straight and rubbed her dry eyes as she saw Sierra watching her. She motioned her hand towards the bustling activity behind her and gave Sierra a weary smile.

"Good morning, Sierra. Have I got a patient for you!"

Sierra leaned back against the doorframe as she watched the nurse pick up the phone and talk to a pharmacist about the patient's medications. Sierra passed her lunch bag from one hand to the other and watched the residents hovering around the patient, competing for space with the lab tech, X-ray tech, and EKG tech.

Sierra could feel the headache pulsating at her temples as she closed her eyes and willed it to stop vibrating like a crazed tuning fork. She massaged her left temple with her free hand as her thoughts raced through her mind. *I'm in no mood for a crash and burn patient today. Please Lord, not today of all days. I slept for four hours and cried for another four. My patience is thin, and I don't have the energy to be sharp this morning.*

Several other day nurses greeted Sierra in the doorway and stepped past her into the staff lounge. Sierra was about to follow them in when she saw her dear friend, Sydney, approach with a huge smile that took a slight chill off Sierra's icy mood. Sydney walked with the sleek movements of a predator seeking out its prey as her short, dark brown hair bounced in intentional disarray around her pretty face. Her chocolate brown eyes always shone with mischief; Sierra had learned early in their friendship that Sydney enjoyed being the class clown. Sierra wasn't sure if that was to hide from past pains or to cover up the insecurities that Sydney refused to believe she had.

"Good morning, Sierra."

"Hi, Syd. I'm not so sure it's a good morning." Sierra stretched her slender five-foot-four-inch frame and gave Sydney a warm hug.

Sydney released Sierra and noticed the bedlam unfolding in room five. They exchanged a frown, knowing the kind of day that awaited them. Sydney placed her hand on Sierra's shoulder. "Think of the bright side, Sierra. After today you're on vacation for two weeks, you lucky dog you."

Sierra smiled and shook her head as they both headed into the staff lounge. "Some vacation. My relationship ended three months ago. My ex-lover is coming over today to move the last of her things out of my house and our long-awaited trip to the Cayman Islands has been cancelled! I'm going to spend the next two weeks sulking, depressed, and driving everyone around me nuts. I plan on bingeing on ice cream and peanut butter and jelly sandwiches, Sydney, so don't try to talk me out of my dietary suicidal ideation's."

Sydney laughed as she watched Sierra slip her lunch into the fridge and lean back against the closed door, closing her brilliant blue-gray eyes and massaging her temples.

Sydney had met Sierra five years before when she first started working in the neurosurgical intensive care unit. They instantly connected and became close friends, a friendship that Sydney cherished. Sydney realized early that she was very attracted to Sierra. Her smooth, olive complexion enhanced the depth of her unique teardrop, blue-gray eyes. Her chestnut brown hair feathered lightly around her face and tumbled onto her slender shoulders. Sydney always admired her professional, no nonsense attitude and strove to make Sierra laugh. Sydney was well aware of Sierra's troubled relationship as they spent hours sharing their innermost feelings.

It was one of those heartfelt talks that floated into Sydney's mind as she watched Sierra. "She is so inattentive to you and your needs, Sierra! She takes you and your relationship for granted. She has no idea what a good thing she has. You deserve better, Sierra. You deserve someone that realizes what a fabulous woman you are," Sydney stated firmly, shocking herself with the intensity of her words.

Sydney bounded from the couch and stood staring out of Sierra's living room bay window. She sensed Sierra even before she touched her shoulder.

"Sydney, I'm sorry. I had no idea you felt that way."

Sydney laughed halfheartedly as she turned to see the tears in Sierra's glimmering eyes.

"The whole time I've been leaning on you as a friend and telling you all about my empty relationship and I had no idea you had feelings for me."

"I didn't want you to know, Sierra. I've been trying hard just to be your friend and respect the fact that you belong to someone else even though that someone else is not worthy of you." Sydney slowly touched her thumb to the warm tear slipping down Sierra's cheek. "I also realized that you had no idea how I felt because you don't feel the same way about me as I feel about you."

Sierra dropped her face and struggled to find the right words.

Sydney touched her thumb to Sierra's chin and raised her friend's face to meet her eyes. "It's not something to feel bad about, Sierra. I believe we have no control over who we are and are not attracted to. It just happens. Chemistry is a strange thing. Especially when it's one sided."

"I never meant to hurt you, Sydney. Your friendship has always been near and dear to me. I would never want to lose that."

Sydney gently guided Sierra into her arms and held her tight. "You're never going to lose me, Sierra. If all you can give me is your friendship, then I feel blessed for that gift from you. I would never do anything to jeopardize that."

Sierra nodded her head slowly as Sydney felt her warm tears against her neck. Sydney tilted Sierra's head and kissed her forehead. "Just give me time to get over you, Sierra. It may take the rest of my sorry life, but I vow someday to tell you that you mean nothing to me."

Sierra leaned back and looked into Sydney's sensitive, chocolate brown eyes. "Gee, don't go that far! I like knowing that you're smitten with me."

Sydney laughed as she hugged Sierra close. "Smitten, what the hell kind of word is that? Lady, I'm nuts about you and that's one of the reasons it infuriates me to hear about your lousy relationship with Linda. Dump the bitch, Sierra, and then give me ten years before I have to see you with another woman."

Sierra laughed as she held Sydney tight. "Regardless of the women that come and go in my life, Sydney, I cherish the thought that you will always be here to stay."

Sydney shook off the memory as she set her leather bag and jacket down on the nearest chair and faced Sierra. "Sierra, listen, I have a great idea. Do you remember my friend the E.R. doc I told you about that owns and operates that resort for spinal cord–injured adults up in Springfield, Ontario?"

Sierra gave Sydney a suspicious look and crossed her arms across her chest. "Yes. What about her?"

Sydney shook her head and leaned back against the pine table. "Don't give me such a skeptical look, Sierra. I'm trying to help you out here."

Sierra inhaled deeply and placed her hand on the arm of her dear friend. "I'm sorry, Syd. Now, what about your friend the selfless, heroic doc that dedicates her life to lifting the spirits of spinal cord–injured adults?"

Sydney squeezed Sierra's hand. "Now, that's a better attitude." They both smiled as they moved out of the way of another nurse trying to get to the fridge.

They gathered their things as Sydney guided Sierra to a quiet corner in the lounge. "My friend, the selfless, heroic doc, also known as Dr. Kaitlin Bradley, runs that resort like a well oiled clock. She's very involved in the day-to-day activities of the resort and has made it a priority to staff the place with experienced professionals. She inherited the resort from her grandparents three years ago and with it a huge inheritance. When she first converted the resort to a getaway for spinal cord-injured adults she had lots of nurses that had worked with her in the past offering to come up for short periods of time to help out. Since then Kaitlin has welcomed any nurses who wanted to come up and volunteer their time at her resort. With more help around she feels the guests get more attention and the nurses get a working vacation.

"It's a gorgeous place right on Sturgeon Lake and it's open all year round. I love going up there in the winter to cross country ski. It's only three hours north of Toronto, and she gives you a free room and feeds you three delicious, warm meals a day for helping her out."

Sierra studied Sydney carefully as she slipped into her lab coat and hung her black Littmann stethoscope around her neck. "How is that different from prison, Syd?"

Sydney burst into laughter and gently smacked Sierra's arm with the bell of her stethoscope. "Get serious, Sierra!"

Sierra playfully rubbed her arm and grimaced at Sydney. "I am serious, Sydney. I need a vacation, not another job!"

Sydney smiled and reached inside her brown leather bag for her pocket protector full of pens, pencils and a pair of bandage scissors. "Wake up, Sierra. You just said you're going to spend two weeks mourning your relationship with Linda that should have ended a long time ago. What a waste of precious vacation time."

Sierra gave Sydney a disapproving frown as she slumped into the nearest chair. She wasn't in the mood to tell Sydney that she was right. She'd rather wallow in the despair of her shattered relationship and cancelled vacation.

Sydney knelt before Sierra and rested her hands on her knees. "I'm sorry, Sierra, but you know I'm so grateful that you finally dumped Linda three months ago. Now it's time for you to get on with your life. I'm sure Kaitlin could really use your help and expertise and it would be the much needed break you deserve from Toronto and from Linda, the good for nothing wench."

Sierra's blood instantly boiled as she sat bolt upright in the chair and leaned menacingly close to Sydney as she whispered, "Stop it, Sydney! I won't have you talk about Linda like that. I spent three years of my life with her and whatever your opinion is of her you fail to remember that I did love her." Tears welled in Sierra's beautiful blue-gray eyes as she shot Sydney an icy stare.

Sydney dropped her head and felt consumed by prickly remorse. She took a deep breath and looked back into Sierra's teary eyes. "I'm sorry, Sierra. I don't think too kindly of a woman that lies and cheats on my best friend."

Sierra wiped at her tears as the night charge nurse, Joan, stormed into the room. "All right ladies and gents, let's get shift report started so I can escape the nightmare happening out there and hand it over to you lovely, highly skilled individuals." Everyone groaned and slipped into chairs as Joan gave Sierra and Sydney an *are you guys okay* look. They both gave her a reassuring smile as Sydney sat down beside Sierra and nudged her shoulder affectionately.

"Think about my offer and let me know by the end of the day. If you decide to go, I'll call Kaitlin and tell her to expect you tomorrow, bright and early."

Sierra reached for a tissue in her pocket and dried her eyes. "I'll think about it, Sydney, but don't get your hopes up that you might be able to get rid of me for two weeks. The way this day is looking we probably won't even have time to use the rest room."

Sydney beamed her a bright smile and whispered, "Do you think that my urinary retention is a hereditary gift? No, ma'am. I have spent my entire nursing career working on seeing how long I can go without emptying my bladder before I find it resting on my sneakers." They both burst into a fit of giggles as Joan turned and gave them a look.

Joan rambled through her report and looked over her bifocals at Sierra as she came to the patient in room five. "Sierra, I've assigned you the new admission. Twenty-seven-year-old male broke into a residence last night, not expecting the owner to be asleep in his reclining chair with his shotgun at his side." They all groaned as they could see the picture run through their minds like an old movie. "The owner was awakened by the sound of breaking glass. Our patient tiptoed into the living room and was about to pick up the TV when the owner swung around in his chair and fired twice." Joan waited till the groans subsided and continued.

"Our patient was shot in the left buttocks and left lower quadrant of his abdomen. We have two entrance wounds and no exit wounds. Those bullets careened through his abdomen like a roller coaster hell-bent on derailing. One bullet completely severed his spinal cord at L-1 L-2 leaving our young burglar a complete paraplegic at the scene. We just received him from the O.R. He is intubated, ventilated and heavily sedated on morphine and ativan. They fused his spine from T-12 to L-3. They repaired a laceration on his liver, removed his ruptured spleen, removed a long section of his perforated large bowel and gave him a colostomy and last but not least, repaired a nick in his bladder. Unfortunately he continues to hemorrhage and the doc's are having a hard time finding the source of the bleeding."

She took a deep breath, carefully removed her bifocals from her face and looked at Sierra. "It doesn't look good, Sierra. His prognosis is poor, and the family is hysterical. They're all wondering how this could have happened to their lovely son." Everyone groaned and rolled their eyes as Joan mindlessly chewed on the arm of her glasses. "I've given him to you as a one-to-one. I know you will be run off your feet with him today."

Sierra headed for the door. "Like today is going to be any different than every other day in this zoo."

The remaining staff laughed as they watched Sierra head out the door to get the report from the exhausted night nurse.

CRITO CRITO CRITO

Sierra silently prayed for this unfortunate young man as she threw herself into her work, moving with the high level of intelligence and dedication of ten years of intensive care nursing. She worked closely with the surgical residents as she bolused the patient with ten liters of lactated ringers intravenously. The hours continued to speed by as she gave him eight units of packed red blood cells, five units of fresh frozen plasma, two hundred grams of albumin, and ten units of single-donor platelets. She pumped all these blood products into him one after the other and watched in frustration as he slowly poured out five liters of his own precious blood from the thin rubber drains poking through his abdominal wall like tentacles. She worked feverishly as her twenty-seven-year-old patient continued to hemorrhage and the residents tried mercilessly to stabilize the patient so they could get him back to the O.R and find the source of his bleeding. The intensity in the room was palpable as his vital signs continually deteriorated with each liter of blood Sierra emptied from his drainage canister.

Eight hours into Sierra's struggling shift, the cardiac monitor alarm went off with a shrill continuous ring. Sierra looked up at the screen and shouted, "V-TACH! Sydney, call a code and bring the crash cart in here now!"

Within seconds the room was filled with residents and nursing staff. Sierra confirmed that her patient had no pulse. A male nurse started chest compressions. The respiratory therapist disconnected the ventilator and connected an ambu bag to the patient's endotracheal tube and began to bag him with one hundred percent oxygen.

Sydney handed Sierra the defibrillator pads and watched as she slapped the two oval-shaped pads on the patient's chest. Sydney charged the defibrillator to two hundred joules. Sierra looked up at the cardiac monitor and saw that the patient's rhythm had deteriorated into an even more ominous rhythm of ventricular fibrillation.

Sydney announced, "Charged at two-hundred joules. Everyone clear? Everyone clear? Shocking at two hundred joules!" Sydney hit two buttons simultaneously on the defibrillator as everyone watched the young patient's lifeless body lurch off the bed as if he'd just landed from a fall off a tall building.

Sierra injected the patient with one milligram of epinephrine intravenously as Sydney charged the defibrillator to three hundred joules.

Sydney made sure everyone was clear as she announced, "Shocking at three hundred joules." The patient's limbs jerked off the bed and slammed down hard as the jolt of electricity raced through his body in a futile attempt to shock his erratic heart to a standstill and allow his own natural rhythm to resume. Sydney repeated the same procedure at three hundred and sixty joules.

Sierra administered another milligram of epinephrine and 120mg of lidocaine as chest compressions resumed and the cardiac monitor showed no signs of spontaneous life. The residents stuck their gloved hands on the patient's neck and groin in a desperate attempt to find a pulse.

After thirty minutes of intense effort to resuscitate the patient, the senior resident looked at his watch, then over at the cardiac monitor. "Stop compressions and let's see what we have."

Everyone turned to the monitor and watched the undulating waves of chest compressions turn into a horizontal flat line with no signs of any electrical activity. The residents confirmed that they had no palpable pulse.

The senior resident snapped his gloves off his hands and threw them on the bed in frustration. "It's been thirty-two minutes without a pulse. We've done everything we can do. Let's call it." He looked down at his watch one final time and wiped his damp forehead on the sleeve of his lab coat. "Time of death: three-thirty. Cause of death: full cardiac and respiratory arrest secondary to massive, uncontrollable hemorrhaging."

Everyone breathed a sigh of defeat as the young resident ran his hands through his hair in frustration. "Sierra, I'll go talk to the family. I'll fill out the death certificate and call the coroner when I come back."

Sierra watched him head out of the room as Sydney reached up and turned off the cardiac monitor.

Sierra stepped quietly to the head of the bed and gently ran her hand over the young patients eyelids and guided them closed. Everyone watched her as she whispered softly, "It's all over now. Your struggle is over. Rest in peace."

Everyone felt a warmth rush over their spines and prickle the hair at the back of their necks as they felt the depth of emotion in Sierra's words.

Sydney disposed of her gloves and slipped on a clean pair as she placed her arm around Sierra's shoulders. "You did a great job, Sierra. You did everything you could do."

Sierra shook her head and looked up into Sydney's warm brown eyes. "After ten years of this shit, you'd think we would be used to this. But it's painful each and every time one dies, regardless of the circumstances."

"I keep telling you to stop being so compassionate and loving, Sierra, but you just won't listen."

Sierra threw Sydney a stare; Sydney gave her a coy, devilish grin that instantly made her heart feel lighter.

Sydney helped Sierra clean up the mess in the room and remove some of the equipment. Together they bathed the patient and placed a crisp white sheet up to the patient's shoulders.

Sierra surveyed the room while she peeled off her gloves and threw them in the nearest trashcan. "I'm going to talk to the family, Sydney. I'll have them come in and say their good-byes when they feel ready."

Sydney finished combing the patient's hair before placing the comb in the patient's bedside table. "Sure, Sierra. Take your time."

Sierra stood in the doorway and watched Sydney disconnect the patient's last intravenous line. "Sydney," Sierra said.

Sydney looked up from her task.

"Thanks for your help and support. That goes beyond this room as well."

Sydney smiled softly. "Sure, now you appreciate me. This morning you were ready to shove me in a biohazard bag and ship me off to some uninhabited biodegradable wasteland."

"Yeah, well, you know, some of us are a little hardheaded and maybe a little tiny bit stubborn," Sierra admitted.

"A little stubborn! Sierra Vaughn, you are the epitome of selfless, stubborn, and hardheaded when it comes to your own well-being. You need to stop putting everyone else before yourself, Sierra. You deserve a lot better than what life has dealt you."

Sierra bit her lower lip in an attempt to fight off the tears struggling to consume her. "Thanks, Sydney. I'll remember that next time I feel like shoving you in a biohazard bag."

Sierra ducked out of the doorway in a real hurry as a roll of gauze bounced off her shoulder and unraveled as it rolled along the floor.

Fifteen minutes later Sierra guided the grief-stricken family into the patient's room. Sierra spent time with them answering all of their questions and sharing their pain before she headed for the doorway to give them their privacy. She rested her hand on the door frame and turned back to watch their sobbing anguish, as she felt her own tears blur her vision.

Sydney gently took Sierra's arm and guided her into the nurse's station. Sydney filled a cup with ice cold water from the water cooler and handed the glass and a tissue to Sierra.

"Thanks, Sydney." Sierra took a deep swallow of the cold liquid before slumping into the nearest chair in exhaustion. "I'm getting so tired of dealing with young male trauma patients whose lives are changed forever by violence or drug and alcohol-related accidents."

Sydney strolled from the nurse's station and peeked into both her patient's rooms to make sure they were okay before turning back to Sierra. "I hear you, girlfriend. So, my dear, burned-out friend—ready to spend two weeks away from all of this, basking on the shores of Sturgeon Lake?"

Sierra took a final drink of water and looked at Sydney over the rim of her cup. "You're relentless, Syd. It doesn't sound nearly as appealing as the crystal blue shores of the Cayman Islands, but two weeks in beautiful northern Ontario sounds like a close second right now."

Sierra rose from her chair and refilled her cup. She leaned back against the counter with Sydney as they both silently came down from their adrenaline rush. "I need to escape the reality of my miserable life and rejuvenate my soul."

Sydney reached for Sierra's cup of water and took a drink. "That's my girl. Bradley Bay awaits you, or 'the Emerald City,' as the resort is more affectionately known, awaits you."

Sierra watched Sydney take another sip of water with a questioning frown on her face. "Why would a resort for spinal cord–injured adults be nicknamed the Emerald City?"

Sydney grinned mischievously as she walked towards the water cooler to refill their cup. "I'll let Kaitlin explain that one to you. I'm sure the two of you will find each other quite fascinating." Sydney turned her back on Sierra and proceeded to pour more water.

"Sydney, would you care to explain what that is supposed to mean?"

Sydney turned and beamed Sierra a feigned innocent look. "You'll see. I can't wait to talk to you in a few days." Sydney erupted into giggles just as a roll of paper tape narrowly missed her head.

⚙ 2

Sierra gracefully guided her Honda Passport around the curving, scenic two-lane highway that led her deeper into the natural wonder of northern Ontario. The beautiful, majestic spruce, pine, and birch trees mesmerized her as she sang along with the song pouring from Melissa Etheridge, claiming to be the only one.

Within three hours Sierra turned onto a paved side road and came upon a huge cedar sign painted with bright yellow block letters that read:

**WELCOME TO BRADLEY BAY.
JUST FOLLOW THE YELLOW
BRICK ROAD TO THE EMERALD CITY.**

Sierra shook her head and laughed as she put her vehicle back in drive. "Well, Dr. Kaitlin Bradley, I hope you're the Wizard of Oz because I certainly have a few things that I wish for."

Sierra drove along the paved narrow road shrouded on one side by the breathtaking expanse of Sturgeon Lake and on the other side by beautiful gangly spruce and willow trees. The lake's peacefulness seemed to embrace her as she stared toward the darkened woods filtered with sunlight. What kind of wildlife lived in those woods? A shiver ran along her spine as she gripped the steering wheel tighter. "God, I hope there are no bears up here. I'll kill Sydney if any furry, four-legged creature dares to share my bed."

Sierra couldn't help but laugh at herself as she became enchanted by the beauty and serenity surrounding her. She smiled as she remembered the last time that she had been north of Toronto. Linda had made reservations for them at a posh resort and spa for a weekend to celebrate their second anniversary. Linda knew that was the closest to camping she would ever get Sierra.

Sierra treasured those memories with Linda and felt the familiar tightening in her chest as the tears welled in her eyes and threatened to distort her vision if she didn't get a grip on her emotions.

Sierra drove past several secluded, gorgeous log homes and cabins that displayed wealth and respect for their surroundings. She glided around a final curve and arrived at the beautiful resort. Sierra blinked her eyes in disbelief at the size and historic elegance of the main estate. She put her vehicle in park and carefully eased her stiff back out of the driver's seat. She took one step away from her vehicle and stood facing the huge, pristine white estate. A pine front porch ran the length of the front of the main house. Sierra could see several groups of people in wheelchairs intently playing cards and board games. The buzz of their excited voices floated from the porch; Sierra felt instantly transported back to her childhood on her grandparent's farm. She smiled at her fond memories as she turned around to face the calm beauty of Sturgeon Lake.

Sierra took two steps closer as she watched several small sailboats slice through the glass surface at a slow respectful pace. Paddleboats launched from the huge square dock as Sierra noticed that only one person in each boat was pedaling. A small group of people standing and in wheelchairs had collected on the dock to watch the boats. Sierra heard their laughter as clearly as if she were standing right beside them.

Sierra took a deep breath of the fresh pine air and felt embraced by the combination of tranquility and festiveness surrounding this elegant resort.

She stretched her back and walked to the back of her vehicle to unload her three, fluorescent orange Samsonite suitcases. Sierra locked the doors to her vehicle and checked her watch. Four-thirty. She was more than ready for a shower and a long, leisurely nap. Sierra reached down to grab a suitcase when she heard the screen door to the main house spring open with a rusty squeak. She shaded her eyes from the afternoon sun as she watched two suntanned, beautiful women walk down the front steps toward her. She guessed them to be ten years older than herself, making them about forty.

The taller, thinner brunette with dark smiling eyes extended her hand. "Hello there. You must be Sierra Vaughn. I'm Sabrina."

Sierra shook her hand firmly. "Hi, yes I am."

Sabrina indicated the shorter, stockier, blond, and blue-eyed woman beside her. "And this is my partner in crime, Logan. We're the resident nurses here at Bradley Bay." Sierra shook Logan's hand and felt instantly encompassed by their natural warmth and charm.

"We've been looking out for you, Sierra, and as soon as we spotted those blinding, bright orange suitcases we knew our nurse from Toronto had arrived."

Sabrina nudged Logan's ribs with her elbow and gave her a *be nice* glare.

Logan reached for her ribs and winced playfully. "What? It's true. We could use those suitcases as flares in an emergency."

Sabrina struggled to stifle a giggle as she turned to see the smile brighten Sierra's vibrant eyes.

"Never mind her, Sierra. We were getting worried about you. We expected you sooner," Sabrina said.

Sierra smiled and tucked her hands into her jeans pockets. "I'm sorry I arrived later than expected. I never meant to worry you both. It took me a while to get myself organized this morning. And I must admit I wavered between coming and not coming and wondering if this is the right thing to do."

"We're glad you decided to come, Sierra. Sydney has mentioned you to us several times over the past several years, and we kept telling her to bring you here. She always brushed that off and said your girlfriend would never allow it," Logan said.

Sierra hung her head in embarrassed shame as Sabrina reached out and touched her arm. "Whatever your reasons are for being here, Sierra, we're just glad to finally meet you. We plan on keeping you so busy that you will have very little time to feel your pain. This is definitely the place to rest a bruised heart and get a new perspective on life."

"Besides we've been dying to meet the one woman in a thousand that has not fallen for Sydney's charm and killer smile," Logan teased.

Sierra blushed with embarrassment and rolled her eyes. "I keep telling Sydney that I'm in her life to remind her that she's not the center of every woman's fantasy as she so adamantly believes. She has an ego the size of Texas, that woman." They all laughed as Sierra felt embraced by these sweet women. "I'm so glad to meet you two. Sydney has told me so much about you both."

"Please only believe half of what Sydney tells you and take the next two weeks to formulate your own opinion. That way we know we might have a small chance of all becoming friends," Sabrina teased.

"I don't think being friends will be much of a problem," Sierra said.

"See, I bet you're already wondering what made you question coming here. Especially with wonderful women like us around to keep you company, and busy to the point of exhaustion," Logan said, as she glanced down at her watch. "We're just grateful you arrived safely and didn't get swallowed whole by a coyote or black bear."

Sierra gave her a horrified look. "Please don't tell me there are bears and coyotes up here because if there are then I'm out of here in a heartbeat. This country is just not big enough for that kind of wildlife and me. I'm terrified of spiders and mice, let alone coyotes and black bears!"

Sabrina and Logan burst into a gregarious laughter as Sierra gave them both a menacing look.

Sabrina reached for one of Sierra's suitcases. "You're safe with us, Sierra. We promise to protect you from the tarantulas and man-eating mice that roam these woods." Sabrina and Logan were stunned as they watched Sierra quickly jump back into her vehicle and start the engine. They both looked at her in shock as Logan reached for the door and gently eased her back out.

"Bri was only kidding, Sierra. Cut it out, Bri. You're scaring this woman to death. She is graciously donating two weeks of her vacation time to help us out and you just about have her running back to Toronto within fifteen minutes of her arrival here."

Sabrina laughed as she set the suitcase down. "I'm just playing with your mind, Sierra. Honest. Now, let's get your suitcases and show you to your room in the main house."

Logan used both hands to haul Sierra's suitcase up the front wheelchair ramp. "Sierra, you're spending two weeks in a resort, not taking a cruise around the world. You certainly wouldn't be labeled a light packer, if that's what you're afraid of."

They all burst into laughter and had to stop on the front porch to catch their breath. Sierra felt instantly welcomed by these two beautiful women who had made the smooth operations of Bradley Bay their goal in life.

"Sydney told me to pack a little bit of everything for the hot days and cool evenings, so that's what I did."

"What you did, Sierra, is over-pack," Sabrina teased, as she headed through the automatic sliding glass doors and into the main reception area that rivaled that of any grand hotel.

A plump, gray-haired woman at least twice Sierra's age sprang out from behind the main desk with more energy than Sierra had on a good day. She walked toward them dressed in an elegant floral sundress, a definite spring in her step.

They all set down their suitcases as Logan turned to Sierra. "Sierra Vaughn, this is Gladys. Gladys is the welcoming committee, the lady of the house, and the overall queen bee. She is the mom we all wish we had."

Sierra smiled as Gladys pulled her into her ample bosom and gave her a warm, motherly hug. Gladys held Sierra back at arm's length and beamed into her with her deep green eyes. "We are so grateful to have you here, Sierra. If there is anything you should need, please don't hesitate to come ask me. Anything at all, do you understand me, young lady?"

Sierra nodded her head obediently as Gladys took one step back from her and assessed her from head to toe. Sierra stood still as Gladys walked completely around her. She finally stopped before Sierra and shook her head. "We're going to have to feed you right while you're here, Sierra Vaughn. You could use some more meat on those bones of yours."

Sierra flushed with embarrassment as she looked down at her slender frame. She knew she had lost five pounds recently, but she didn't think she looked that bad.

Logan stepped beside her and placed her hand on Sierra's back. "You'd think you were a concentration camp victim the way Gladys talks."

"Gladys is Dr. Bradley's aunt. We love Gladys to death even though she feels we all need to look like the Michelin Man to be healthy," Sabrina said.

Gladys swatted Sabrina's behind and shooed the girls away after giving Sierra another bone-crushing welcome hug.

Logan guided their little entourage through the main living area as Sierra saw the large groups of guests in wheelchairs interacting as if this were a family reunion of an especially large family. Sierra was mesmerized by the architecture of the house and the well-preserved details in the woodwork. The antique furniture was draped with flowery, bright cushions. Every room was huge, with double doorways and inlaid oak hardwood floors.

"This house is gorgeous. Who does it belong to and how old is it?"

Logan set down Sierra's weighty suitcase at the bottom of the massive, wide staircase. "It is a breathtaking place. The house was built in the early 1920s by Kaitlin's grandparents. They had a sawmill in the area and built this home with their own hands. It's been renovated a few times over the years as you can see. Recently all the doorways were widened to allow for easy access for all our wheelchair guests, and a huge automatic sliding glass door was installed at the front foyer. It has ten thousand square feet of living space and twenty bedrooms on the second floor. It has been passed down to Kaitlin from her grandparents, and she has done wonderful things with this place. There are also twenty cabins along the edge of the lake that belong to the resort. Kaitlin still rents those to families that have been coming to vacation at Bradley Bay for generations.

"The most remarkable thing Kaitlin did was turning the main estate into a resort for spinal cord–injured adults when it was once a very lucrative family resort."

"Why did she decide to change the resort to focus on spinal cord–injured adults?"

Logan reached for the suitcase and pointed toward the elevators. "You are going to have to meet Kaitlin and find out that answer for yourself, Sierra. Now, let's get in an elevator and see if the maximum weight allotted will match the weight of these bags."

Sierra rolled her eyes as Sabrina hit the elevator button. "Next time, Sierra, bring suitcases with wheels."

Sierra shook her head as the elevator doors slid open. She grabbed two of her suitcases and stepped into the empty elevator with ease. She set down the suitcases and reached for the third as Sabrina and Logan looked at her in awe. Sierra set the suitcases down together and stood with her hands on her hips. "Are you too wusses coming or shall I find my own way?"

Sabrina and Logan slowly stepped into the elevator. Sabrina hit the second floor button as Logan squeezed Sierra's biceps. "For a concentration camp victim, you certainly do have muscles." The elevator doors slowly closed and surrounded them in their laughter.

On the second floor, Logan guided them down a long hallway to the west wing of the building. She slipped her key into a lock and opened a door, guiding Sierra in first.

Sierra set her suitcase down on the polished oak floor and looked around the quaint, small room that was no bigger than her old university dorm room. It was furnished with a double bed, a small secretary's desk and chair, a tiny fireplace, and had just enough room for a loveseat. Sierra walked around the room in stunned disbelief not sure of what she had expected to walk into, but it certainly wasn't this petite room.

Logan and Sabrina watched her walk into her tiny bathroom and take in the small sink, toilet, and shower that would leave her barely enough room to stand and dry herself off. Logan and Sabrina tried hard not to laugh at the look of total shock in Sierra's beautiful blue-gray eyes. They watched her walk slowly around the double bed and gently touch the intricate white and rose Mennonite quilt adorning the bed. Sabrina and Logan gave each other a playful wink and dropped into the rose colored loveseat.

Sierra sat on the edge of the bed as she struggled to gather her thoughts.

Logan nestled into Sabrina's outstretched arm and fit perfectly to her contours as they have for many years.

Sabrina smiled at the forlorn expression on Sierra's face. "Sorry this isn't the Radisson, Sierra. This is one of the smallest rooms in the resort, so we reserve it for the walking guests. Our wheelchair guests use all the bigger rooms. Do you think you could survive in this room for two weeks?"

Sierra looked away from their warm smiles and traced her finger along the delicate stitching in the quilt. "This room is very pretty, just a little smaller than I expected for the size of the house. I don't mean to come across as ungrateful or unappreciative. It's just that these two weeks were planned for a trip to the Cayman Islands. It just made me sad to think of where I thought I would be instead of where I am."

Logan reached out and touched Sierra's jean-clad leg. "We're sorry your original plans were changed, Sierra. This room is rather small and rustic but you won't be spending much time in here if that makes you feel any better."

Sierra gave them a questioning scowl. "You guys don't plan on working me to death, then feeding me to those woman-eating mice and tarantulas, do you?" They all burst into laughter as they enjoyed their blossoming friendship.

Sierra kicked off her Dr. Martens sandals and tucked her legs under her as she enjoyed their playful banter.

"How long have you two been together?" Sierra said.

Sabrina rested her hand intimately on Logan's shoulder and held her close. "We will be celebrating our tenth anniversary this summer."

Sierra gave them a beautiful smile. "Ten years, wow! I applaud you guys. That's so terrific. I couldn't keep my relationship alive for three years, let alone ten."

Logan reached for Sierra's hand and gave it a gentle squeeze. "Sydney told us very little about your relationship. Maybe someday by a crackling fire and with a glass of wine you will tell us about it."

Sierra smiled at their warmth and bit her lip to fight back her tears. "I'd like that." Sierra quickly cleared her throat and changed the subject. "How long have you two lived here at Bradley Bay?"

Logan slowly released Sierra's hand to allow her the distance to collect herself. "We've been working for Kaitlin for three years, ever since she opened up the Emerald City. We met her when she was doing her residency in Toronto where we worked in a Neurosurgical intensive care unit. We clicked immediately and when she had started the planning process for Bradley Bay she called us up and offered us the job of keeping a watchful eye over all the wheelchair bound guests. We eagerly accepted the offer to escape Toronto and live in this oasis. We both have been in nursing for twenty years so we were more than eager to escape the rat race."

"That's a fascinating story. I look forward to spending these two weeks with you guys and getting to know you better."

Sabrina glanced at her watch and eased off the loveseat. She extended her hand to Logan and helped her to her feet.

"Speaking of Kaitlin, we'd better show you around the place and get ourselves to the dining room so we can help feed some of the quadriplegic guests."

Sierra gave them a shocked look. "I was hoping to grab a shower and a nap."

Sabrina laughed as she stepped toward Sierra and guided her to her feet. "Are you kidding, girl? Now you're sounding ungrateful and unappreciative. There is no time for the finer things in life here at Bradley Bay. There is work to be done. You're not a paying guest, so don't expect any of the luxuries you normally afford yourself everyday."

Sierra groaned with discontent as she allowed Sabrina to guide her back into her sandals. Sabrina guided her toward the door, but Sierra gently pulled Sabrina to a stop.

Sierra turned and looked out the beautiful picture window beside her desk. Sabrina and Logan watched her walk to the window and take in the gorgeous view of Sturgeon Lake and the surrounding log homes. Sabrina and Logan joined her at the window. Sabrina smiled and watched Sierra's mesmerized expression.

"Beautiful, isn't it?" Sabrina said, as she swept her hand across the view and guided Sierra's eyes to the nearest log home on the lake. "That's our house there. You're welcome anytime, Sierra, so please don't ever hesitate to visit us."

"Oh, sure. First you're telling me that I won't have any personal time for anything, and now you're inviting me to come visit. Hypocrites."

Sabrina reached for Sierra's chin and guided her to look down at the ground below. "It's a mighty long fall from here, Ms. Vaughn, so I highly recommend that you watch that sharp tongue of yours."

Sierra swallowed hard and wisely moved one step back from the window. "I look forward to visiting you in your home," Sierra said. She turned back to the window and noticed a sprawling, rustic log house a short distance beyond Sabrina and Logan's home. A beautiful cedar deck surrounded the home, affording a view of all directions of this lush area. Rich, plush patio furniture adorned the deck and a midnight black cat sat atop the cedar railing, bathing herself in the afternoon sun.

Sierra pointed to the log home. "Who lives in that beautiful home?"

Logan followed Sierra's gaze. "That is the residence of Dr. Kaitlin Bradley. It's a gorgeous place. Now, speaking of Kaitlin, we'd better get our butts in gear before she sends the Mounties out looking for us."

Sabrina and Logan guided Sierra to the door. Logan handed her the room key and watched her hesitantly lock the door. Sierra saw the playful smiles in their eyes and frowned. "I felt like a bath anyway and since there is no bathtub I might as well be put to work."

"Mighty chivalrous of you, Ms. Vaughn. Mighty chivalrous," Sabrina teased.

"See you're not such an ungrateful, unappreciative girl after all," Logan said.

Sierra tucked the key into her jeans as she followed Sabrina and Logan down the long hall and down the elegant staircase.

Sabrina and Logan showed Sierra around the grounds and gave her a good idea of what her roles and responsibilities would be while she was at Bradley Bay.

"Okay, now I know what my job is around here. What is it exactly you two will be doing while I'm off taking care of the guests' physical needs, organizing their activities, and running their physical therapy sessions?"

"Oh, did we forget to tell you, Sierra? We're going to the Cayman Islands for the next two weeks," Logan announced.

Sierra stopped dead in her tracks and gave Sabrina and Logan a shocked look that sent them into a fit of laughter.

They both reached for one of Sierra's arms and pulled her forward.

"Come along you gullible little thing, you. That should teach you to mind your manners and just be a good free slave while you're here," Sabrina said.

"We're just playing with you, Sierra. Any help you can give us around here will mean more attention for the guests and that's all that matters. We promise to make sure you have plenty of relaxation time for yourself. It probably will be between the hours of midnight and six a.m., however, you will be amazed at what one can do out here to unwind at those hours," Logan said.

Sierra groaned and rolled her eyes. "Yeah, if I was a bat."

They burst into laughter as Sabrina guided them toward the huge redwood dock on the lake.

Sierra saw two young men in wheelchairs guiding a model-motorized boat across the water with professional ease. Nearby, a young woman awkwardly readjusted herself in her electric wheelchair. A woman knelt before the wheelchair and helped to reposition the young woman's leg straps.

Then the woman stood. Sierra was awestruck by her delicate profile and aura of self-confidence. The woman tilted her face to the early evening sun, casting a shadow across her high cheekbones and down to her strong jaw. Her small chin tilted downward as the sun illuminated her slender nose and full, rosy lips. Sierra was mesmerized as she watched her take a seat on the cushioned bench beside the guest in the wheelchair. The woman's long, light brown hair blew freely in the gentle breeze as she smiled easily with her eyes. She was looking out onto the lake and pointing at the model boats as the woman in the wheelchair laughed at her comment. They looked so comfortable together. Sierra stepped closer and saw how the woman had one leg curled under her on the bench and seemed at ease with the flow of her slender, athletic body. A fluttering sensation clenched at Sierra's belly as she cautiously rested a hand over the tingling area, convinced it had to be her empty stomach talking to her and nothing more.

Both women turned as they heard Sabrina's voice. "Hey, you two. There's someone we want you to meet."

The guest in the electric wheelchair slowly spun her chair around and quickly appraised Sierra from head to toe. She tilted her head and whispered to the woman beside her, "Now that's a babe."

The woman on the bench stood with a commanding presence as she discretely tweaked Jennifer's ear. She was acutely aware of Sierra's flawless olive skin and exotic blue-gray eyes. It was those eyes that pierced Kaitlin and threatened to delve into corners that Kaitlin refused admittance to any woman. This woman would not be an exception. The self-confidant tilt of her chin and stubborn stance challenged Kaitlin to shake her resolve. She refused to acknowledge the unfamiliar surge of desire swelling in her chest and focused on the more familiar anger burning in her belly.

Sierra felt shaken by the woman's intense, cold stare and stepped close enough to see the brooding emotions swarming in her emerald green eyes. Sierra was in awe of her energy as she struggled to look away from those scrutinizing eyes that conveyed so many conflicting emotions all struggling to surface and escape. Sierra wasn't sure if she was struggling to maintain control or willing Sierra to be intimidated by that icy stare. Sierra was ready to tell her what she could do with that icy stare.

Sabrina placed her hand on the shoulder of the woman in the wheelchair and gave her a beautiful smile. "Jennifer, this is Sierra Vaughn. She's the nurse we were telling you about who has come up from Toronto to give us a hand for the next two weeks."

Jennifer was a pretty woman in her thirties. The atrophied muscles in her hands and the limited movement of her arms indicated that she must be an incomplete quadriplegic. Sierra watched as Jennifer struggled to extend her young withered hand toward her. Sierra took her hand and held it warmly.

"Hello, Jennifer. It's a pleasure to meet you. I hope you'll give me a better tour around this magical place than these two did."

Jennifer slowly laid her hand back down in her lap. "That's a deal. Tomorrow, I'll be your official tour guide of the Emerald City. You wouldn't have to twist my arm to get me to show a beautiful woman around this piece of heaven. I am at your service in whatever capacity I can be of assistance, Sierra. All you have to do is ask."

"Thank you, Jennifer. I appreciate that. I may need all the help I can get with the tasks Sabrina and Logan have assigned me."

"Since when have you become such a helpful little lass, Jen? Whenever Logan and I ask you to help out you whine at us that you contribute by teaching your computer classes to the guests and we are to remember that you are here on vacation and not the hired help. You're going to be very busy with your classes and Sierra is going to be way to busy to have you lusting after her."

"One thing I did not lose in my motorcycle accident is my lust for women. Thank God. Now, if you lovely ladies will all excuse me, I need to get ready for dinner." They all said good-bye as they watched her maneuver her electric wheelchair expertly along the wooden walkway leading to the main estate.

Logan turned to Sierra and touched her arm. "Sierra Vaughn, this is Dr. Kaitlin Bradley. Katie, this is Sierra."

Kaitlin extended her hand and shook Sierra's. Sierra was stunned by the intensity of her grip as she stared into those brooding emerald eyes.

"Well, Sierra Vaughn, I see that you did decide to show up and I noticed that you brought enough luggage to put on a fashion show for the guests."

Sierra was stunned by her stinging sarcasm as she felt the bile splash against her stomach wall. She swallowed hard and tried desperately to control her voice. "I didn't realize that I had a specific time of arrival established for me, Dr. Bradley, and yes, I brought a lot of clothes only because I obviously had no idea what to expect, so I over-packed."

Sabrina and Logan shared a bewildered look as they watched the exchange unfold before them.

"Well, then, Ms. Vaughn, is Bradley Bay what you expected?"

Kaitlin's rude, icy demeanor instantly incensed Sierra as she felt her emotional floodgates strain with this assault. "It's more rustic than what I expected, Dr. Bradley, but I'm sure I'll manage for the next two weeks. I'm not a quitter. I'm committed to staying and helping Logan and Sabrina, whether you want me around or not!"

Sierra's flaring emotions and blazing blue-gray eyes fascinated Kaitlin. Her smooth olive complexion deepened with anger as Kaitlin watched her raise her tiny chin in stubborn defiance. Her slender, willowy frame stiffened to do battle; Kaitlin wanted to see if she could shatter that facade of control and self-confidence.

Kaitlin was astounded by the anger this woman incited in her for no apparent reason as she lashed out irrationally. "Stay if you wish, big-city girl, but know that we're not here to pamper you or cater to your every whim and desire. We have too many other guests who have real complaints and real worries to waste our time coddling you." Kaitlin moved one step closer to Sierra as Sabrina and Logan dropped onto the dock bench in shock.

"You don't owe us anything, Sierra Vaughn, so feel free to pack your fluorescent orange bags and head back to the big city anytime if we don't meet your big-city needs. You have nothing holding you here and we don't owe you anything. If you want to stay and help, that's great, but I expect that you will pull your weight like the rest of us without too many complaints."

Sierra was outraged by Kaitlin's rudeness. She swallowed hard against a dizzying wave of nausea. Sierra took one measured step toward Kaitlin's fiery green eyes and struggled to find her usual self-control. "I'm here to fulfill my promise to help, Dr. Bradley, and that I will do. Your lack of social graces and appalling manners don't scare me. I have been up against a lot worst situations than your disgraceful rudeness, Dr. Bradley, so please don't be disappointed when I tell you that your childish temper does not intimidate me."

Tears welled in Sierra's eyes as she spun on her heels to face a stunned Sabrina and Logan. "Ladies, I'll meet you in the dining room. I believe there are some quads that need my assistance with their meals." With that, Sierra walked briskly toward the main house and roughly shoved her hands into her pockets, struggling to contain the unusual raging anger that careened through her veins. She reluctantly lost the battle with her tears as her cheeks became drenched.

They all watched Sierra walk away in a shroud of emotion. Sabrina and Logan slowly stood before Kaitlin. Kaitlin was astonished by Sierra's composure and inner strength as she watched her slumped shoulders disappear into the main estate as a sharp pain of self-disgust rammed into her gut.

Kaitlin cursed herself as she saw the look of disbelief and anger in Sabrina and Logan's eyes. She took one small step back.

Sabrina reached out and grabbed her by the arm and held her still. Logan stood before her and looked her straight in the eye.

"What the hell was that all about, Dr. Bradley? The woman is a doll and she gives us two weeks of her precious time and you act like she's a Russian spy coming here to take away all of our trade secrets!"

Kaitlin dropped her head in embarrassment. Sabrina reached toward her chin and tilted Kaitlin's face to meet her enraged eyes. "You don't even know the girl and you exploded all over her head like that for no reason at all. What the hell provoked that emotional assault? What did she ever do to you, Katie?"

Kaitlin eased her face out of Sabrina's hand. She shyly turned and looked out at the lake as she slipped her hands into her pockets and wished she knew why that woman provoked such anger in her. She refused to analyze the unsettling stir of intrigue and desire gripping her chest. She refused to allow another woman to burrow into the remains of her splintered heart. Sierra's blue-gray eyes swam before her as she marveled at her ability to reign in her anger and fight back with unyielding tenacity. Kaitlin wondered what it would be like to see all that fire and intensity unleashed.

She took a deep breath before turning back to face Sabrina and Logan. "I had a really shitty shift at work last night. I had two patients come in full cardiac arrest and I lost them both. The nursing staff were in particularly bitchy moods and I was sick of it! So the last thing I wanted to be confronted with was another nurse who felt she had special privileges. Besides, I sensed she's disappointed by Bradley Bay and doesn't really want to be here in the first place."

"That's it, Kate? What a pathetic excuse. You have a shitty night at work, so you decide to take it out on a total stranger who has come here to help you without even knowing you? As for her not wanting to be here, she admits to wishing she were elsewhere for her vacation, so give the girl a break. She has the desire and the unselfish will to help us, so let's not look a gift horse in the mouth. We know you better than this, Kate, and we would think that there is more to this than a lousy night at work. This is totally out of character for you and I'm far from impressed," Sabrina seethed.

Kaitlin looked down at her feet and felt the cold discomfort of shame envelop her body.

"We've never seen you treat anyone like this, Kate. You're always the one that rolls out the red carpet for anyone that comes to help us, and you never hesitate to make her feel like part of our family. You're one of the most incredible women we know, Katie, but tonight your behavior, to quote Sierra, was appalling and disgraceful! Now, you'd better get over your self-pitying feelings of your lousy night and get your sorry ass into the dining room and deliver the hugest apology of your life. You had no right to treat her like that, Katie. If Sierra does not find your apology suitable, then we're just going to have to tie an anchor around your neck and throw you into the cold lake. Got it, Dr. Bradley?"

Kaitlin fiddled with the edge of her belt and stared down at her shoes. Logan and Sabrina couldn't help but smile at her childlike pout.

"You two have certainly become protective of this complete stranger in a short period of time."

Sabrina took Kaitlin by the shoulders and turned her toward the main estate. "Sierra is not a complete stranger, Kate. She is family, so move it or it's 'woman overboard.'"

Kaitlin looked back and gave Sabrina and Logan a forlorn look. "I need to change first. Then I'll see you guys in the dining room. Okay?"

Sabrina and Logan gave her a parental scolding look as Sabrina leaned intimately close to Kaitlin's beautiful, soft face. "You have exactly fifteen minutes to get your sorry ass in that dining room and deliver that apology, Dr. Bradley. Is that clear?"

"Yes, Mother," Kaitlin drawled.

Sabrina turned Kaitlin around one final time as they both smacked her bottom and enjoyed hearing her complaints of physical abuse all the way back to the main estate.

ᘒ 3

Kaitlin stood in the doorway of the spacious, glassed-in main dining room and took a deep breath. She nervously tugged on her black silk shirt and toyed with the crisp pleats on her khaki slacks as she watched the dining room staff serve the few remaining guests. She scanned the room and saw Sabrina, Logan, and Gladys eating together and talking quietly. Kaitlin walked toward their table and scanned the room one final time. She felt a strange flutter of mixed disappointment and relief that Sierra was nowhere to be found.

Sabrina watched Kaitlin approach as she set down her fork and wiped her mouth on her red linen napkin. "Well, look what the cat dragged in."

Everyone looked up at the guilty concern in Kaitlin's eyes as Sabrina looked at her watch. "Instead of fifteen minutes, it only took you an hour and a half to get here. Very convenient, Dr. Bradley. Just enough time to miss Sierra."

Kaitlin slipped her hands into her pockets and frowned as she felt everyone's parental disapproval. She felt properly chastised and uncomfortable being on this end of the stick. "I was paged by the E.R. doc on tonight and he wanted to know about the two cardiac arrests last night. I filled him in on what happened and we ended up talking longer than I had expected. I didn't purposely stay away this long, Sabrina. Give me a break. You guys know me better than that. Besides, I'm absolutely starving, and where's Sierra anyway?"

Logan gently pushed her plate away and wiped her mouth. "She helped us feed several of the quads, then when we invited her to come eat with us, she said she wasn't very hungry. Gladys wouldn't let her escape that easily so she made her a turkey sandwich and gave her a can of Diet Pepsi. Sierra said she was going to take her little picnic and sit by the lake so she could clear her head and soothe her soul."

Kaitlin looked down at the stern expression on her dear aunt's face and bent down to kiss her cherub cheek. Silently praying to ease the explosion that was about to erupt.

Gladys crossed her arms across her bosom and gave Kaitlin a grunt of disapproval. "What are you waiting for, Katie? You're not getting one crumb of supper till you get yourself out there and apologize to that sweet, delightful girl. Don't even try and talk your way out of it because I will not hesitate to take you over my knee and deliver the spanking that you deserve for your pitiful behavior this afternoon. And don't think for one minute that because you're thirty-three that I would even hesitate to spank you. I never raised you to be rude and hateful, Kate. Now get out there and apologize to our Sierra."

Kaitlin grimaced at her aunt and turned to Sabrina and Logan. "Tattletales."

They all burst into laughter as Kaitlin dropped her head in frustration and stormed out of the dining room.

Kaitlin stormed through the sliding glass doors and onto the homey front porch. The balmy night air warmed her skin, and the fresh scent of blossoming lilac bushes surrounded her. She rested her hands on the pine railing and leaned her hips forward as she saw a tiny figure sitting on the edge of the well-lit dock.

Kaitlin headed down the front steps and walked across the shuffleboard courts. She walked across the wooden volleyball platform and gingerly stepped through the beach sand of the horseshoe pit. Kaitlin stopped and squinted her eyes to see if that really was Sierra sitting there alone looking out onto the glistening lake. She saw her thick mane of chestnut hair flow over her soft pink T-shirt and watched as her slender shoulders rose and fell. The sight of Sierra crying enveloped Kaitlin in shame as she ached to take her in her arms and protect her from such raw pain; pain she herself had caused. Kaitlin roughly shoved her hands into her pockets and moved forward, shaking her head and muttering under her breath, "Shit!"

She stepped quietly onto the dock and eased herself down beside Sierra.

Sierra gasped with fright as she turned to see the intruder. She looked into Kaitlin's concerned emerald eyes, then quickly broke their gaze. She abruptly turned, gathered the remaining half of her turkey sandwich and can of Diet Pepsi and rose quickly to her feet.

Kaitlin felt an unusual depth of compassion and concern as she saw the tears tumble from those mesmerizing blue-gray eyes. Kaitlin quickly jumped to her feet and reached to stop Sierra from walking away. "Sierra. Please don't go. Please let me apologize."

Sierra turned to face Kaitlin as a fresh wave of tears washed over her cheeks. "I need to go, Dr. Bradley. I would hate to have you see me like this and think I was a big-city baby that needed pampering and coddling. Because I would never want that or ask for that from you!" Sierra jerked her arm away from Kaitlin's grasp and took two steps away.

"Sierra, if you don't give me a chance to apologize, Sabrina and Logan are going to tie an anchor around my neck and throw me in the lake."

Sierra stopped in her tracks and fought the urge to burst into laughter as she visualized Sabrina and Logan delivering their threat.

Kaitlin sensed Sierra's hesitation as she struggled to find the words to soothe her tortured heart. "And I'm starving and Gladys won't feed me till you have accepted my apology. Even worse, she's threatened to spank me."

Sierra unsuccessfully tried to suppress a giggle as she turned and walked directly up to Kaitlin. "Well then, Dr. Bradley, I hope that you're a good swimmer. Otherwise, when they do your autopsy, they're going to find you with an empty stomach and a red bottom!" Sierra quickly turned on her heels and walked away as she heard warm, caressing laughter behind her.

Kaitlin quickly caught up to her and gently took her arm. "Sierra. Please. Just give me a few minutes to apologize for my appalling manners and childish temper, as you so kindly described it this afternoon."

Sierra couldn't help but smile as she stared into those intense emerald eyes. She wanted to bolt and hide from this intriguing woman but instead found herself riveted to the spot and very acutely aware of the touch of her hand.

Kaitlin gestured to the padded dock bench and tenderly rested her hand on Sierra's elbow. "Please, Sierra. Just a few minutes of your time. Then you can be rid of me, and I can be absolved of my sins."

Sierra took one step closer to Kaitlin's pleading eyes. "I've got news for you, Dr. Bradley. It would take you a lot more than a few minutes of my time and at least three visits to a confessional for you to be absolved of your sins of this afternoon."

Kaitlin's deep laughter deflated Sierra's anger as it caressed her with its genuine delight. "I see. Well, maybe we can start with those few minutes and then I'll try and fit in some time with my priest."

Sierra glared menacingly at Kaitlin and wondered why she felt so enamored with this temperamental woman. Sierra ached to see beyond those glimmering eyes that shielded something deep within.

Kaitlin gently guided Sierra by the elbow to sit on the padded dock bench and slipped in beside her. Sierra took a tissue from her jeans pocket and dried her eyes as Kaitlin looked out onto the lake and watched the moonbeam dance across the glassy surface.

Sierra watched Kaitlin's soft profile and admired the high cheekbones, tiny nose and full, sensuous lips. Her light brown hair floated effortlessly with each gentle breeze like a kite in natural flight. Sierra heard a low grumbling sound and looked down at her soda and remaining turkey sandwich. "Your stomach's growling. I would offer you the other half of my delicious, mouth-watering turkey sandwich and soda, but Gladys would probably spank me if I did that before I accepted your apology."

Kaitlin turned to see the beautiful gentle smile curl the corners of Sierra's pillowy lips. Her olive skin glistened in the moonlight as Kaitlin ached to reach up and run her fingers through her wind-blown, feathery brown hair. Her exquisite blue-gray eyes captivated Kaitlin; she marveled at Sierra's natural beauty without a hint of makeup.

Kaitlin reached for the soda in Sierra's hand. "I won't tell if you don't." Sierra watched Kaitlin put the can to her lips and take a big sip.

"That all depends on whether or not your apology is good enough for me to save you from Gladys's heavy hand."

Kaitlin held the soda can in both hands. "Aunt Gladys has raised me like her own daughter since the age of five and has never, ever spanked me. At thirty-three, it's a little late for her to start, don't you think?"

Sierra crossed her arms across her slender abdomen and leaned back against the padded bench. "Maybe if she had started much earlier then you wouldn't be so rude and hot-tempered at the age of thirty-three, don't you think?"

Kaitlin leaned back into the cushions and smiled as she took another sip of Pepsi, never taking her eyes off the playful twinkle in those blue-gray eyes. "Touché, Ms. Vaughn, touché."

Sierra waited until she was finished, then reached forward and took the soda from her hand. "All right, that's enough Pepsi for you. Let's hear your excuse for your pathetic temper tantrum this afternoon."

Kaitlin couldn't help but smile at Sierra's directness as she watched her set the sandwich and soda can down on the bench beside her. Kaitlin took a deep breath and nervously cleared her throat. "I'm really sorry about the way I treated you today, Sierra. I was a real bitch, and I had no right to treat you like that. I really lost it with you this afternoon. I rarely lose control like that."

Sierra tilted her head and leaned in closer. "What was it, Dr. Bradley? What made me the target of your wrath?"

Kaitlin ran her hand through her hair nervously and looked out onto the calm lake. How did she begin to explain something she herself did not understand?

"You're very direct, Ms. Vaughn, and you're not going to make this easy for me are you?"

"No, I'm not. I want you to suffer like I did this afternoon."

Kaitlin looked back into Sierra's misty eyes and saw a depth of pain and hurt that she felt only she understood. Those blue-gray eyes screamed of honesty, innocence, and distrust. Kaitlin wished to erase all the painful emotions swimming in that shimmering blue depth and fill it with warmth and laughter.

Sierra watched the bright glow in Kaitlin's deep emerald eyes as Kaitlin leaned forward and cleared her throat.

"I work in the E.R. of the community hospital in this area. Last night I had two men, both in their forties, come in full cardiac arrest. We worked feverishly on both of them, but inevitably they both died. The families were devastated, and the nurses and I were stunned. Both men had existing cardiac disease, but it's still devastating to lose them at such a young age. And two in one night. That was the hard part. I felt so defeated. I keep going over both arrests trying to understand what more we could have done. What more I could have done to save their lives."

"Is there anything else you or the nurses could have done?"

Kaitlin leaned her elbows on her knees, wringing her hands together as she hesitated slightly. "My head knows we ran those codes flawlessly. Both those men were pretty far gone by the time we got them."

"Then you know you were fighting a losing battle, Kaitlin."

"Nevertheless, it was a battle I was determined to win. I haven't lost young patients like that in a very long time. We gave it everything we had, and it left us all totally drained in the end. I dealt with it by withdrawing into myself. The nurses dealt with it by becoming bitchy and irritable for the rest of the night. By the time I got home this morning, I didn't care if I saw another human being for a very long time. I just wanted to bury my head under my pillow and wallow in my misery."

"What pulled the ostrich's head out of the sand?" Sierra said.

Kaitlin couldn't help but smile as she leaned back into the cushioned bench and admired Sierra's insight.

"This afternoon, someone rang my doorbell incessantly. With the mood I was in, you can imagine my temperament when I forced myself to put something on and see who was going to be the next local murder victim."

Sierra shielded the grin on her lips with her hand. Kaitlin loved to see the warmth and intrigue in those entrancing eyes.

"I'm so glad you find this humorous, Ms. Vaughn. I went down my stairs with a full head of steam and jerked my front door open. There, sitting in her electric wheelchair, was Jennifer. She had tears in her eyes and in her hand was a tiny sparrow with a broken wing. She gently stroked the little sparrow with the little control she has in her contracted hands and looked up at me and said, 'Can you help me, Kate? I think this little guy is in trouble.' Here is a woman who is a quadriplegic with no use of her legs and minimal use of her arms and she's holding a tiny sparrow with a broken wing and crying for its pain. Man, did I feel like a shmuck! Jennifer never ceases to amaze me. She has an uncanny way of slamming reality right in my face and making me realize how screwed up my priorities are sometimes."

"Jennifer made you see the sunlight beyond the darkness of your pillow," Sierra said.

Kaitlin nodded in agreement.

"What happened to the sparrow, Kaitlin?"

Kaitlin felt an unusual warmth caress her chest with the way Sierra said her name. "It died in Jennifer's hands. Together we buried it in a place where she can visit. It's amazing how much love and compassion Jennifer has regardless of the difficult things she has had to deal with. That's what put me in my place today. She has been through so much and still has so much to give. I on the other hand felt like I failed last night and wanted to hide forever. People like Jennifer just keep on going and handle everything that comes their way with grace and dignity. Physically challenged people have so much to teach us."

Sierra placed her hand on Kaitlin's knee. "Then today was not a total loss, Dr. Bradley. You learned something about yourself and those around you. And thanks to a few bitchy, irritable nurses and a lousy night at work, I was gifted with the essence of your anger."

Kaitlin began to speak as Sierra touched her full lips with her fingertips. Time stood still. That simple touch crackled and exploded between them like a brilliant fireworks display.

"I understand, Kaitlin. You've already apologized. I appreciate you explaining what happened last night and sharing your pain with me. I know that was not easy for you."

Sierra slid her fingertips from Kaitlin's lips and had to entwine her hands together to control the surge of heat and fluttering she felt cascade throughout her entire being.

Kaitlin's lips tingled and ached for the touch of Sierra's hand. They both sat transfixed and absorbed in each other's magnetic energy until Kaitlin nervously looked away. "Thank you for accepting my apology and being such a good listener."

"I sense you don't feel comfortable sharing your pain with too many people, Dr. Bradley."

"You're right about that, Ms. Vaughn, but there is something about you that makes me pour my soul out."

"It could be that I hold the only scrap of food you could be looking at tonight."

Kaitlin's heartfelt laughter embraced Sierra with its warmth. "When Sydney called me at work last night and told me you were coming, she told me that you were a real spark. Well, she wasn't kidding. You're a fascinating woman, Ms. Vaughn."

"Well, thank-you, Dr. Bradley. I'll take that as the first compliment you've given me."

Kaitlin leaned forward and slowly brushed a long strand of chestnut brown hair off Sierra's shoulder. She wound it around her finger and watched it slip from her grasp with the next gentle breeze. "She also told me you guys had an equally horrible shift yesterday. Tell me about your patient that died, Sierra."

Sierra felt a warmth surge in her belly as she shared the events of her last shift with Kaitlin and told her all about the twenty-seven-year-old patient who hemorrhaged to death.

"That's a nightmare, Sierra. That's one of the benefits of working the E.R. in a town three hours north of the city. I don't have to deal with the big-city violence." Kaitlin rested her elbow on the back of the bench and forced herself to lean back from Sierra's enticing chemistry. "But being a big-city girl, that probably suits you best."

Sierra closed her eyes and leaned her head back against the redwood railing. "Violent death doesn't suit me, Dr. Bradley. And stop calling me a big-city girl. Just because I was born and raised in Toronto doesn't mean that I want to spend the rest of my life there."

Sierra turned her head to face Kaitlin and heard her stomach growl in protest. Sierra picked up the half sandwich and Diet Pepsi and offered them both to Kaitlin. "You'd better take these before your stomach starts to really scream at me."

Kaitlin looked down at Sierra's hands. "Are you sure you don't want any more of your sandwich, Sierra?"

"I'm sure. Please have the rest before your stomach organizes a violent revolt against me."

"Does that mean that you've accepted my apology?"

Sierra gave her a glowing smile that cascaded from her beautiful face into Kaitlin's heart.

"Apology accepted."

A glorious smile exploded across Kaitlin's face as she reached for the sandwich and felt Sierra tug it back gently. Kaitlin looked up into her brilliant eyes and saw a burst of mischief race across her smile.

"Don't you ever treat me like that again, Dr. Bradley, because I can promise you that I will make sure my guard dogs keep their anchor and spanking handy."

Kaitlin frowned and tugged the sandwich away from Sierra's hand. "How did you manage to win those three over so quickly, anyway?"

Sierra laughed and took the plastic wrap from Kaitlin's hand and watched her eagerly bite into the sandwich. "I was just my usual charming self. Something that obviously failed to win you over this afternoon."

Kaitlin lifted the can to her lips and peered at Sierra over the edge. "That charm has certainly shone bright this evening."

Sierra blushed slightly and felt unusually warmed by Kaitlin's closeness. She looked down at her hands; stunned by the ease to which Kaitlin could vibrate her senses.

Kaitlin took another bite of her sandwich and watched Sierra carefully. "Sierra, why didn't you eat a proper meal tonight? Half of a turkey sandwich can't possibly be enough for a big-city girl that made the three hour drive from Toronto to Springfield."

Sierra looked directly into Kaitlin's concerned eyes. "Someone who shall remain nameless, destroyed my appetite."

Kaitlin frowned as she looked into Sierra's emotional, glistening eyes. "Oh. I see."

Sierra laughed softly at Kaitlin's discomfort and watched a pair of loons glide along the lake and dive below the surface, only to reappear fifty feet away. "I usually have trouble eating when I'm upset, so you'd better back off, Dr. Bradley. Otherwise, I will leave here at the end of two weeks looking like the concentration camp victim that your aunt already thinks I am."

Kaitlin choked on a sip of Pepsi as she tried to laugh and swallow at the same time. Sierra gently rubbed her back until she caught her breath.

"That sounds like my adorable aunt Gladys to insinuate something like that." Kaitlin felt the warmth of Sierra's hand on her back long after she moved it away.

Sierra turned in the bench to face Kaitlin and was struck by the reflection of the dock lights in her eyes. "You mentioned that

Gladys raised you since you were five. What happened to your parents?"

Kaitlin leaned back into the bench as Sierra saw the intense emotions darken her bright eyes. "My parents were both archaeologists. Not exactly a profession that's in high demand in Canada."

Sierra was thoroughly impressed. "Wow."

Kaitlin laughed at her excitement as she continued. "They never had any intention of having kids, so I was a dent in their career plans. They hauled me all over the world with them until I turned five, when they knew they had to put me in school. Gladys always disapproved of the places they hauled me off to and I was really too young to appreciate the beauty of their travels. So, to make a long story short, Gladys and my uncle offered to take me in and get me a proper education and we have been inseparable since. Gladys's husband died when I was only ten of stomach cancer, and it was his suffering that inspired me to be a doctor. I loved him like a father and I still miss him dearly. Gladys is very special to me and I love her deeply. I credit her for the person that I am today."

The depth of warmth in Sierra's intense eyes mesmerized Kaitlin as she forced herself to look away. "I don't think that today would be a fine example of the person I really am and Gladys's threats to spank me speak for themselves. I'm sure she wouldn't hesitate to send me back to my mother after the way I treated you today."

Sierra felt enthralled by Kaitlin's childhood. "Where are your parents now?"

Kaitlin frowned and took a deep breath. "My father died ten years ago in a mine explosion in Argentina while they were excavating a new site. The whole thing was rather fishy, but finding out what really happened there is more than anyone is willing to take on."

"I'm sorry, Kate. That's a terrible way to lose your father."

Kaitlin looked away and followed the moonbeam to the opposite shore. "He kept promising me that he would retire early and come take over Bradley Bay from my grandparents so that we could all live up here and spend the time together that we never had during my childhood. Obviously that never happened and I ended up running the resort when my grandparents passed away three years ago. I lost the opportunity to have a relationship with my father and that always made me appreciate the time that I do have with the special people in my life."

Kaitlin turned in her seat to face Sierra and tucked her leg beneath her. "When I moved to Toronto to go to med school I really missed Gladys and my grandparents. I would take every opportunity I could to escape the city and come back home to Bradley Bay. My grandparents were such a huge part of my life. They were incredibly adventurous and entrepreneurial. They settled in this area and saw great potential for growth and development. They took over the lumber business in town and used their wealth to strengthen the town and it's people. They donated money to build several wings at the hospital and had a new nursing home built. They served on the town counsel my entire life and helped promote businesses and expansion. Springfield has grown from a sleepy northern town to a busy, eclectic mix of enterprise, city refugee's, and artsy yuppies. As a result this town has attracted a large following of gay's and lesbians. I'm not sure that the town was ready for that but the overall feeling here is one of acceptance.

"I loved my grandparents dearly and I've missed them so much since they passed away. I had them buried in a special plot here on Bradley Bay. It's what they wanted. It's really important to Gladys and my mother to have their parents be a part of the town they helped to create."

Kaitlin saw the stunned look on Sierra's face. She looked away and fiddled with the pleat on her khaki slacks. "I didn't mean to go on like that, Sierra. I haven't talked about my grandparents in a long time."

Sierra reached out and rested her hand on Kaitlin's arm. She was engulfed by the enthusiasm and love pouring from Kaitlin as she talked about her family. She momentarily stepped out from behind her fortress walls and shared a part of her sensitive heart. When she saw that Sierra felt her passion she slipped behind those walls and locked the door to her deepest thoughts and feelings. What caused that quick retreat? What caused this woman such pain that she refused to share herself unconditionally? Sierra had a feeling there were many layers to be peeled away before she would find all those answers. Answers she ached to find.

"You were hardly going on and I loved hearing about your family. Your family is very special to you, Kaitlin, and that is something to always treasure. What your grandparents have done for this town is remarkable. I'm sure they are as proud of you as you are of them."

Kaitlin uncurled her leg and felt the vehement heat radiating from Sierra's gentle touch. "My grandparents had a vision and fulfilled that vision. I'm so proud of them for that."

Sierra sensed she was treading on rocky terrain as she gently squeezed Kaitlin's arm. "I can see that. What happened to your mother, Kaitlin?"

Kaitlin abruptly looked away from Sierra and stared out at the lake. Sierra could feel the tension in her arm wind her like a tight coil.

"She lives here in the area."

Sierra felt Kaitlin emotionally slip away as she gently touched her chin and guided her face back to her. Tears threatened to spill from those brilliant emerald eyes. Sierra felt consumed by her pain. "I'm sorry, Kate. I didn't mean to dig up painful memories. Your eyes scream of your pain, regardless of the way you try so hard to bury it. Whenever you want to talk about anything, Kate, I will always be here to listen. Please remember that."

Kaitlin hesitantly slipped her chin from Sierra's tender hand and felt stunned by her insight and awareness. Kaitlin looked down at her hands and felt acutely aware of Sierra's loving warmth. "Stop reading me so well. I work hard at maintaining my protective walls, you know."

Sierra brushed a loose strand of hair away from Kaitlin's eyes. "Your emerald eyes are the windows to your soul."

Kaitlin smiled as Sierra leaned back against the cushioned bench. They both sat in peaceful silence and enjoyed the serenity around them and the intensity of their new friendship.

"Are you close to your family, Sierra?"

Sierra continued to stare at the stars and three quarter moon as she smiled at her warm memories. "Very close. My parents are both real estate agents. They waited till their business was well established before they had me and ended up only having me. They sold their business and retired five years ago. My parents are now in their seventies and call me their greatest acquisition. They bought me my house in Toronto when I graduated from nursing school as a graduation gift. They are both very special people and spoil me rotten all the time. They are very near and dear to my heart, so it's easy for me to understand your deep love for your family. I feel the same love for mine. I called them earlier to let them know I'd arrived safely. They told me to have a wonderful time. Wait till I call them tomorrow and tell them what a wonderful time I've had so far."

Kaitlin quickly looked away from Sierra's menacing stare. She couldn't help but smile at Sierra's tenderness towards her parents. Here was someone who would take family and personal commitments as seriously as she did. "Maybe you could give me a couple of days to make up for today before you report back to your parents."

"Why don't I just invite my parents up here so you can explain to them yourself why you treated me like a useless piece of baggage upon our first meeting."

Kaitlin slowly eased herself back from Sierra as the challenge in Sierra's eyes let Kaitlin know she was up against an unyielding force. "Geez, Sierra, remind me to have the phone cable disconnected in your room."

Sierra couldn't help but laugh as she marveled in the look of terror and pure guilt in Kaitlin's shining eyes. "Leave the cable

44

connected, Dr. Bradley, and I'll give you those few days to make up for your deplorable behavior."

Kaitlin extended her hand. "You've got yourself a deal, big-city girl."

Sierra slipped her hand into Kaitlin's and felt the surge of liquid fire race from her tingling palm to the center of her belly. "I expect you to take this deal very seriously, Kaitlin."

"I promise not to unload on you like that again, Sierra."

"I don't mind you sharing your frustrations with me, Kate. Just don't ever treat me like that again. I didn't deserve that and I won't tolerate that behavior from you again."

Kaitlin was mesmerized by the defiant tilt of that tiny chin and the unshakeable self-respect. A rush of excitement and attraction swirled around Kaitlin's chest as she faced this astonishing woman. "I promise not to mess with the big-city girl."

"Good." Sierra's heart beat an erratic pace as each nerve ending felt like it was acutely aware of Kaitlin's touch. She had to slip her hand from its resting place in Kaitlin's to try and ease the chaotic hum vibrating throughout her entire being.

Sierra leaned back against the padded bench and rested her hand on her chest. She studied the black canvas littered with brilliant stars and felt awed by their abundance. "Does the night sky always look this beautiful over Bradley Bay?"

Kaitlin looked up at the twinkling diamonds that never ceased to capture her attention. "Yes, it's always a spectacular sight each and every night. No two nights are ever the same. I have a telescope on my front deck that gives me a breathtaking close-up glimpse of all the different constellations. You'll have to come to my place and look through it some night to see what I mean."

Sierra turned to Kaitlin and watched her elegant profile as she gazed at the stars. "I'd really like that."

Kaitlin reached forward and brushed a silky strand of chestnut hair over Sierra's shoulder. "Sierra, I really appreciate you being here to give us a hand over the next two weeks. It means a lot to me that we give the guests as much professional attention as we can provide."

Sierra watched the many questions struggle to escape those emerald eyes as she forced herself to look away. "I must admit, Kate, Bradley Bay was not my first choice of where I wanted to spend my two-week vacation." Sierra looked up into Kaitlin's warm eyes. "Six months ago I booked a vacation to the Cayman Islands as a surprise for my ex-lover, Linda. I thought it would be the vacation we needed to get our struggling relationship back on its feet. We had been together for three years and now when I look back I realize what an emotional struggle those years really were. Linda was very controlling and domineering. I never really saw it until I realized how much I compromised of myself to make her happy. In the end I started feeling like one of those dolphins on the Greenpeace specials that was caught in the fishermen's nets. I needed desperately to be set free but had no idea which way to turn. All of my friends saw it long before I realized what was happening, and that's humiliating."

Kaitlin wiped away the tear coursing down Sierra's soft cheek as she watched her close her eyes and take a deep breath. "I was determined to give our relationship a fighting chance even though people kept telling me to dump her and move on with my life. They all felt I deserved better, but nobody stopped to see how much I loved her."

Sierra took a gasping breath and struggled to control her tears. "Three months ago I had gone into work to do a night shift because they were short staffed. By eleven o'clock at night I had transferred both of my patients out of the unit and onto the neurosurgical floor. The patient census in the unit was low, so they asked me if I wanted to go home. I was ecstatic. I knew that Linda would be really surprised so I stopped and picked up a bottle of wine and thought it would be a perfect night to surprise her with the tickets to the Cayman Islands." Sierra stopped to catch her breath and quickly dried her eyes. "Nobody was as surprised as I was when I tiptoed into our house and heard some very interesting sounds coming from our bedroom. I found Linda and her ex-girlfriend very busy beneath our sheets."

Kaitlin covered her eyes with her hands and groaned, "Oh God, Sierra, no!"

Sierra laughed halfheartedly as she recalled the nightmare of that night. "I took that bottle of wine and hurled it against the wall. The explosion of glass and wine caught their attention immediately."

Kaitlin laughed softly through her hands as she watched Sierra intently. "What happened next, Sierra? How did you handle that mess?"

Sierra leaned back against the cushions and dried her eyes. "I went into the living room while they both scurried to get dressed and tried to figure out how they were going to explain their little affair. Linda saw her ex to the door and we spent the rest of the night talking, screaming, and crying. Linda admitted to having several affairs throughout our three years together, and that made me sick! I felt so naïve and deeply betrayed. Here I was pouring my heart and soul into maintaining our relationship, and she was screwing every woman she could find. She told me she always knew that our relationship was doomed and since it was my house she thought she would just stay around as long as possible until I threw her out. Isn't that one of the most pathetic stories you've ever heard? I'm thirty years old and I gave my life and my love to a woman who used me and played me for a fool." Sierra bolted from the bench in a flurry of emotional frustration and walked to the edge of the dock.

Kaitlin allowed her a few minutes to get herself together. Her eyes were drawn to the slender fit of Sierra's jeans and long, shapely legs. Kaitlin shook her head of her intimate thoughts and brought herself back to Sierra's pain. Kaitlin rose from the bench and stood beside Sierra, resting her hand intimately on her lower back.

Sierra ran her fingers through her hair and stared down into the onyx water.

"I'm sorry you had to go through that pain, Sierra. As much as you hate to hear it, it was probably a blessing in disguise that you went home early that night and found what you did. Otherwise Linda might have gone on to betray you."

Sierra turned to Kaitlin. "Unfortunately, I had to be slapped in the face with Linda's infidelity before I could see her for what she was. I was so trusting, Kate, and so damn naïve. I learned some painful lessons, and I hope never to be hurt like that again. For the past several months I've felt like a train with no headlight. I realized that I've been barreling along the track that Linda laid down for me. Now it's time that I turn on my own light and find my own track."

Kaitlin gently rubbed Sierra's back. "Linda has no idea what a gem she has lost."

Sierra smiled through her tears as she allowed Kaitlin to guide her back to the bench.

Kaitlin gently placed her arm around Sierra's shoulders and smiled as Sierra rested her head back against her arm.

Sierra looked up at the sparkling stars and caught her breath as Kaitlin watched the light return to her eyes.

"Thank you for sharing your personal life with me, Sierra. I'm also really grateful that you didn't have a bottle of wine in your hands when I yelled at you this afternoon."

They both burst into laughter as Sierra turned her head to look into Kaitlin's sparkling eyes.

"That was the first time in my life I had ever thrown anything, Kate, but you'd better watch yourself because I'm sure with practice my aim could get better."

Kaitlin forced herself to look away from those soft, moist lips that lay so close.

Sierra was stunned by her desire to snuggle deeper into Kaitlin's arms as she cleared her throat and forced herself to sit up. She looked over at the warmth in Kaitlin's eyes and rested her hand on her arm.

Kaitlin instantly felt the tender warmth of her touch. A surge of heat mushroomed in her belly and flowed to her thighs.

Kaitlin was shocked by her intense response as her chest warmed with a tingling sensation that she had not felt in years. They both felt the intensity between them as their eyes locked in an intimate dance.

Sierra nervously looked down into her lap. "How do you do it, Kate? How do you work as an E.R. doc and keep this remarkable place going?"

Kaitlin stared back at the sprawling main estate. "I love being an E.R. doc, Sierra. I only work one twelve-hour night shift a week to keep up my skills, and the rest of the time I dedicate to this place. My grandparents left me a sizeable inheritance so I can easily balance my time between here and the hospital. The money they left me also allows me to run Bradley Bay the way I like to."

Sierra watched her look out onto the lake and saw years of tumultuous emotions tumble across her eyes. "That's incredible what you've done here, Kate. You've created an oasis where spinal cord–injured adults can come and interact with each other and with nature."

Kaitlin felt embraced by Sierra's unconditional warmth. "I couldn't do it without Sabrina, Logan, and Gladys. I call them my three musketeers. They have given me three years of blood, sweat, and tears to help me make my vision a reality. When my grandparents owned and operated Bradley Bay, it was a thriving family resort. The same families came back every year generation after generation." Kaitlin suddenly looked away as Sierra was enchanted by her story.

"If it was so successful why did you convert it to a resort for spinal cord–injured adults? What inspired your vision?"

Kaitlin turned back to Sierra with eyes filled with pain just as they heard the three musketeers approaching. Together they watched them walk closer.

Sierra could see the small boat anchor and chain dangling from Sabrina's hands.

Kaitlin quickly jumped to her feet. She guided Sierra to her feet with pleading in her voice, "Please, Sierra, save me."

Sierra guided Kaitlin to stand behind her. Sierra basked in the burning intensity of her warm hands resting on her shoulders.

The three musketeers stood before them and glared over Sierra's shoulder at Kaitlin. Sierra raised one hand and laughed softly. "Wait, ladies. I have accepted Kate's meager apology, and I think we should give her a chance to prove that she can behave like the gracious welcoming committee that you all say she can be."

Sabrina carefully set the anchor down on the dock as Kaitlin playfully leaned against Sierra's back and exhaled deeply. They all burst into laughter as Sierra reveled in the warmth of Kaitlin's body against her back. Sierra turned to see Kaitlin's triumphant smile as she turned back to the girls and gave them a mischievous wink.

"Kate has promised me that from this moment on, she will be on her best behavior and that she will not hesitate to fulfill my every whim and desire."

Kaitlin's jaw dropped open as Sabrina, Logan, and Gladys laughed hysterically at her obviously shocked reaction. Sierra turned slowly and enjoyed every moment of Kaitlin's utter surprise.

Gladys stepped toward Kaitlin and wrapped her warmly in her arms. "That's my girl. I knew you would make it up to Sierra for treating her so badly."

Kaitlin turned her head and fired Sierra an *I'll get you for this!* look as Sierra burst into giggles.

They all settled close on the cushioned bench and spent the next hour talking about the planned activities for the next day.

Gladys tried to conceal a yawn as she rose from the dock bench. "Good night, ladies. This old gal is getting her weary bones to bed. I suggest you all do the same, since tomorrow will be another busy day. This place is booked to capacity, and we have a lot of things planned." Gladys hugged and kissed Sabrina and Logan warmly. She stood before Sierra and held her close. "I can promise you that tomorrow will be a better day, Sierra." Gladys threw Kaitlin a scolding look before turning back to

Sierra. "I feel confident that you will feel much more welcome and appreciated than you did today."

"It didn't turn out to be such a bad day after all, Gladys. That niece of yours is not as wicked as I thought she was." Gladys hugged her tight before stepping toward Kaitlin. Kaitlin took several measured steps backwards till she reached the edge of the dock.

"Keep on going, Katie. A good dunking is about what you deserve tonight, regardless of Sierra graciously forgiving you." Gladys reached for Kaitlin and squeezed her tight in her arms before reaching behind her and firmly smacking her bottom.

"Ouch," Kaitlin whined, as she rubbed her own bottom.

"Now, I left you a plate of food in the main kitchen if you feel you finally deserve to be fed," Gladys stated firmly.

Kaitlin took Gladys's chubby face in her hands and held her close. "Sierra shared her sandwich with me, so there. At least she was thoughtful of my growling stomach, compared to the rest of you wretched women."

Gladys held Kaitlin close as she attempted to look stern. "You'd better pay attention to who is being kind to you, Katie, and realize it's best not to cut off your nose to spite your face." Gladys pinched Kaitlin's tiny nose before hugging her tight and waving good-bye to everyone.

Sabrina reached down to pick up the discarded anchor and looked at Sierra. "Do you want us to give you a wake up call at seven o'clock, Sierra, or are you going to manage to get your city buns out of bed by yourself?"

Sierra frowned and playfully swatted Sabrina's arm. "I think I can manage to get myself out of bed at that ungodly hour without you two barreling down my door. However, I would like to remind you guys that I am on my vacation. Tell me now if you both plan on torturing me like this for the next two weeks because you could seriously damage my usually sunny, charming personality."

Logan leaned closer to Sierra's smiling eyes. "Welcome to the Emerald City, Sierra. One thing we can promise you is that the yellow brick road will guide you to your bed every night in an exhausted heap."

They all laughed at Sierra's grimacing expression.

Sabrina touched Kaitlin's arm. "We've already made sure that the quads and paraplegics transferred into bed okay. We'd like to make a final check and make sure they have everything they need. If you give us fifteen minutes, we'll walk you home."

"That would be great as long as you guys promise me you don't have plans for that anchor when Sierra's not here to protect me."

Sabrina leaned intimately close to her glowing face. "You'd better do good on your promise to behave yourself, Dr. Bradley, or you could easily become a very tasty treat for the Loch Ness monster that lurks in this lake." Kaitlin gasped with terror and jumped back behind Sierra.

Sabrina and Logan hugged them both warmly and headed toward the main estate.

Sierra turned to Kaitlin and felt enveloped by the warmth of her brilliant smile. "Those two are absolutely adorable," Sierra said.

The deep bond forged between Sierra and the three musketeers amazed Kaitlin. "Yes, they are adorable and very special." Kaitlin looked into Sierra's bright eyes and hated to end their time together. "Are you sure you're not hungry, Sierra? I could whip you up something in my kitchen. I'd hate to have you go to bed on an empty stomach."

Sierra rested her hand on Kaitlin's arm. "I'm fine. Will you please stop worrying about my withering frame?"

Kaitlin frowned as Sierra laughed at her expression. "You must still be hungry, Kate. I'm sure half my sandwich will only silence your growling stomach for a short while."

Kaitlin luxuriated in the gentle touch of her hand. "Actually, I feel fine. That was the most delicious turkey sandwich I've ever shared."

They both stood awkwardly as they hesitated to say good night.

Kaitlin gestured toward the main estate. "You must be tired after your long day, Sierra. Let me walk you back to the house." Silently, Kaitlin rested her hand on Sierra's elbow and guided her forward, as they leisurely walked back to the main estate side by side.

They were both lost in their thoughts of the emotional day as they stopped at the front steps. When they stood facing each other, Kaitlin gave Sierra an impish grin. "I hope that you'll let me know your every whim and desire, since I hear that I've promised to fulfill them while you're here."

Sierra burst into playful laughter and gave Kaitlin a devilish smile. "Oh, don't worry about that, Dr. Kaitlin Bradley. I'm determined to ask anything and everything of you so that by the end of these two weeks you will feel thoroughly cleansed of your deplorable behavior."

Kaitlin playfully dropped her face into her hands and muttered, "God help me."

Sierra thoroughly enjoyed their lighthearted banter as she hesitantly reached up and ran her hand over Kaitlin's soft hair.

Kaitlin slowly raised her face from her hands and looked into Sierra's intense eyes. Everything else ceased to exist as they absorbed each other's sizzling, magnetic chemistry. Kaitlin intently moved one step closer and took Sierra's soft hands in her own. They were both mesmerized by the intensity of their touch as Kaitlin looked down at their entwined hands. "Thank you for accepting my apology, Sierra, and for being such a good listener. I promise to be on my best behavior for the next two weeks."

Sierra glided her thumbs over the back of Kaitlin's strong hands. "I look forward to seeing that, Dr. Bradley." Sierra squeezed Kaitlin's hands. "Thank you for coming to talk to me. I will always cherish my time with you tonight. I hope you continue to let me in behind your walls to learn more about the real Dr. Kaitlin Bradley. I also look forward to the time when you are ready to explain to me what inspired your vision to convert Bradley Bay. I would also love to hear how it got its nickname, the Emerald City."

Kaitlin felt warmed by Sierra's close proximity. "You have a lot of questions, big-city girl. You'd better stay two months instead of two weeks if you seek all those answers."

They heard the screen door squeak and looked up to see it slam shut behind Logan. Sabrina and Logan bounced down the front steps hand in hand with beautiful, tired smiles.

Sierra hesitantly released Kaitlin's hands. She stepped toward Sabrina and Logan and hugged them warmly. She bid everyone good night as she headed up the first two steps. She stopped and turned back to Kaitlin. "Good night, Dr. Bradley. Sweet dreams."

Kaitlin jammed her hands into her pockets and frowned. "Don't I get a hug too?"

Sierra laughed as she climbed the remaining steps to the front porch. She turned as she reached the top and gave Kaitlin a gentle wink. "I only give my hugs to people that will appreciate them. You, my friend, have yet to appreciate me."

Sabrina and Logan whistled and cheered Sierra's retort as Kaitlin stood in frustrated shock and watched Sierra wave good night.

CRITOCRITOCRITO

Sierra dropped her room key onto her tiny desk and stepped toward the picture window. She wrapped her arms around herself and leaned her forehead against the cool glass, gazing out on the calm lake. Sierra's mind was filled with thoughts of Kaitlin as she listened intently to the shrill, chirping sound of the crickets that pierced through the still night. She shook her head to clear her racing thoughts and spiraling emotions as she noticed movement on Kaitlin's back deck.

Sierra squinted to get a better look and watched Kaitlin walk to her back railing. She leaned back against the railing and picked up the midnight black cat and held it close to her chest.

She gently massaged its face and head as she stared off in the distance.

Sierra was spellbound watching her fluid movements as she saw Kaitlin start to walk back into her house, then stop suddenly. Sierra smiled shyly as she realized that Kaitlin saw her watching. Sierra watched Kaitlin gently place the cat down on a lounge chair.

Kaitlin looked up at Sierra and placed her hands along the side of her head and tilted her head sweetly to signal for Sierra to go to sleep.

Sierra placed the palm of her hand against the window to signal for Kaitlin to wait. She stepped away from the window and grabbed a piece of paper and black marker from her suitcase and started writing in big block letters. Sierra replaced the cap on the marker and stepped back toward the window. She laughed softly as she saw Kaitlin standing on her front deck beside a large telescope. Sierra glided her window open and placed her note against the screen.

She could see Kaitlin bend before the telescope and laugh as she read:

STOP THINKING AND TUCK YOURSELF INTO BED, DR. BRADLEY. I HAVE PLANS FOR YOU TOMORROW. YOU'LL NEED ALL THE REST YOU CAN GET.

Sierra enjoyed watching Kaitlin laugh as she slowly took her sign away from the window.

Kaitlin shook her head at Sierra's sense of humor. She slowly raised her hand and waved good night. Then she blew Sierra a kiss.

Sierra's breath caught in her chest as she leaned back from the window and waved, aching to lean into those lips that formed that kiss.

⚙ 4

Sabrina, Logan, and Sierra spent two hours assisting several of the paraplegic and quadriplegic guests to shower and dress for breakfast. They worked closely with their family members to enable the spinal cord–injured guests to achieve their maximum independence.

The girls assisted several of the quads with their breakfast and finally settled down at their own table to enjoy a warm, hearty meal of French toast and crispy bacon. They divided their duties for the rest of the morning and headed off in different directions, promising to meet back in the dining room at eleven-thirty.

೮೩ಖಿ೮೩ಖಿ೮೩ಖಿ

Kaitlin walked along the lane from her home to the main estate. She closed her eyes as she felt the warm rays of the midmorning sun bathe her face. Her heart brimmed with an unusual happiness as she heard the unmistakable joyous sound of Sierra's laughter.

She stopped as she saw a circle of wheelchairs on the volleyball platform. Sierra was bouncing from one quad to the next with exuberance as she held a bubble wand before their mouths and watched them blow huge bubbles into the circle. Kaitlin's black cat, Licorice, was positioned in the center of the circle springing continuously from her hind feet trying to swipe at the bubbles and eliciting a roar of laughter from a large group of people watching her from outside the circle.

Kaitlin felt a rush of tingling excitement as she began walking toward Sierra and her festive little group. She squinted against the bright sun as she admired Sierra's slender frame dressed in a stylish pair of beige shorts and matching striped T-shirt.

Sierra dipped her wand into the liquid soap solution and positioned it before Jennifer's mouth. Jennifer gently blew a trail of glistening bubbles over Licorice's head and watched her completely flip in midair to catch those elusive air pockets. Everyone burst into laughter and applauded as Sierra looked up and saw Kaitlin approach.

She inhaled sharply as her heart raced in her chest. The look of intense warmth she saw in Kaitlin's eyes spread like a rippling pond through her soul. She felt herself being drawn towards that sensual energy with a force like no other she had ever experienced.

Kaitlin felt consumed by an instantaneous rush of heat as she saw the unrestrained yearning gleaming from that blue-gray depth. She craved to unleash the intensity and need behind that look.

Jennifer looked up and saw Sierra frozen in her spot, as the liquid soap dribbled from the wand and over her hand. Jennifer followed her unwavering gaze and smiled as she saw the reason for her stunned state.

"Good morning, Dr. Bradley. Would you care to join us in the playful torture of your entertaining cat?" Jennifer said.

"Good morning, Jen, Sierra." Kaitlin greeted the crowd warmly as she stood before Sierra and Jennifer. She looked down as Licorice pranced toward her and rubbed herself along her shins. Kaitlin bent down and scooped Licorice into her arms and rubbed her soapy head. "What are they doing to you, Licorice?"

Sierra forced herself to breathe evenly as she finally realized that her hand was covered in soap and dropped the wand into the solution. "I was assigned to do the breathing exercises with this lovely group of people so I was trying to make a game of it. It turned into a real party when Licorice here decided to be my little assistant." Sierra reached forward and rubbed the beautiful black cat's chin as she found herself lost in Kaitlin's shining emerald eyes.

Kaitlin forced herself to look away from Sierra's engaging eyes and looked down at Licorice. "No wonder I couldn't find you to feed you this morning. You went off and found yourself a job."

Kaitlin bent forward and placed Licorice in Jennifer's lap. Licorice gladly curled into a black ball of fur as Jennifer gently ran the back of her withered hand over the spoiled cat's head.

Sierra looked over the circle of quads and at their waiting family members. "I think we've done enough heavy breathing for one day, guys. It's getting close to lunchtime. Why don't we give your lungs a rest and meet back here tomorrow morning at the same time and see what sort of tricks Licorice will have in store for us."

They all thanked Sierra for her kindness as family members or friends slowly guided each wheelchair off the wooden platform.

Jennifer grinned as she watched Kaitlin and Sierra squirm in each other's allurement. She held Licorice close in her lap and absorbed the intense chemistry exploding between these two women. "Sierra, my guided tour of the Emerald City leaves after lunch. Don't miss the bus since you're the only scheduled guest on my tour."

Sierra gave Jennifer a warm smile. "I wouldn't miss that tour for the world, Jennifer. That gives me enough time to help out with lunch and check on Sabrina and Logan and see if they need a hand with anything. Why don't I meet you on the dock at one o'clock?"

"Sounds good. See you then."

Jennifer's mother, Anne, slowly guided her chair to the platform ramp. "Put your hiking boots on, Sierra. Jen's guided tours don't miss a nook or cranny of this huge place. She travels in this wheelchair like she did on her motorcycle. Fast and furiously."

"Thanks for the tip, Anne. I'll be ready. I hope I'm not interfering with any plans you had with Jennifer."

"Not at all, Sierra. This gives me the opportunity to catch a nap before Jennifer and I go sailing. It doesn't satisfy Jen's need for speed but it gives us a really tranquil time out on the lake together. It's times like that that I really cherish here with Jennifer."

"If you'd only let us take the motorboat out I could really show you a good time, Mom."

"Forget it, Jennifer. The last time Katie let you steer the motorboat you almost rammed the dock and got us all killed."

"Please, I had a reason. There was that group of teenage girls sunbathing topless by one of the cabins. I was momentarily distracted. I can do better with practice."

"Do what better with practice? Steer the boat or watch topless women? God knows you don't need any practice at pursuing women."

"Since I got that mastered, I just need to practice steering the boat. What do you say, Mom?"

"Jennifer, let's just stick to sailing for now so that you don't give your old mom a heart attack, okay?"

"Party pooper."

Kaitlin and Sierra waved good-bye as they watched Jennifer take control of her electric wheelchair. She loosely gripped the control stick on her side rail and guided her wheelchair toward the lake as her mother strolled beside her in endless debate.

Kaitlin turned to Sierra and reached into the soapy solution to pull out the wand. Sierra watched her raise the wand to those sensuous lips and blow a steady stream of big bubbles skyward. Kaitlin dipped the wand again and looked into Sierra's eyes. "I haven't done this since I was a kid."

Sierra was enchanted as she watched Kaitlin's full, rosy lips tease a huge bubble from the wand.

"That was incredible what you did with those quads, Sierra. Getting them to blow bubbles to expand their lungs is a brilliant idea. How did you come up with that exercise?"

Sierra felt extremely aware of every tingling cell in her body as she eased herself one step back from Kaitlin's intoxicating essence. She nervously wiped at a trail of soap dripping from her thumb as she willed her heart to slow its erratic pace. "Sabrina and Logan gave me a bag of balloons to get them to blow up but I hate blowing up balloons. It gives me a headache, so I couldn't think of torturing the guests like that."

Kaitlin laughed softly at Sierra's grimacing expression as she dropped the wand into the container. "I found this bubble maker behind the main desk, and Gladys told me to take it and have fun. But I never imagined that it was going to turn into a circus with Licorice being my star performer."

Kaitlin took the container from Sierra and replaced the lid. "You were wonderful with them, Sierra. I've never seen them enjoy their breathing exercises like they did with you and Licorice."

Sierra blushed deeply as Kaitlin took her by the soapy hand. "Come on, let's get you inside so you can get the soap off your hands. Thanks to you, I'm going to have to bathe Licorice just to get all the soap out of her fur. Otherwise, she's going to be licking herself for days."

They both laughed as Sierra followed Kaitlin into the main office behind the reception desk. The room was spacious and cozy. Two walls consisted of large, semicircular bay windows overlooking Bradley Bay and the wooded area. A massive antique rolltop desk sat in one corner cluttered with invoices and opened mail. Adorning the top of the desk were several pictures of Kaitlin at different ages. Sierra guessed it was Gladys's desk.

Nestled in a far corner was an ornate oak executive desk and chair. The desktop was immaculately neat and organized with a single picture of the three musketeers—undoubtedly, Kaitlin's desk. Below one bay window was a modern computer table, loaded with the latest in computer technology.

Kaitlin guided Sierra to the sink in the office bathroom and reached for the pink hand towel. Sierra thanked her and dried her hands as she watched Kaitlin wash her hands.

"Your cat is beautiful, Kate. How did you come up with her adorable name?"

Sierra handed the towel back to Kaitlin and enjoyed her closeness in the small feminine bathroom adorned in pastel colors of pink and gray. "She's a wonderful cat. I found her as a tiny ball of whimpering black fur under my back deck about a year ago. She and I became instant roommates. As for her name, I love black licorice, so that's how she got her name."

Sierra leaned back against the counter. They both luxuriated in the intensity between them as Sierra gave Kaitlin a breathtaking smile. "Good morning, Dr. Bradley. How did you sleep last night?"

Kaitlin replaced the towel on the towel rack and leaned her hip against the counter. "Very well, thank you. How did you sleep, Ms. Vaughn?"

"Very well, actually. However I have one complaint that I would like to lodge with the complaint committee."

Kaitlin couldn't help but laugh at Sierra's playful charm as she gave her a dubious look. "Since I'm assigned to taking care of your every whim and desire, you'd better let me hear this complaint."

Sierra thoroughly enjoyed her playful control over Kaitlin. "My bed squeaks."

Kaitlin burst into laughter. "Your bed squeaks?"

"Yes, my bed squeaks."

Kaitlin gave her a seductive stare and leaned intimately close to her attractive eyes. She watched her dark, lush eyelashes flutter rapidly as Kaitlin inhaled her enticing vanilla scent. "When does your bed squeak?"

Sierra gently grabbed the collar of Kaitlin's elegant white linen blouse and pulled her even closer. "It squeaks when I sit on it, when I lie down, and each and every time I roll over during the night. I'm amazed you couldn't hear my bed from your place." Sierra released Kaitlin's collar and watched her slowly back away.

"Well, if you weren't such a restless sleeper then maybe you wouldn't wear out the bed frame and springs."

Sierra blushed sweetly. "I'm not a restless sleeper, Dr. Bradley." Sierra shyly looked down at her hands. She wondered what Kaitlin would think if she knew she was the cause of her sleeplessness. "I just had a lot on my mind last night, and that's no excuse for my squeaky bed."

Kaitlin gently touched Sierra's chin, guiding her eyes back to her. "If I have your permission to let my staff enter your room, I'll make sure somebody takes care of the problem before you lay your beautiful face back down on your pillow tonight." Kaitlin slowly, hesitantly, released her hand and stared at the beautiful smile on Sierra's moist lips.

"You have my permission. While you're at it, Dr. Bradley, could you have them put someone in my bed that would give me a warm, fuzzy feeling all night?"

Kaitlin burst into her rich, deep laughter and looked at Sierra with a smoky, seductive look in her eyes. She leaned intimately close to her and whispered, "I'll see what I can do to fulfill that desire, Ms. Vaughn."

Sierra could no longer fight the urge as she reached up and slowly traced her fingertip along Kaitlin's soft cheek. "I would appreciate that, Kaitlin Bradley."

Kaitlin gazed into Sierra's eyes and struggled to control the raging desire to take her into her arms and kiss her passionately. Kaitlin breathed a sexually frustrated groan and leaned back against the bathroom vanity. She closed her eyes in an attempt to control the fevered emotions Sierra spun within her in such a short period of time.

Sierra was gripped by their mutual longing as she reached up and tenderly brushed a stray strand of hair from Kaitlin's eyes. She was awestruck by the depth of passion peeking beyond those titanium walls.

Kaitlin opened her eyes and peered deeply into Sierra's eyes.

"I should go and help Sabrina and Logan with lunch before I hop on Jennifer's tour bus."

Kaitlin took a deep breath and gently touched Sierra's arm. "Before you go, I have something for you." Kaitlin guided Sierra across the room. "I put this in my desk this morning when you were busy in the dining room." Kaitlin slid the middle drawer open and pulled out a small flat package wrapped in pretty pink tissue paper and secured delicately with burgundy ribbons and bows.

Sierra watched as Kaitlin turned with the gift. "How long have you been up this morning?" Sierra asked.

Kaitlin shyly stepped before Sierra with the package balanced lightly in her hands. "I've been up since six o'clock. You're not the only one who was a restless sleeper last night."

Sierra smiled brightly into Kaitlin's sensitive emerald eyes and carefully accepted the gift from her outstretched hands. Sierra flushed with excitement as she slowly ran her fingertip across the shiny ribbons.

Kaitlin watched her with rapt amazement. She gently touched her chin with the soft pad of her thumb. "Go ahead. Open it."

Sierra carefully removed the crinkly tissue paper and handed it to Kaitlin. She stared down in wonder at the beautiful red velvet journal in her hand. Sierra ran the palm of her hand across the plush velvet cover. She carefully opened the journal and read the inscription written in Kaitlin's elegant penmanship.

Dear Sierra,

> *I hope that your memories of Bradley Bay touch your heart as you have already touched mine.*

Love, Kate

Sierra raised her face to look into Kaitlin's magnificent eyes. "It's beautiful, Kate. It's truly beautiful."

Kaitlin brushed a stray strand of hair away from Sierra's eyes. "I thought you might like to record your adventure here at

Bradley Bay so you will always have something to remember us by when you leave."

Sierra looked intently into Kaitlin's searching eyes and took a deep breath. Kaitlin had no idea how profoundly affected she already was by her and Bradley Bay.

"I also put my home phone number and pager number in there so you won't have to flash me cue cards every night out your bedroom window."

"But that was so much fun," Sierra said.

Kaitlin slipped her hands into the pockets of her classy black pleated shorts and said sarcastically, "I really enjoyed being told to go to bed like that." They both laughed warmly as Kaitlin watched Sierra gingerly close the journal and caress the front cover.

"This is one of the most touching gifts I've ever received, Kate. Thank- you."

Kaitlin smiled at Sierra's reaction and tenderly touched her soft cheek. "You're very welcome." Kaitlin looked down at the journal and touched it with her finger. "Make sure you just write nice things about me in there."

Sierra tilted her head. "You'd better continue to show your sparkling charm and tender heart, Dr. Bradley, or you may not be mentioned at all."

Kaitlin gasped in horror as she reached for the journal and tried to pull it away from Sierra's hands. Sierra easily tugged her journal back and held it tight against her chest. They both laughed warmly as Kaitlin looked down at her watch and sighed. "I should probably head into town to pick up the stationery and medical supplies that Gladys ordered."

"Do you have to go?"

Kaitlin leaned closer to Sierra's beautiful pillowy lips. "I would have invited you to come with me, but I understand that Jennifer has already booked your time."

Sierra reached forward and gently tugged on a button on Kaitlin's blouse. "That's correct. If you want to have time with me, Dr. Bradley, you're just going to have to stand in line."

Kaitlin threw her head back and laughed. "I see. I'll keep that in mind, Ms. Vaughn, you popular little thing, you." They both laughed as Gladys bounced into the room with a glow of loving energy.

She instantly saw Kaitlin and Sierra and squealed with delight as she hugged and kissed them both.

Sierra held her journal out to Gladys. "Look, Gladys. Kate gave me a gift."

Gladys held the beautiful, rich journal in her hands and gave Kaitlin a loving smile. "What a lovely gift, Katie. Sierra, I hope these pages are filled with as much love and enthusiasm as you have given us."

Sierra smiled as she took her journal from Gladys. She hated to leave this loving circle. She shyly looked from Gladys to Kaitlin. "I should go and help with lunch." Sierra stepped toward Gladys and hugged her tight as the phone rang at the reception desk. Gladys kissed the tip of Sierra's tiny nose. "Excuse me, ladies, while I grab that."

Sierra set her journal down on Kaitlin's desk and stepped toward her smiling eyes. She gently slid her hands onto Kaitlin's slender waist and felt her tremble beneath her touch. Sierra whispered softly, "Come here, you," and stepped into the loving warmth of Kaitlin's arms. Sierra felt the softness of Kaitlin's cheek against her forehead as they fit perfectly in each other's embrace.

Kaitlin glided the open palm of her hands slowly along Sierra's back and held her close as she heard a soft, sensuous moan escape her lips. Their hips met in an intimate union as Kaitlin felt a caressing heat burn between her thighs. Kaitlin brushed her face in Sierra's hair and inhaled the gentle scent of lemon and vanilla.

Sierra slowly outlined the contours of Kaitlin's back and held her tight against her as she felt a blazing arousal and vitality coursing through her veins. Sierra tilted her head up and brought her lips to Kaitlin's ear, whispering seductively, "Thank you."

Kaitlin smiled and nuzzled her cheek against Sierra's. "You're welcome. Thank you for feeling I finally appreciate you enough to deserve one of your earth-shattering hugs."

They both laughed softly and hesitantly leaned back. Sierra was mesmerized by the glimmering glow in those emerald eyes. That unusual fluttering sensation beat a rapid pace in Sierra's belly; competing with the erratic pace of her heart. She basked in the emotions assaulting her senses as she floated on the intense waves of heat cascading from Kaitlin's hands on her waist.

Kaitlin was stunned by the passion and sensuality between them, as they stood suspended in time, basking in their intimate contact. She had never felt so acutely aware of every sense of sight, smell, touch and sound as she was holding Sierra in her arms.

Gladys bounced back into the room and stopped suddenly as she saw their warm embrace and felt the depth of emotion flowing continuously between them.

Sierra and Kaitlin turned and smiled at the look of pure joy in Gladys's eyes. Sierra sheepishly cleared her throat as she leaned up toward Kaitlin's face. She kissed her soft cheek, allowing her lips to linger as she absorbed her heat and subtle perfume. She took one step back from Kaitlin and smiled at the look of smoldering passion in her eyes. Sierra reached forward and gently touched her chin. "Please drive safely into town, Kate. I'll see you when you get back."

Kaitlin was speechless as she watched Sierra pick up her journal and hug it tight. Sierra leaned toward Gladys and kissed her cheek before she waved good-bye and stepped out of the office.

Gladys exuded pure joy as she stepped toward Kaitlin's beaming smile. "I haven't seen that look of bursting love in your eyes since that Christmas we bought you that tiny golden retriever puppy. He jumped out of that gift box and into your arms and licked your face for hours."

Kaitlin burst into laughter as she fondly remembered her many beautiful Christmases with Gladys.

Gladys stood before Kaitlin with eyes filled with maternal love and cupped her glowing face in her hands. "She's a very special woman, Kaitlin. You've been alone for a year now. It's time you let go of the past and allowed someone to share your future." Gladys watched the pain cloud Kaitlin's eyes as her heart ached for her happiness. "Follow your heart, Katie, and see if that beautiful puppy that just bounced out of this office will accept your love as that furry little puppy did for many, many years."

"She's leaving in two weeks to go back to the big city, Gladys. I have to remind myself of that. What do I have to offer Sierra here?"

Gladys was shocked and appalled by Kaitlin's unusual self-defeating attitude. She took her firmly by the shoulders and held her still. "You, Kaitlin. That's what you have to offer her here. That's more than most women could wish for!" Kaitlin laughed shyly and reached for a tissue. "For three years now, Katie, you've been taking care of everyone else and ignoring your own happiness. I see the way that you and Sierra look at each other. It's the same look I shared with your uncle since the day I fell in love with him."

Kaitlin leaned her forehead against Gladys's. "I'm so scared, Gladys. I'm so afraid to fall in love again."

Gladys held her close and whispered softly, "I know, sweetheart. I know."

⚙ 5

Sierra stopped to pick a handful of brilliant yellow buttercups as Jennifer slowly rolled along the nature trail cleared for wheelchair accessibility. Towering spruce trees lined the trail and embraced them into its majestic beauty.

Jennifer slowly raised her arm and pointed out a beautiful pair of blue jays hovering by their nest. She continued on for several feet and showed Sierra the spot where Kaitlin buried her little sparrow.

Sierra gently placed a single buttercup in the palm of Jennifer's hand and watched her carefully balance it as she admired its simple elegance.

Sierra raised the delicate flower to her nose as she kept in step with Jennifer's chair. "When you think about your accident, Jennifer, do you ever wish you'd never owned a motorcycle?"

Jennifer gazed up at the midday sun. "I've had five years to think about that, Sierra, and as crazy as it sounds, I feel very grateful for the time I had on my Harley."

Sierra turned to look at Jennifer and saw the intense sadness in her eyes.

"I was in my late twenties at the time and nothing in my life gave me the feeling of freedom and control like I had when I rode my motorcycle. Nothing. I had ridden it for ten years and never had an accident till that fateful rainy morning. I was in such a damn hurry to make it to my classes at the University of Toronto that I didn't even see the car pull out of the parking spot right in front of me. The roads were so slick from the rain that I lost control of my bike and slammed head on into a streetcar and instantly became a C5 incomplete quad." Jennifer focused on the trail ahead and laughed sadly. "My ex-lover, Chelsea, always said I was meant to be on wheels, but these weren't exactly the type of wheels I had in mind."

Sierra laughed softly at Jennifer's sense of humor and gently squeezed her shoulder.

"I'm thirty-three years old, Sierra, and I've been a quad for five years. Chelsea left me a year after my accident because she just couldn't handle the altered lifestyle. When she left me I fell into a deep depression. Then one day I realized that my life span was already greatly diminished by my accident so I wasn't going to waste my precious time on regrets and self-pity. I still have my down days like anyone else but I feel grateful for the wonderful years I had with my legs and now I'm trying to have the same positive attitude about my wheels."

"You're an inspiration, Jennifer. To the other quads and to all of us with legs."

"It really makes a difference to be able to hold a job like anyone else. I love my work at the motorcycle dealership. I do everything from sales to searching the Internet to find parts for vintage bikes. It makes me feel like a whole person and not just a burden to those around me."

"You haven't let your physical limitations slow you down from leading a fulfilling life, Jennifer, and that's truly remarkable. Not many people would have bounced back from a devastating injury like yours and done as well as you have."

Jennifer smiled as they finally reached the crest of the hill. She stared out at the breathtaking view of Bradley Bay and marveled at the cabins that speckled the lakeshore. "This is my most favorite spot. I love coming up here to think. I'll just sit for hours and watch everyone enjoying themselves out on the lake. I once told Kaitlin that I was going up to my summit and ever since that day she has nicknamed this spot The Summit. She had this viewing platform built so we could safely sit here in our wheelchairs and enjoy the view."

Sierra squeezed Jennifer's shoulder as she admired her inner strength. Sierra sat on the bench beside Jennifer as they stayed and talked about Jennifer's hopes and dreams.

Jennifer directed her electric wheelchair back down the nature trail as Sierra stepped in beside her. "This place deserves a lot of the credit for my emotional strength, Sierra. I met Sabrina, Logan, and Kaitlin when I was hospitalized for my accident. They all looked after me, and I adored them for their kindness and positive attitudes. Every time I would go back for my doctor's visits I would always visit with Kaitlin. When she moved up here, she wrote me and invited me to Bradley Bay. I've been coming every summer and winter for three years now. This place always makes me feel normal—unlike when I'm at home and everybody stares at me like I'm some creature from the black lagoon."

Sierra laughed as Jennifer rolled her eyes playfully. "Bradley Bay gives me the opportunity to meet people who have shared similar struggles and experiences. People who can really understand my life without feeling the need to shower me with pity. Besides, it's a great place to cruise chicks."

Sierra laughed at Jennifer's spunk and rested her hand on her shoulder. "That a girl! That's the attitude."

Jennifer gave Sierra an impish smile and carefully maneuvered her chair around a bend. "The one person besides Kaitlin that really made me see that I could lead a full, meaningful life was Quinn."

Sierra stopped to pick several white daisies and asked, "Who's Quinn?"

Jennifer suddenly stopped her wheelchair and spun around to face Sierra. Jennifer's expression was shocked as she slowly shook her head. "I'm sorry, Sierra. I thought Kaitlin would have told you about Quinn."

Sierra stepped closer to Jennifer and gave her a questioning frown as Jennifer took a deep breath. "Quinn was Kaitlin's lover. She became a quad three years ago in a freak pool accident. Sadly, she died one year ago from pneumonia."

CRIOCRIOCRIO

Kaitlin entered the final inventory figures into her computer and clicked back onto the main screen before she headed into the kitchen for a glass of orange juice. She reached into the cupboard for a glass and looked out her huge kitchen bay window. Sierra was climbing her deck stairs with determination in her step and tears in her eyes. Kaitlin instantly felt concerned and set the glass down on the large, white speckled island in the center of her kitchen. She stepped toward her sliding glass door and slid it open just as Sierra walked toward her and crumbled into her arms. Kaitlin held her tight and caressed her head as she felt her sob against her. "What is it, Sierra? What's happened?"

Sierra leaned back and allowed her tears to flow, as she stayed cocooned in Kaitlin's arms. "You should have told me, Kate. I had no idea. I never imagined in my worst nightmares. Then I yelled at you, and, oh God, I feel so bad!"

Kaitlin was stunned as Sierra bombarded her with her emotions. Kaitlin took her teary face in her hands and held her still. "What're you talking about, Sierra? You've completely lost me."

Sierra stepped back from Kaitlin's warmth and ran her hands through her hair in frustration. "I'm talking about Quinn, Kate. You should have told me about Quinn."

Kaitlin leaned back against the back of her floral print couch and took a deep, emotional breath. "Jennifer told you."

Sierra's eyes flashed with emotional intensity as she stepped intimately close to Kaitlin's concerned eyes. "Yes, Jennifer mentioned Quinn to me and I would much rather have been told by you."

Kaitlin exhaled a frustrated breath and reached forward for Sierra and pulled her intimately close. "I was about to tell you last night on the dock, Sierra, till a boat anchor came toward me with my obituary written all over it!" They both laughed as Sierra dried her eyes.

"At least if I'd known, I would've understood your less-than-sunny disposition."

Kaitlin looked at Sierra with a flood of anger in her eyes. "Just because my lover was a quad, Sierra, does not in any way give me the right to be a bitch and treat you as badly as I did yesterday. That's exactly the reason why I don't share my personal life with people. I don't need any pity or excuses for my behavior." Kaitlin attempted to move away from Sierra, but Sierra reached for her face and held her still.

They stared into each other's emotional eyes as Sierra spoke softly. "I'm not trying to give you excuses for your deplorable behavior, Kate, or shower you with pity. I'm just asking to be invited into your world so I can understand what makes you such an incredible woman."

Kaitlin felt enveloped by Sierra's passionate warmth as she closed her eyes and leaned her forehead against Sierra's. Sierra held her tight and caressed her silky hair. Kaitlin leaned back and took a deep breath. "Come on, you. Come in so I can tell you my story from the beginning."

Kaitlin took Sierra's soft hand and guided her into the large, spacious kitchen. The sun streamed in from the bay window and illuminated the pristine white kitchen. Pine cupboards lined one wall with an antique baker's shelf and round table adding to the kitchen's warmth.

"Can I get you something to drink, Sierra? Pepsi, coffee, tea, orange juice, water?"

Sierra slowly turned to absorb the beauty of Kaitlin's cozy, sun-filled home. "Orange juice, please."

Kaitlin watched Sierra absorb the design of her home with awe as she walked slowly around the kitchen island and stopped at the steps leading to her sunken living room.

Sierra was stunned by the wide-open concept and elegant, feminine furniture that creatively divided the huge area into a living room, dining room, and office. Sierra's eyes followed the ornate, pine spiral staircase up to the second story loft. Her eyes followed the pine railing across and rested on a gorgeous pink, burgundy and white Mennonite quilt draped elegantly over the railing, partially obscuring the view of an open doorway. Sierra's mind raced wildly as she conjured up visions of Kaitlin lying on her bed beyond that quilt.

Kaitlin stepped toward Sierra and smiled at the look of wonderment in her eyes as she handed her a glass of orange juice.

"Thank you. Your home is gorgeous, Kate. It's like something you see in those home design magazines. It feels so warm and cozy."

Kaitlin took a sip of juice from her own glass. "Thank you. I'm glad you like it. I've made a lot of changes in the past year, after Quinn died. I really like how it turned out." Kaitlin took Sierra by the elbow and guided her down the steps. "Come into the living room so I can tell you about Quinn before you accuse me of hiding something else from you."

Kaitlin guided Sierra onto a tan, plush loveseat that afforded them a breathtaking view of the lake. They settled in close together and set their glasses down on the glass coffee table.

Sierra settled back into the thick cushions and gently took Kaitlin's hand. She watched their fingers slowly entwine and felt enthralled by Kaitlin's soft touch. "I'm sorry for barging in here uninvited. I was just shocked when Jennifer told me your lover was a quad."

Kaitlin instantly felt the heat surging through her body from Sierra's touch. "You're welcome in my home anytime, Sierra, so don't apologize. However, that was quite a grand entrance. I can't say I've ever had a woman storm into my house like that before." They both laughed as Sierra gently squeezed Kaitlin's hand.

"I always like to leave a lasting impression."

Kaitlin burst into laughter as she leaned closer to Sierra. "You, Sierra Vaughn, have definitely left me with a lasting impression of these past two days."

Sierra's breath caught in her throat as she forced herself to calm her unsteady heartbeat. "All right, enough of the small talk, Dr. Bradley. Spill your guts, and then I'll decide whether I'll forgive you for withholding this information from me."

Sierra watched Kaitlin take another sip of orange juice and slowly set her glass down with an impish smile in her eyes. She leaned back into the couch and curled one leg under her as she placed their entwined hands on her thigh.

"Quinn was a pediatrician. We met at an emergency trauma conference in Vancouver." Sierra watched years of cherished memories float across Kaitlin's eyes. "We'd been together for eight years, and at the time we were living and working in Toronto. Three years ago, on a hot summer July day, I threw a surprise birthday party for Quinn's thirty-second birthday. All of our friends and family were there having a great time around the pool."

Sierra watched as Kaitlin stared out over the lake and saw nothing but her painful memories. Kaitlin dropped her head as her tears drenched her cheeks.

Sierra slid closer and placed her hand on Kaitlin's back. Kaitlin quickly wiped away her tears and bit her lower lip to control the floodgate of emotions tearing at her heart.

"Quinn's older brother was horsing around with her and innocently pushed her into the pool. Quinn fell awkwardly and curled as soon as she hit the water. She hit her head on the side of the pool and at that instant became a complete C5 quad. Everyone thought she was fooling around when she didn't come up right away, but I knew something was wrong. I jumped in after her and brought her to the surface as she gasped wildly for air. Her body was completely limp in my arms and she had a big gash on her forehead. I knew by the look of terror in her eyes that something terrible had happened." Kaitlin ran her hand through her hair to try and ease the horrible memories as she saw it over and over again as if the incident had just happened yesterday.

"From that moment on, the only part of Quinn's body that could feel my touch was her shoulders, face, and head. She was left with minimal movement of her arms and no sensation from beneath the shoulders down. She was robbed of the ability to feel my hugs or need my caresses."

Sierra was consumed by Kaitlin's tragedy as she held her close and allowed her to drain her sorrow. "Oh my God, darling.

How horrible. Her brother must have been beside himself with grief!"

Kaitlin shook her head sadly and reached for more tissues on the coffee table. "So much so that two months after Quinn's accident he shot and killed himself."

Sierra gasped in horror and leaned back in the couch. "Oh my God!"

Kaitlin dried her eyes and took a deep breath. "It was such an emotionally devastating time for everyone involved, especially Quinn. She was grieving the loss of her body and her brother."

Sierra struggled to absorb the whole tragedy as Kaitlin held her hand tenderly. "It was a nightmare for months. Quinn spent one month in hospital and every day she begged me to let her die."

Sierra gently wiped away Kaitlin's tears as she handed her a fresh tissue.

"Quinn loved it at Bradley Bay. We had always planned on retiring up here. After she completed six months in a rehabilitation facility, we moved up here. She was very bitter and angry and always said she felt like a useless burden to me. I did everything in my power to make her realize that she was still the same woman that I loved." Kaitlin sighed deeply and stared out over the calm lake. "Sadly, I realized that my love wasn't enough, so I tried hard to give her reasons to live. My grandparents both passed away shortly after we moved up here, so Quinn and I started running the resort. I gave her as much responsibility as she could handle from her electric wheelchair and I saw how it brought meaning and purpose back to her life. I learned that everyone needs to feel useful and productive and that's no exception for paraplegics and quadriplegics. With time I slowly started to get my happy, vivacious Quinn back. One night we were sitting on our back deck and she turned to me and told me I was like the Wizard of Oz." They both laughed softly as Sierra gently caressed Kaitlin's back. "You remember from the movie how the cowardly Lion asked the Wizard for courage, the Scarecrow wanted a brain, and the Tin Man wanted a heart? Quinn felt that I helped to get her back on the yellow brick road where she was granted all three.

"We talked about how it would be great to help other quadriplegics along their bumpy road of rehabilitation and acceptance in an unconditionally loving environment. That's how we came up with the idea to convert the main estate into a resort for spinal cord–injured adults. We wanted to create a safe haven were they could come up here and be with their own kind and receive counseling and physiotherapy and hear motivational talks from other spinal cord–injured adults who have successfully rejoined the workforce. Bradley Bay provided the perfect emotional and spiritual retreat that we could create. We still rent the twenty cabins along the lakes edge to the families that continue to come vacation here at Bradley Bay year after year. That allows us the financial balance we need to keep this dream alive.

"Quinn was an excellent motivational speaker and ran the most inspiring group therapy sessions. She introduced me to one of her groups as the Wizard of Oz and one of the guys in the group said that if I was the Wiz then they must be in the Emerald City. That's how Bradley Bay became known as the Emerald City. Our goal was to have quadriplegic and paraplegic adults come here to discover their potential and not focus on what they'd lost. They have to learn to get back on the yellow brick road mentally and emotionally stronger in order to find their own way home. I wanted to create a place that made them feel safe and secure, kind of like the way I feel every time I look at a lighthouse and see that beacon of light."

Sierra was deeply engrossed in Kaitlin's story as she watched her stop to catch her breath. Sierra gently brushed a stray strand of hair away from Kaitlin's eyes and felt engulfed by her dedication and intensity. "What a beautiful story to come from such a horrible tragedy."

Kaitlin took a sip of her orange juice before offering Sierra her own glass. Sierra took a sip and set the glass down. "What happened to Quinn, Kate? Jennifer said she died of pneumonia a year ago."

Kaitlin looked away from Sierra's tender eyes and basked in the warmth of her soft hand. "Quinn had a cold for a couple of days that got worse instead of better. I took her in for a check up and the X-ray showed that she had pneumonia. She adamantly refused to be hospitalized and receive intravenous antibiotics so we went home on oral antibiotics, praying that it would be the answer.

"After Quinn's accident she had me rewrite her living will and medical power of attorney. She made herself a 'do not resuscitate' should anything happen. We went over every life-threatening complication of being a quadriplegic, and she made me promise and sign in writing that I would not do anything to prolong her life for any reason whatsoever. That was so painful for me to make my thirty-five-year-old lover a 'do not resuscitate.'

"As the days passed, Quinn's pneumonia only got worse, and I begged her to let me admit her into the hospital. She refused, and I was so frightened at how calm and peaceful she was during that whole ordeal. I was not ready to lose Quinn, but she was more than ready to die. I told her we could still have another ten years together if she let me treat her pneumonia properly. She said that was the main reason why she refused treatment. She knew I would always be at her side and she was grateful to finally be able to give me my life back."

Sierra felt her own tears sting her cheeks as she watched the tears flow from Kaitlin's emerald eyes.

"Three days later, I held Quinn in my arms as she took her last breath and her soul left me forever."

Sierra guided Kaitlin into her arms and held her close as anguished tears flowed from her eyes. Sierra leaned back and tenderly wiped away Kaitlin's tears, whispering, "I'm so sorry for what happened to you and Quinn, sweetheart. You've truly been to hell and back and created an invaluable institution from your grief."

Kaitlin smiled through her tears and reached up to touch Sierra's damp cheek. "There are so many days, Sierra, that I beat myself up for allowing Quinn to die like that when I could have done so much more. But I had to respect her wishes. There was no other way. Then there are days that I am grateful that she has gone on to a better place. I know that she is at peace now and I feel in my heart that she is with her brother again. He will take good care of her for me."

Sierra leaned forward, rested her forehead against Kaitlin's, and reached up to hold her face in her hands. "You did everything you could, Kate. You can't continue to beat yourself up for granting someone their wishes." Sierra slid her thumbs over Kaitlin's soft cheeks and gazed into her stormy eyes. "Tell me, Dr. Bradley. If you could ask for anything from the Wizard, what would it be?"

Kaitlin leaned back slightly and looked deeply into Sierra's brilliant blue-gray eyes. "I would ask for the Lion's courage, the Scarecrow's brains and the Tin Man's heart to continue to keep this dream alive."

Sierra smiled deeply and leaned intimately close to Kaitlin's shimmering emerald eyes. "You, my dear girl, have the courage, the brains, and the heart to keep all your dreams alive."

Kaitlin was overwhelmed by Sierra's compassionate warmth and sensuality. She stared at Sierra's pillowy lips and ached to fulfill her burning desires. Her longing and reawakened need terrified her. She quickly got to her feet and went to stand before the floor-to-ceiling picture window.

She wrestled with her conflicting emotions as she watched the gentle ripples glide across the lake and lap at the grassy shore. Her life with Quinn seemed like it had taken place a million years ago; she thought of how difficult the past year had been grieving for her lover. She worked so hard to rebuild her life and put the past behind her knowing that some of that pain would never die. Sharing her past with Sierra had laid her vulnerable to those painful wounds, yet she felt soothed and eased of a burden she had carried alone.

Kaitlin had vowed to herself that she would never love like that again and have to deal with that kind of loss and pain, until Sierra. Sierra seemed to miss that road sign and bowl into her life unheeded. She forced a surge of light and energy into all of her senses making Kaitlin feel like she was the one awakening from a deep sleep. Everything was brighter, warmer, fresher, and lighter when Sierra was around. How was she going to protect her own heart when it had already surrendered to the blue-eyed enemy?

Sierra watched Kaitlin struggle with her emotions as she stood staring out onto the bay. She yearned to go to her and hold her close but sensed that she needed time and space. Sierra admired her inner strength and watched Kaitlin standing before that window with such elegant beauty and grace. Beauty displayed so subtly in a white linen, sleeveless blouse and pleated black shorts. Shorts that displayed her endless, shapely legs to perfection.

Sierra watched her sigh as a deep frown creased her brow. "What is it, Kaitlin? What's wrong?"

Kaitlin turned and looked back at Sierra's concerned expression. She nervously looked back out the window and shoved her hands into her black shorts. "I'm not very good at expressing myself when it comes to this emotional stuff, Sierra, so please bear with me."

Sierra rose from the couch and stood before Kaitlin.

Kaitlin reached forward and slowly ran the soft pad of her thumb along Sierra's full lower lip and whispered in a husky voice, "I've been having a real hard time convincing my heart that you're going home in two weeks. Instead, it's been very disobedient and gone ahead and fallen in love with you anyway."

Sierra closed her eyes as her heart bounded in her chest. She struggled to breathe evenly as she wallowed in Kaitlin's alluring touch. "That makes two very disobedient hearts. I think we should send them both to the time out corner and make them atone for their sins."

Kaitlin laughed as her thumb trailed along Sierra's firm jaw and across her soft cheek.

"There is one other thing I would ask the Wizard for if I'm allowed just one more wish," Kaitlin said.

Sierra was lost in Kaitlin's passionate eyes and her body's throbbing need. She closed her eyes and luxuriated in Kaitlin's feathery touch as she said softly, "What would that wish be, Dr. Bradley?"

Kaitlin slowly leaned closer to Sierra's moist, slightly parted lips and whispered in a smoky voice, "I would ask for you."

Sierra opened her eyes and saw the unbridled desire and want in Kaitlin's eyes. Sierra glided her hands into Kaitlin's silky hair and gazed deeply into her emerald eyes. "I love you, Dr. Kaitlin Bradley."

Kaitlin's smile burst across her face as she slowly slid her hands along Sierra's arms and onto her slender waist.

"I love you, Ms. Sierra Vaughn."

Sierra's heart beat rapidly in her chest as she watched Kaitlin lean intimately close. Their eyes never wavered from their intense contact as their lips tenderly met, softly, slowly, teasingly as Sierra closed her eyes and breathed a soft, passionate moan.

Kaitlin breathlessly leaned back and watched Sierra slowly open her heavy-lidded eyes. Her moist, slightly parted lips set Kaitlin's entire being on fire. A heightened, tingling sensation took Kaitlin by surprise as it lapped at her breasts and thighs.

Sierra ached for much more as she guided Kaitlin closer and brushed her lips with soft, caressing kisses, escalating their aching desire as their kisses become more hungry and impatient.

Sierra gently guided her tongue across Kaitlin's lower lip as she heard a low erotic gasp escape from Kaitlin's throat.

Kaitlin slowly glided her hands up along the contours of Sierra's back and into her thick brown hair. She held Sierra's head still as she slowly delved between her parted lips and tasted Sierra's sweet mouth. Kaitlin wanted to immerse herself in that honeyed cavern as she took as much as Sierra gave. Kaitlin gasped as their tongues met and danced to their own feverish beat.

Sierra leaned her forehead against Kaitlin's cheek and tenderly floated her fingertip across her moist, warm lower lip as they both struggled to catch their breath.

Kaitlin slowly opened her clouded eyes and glided her hands down Sierra's back and onto her shapely hips. "You, Sierra Vaughn, melt me."

Sierra grinned from ear to ear as Kaitlin kissed the tip of her exploring finger. "You, Kaitlin Bradley, rock my world."

Kaitlin tenderly glided her hands over the contours of Sierra's lower back and held her intimately close. "I've never been with another woman or even remotely interested in another woman since Quinn. Then one day this gorgeous, blue-eyed, spectacular woman walks out onto my dock and calls me disgracefully rude and lacking in social graces and completely spins my heart and desire out of control."

Sierra giggled sweetly as Kaitlin's feathery touch consumed her with a heated arousal. "You took my breath away when I saw you on that dock, Dr. Bradley. You deserved to be put in your place, regardless of how intensely you shook my senses."

They swayed against each other as Kaitlin took Sierra's fingertip into her mouth and watched her close her eyes and emit a throaty gasp. Kaitlin toyed with Sierra's finger then crushed her lips to Sierra's with impassioned demand.

Sierra was overwhelmed by her raging need as she arched against her, wanting to feed the fire that blazed between them. Sierra felt Kaitlin's ragged breath against her swollen lips as she lay soft exploring kisses along the edges of her mouth. She nipped at her full lower lip, gently sucking it into her mouth and tracing it with her tongue. Sierra's tongue dipped deeper and savored her heady taste as their tongues met and shared an explosive kiss of passion and discovery.

Kaitlin held Sierra tight as she let her lips linger against the silky smoothness of Sierra's forehead. She was immersed by the

81

peace of holding her in her arms as she whispered softly, "Do you forgive me for not telling you about Quinn myself?"

Sierra turned to linger her lips against Kaitlin's soft neck. "You keep kissing me like that, Dr. Bradley, and I'd forgive you for anything."

Kaitlin brushed her lips against Sierra's cheek and leaned toward her lips, kissing her slowly, teasingly. "I'll remind you of that every once in a while, Ms. Vaughn."

Sierra leaned back slightly and trailed her thumb over Kaitlin's chin. "You think you have found your power over me, do you, Dr. Bradley?"

Kaitlin leaned closer to touch her tongue to Sierra's lower lip, eliciting the moan that rocked her soul. "Yes, Ms. Vaughn. I believe I now know how to turn you into putty."

Sierra laughed softly and wrapped her arms around Kaitlin, hugging her tight. "You certainly do turn me into putty, my love. Without a doubt."

Kaitlin held Sierra close and caressed her soft hair, inhaling its subtle lemon scent. "You realize this is pure torture for me since I have to go into work tonight and won't be able to spend this evening in your wonderful company."

Sierra leaned back slightly and felt a searing heat with each stroke of Kaitlin's soft hand. "Good. It'll give you more time to appreciate me."

Kaitlin dropped her head back and burst into her heartfelt laughter as her phone intruded on their playfulness. Kaitlin emitted a frustrated groan as she guided Sierra back to the couch and reached for her cordless phone on the coffee table.

Sierra leaned back against the cushions and smiled as she heard Kaitlin say with controlled impatience, "Yes?" Sierra leaned forward and ran her fingers through Kaitlin's shiny hair as she saw the expression soften on her beautiful face.

"I sound irritated, Sabrina, because you're interrupting me at a most inopportune time."

Sierra watched a shy smile curl the corners of Kaitlin's soft lips.

"Yes, Sierra is with me. Do you get the picture yet, Bri?" Kaitlin sighed and closed her eyes. "If I wasn't on the phone with you, Bri, I might have the opportunity to do delicious things to her beautiful body, but at this very moment my hands are occupied holding the phone!" Kaitlin rolled her eyes and watched the beautiful light in Sierra's eyes. "No! You can't talk to Sierra. Her hands are very busy melting me at this moment."

Sierra laughed softly as she continued to float her fingers through Kaitlin's hair.

Kaitlin's expression grew serious as she said, "Is he hurt bad, Sabrina?" Kaitlin listened a few minutes longer and said, "We'll be right there." Kaitlin said good-bye and replaced the phone in its cradle.

"What's wrong, sweetheart?"

"One of the paraplegics fell out of his chair while reaching for his fishing pole on the dock. Sabrina said he just scraped both knees, but we should go down and have a look."

Sierra took Kaitlin's hand and guided her to her feet. They both reached for their glasses and headed into the kitchen.

Kaitlin took Sierra's glass from her and placed them both in the sink. She rested her hand on Sierra's lower back and guided her to the sliding glass door leading to her back deck. Kaitlin stopped Sierra just before she stepped outside.

Sierra looked up into Kaitlin's radiant emerald eyes.

"I just want to thank you for coming to talk to me, Sierra. I'll always cherish this time I had with you."

Sierra leaned forward and rested her hand on Kaitlin's tummy. "For a girl who feels she has trouble expressing herself when it comes to emotional stuff, you certainly don't seem to have trouble finding the words that warm my heart."

They both stared intently into each other's eyes as Sierra glided her hands along Kaitlin's waist and rested them on her hips.

"I have a desire I'd like you to fill, Dr. Bradley, seeing as how you're the one assigned to fulfilling my every whim and desire."

Kaitlin took Sierra's face in her hands and leaned intimately close to her lips. "And what desire is that, Ms. Vaughn?"

Sierra gave her a seductive smile as she eased her thumbs lightly over Kaitlin's sides. "I desire you."

Kaitlin felt a burst of liquid heat cascade into her chest and spiral down to her thighs as she leaned toward Sierra and kissed her until they were both breathless and aching for more.

CEDCEDCED

Kaitlin and Sierra walked down to the crowd gathered on the dock. Sabrina and Logan greeted them warmly as Kaitlin knelt before Michael, the twenty-five-year-old paraplegic who had fallen out of his wheelchair. She could see the concern and embarrassment in his eyes as she squeezed his hand and gave him a reassuring smile.

"All right, Humpty Dumpty, let's have a look at these legs of yours," Kaitlin said. Everyone laughed as Michael dropped his eyes in embarrassment.

"Sorry about this, Dr. Bradley. I was just trying to exercise my independence. Instead, I almost executed a perfect nosedive into the lake. I would have been doing some serious dog paddling if Sabrina and Logan hadn't grabbed me by the seat of my pants."

"They're just lucky they got you in time, or else they would be the ones doing some serious dog paddling."

Sabrina and Logan pretended to look horrified as they clutched their chests in disbelief.

"Next time, mister, try to retrieve your fishing pole with your fingers and not your lips and none of us would be in this predicament," Logan fired back. Everyone burst into laughter as Kaitlin began meticulously assessing Michael for any injuries.

Jennifer's concern was etched on her face as she eased her wheelchair closer and watched Kaitlin gently touch Michael's knees. "You would think that he would have learned after his parachuting accident not to throw himself out of anything anymore. Instead, the fly boy decides he wants to throw himself out of his wheelchair and see if he can crack his thick skull this time."

Michael threw Jennifer an indignant stare. "Listen to Ms. Evel Knievel. Like you're one to talk. Just come closer and kiss me better."

"Did I forget to mention. I gave up kissing boys in kindergarten. Girls are so much more satisfying."

"Play nice you two," Kaitlin scolded.

"Well, that's what he gets for scaring us to death like that. In the three years that we've known each other I've never seen him fall out of that chair. I really thought he had hurt himself."

"Were you worried about me, Ms. Knievel? Come over here so I can kiss you."

"Yuck. Save it for your girlfriends that really appreciate your machismo, fly boy."

Michael reached for Jennifer's tiny hand and squeezed it gently as they shared a smile of endearing friendship.

Sabrina turned to Sierra and whispered in her ear, "That's a beautiful smile you're wearing, young lady."

Sierra gave Sabrina and Logan a mischievous smile and turned to watch Kaitlin gently flex and extend Michael's flaccid legs. "That's Kate's fault. She has the most amazing lips."

They all smiled as Logan gently touched Sierra's hand. "We're thrilled to see what's happening between the two of you, Sierra. You're both very special to us, and Kate couldn't have asked for a better woman."

Logan's warmth blurred Sierra's eyes with tears as she gave them both a joyous smile. Sierra turned back to watch Kaitlin gently assess Michael's ribs and spine. Sierra was enthralled by Kaitlin's professionalism and tenderness as she wondered what it would feel like to have those hands touch her own heated skin. She wondered if those hands were willing to reach out and risk loving again. Or would a two-week affair be all she wanted from her?

Kaitlin rose to her feet and brushed off her knees. "Seems like your scraped knees are your only injuries, Mike. I don't detect any fractures or dislocations, so we're lucky. Sabrina and Logan will cleanse and dress your knees for you and we'll watch for any swelling over the next couple of days. Then I want you to write out one hundred times, how you will never reach for your fishing pole like that again."

"Sorry again for all the fuss, Dr. Bradley."

Kaitlin ruffled his blonde hair and gave his shoulder a gentle squeeze. She reached for his fishing pole leaning against the dock bench and handed it to him as she turned and saw Sierra's moist eyes. She stepped toward Sierra and touched her cheek. "Are you okay, sweetheart?"

Sierra gave Kaitlin a sweet smile and stepped toward her. "Sabrina and Logan made me cry."

Sabrina and Logan gasped in horror as they both grabbed Sierra and dragged her, fighting and screaming, to the edge of the dock. Everyone gathered to watch Sierra's playful plight as she begged mercilessly for them to let her go.

"Pleeeeease, you guys. I don't want to go in the lake. It's cold and I'm terrified of having slimy little fish rub against my legs."

Everyone laughed at Sierra's plea for release as Sierra turned to Kaitlin with pure distress in her eyes. "Please, Kaitlin, help me."

Kaitlin crossed her arms across her chest and leaned back against the redwood railing with a devilish grin on her face. "What was it that you said about me having appalling manners and being disgracefully rude?"

Sierra was stunned into silence as Sabrina beamed her a huge grin. "Yes, and I do believe you questioned our roles and responsibilities compared to yours on our first tour of Bradley Bay. What kind of way is that to treat your hostesses? I think you need to be taught a lesson, young lady."

Everyone on the dock was enthralled by Sierra's dilemma as they waited for Kaitlin to rescue her.

"Can't I just write out one hundred lines like Michael?"

Sabrina counted to three, and then she and Logan introduced a screaming Sierra to the cool depths of Sturgeon Lake.

The crowd gasped and applauded as Kaitlin walked to the edge of the dock in stunned disbelief that Sabrina and Logan actually had thrown Sierra in. She turned to them both and smacked both their shoulders as they watched Sierra gracefully swim to the surface and take a deep breath.

"God! This water is freezing!"

Everyone laughed as Sierra floated effortlessly and wiped the water from her eyes. She glared up at the three beautiful faces looking down at her. "I'll get you guys for this. Mark my words. Revenge is so bittersweet."

Sabrina and Logan burst into laughter as Kaitlin squatted down and extended her hand to Sierra. "I'm sorry, Sierra. I honestly didn't think these two thugs were going to throw you in."

Sierra gave her a menacing scowl as Logan and Sabrina continued to giggle. "I hope you don't mind me using that line next time those two thugs threaten to tie an anchor around your neck, my sweet Kate."

Kaitlin gave her a guilty pout and extended her hand further. "Let me help you out, Sierra, before the Loch Ness monster starts nibbling on your toes."

Sierra faked panic and swam quickly toward Kaitlin. She approached to within inches of Kaitlin's hand and began throwing arms full of water at the guilty parties. Sabrina, Logan, and Kaitlin squealed as they jumped out of the way of the icy cold water. Everyone on the dock applauded Sierra's counterattack as they enjoyed her jubilant smile and watched her swim away.

Kaitlin stepped to the edge of the wet dock and placed her hands on her hips. "Sierra Vaughn, get back here right now before a school of slimy fish rub themselves all over your body!"

Sierra stopped her front stroke and looked back at Kaitlin. "Catch me if you can, Dr. Bradley."

Kaitlin exhaled a frustrated groan and muttered, "I'm going to kill that woman!"

Everyone watched Kaitlin easily slip into a moored fifteen-foot Coleman canoe, release the ties, and paddle rhythmically toward Sierra. They moved to the edge of the dock to watch the events unfold before them.

Kaitlin easily maneuvered the canoe alongside Sierra and placed the paddle inside the boat. She sat comfortably in her seat and beamed Sierra a gorgeous smile. "Caught ya!"

Sierra laughed at Kaitlin's triumphant smile and swam to the edge of the canoe. Kaitlin reached for Sierra's cold hand and held it tight. "I really am sorry, sweetheart. I never thought they would toss you in like that. Please let me get you out of that cold water before you catch a nasty cold."

Sierra wiped the water from her eyes and smiled sheepishly. "That's all right, sweetheart. I'll get even with them. However, I do have one question for you."

Kaitlin gave her a suspicious look and brushed the wet hair from her eyes. "What question is that?"

Sierra grinned like a cat about to pounce on its prey. "Can you swim, Dr. Bradley?"

Kaitlin felt apprehension building in her stomach as she answered slowly. "Yes. Why?"

Sierra slowly began rocking the canoe and grinning from ear to ear. "Because, I thought you might like to come in here and get wet with me and share in this lovely, ice bath."

Kaitlin gripped the edges of the swaying canoe and glared dangerously at Sierra. She leaned close enough so only Sierra could hear. "First of all, Sierra, I was wet before we got anywhere near this lake, and secondly, don't you dare toss me in. I'm terrified of slimy fish and the Loch Ness monster."

Sierra laughed deeply and jerked the canoe toward her as she watched Kaitlin dive in beside her. Thunderous applause erupted from the crowd on the dock as Sierra reached for Kaitlin and guided her to the surface. Sierra burst into laughter as she held on to the canoe with one hand and held Kaitlin securely against her with the other. She watched her wipe the water away from her shocked emerald eyes and shiver from the cold.

Kaitlin opened her eyes and glared at Sierra as she splashed water at her. "You little shit!"

They both burst into laughter as Sierra rested her hand intimately against Kaitlin's lower back. Kaitlin wrapped her legs around Sierra's and brushed the hair from her eyes. They held each other close as Sierra looked down at Kaitlin's drenched white blouse and enjoyed the sight of her erect nipples.

Kaitlin laughed at the beautiful expression on Sierra's face and enjoyed the view through her wet cream T-shirt. "We're both rather cold, I see."

Sierra blushed sweetly as Kaitlin was astounded by the intensity of their attraction. Kaitlin brushed the water from Sierra's long, dark eyelashes and leaned intimately close to her wet face. She watched a single drop of water slip down Sierra's cheek and settle on the center of her pillowy lower lip. Kaitlin was acutely aware of the watchful crowd on the dock as she ached to catch each drop of water with her tongue.

Sierra was spellbound watching Kaitlin's blazing eyes as she floated her hand beneath her blouse and touched the cool skin of her lower back. Kaitlin closed her eyes and absorbed Sierra's caress. "We'd better get out of this lake before we either freeze to death or spontaneously combust," Sierra said.

"I vote for spontaneous combustion," Kaitlin teased, as they heard the water churning near them. They both looked toward the dock and saw Logan and Sabrina approach in a paddleboat.

Sabrina saluted them as she floated in beside them. "Ahoy, mates. Do you two plan on clinging in the lake till you get frostbite and have to have certain parts of your anatomy amputated, or would you rather hop on our cruise ship and wrap yourselves in these lovely, white terry cloth robes we brought you?"

Sierra turned Kaitlin toward Sabrina and Logan's outstretched hands and helped to ease her out of the water.

"Sierra and I voted on spontaneous combustion," Kaitlin said, as she eased into the paddleboat.

Sabrina and Logan looked at her as if she had lost her mind. "You've been in the water too long, Dr. Bradley. What the hell is she talking about, Sierra?" Logan said.

Sierra shivered from the cold as she eagerly accepted their help to get out of the lake they had thrown her into. "I'll explain it to you guys when my body temperature climbs out of the subzero mark." Kaitlin eased Sierra into the seat beside her and wrapped her in a warm terry cloth robe.

Logan and Sabrina expertly turned the paddleboat around and safely returned them both to the cheering crowd.

Logan tied off the paddleboat and canoe before they took Michael up to the main resort to dress his knees. Jennifer was right at his side.

Kaitlin walked Sierra up to the main estate and watched as she sighed and nuzzled the terry cloth robe tighter around her. "This robe smells like your sweet perfume," Sierra said.

Kaitlin watched Sierra bury her little nose in the collar of the robe. "That's my robe you're wearing. Sabrina and Logan must have gotten them from my change room off my back deck."

Sierra hugged the robe tight. "You can keep it if you like, Sierra. It certainly looks very alluring on you."

They arrived at the front of the resort as Sierra gently tugged on the belt of Kaitlin's robe. "Thank you, Kate. I would love to keep your robe." Sierra wrapped her finger around the belt as she hesitated to say good-bye. "I guess we should both get inside and into a warm shower."

Kaitlin tugged the collar of Sierra's robe higher around her beautiful face. "I'd rather you came and joined me in my shower."

Sierra was moved by Kaitlin's passion and warmth as she stared into her shimmering eyes. "If I join you in the shower, Dr. Bradley, you'll never get to work tonight. You'd better shower alone this time and come meet me in the dining room so we can have dinner together before you have to go."

"I guess I'll settle for dinner with you this time," Kaitlin said, as she slowly backed away from Sierra. "But be careful, Ms. Vaughn. I don't hand out invitations to my shower freely. You may have just missed your one and only opportunity."

Sierra slipped her hands into the thick terry cloth pockets of her robe. "I'll consider that invitation as a rain check and use it at a more opportune time, if that's okay with you, Dr. Bradley."

"A more opportune time. Hmmm. I just hope we don't spontaneously combust before then."

Sierra laughed at Kaitlin's humor as she watched her blow her a kiss and walk on toward her home.

Kaitlin stopped a few feet away and looked back at Sierra still riveted to her spot. She gestured toward the main house and watched as Sierra pulled the collar tighter around her neck and inhaled the subtle scent of Kaitlin's lingering perfume. Kaitlin felt overwhelmed with longing as she watched her wave and climb the stairs, before slipping in the front door.

છ૪ાઉ૪ાઉ૪ા

Kaitlin stood before her floor-length mirror and tucked her gray and white silk shirt into her classy black pleated trousers. She began buttoning her cuffs as her bedside phone rang. She sat on the edge of her bed and cradled the phone against her ear as she continued to work on her cuffs. "Hello?"

Sierra lay on her back across her new bed. "Hello, Santa Cláus!"

Kaitlin grabbed the phone in her hand and laughed softly. "Do you like your gifts, Sierra?"

"Hang on one second and tell me what you hear."

Kaitlin listened intently and only heard Sierra's sweet laughter.

"That was the sound of me bouncing on my new bed with no squeaks."

Kaitlin laughed and held the phone close.

"Kate, I didn't expect you to buy me a whole new bed."

Kaitlin felt tickled by Sierra's pleasure. "I would do anything to make you happy, Sierra, and since I'm the quality assurance committee around here, I feel I need to test out the quality of that new bed with you. To ensure customer satisfaction, of course." Kaitlin loved the sound of Sierra's laughter filling her home.

"Well, then, my quality assurance committee, when would you care to run that customer satisfaction test?"

Kaitlin groaned in frustration and dropped back onto her bed. "My body aches for your touch, Ms. Vaughn, so right now would suit me just fine. Unfortunately, I have this little matter of work to attend to this evening."

"Since you'll not be able to meet my every whim and desire this evening, it seems that I've been given another adorable little companion to take your place."

"I couldn't resist when I saw that beautiful little teddy bear dressed in little pink p.j.'s and a matching nightcap. I hope she can provide the warm, fuzzy feeling that you're looking for."

"You, Dr. Bradley, are giving me an incredibly warm, fuzzy feeling as we speak. This little bear does have the cutest pink p.j.'s. P.J.'s. I like that. I think we should name our little friend P.J. What do you think, Kate?"

Kaitlin felt encompassed by Sierra's tenderness and warmth. She checked her watch and rose to her feet. "I like that name. I like it very much."

"Thank you for the new bed and beautiful teddy bear, Kate. You've touched my heart. I finally have something nice to write about you in my journal."

Kaitlin walked to her bedroom window and looked toward the resort. She looked up to Sierra's window and leaned against her window frame. "Your heart is not the only part of your body I ache to touch, Sierra."

"That wouldn't be very difficult at this moment, Dr. Bradley, since I slipped from the shower into your snuggly robe."

Kaitlin groaned and rested her forehead against the cool glass. "Please stop teasing me like that, Sierra."

"You deserve to be tortured, Dr. Bradley. Now, stop filling me with empty promises and come meet me in the dining room."

"Okay. And Sierra ..." Kaitlin saw the silhouette of Sierra's feminine figure step before her picture window as she watched her place the palm of her hand against the glass.

"Yes, Dr. Kaitlin Bradley?"

Kaitlin placed her hand against the glass. "I love you."

"I love you, Kate. Very, very much."

CREOCREOCREO

Sabrina, Logan, Gladys, and Sierra talked excitedly as they finished their plates of poached salmon, roasted baby potatoes, and steamed asparagus as Kaitlin excused herself to get everyone some dessert.

The dining room staff cleared their plates as Kaitlin returned carrying a huge serving bowl heaped with assorted flavors of Baskin-Robbins ice cream. She placed the mouth-watering creation before a shocked Sierra and lit the single candle perched precariously atop the icy treat. Everyone applauded Kaitlin's surprise as she handed each of them a spoon and took her seat beside Sierra, who looked at her with beautiful, questioning eyes.

"Whaaaat is this all about, Dr. Bradley?"

Kaitlin leaned back in her chair and gave Sierra a mischievous smile. "Sydney paged me when I was in town today and asked me how you were being treated and if you were enjoying your time here at Bradley Bay."

Sierra leaned closer to Kaitlin and felt embraced by her loving eyes and playful charm as she awaited her response.

"I told her you've never been treated so well in your entire life." Everyone burst into laughter as Kaitlin reached forward and brushed a stray strand of hair away from Sierra's shiny eyes. "I told her that Sabrina, Logan, and Gladys protect you like a rare Fabergé egg, and I, of course, am treating you with my usual gracious good manners."

Sierra scowled at Kaitlin and playfully tugged her closer by the collar of her elegant silk shirt. "Liar," Sierra hissed.

Kaitlin burst into her soft laughter and leaned forward to kiss the tip of Sierra's tiny nose. "Sydney also told me on the phone that before you decided to eagerly and willingly come to Bradley Bay and expose yourself to our unique northern hospitality, you were determined to sulk and be depressed for these two weeks and binge on ice cream and peanut butter and jelly sandwiches."

Sierra dropped her head onto her arm in embarrassment.

"I told Sydney that I felt you've had enough of sandwiches after your first night here, but I did promise to fulfill half of your dietary suicidal ideation and treat you to your favorite flavor of Baskin-Robbins ice cream."

Kaitlin leaned intimately close to Sierra's blushing cheeks as the gentle scent of vanilla floated into her senses, eliciting a wave of desire to sprint across her chest. Kaitlin forced herself to sit back as she picked up her spoon and tapped on the ice cream. "This is your favorite, world class chocolate. This is Gladys's, maple walnut. This is Sabrina and Logan's, mint-chocolate chip."

Before Kaitlin could finish, Logan dipped her spoon into the delicious mint dessert just as Kaitlin smacked her spoon with her own. "Just one minute, young lady. Sierra hasn't blown out her candle yet."

Logan quickly plunged her spoon deeper and scooped some mint-chocolate chip ice cream and devoured it with glee. They all laughed at her playfulness as Kaitlin gave her a scolding look. She returned her attention to the festive-looking mound of melting ice cream and pointed one final time.

"And this is my favorite, strawberry. I prefer strawberry milkshakes, but it would have been really gross if I'd bought us all milkshakes and poured them all in a bowl." Kaitlin playfully squished her face in disgust.

Sierra smiled as she rested her hand on Kaitlin's and looked up at the flickering candle; Kaitlin watched it reflect in her exquisite blue-gray eyes.

"What's the candle for, Kate? It's not my birthday."

"This is the Emerald City, Sierra. A place where wishes come true regardless if it's your birthday or not. So please, make a wish and blow out your candle before Logan goes through mint-chocolate chip withdrawals."

Sierra gazed deeply into Kaitlin's passionate eyes and felt consumed by her intensity. She slowly scanned the smiling faces around her and leaned toward the flickering light. She closed her eyes and hesitated momentarily before she gently blew out the candle. Everyone burst into applause and whistled as Kaitlin removed the candle and invited everyone to dig in.

Kaitlin sat back in her chair and marveled at Sierra's shapely body dressed in an ethereal green, sleeveless slip dress. Kaitlin admired her slender shoulders and feminine curves as Sierra brought a spoonful of strawberry ice cream to her waiting lips.

Sierra's eyes flowed with desire as she watched Kaitlin enjoy the sweet treat. Sierra returned with another spoonful and slipped it between Kaitlin's moist lips and gave her a seductive smile. "Thank you for the delicious surprise, sweetheart. You truly never cease to amaze me."

Kaitlin fed Sierra a spoonful of her world-class chocolate ice cream and had to force herself to look away from those sensuous lips. "You're very welcome, my love. I was happy to fulfill your dietary suicidal ideation."

Sierra was mortified as she looked away shyly. "Sydney's such a snitch. I'll fix her next time I see her."

Kaitlin laughed as she watched Sierra take a scoop of her ice cream and sigh with pleasure. "So, tell me, Ms. Vaughn, after being at Bradley Bay for two days, do you still regret canceling your trip to the Cayman Islands?"

Sierra picked up her linen napkin from her lap and wiped her mouth as she leaned intimately close to Kaitlin's moist lips. "There's no place on earth I would rather be than here with you."

Kaitlin felt a mushrooming excitement in her chest as she watched Sierra take another spoonful of ice cream before wiping her mouth on her linen napkin.

95

Sierra looked up into Kaitlin's blazing eyes and slowly guided her to her feet. "Come with me, Dr. Bradley. It's almost six o'clock and unfortunately I have to get you off to work."

Kaitlin followed Sierra out of the dining room after kissing Gladys, Sabrina, and Logan good night.

Sierra took Kaitlin through the kitchen and stopped to pull a lunch bag out of the huge stainless steel fridge. Kaitlin looked down at the bag Sierra placed in her hands and back into Sierra's flushed face. Sierra shyly admitted, "I had Gladys show me around the kitchen. I made you a turkey sandwich for work, and I put in carrot sticks, pretzels, two apples, an orange, and a can of Diet Pepsi."

Kaitlin was stunned as she saw the pleased anticipation in Sierra's eyes. "I am truly touched that you did this for me, Sierra. I usually make myself lunch to take to work, but I have been rather distracted today."

Sierra's smile exuded happiness as Kaitlin leaned against her and whispered against her lips, "You're really something, Ms. Vaughn. Do you know that?"

Sierra stared at Kaitlin's moist, slightly parted lips and could no longer restrain herself. She leaned toward her and kissed her softly, feeling a slow-rolling ball of burning passion tumble from her hot lips and down to her thighs.

Kaitlin hesitantly leaned back with eyes brimming with passion. "I certainly don't need the lake to make me wet around you, Sierra Vaughn. You have such incredible lips, young lady."

Sierra blushed shyly and took Kaitlin by the hand. "We'd better get you into your vehicle before I kidnap you and tie you to my new bed and fulfill my uncontrollable desire for you."

They both laughed softly as they walked hand in hand to Kaitlin's home and stood on her driveway beside her gold Ford Explorer.

Kaitlin unlocked the door. She reached across to place her lunch on the passenger seat before she turned back to Sierra.

Sierra nervously straightened the collar of Kaitlin's silk shirt. "I'd really like to come by the hospital later and visit you if that's okay, Kate."

Kaitlin burst with excitement as she reached forward and slipped her hands onto Sierra's slender waist. "I'd really like that, Sierra. I'd like that a lot."

"I'll just finish all my chores here first. You know, like milking the cows, rounding up the sheep, grooming the horses, and if I have time I'll gather a basket of fresh chicken eggs so I can make you breakfast in the morning."

Kaitlin burst into laughter and held Sierra tight against her. "You have an incredible sense of humor, Ms. Vaughn. What does a big-city girl know about gathering chicken eggs anyway?"

Sierra eased her hands along Kaitlin's silky arms and onto her strong shoulders. "Oh, I'm just full of surprises, Dr. Bradley. Just you wait and see."

Kaitlin laughed as she glided her hands across Sierra's smooth back. She openly looked her up and down and smiled seductively. "You look absolutely beautiful in that dress, Sierra. Extremely distracting and absolutely stunning."

Sierra blushed and looked down at her green slip dress. "I thought I would put on a fashion show for you since I seem to have brought so many clothes."

Kaitlin looked shyly away from Sierra's scolding look as the memories of their first encounter stung her heart. "I really was mean to you when we first met, Sierra. Please believe me when I say I feel horrible about the things I said."

Sierra smiled and held Kaitlin's distraught face in her hands. "Don't fret, Dr. Bradley. I intend on making you eat your words."

Kaitlin slid her hands sensuously along Sierra's lower back. "I was hoping that you would just forgive and forget, my darling."

Sierra grinned playfully and leaned closer to Kaitlin's soft lips. "Not on your life. I'm a Scorpio, you know. We don't forgive very easily, and you must always beware of my stinging tail."

"I've been very aware of your sexy tail since the first time you walked away from me on that dock," Kaitlin whispered, as she leaned forward and placed tiny, gentle kisses along Sierra's lower lip. She leaned back slightly and watched the heavy veil of uninhibited passion cloud Sierra's eyes before talking her lips with a fierce hunger.

Kaitlin leaned her forehead against Sierra's and struggled to catch her breath. She seductively glided her hands over Sierra's sexy bottom and whispered against her lips, "I have not stopped watching your gorgeous tail since the moment you tried to stomp away from me on the dock."

Sierra closed her eyes and sighed deeply as she basked in Kaitlin's intimate touch. "You keep touching me like that, Dr. Bradley, and I'm definitely going to make you late for work."

Kaitlin pressed a lingering kiss to Sierra's forehead and inhaled the subtle scent of her lemon shampoo and vanilla hand cream. "Promises, promises."

Sierra checked her watch and guided Kaitlin into her Explorer. Kaitlin hesitantly started the engine and glided her window down. Sierra stretched her five-foot-four-inch frame on her tiptoes and leaned in the window to kiss Kaitlin one more time.

"Have a good night, sweetheart. Please don't let any bitchy nurses get you down."

Kaitlin reached out her window and traced her fingertips along Sierra's chin and over her cheek.

"I don't plan on it. That night got me in enough trouble to last me a lifetime." Kaitlin trailed the soft pad of her thumb over Sierra's pillowy lower lip. "I hurt someone I have come to care very deeply about, so I plan on leaving my bad nights at the hospital from now on."

Sierra tilted her head and leaned her face into the open palm of Kaitlin's soft hand.

"Good night, beautiful lady. I look forward to seeing you later," Kaitlin said.

Sierra stepped back and stared into Kaitlin's emerald eyes. "Good night, Kaitlin. I will definitely see you later. Please drive carefully, babe. I hear there's tarantulas and man-eating mice in these woods."

Kaitlin looked at her in shock. "Who told you that?"

"Sabrina and Logan."

Kaitlin laughed at the look of discomfort on Sierra's elegant face. "Those two thugs certainly enjoy getting a rise out of you, Ms. Vaughn."

Sierra smiled beautifully as she reached out her hand and grazed her fingertips against Kaitlin's before blowing her a kiss. She stepped back and waved as she watched the Explorer's taillights disappear among the majestic spruce trees. Her hand automatically rested over her heart as she felt an astonishing love like she had never experienced before.

⚙ 6

Sierra followed Gladys's directions carefully and pulled off the highway and into the heart of Springfield. She turned off her CD player and stared around her in awe as she passed the historic downtown section with it's flamboyant brick architecture, lushly landscaped medians, and welcoming storefronts. Curved wrought iron lights lit the streets brightly as Sierra passed several restaurants, grocery stores, jewelry store, sporting goods store, antique shops, book stores; new and used. It had to be close to store closing time yet dozens of people strolled along the cobblestone sidewalks and lounged on the wooden benches. Mostly men, probably waiting for their wives to emerge from the stores. On one street corner fast food restaurants faced each other menacingly.

Sierra referred to Gladys's directions and turned left off the main street, passing an Art gallery, stained glass shop, Crystal and Gems store and a Bed and Breakfast. Signs at the next light indicated the direction to turn to reach the Golf and Country Club, Springfield Mall, Sheraton Hotel, tennis center and Water Park. Sierra waited at the red light and leaned back into her seat.

"Well, this town certainly has a lot of things going on. This town is almost as fascinating as you, Dr. Bradley."

Sierra eased through the green light and passed a sprawling, brilliantly lit structure and craned her neck to read the sign: Rainbow Lodge. Nursing Home. Sierra wondered if this was the nursing home that Kaitlin's grandparents had built before they passed away.

Sierra saw the sign for Springfield Community Hospital and made a quick detour before heading onto her destination.

Sierra approached the automatic glass emergency doors and stopped just inside the doorway to readjust her purse strap over her shoulder. She looked into the emergency department and saw a little boy holding his mother's hand and dragging a well-worn teddy bear in the other. He turned back and waved good-bye to Kaitlin.

Sierra stepped back to allow them through the doors as the little boy stopped and held out his bandaged arm to his mother. "Look, Mommy. That nice lady doctor put a happy face sticker on my ouchy for being such a good boy."

Sierra exchanged a warm smile with the boy's mother.

"That's a beautiful sticker, son, but we need to talk about you slowing down when you ride your tricycle."

Sierra watched them head into the balmy night air as the teddy bear smiled back at her through his one button eye.

Kaitlin stood at the nurse's station and completed her note on the boy's chart. The E.R. charge nurse, Kelly, came to stand before her. Kaitlin looked up into Kelly's face; it always reminded her of Meg Ryan. Kelly leaned close to Kaitlin and whispered, "Now that is one gorgeous woman walking through our doors. I'd be more than happy to fix what ails her."

Kaitlin turned around to face the emergency entrance and smiled from ear to ear. Their eyes met instantly as Kaitlin watched Sierra float toward her with a large, paper shopping bag in one hand. Kaitlin turned and clipped her gold Cross pen in her lab coat pocket and looked at Kelly. "You're absolutely right, Kelly. That is one ravishing woman. I think I'll go introduce myself."

Kaitlin's unusual forwardness stunned Kelly as she watched her walk toward the gorgeous creature and envelop her in her arms. The other two E.R. nurses came to stand beside Kelly and watched Kaitlin in her intimate embrace. Kelly crossed her arms and leaned back against the counter.

One of the nurses asked, "Who's that?"

Kelly scoffed and shook her head. "Introduce yourself, my ass, Dr. Bradley. You owe us an introduction to this mystery woman by the looks of that hug."

Sierra leaned back and set her shopping bag and purse on a chair as she gave Kaitlin a radiant smile. She stood tantalizingly close as she tugged on the lapels of her crisp, white lab coat. "That little boy that just left here said that the nice lady doctor gave him a happy face sticker for being such a good boy. If I'm a good girl, would you give me a happy face sticker, nice lady doctor?"

Kaitlin's eyes lit up mischievously as she allowed her eyes to linger over Sierra's beautiful green slip dress. "Certainly, and I know exactly where I'd like to put that happy face sticker."

Kaitlin and Sierra hesitantly stepped aside as the radiology tech guided his portable X-ray machine past them on his way to the elevator. The hallway was finally clear as Sierra rested her hand on Kaitlin's arm; they both struggled to keep a respectable distance. "It's so nice to see you, Kate. I missed you terribly this evening."

Kaitlin brushed a strand of hair over Sierra's delicate, naked shoulder. "I have missed you more than words can say, Ms. Vaughn. I've been consumed with thoughts of you and that makes it very difficult for me to concentrate on my work."

Sierra blushed beautifully as Kaitlin enjoyed the brilliant sparkle in those blue-gray eyes. "Speaking of work, my darling, did you get all your chores done this evening?"

Sierra smiled as Kaitlin could feel the intense heat from her touch. "I certainly did. I set up a video in the library for some of the guests. I sat in on a fascinating speaker who has been a quad for five years and now owns a graphic design company. I joined Sabrina's group therapy session, and then I set up several games of chess, Trivial Pursuit, and Scrabble on the front deck for the guests who wanted to be intellectually stimulated. And last but not least, I helped Sabrina and Logan assist several of the quads into bed."

Kaitlin was thoroughly impressed by Sierra's hard work, enthusiasm, and dedication, but she gave her a playfully disappointed look. "Is that all, Ms. Vaughn? What about milking the cows, rounding up the sheep, grooming the horses, and collecting fresh chicken eggs for my breakfast?"

Sierra placed her hands on her slender hips and stepped menacingly close to Kaitlin's impish smile. "Don't push your luck, Dr. Bradley. I'm already overworked and underpaid."

Kaitlin burst into her rich laughter, loving the scowling look in Sierra's eyes. Kaitlin's expression grew serious as she reached forward and gently touched Sierra's cheek. "I really appreciate your hard work and dedication, Sierra. You continuously give warmth, charm, and love to Bradley Bay, and to me."

Sierra melted to Kaitlin's feathery touch as she stared into those intense emerald eyes. "I really love Bradley Bay and its people, Kate."

Kaitlin dropped her hand and looked down at her feet shyly. "When you first arrived, I felt you were really disappointed by what you saw."

Sierra reached forward and gently touched Kaitlin's chin, raising her face to meet her eyes. "When I first arrived at Bradley Bay, I was disappointed with my life, not yours, Kate. And now you have completely turned my life upside down and opened my eyes and my heart to an incredible world and a wondrous love." Sierra was lost in Kaitlin's emotional emerald eyes as she heard a woman clear her throat behind Kaitlin.

Kaitlin turned around as they saw the three E.R. nurses leaning against the nurse's station, waiting impatiently to meet this woman who obviously captivated their dear Dr. Bradley's complete and undivided attention. Kaitlin smiled and sheepishly cleared her throat. She took Sierra by the elbow and guided her closer to the eagerly awaiting crowd.

Kaitlin introduced her as Kelly extended her hand and gently held Sierra's. "So you're the neurosurgical nurse from Toronto that Kate was telling us about." Sierra smiled as Kelly turned to Kaitlin and gently smacked her arm. "It's about time you found your manners, Dr. Bradley, and introduced us."

Sierra laughed softly at Kaitlin's shy smile. "Manners are something that my dear friend seriously lacks," Sierra said.

Kaitlin dropped her face in embarrassment as Sierra happily explained how Kaitlin treated her when she first arrived. "And she even stood by and let Sabrina and Logan throw me in the ice cold lake today!"

Everyone looked at Kaitlin in shock as Kaitlin quickly turned and looked around the empty emergency department. "Why is it there are no patients in here when I seriously need something to do?"

They all burst into laughter at Kaitlin's discomfort and watched her unsuccessfully try to hide a shameful smile.

Kelly glared at Kaitlin and reached forward to touch Sierra's hand. "If you need a break from the obviously ill-mannered, cranky, crabby Wizard, then you just come visit me and I'll show you some true northern hospitality."

Kaitlin threw Kelly a look that could kill as Sierra laughed at her obvious jealousy. "Thank you, Kelly. I'll keep that in mind. However, to be fair to Kate, I understand she had a horrible night with two cardiac arrests and a team of irritable nurses the night before we met."

All three nurses suddenly looked consumed with guilt and could no longer look Sierra in the eye. Kelly shuffled her feet and took a deep breath as she coyly looked at Kaitlin. "We were rather uncharacteristically bitchy and mean to Katie that night."

Sierra looked at them with a maternal scolding look. "Thank you so much, ladies, because I'm the one that bore the brunt of your uncharacteristically bitchy behavior."

They all looked at Sierra like children who had been properly scolded. Kaitlin smiled with glee and stuck her tongue out at them.

Sierra saw Kaitlin's playful scorn and gently placed her hand on her waist. "That does not in any way excuse your behavior that day, Dr. Bradley." The nurses all applauded Kaitlin's reprimand and happily stuck their tongues out at her.

Sierra was deeply impressed by the affection and respect between Kaitlin and her coworkers. They were quick to tease Kaitlin and even quicker to compliment and protect her. Sierra felt their bond was like sisters that would always be there for each other. She loved observing Kaitlin in her element and watching another layer slowly slip away.

Sierra chatted easily with everyone as Kaitlin marveled at the depth of her intelligence and personality. She embraced everyone in her conversation and carried herself with grace and confidence well beyond her years.

The nurses all laughed at Kaitlin's account of Sierra dumping her in the lake. Sierra was filled with a sense of belonging and acceptance that was much more difficult to earn in a big-city hospital.

Sierra suddenly remembered her shopping bag and reached out to touch Kaitlin's arm. "I almost forgot. I brought you guys a treat." Sierra headed back to the emergency room entrance to pick up her shopping bag and purse.

Kelly leaned toward Kaitlin and whispered, "I certainly would not mind curling into that backside every night."

Kaitlin lightly smacked Kelly's shoulder. "Back off, missy."

Kelly playfully rubbed her arm. "If you don't claim her soon, Katie, I would be more than happy to invite that gorgeous woman into my bed and into my heart."

Kaitlin frowned as she watched Sierra gracefully walk back toward them. "Too late, Kelly. She already owns my heart."

Kelly stared into Kaitlin's intense eyes, wondering how long Kaitlin would fight this before surrendering to the happiness being offered her. She prayed Kaitlin would open her heart to Sierra and allow her to fill it with the joy she deserved. A little playful competition should help to pry open that welded heart.

Sierra handed Kaitlin the large paper bag. "Could you please hold this open for me, Madame?"

Kaitlin happily took the handles. "Anything for you, Madame."

Sierra reached deep inside and pulled out a bakery box and handed it to Kelly. "Freshly baked muffins from the kitchen of Bradley Bay to make everyone's tummies happy."

Kelly closed her eyes and inhaled the delicious, fresh-baked smell. "Oh, Sierra. You're wonderful. I'm going to have to find some way to repay you for your kindness."

Kaitlin instantly glared at Kelly and kicked her foot. Kelly yelped with imaginary pain as Sierra looked from Kelly to Kaitlin and smiled at Kaitlin's jealousy.

Sierra reached inside the bag and pulled out a pound of freshly ground Starbucks Colombian coffee and placed it on top of the muffin box. "That goes with the muffins and hopefully will help to keep you guys bright-eyed and bushy-tailed all night." Everyone was shocked by Sierra's kindness and generosity as she reached in one final time and took the bag from Kaitlin. She set the bag aside and handed Kaitlin a Baskin-Robbins strawberry milkshake and a big bag of black licorice.

Kaitlin stared at her treats and beamed with joy. "Sierra! What a wonderful surprise. These are my favorites."

Sierra beamed with pride and blushed beautifully. "I know. I hope you enjoy them."

Everyone smiled at the depth of warmth between Kaitlin and Sierra. The nurses slowly moved away from them and toward the staff lounge. "We'll call you guys when the coffee's ready."

Kaitlin looked toward the slowly moving threesome. "That would be great. I'm going to take Sierra outside to the gazebo. Call me if you guys need anything."

They nodded with a sweet, knowing smile as Kelly twisted her head back. "Can I come?" Kelly said, just as she was violently hauled into the staff room.

Sierra and Kaitlin both laughed as Kaitlin leaned her forehead against Sierra's and growled playfully. "Will you please stop being so damn charming and adorable before you have every lesbian in this town beating a path to Bradley Bay to meet you."

Sierra reached up to touch Kaitlin's glowing smile. "I'm sorry. I'm just being me."

Kaitlin laughed at Sierra's sweet innocence and tenderly kissed her forehead. "Yeah, well, just being you is what sends women's hearts aflutter."

Sierra traced her fingertip across the lapel of Kaitlin's lab coat. "Is that what I do to your heart, Dr. Bradley?"

Kaitlin leaned intimately close to Sierra's moist lips. "You, Sierra Vaughn, make my heart skip several beats. You'd better watch it, young lady, or you could put me into a lethal arrhythmia."

Sierra stared achingly at those sensuous lips and had to remind herself of where they were just as she heard, "Kelly! Get back in here!"

They both turned to see Kelly dodge back out of the doorway and proclaim, "I'm so jealous!"

Kaitlin held her milkshake and licorice in one hand and took Sierra by the elbow. "Come with me, little Miss popular. Privacy seems to be at a premium around here."

Sierra laughed as she allowed Kaitlin to guide her outside into the balmy night air.

They stepped into a beautiful wood frame gazebo and sat on a bench together. The blossoming petunias, snapdragons, and sweet Williams embraced the gazebo in a halo of purples and pinks.

"This is such a pretty place, Kaitlin."

"I really like it here. It's very private. Usually only the E.R. staff come out here. I make a point to escape out here sometime during the night to collect my thoughts." Kaitlin took a sip of her strawberry milkshake and sighed with pleasure before handing it to Sierra. "This is delicious, Sierra. Thank you so much for my gifts. I'm really touched that you did this for me."

"You're very welcome, Dr. Bradley. It was my pleasure."

Sierra took a sip of the creamy milkshake and settled back in the bench. She watched Kaitlin tear open her bag of licorice with childlike exuberance and hand her one. They chewed happily as Sierra sighed. "I wonder what it's like to work in the intensive care unit of a smaller hospital?"

Kaitlin abruptly stopped chewing as she watched Sierra's sensuous lips surround the straw of their milkshake. "Why do you ask, Sierra? Is the big-city girl thinking of making a major career change?"

Sierra smiled as the straw slipped from between her lips. "Yes, as a matter of fact. I've been thinking of the possibilities."

Kaitlin frowned and leaned closer to Sierra. "Think really hard about what you're saying. It's a whole different world and pace out here, Sierra. This hospital only has one hundred beds compared to the one thousand beds at your hospital. That's a huge difference not only in size but funding, resources, and availability of services. It may not be as progressive or modern as you are used to."

Sierra scanned Kaitlin's serious eyes and looked down at the milkshake in her hands. "You're not being very encouraging, Dr. Bradley."

Kaitlin closed her eyes as she struggled to control her desire to beg Sierra to alter her entire life for her. "Sierra, I'm only telling you the way it is because I don't want you to make any hasty decisions that could ultimately make you very unhappy because of what's happening between us. Your happiness means the world to me, Sierra. I want you to think seriously about what you're saying. I would never ask you to sacrifice your career and happiness to be with me in this town until you knew exactly what you're getting yourself into and felt one hundred percent sure that this is what you wanted. You need to know what living up here with me would mean to your life, especially when you're used to living in Toronto and being a heartbeat away from all the energy and excitement."

Sierra felt a disheartening heaviness fill her chest as she looked away from Kaitlin's moist, emotional eyes. She leaned her head back against the gazebo frame. "I have lived in Toronto my entire life, Kate, and never have I felt the energy, excitement and love I feel at Bradley Bay. It's not the city that makes it all happen, Kate. It's the people. You and everyone at Bradley Bay have made me feel so loved and needed and alive—I have never felt that from any group of people in any city. The warmth and kindness is so palpable in this town. It's such a contrast to the cold fear that permeates city living."

Sierra turned in the bench to face Kaitlin and felt searing hurt and anger burn in her stomach. "If it's an excuse you need to say good-bye, Dr. Bradley, then don't use this town or its sleepy, loving ambiance. You just have to look at me and tell me that we'll only just be friends. That I can handle. I can't handle you pushing me away on the pretense of what will or will not make me happy when it's being with you that fills me with an excitement and happiness like I have never felt in my entire life."

Kaitlin was astounded by Sierra's articulate insight and intense emotions. She reached up to wipe away Sierra's fallen tears as Sierra intercepted her hand and brought it to her lips. She kissed it softly as her tears spilled onto their hands.

Sierra set the milkshake on the bench and rose quickly, struggling to control the sob in her throat. "I should probably go and let you get back to work."

Kaitlin swiftly took Sierra by the waist and sat her back down on the bench. She knelt before her as she felt anger burn in her belly. "Don't you dare do this to me, Sierra. Nothing makes me angrier than if you walk away from me when you're upset like this. Whenever either one of us is upset about something, we're going to sit down and talk about it rather than running away. Understood?"

Sierra allowed Kaitlin to wipe away her tears as she answered softly, "Understood."

Kaitlin slipped in beside her and handed her several tissues from her lab coat pocket. Kaitlin allowed Sierra time to dry her eyes as they sat close.

Sierra folded her hands in her lap and took a deep, emotional breath. "I'm sorry. I didn't intend for our visit to turn out this way."

Kaitlin gently touched Sierra's damp cheek. "I don't want you to ever apologize for sharing your heart and mind with me, Sierra."

Sierra smiled and toyed with the edges of her tissue.

Kaitlin leaned back against the bench and glided her fingers into Sierra's hair and gently turned her head to face her. "Sierra, when Quinn became a quadriplegic, I was forced to make some major changes in my life. I had no regrets over moving or working here for Quinn's happiness. But somewhere along the way I lost what was important to me because my life revolved around Quinn's needs. When I lost her, I realized I lost myself. I felt emotionally isolated in my pain and started to realize how bitter and unhappy I was. It took me a long time to step out of the shadows of being a primary caregiver to look at what I needed and wanted from my life. I have finally come to appreciate the beautiful things in my life and the wonderful people who surround me. I knew that someday I would like to share my life at Bradley Bay with a very special woman."

Kaitlin reached up and gently caressed Sierra's warm cheek. "You have no idea the depth of my love for you if you think I could blow you off that easily. It's really important to me that you take the time to make sure this is what you want, Sierra, because I never want you to experience the isolation and unhappiness that I did. It would greatly affect our relationship, and I never want to put you through that kind of pain. I would never intentionally hurt you, Sierra. I need you to believe that."

Sierra watched the sincerity and fear burn in Kaitlin's eyes. She reached up and touched the tight line of her lips, willing the distress to soften its hold. "Something in you wants to make it difficult for me to love and care about you and be a part of your life. I'm not sure if it's because you're terrified of loving and losing again or because you just refuse to believe that I could possibly love you as deeply as I do. It isn't a tragedy that brought us together, Kate. It's the pure, simple damn luck of my falling in love with you."

Kaitlin laughed and leaned closer to Sierra. "Damn luck?"

Sierra looked shyly at Kaitlin and struggled to hold herself back from taking her in her arms and holding her forever. "Yes, Dr. Bradley. Damn luck. You're determined not to make this easy for me and I'm not sure if I'm up for another emotional struggle."

Kaitlin frowned as a serious cloud darkened her eyes. "I'd rather you struggled with understanding the reality of living here and sharing my life at Bradley Bay now, Sierra, rather than two or five years down the road. I'm terrified that my big-city girl will feel that my love and what I have to offer just isn't enough for what you need."

Sierra jumped from the bench and knelt before Kaitlin, taking her face in her hands. She stared deeply into her brooding emerald eyes and fought to rein in her temper. "Damn you, Kaitlin Bradley! Your love was enough for Quinn, and it certainly is enough for me. Your lover became a quadriplegic, Kate, and no amount of love was ever going to ease that devastation or bring back what she really wanted, which was her life and limbs. Stop blaming yourself for Quinn's unhappiness. Your love and devotion was more than she could ever have asked for, but that's not what she wanted most, Kate. Stop believing that Quinn's depression was a direct reflection on you or any lack of your love. You were wonderful to her and without you she would never have enjoyed the time she had before her death."

Sierra brushed her thumbs beneath Kaitlin's anguished eyes as she saw the years of devastation and isolation consume her. "You have to somehow put it all behind you, Kate. Let me help you. Give our love a chance and believe that you and I can find happiness together. You deserve that, Kate. More than anyone I know. Your love fills me so completely, and it infuriates me that you question whether that love would be enough for me. It was enough for Quinn, and it is certainly enough for me. Now, back off the painful memories, Dr. Bradley, and ditch the low emotional self-esteem. Allow me the opportunity to learn everything about you and your world. We need to decide together what we both want and need before I pack my fluorescent orange suitcases and go back to the big city filled with noise, pollution, crime, traffic, and indifference. Maybe when I leave, you will really appreciate the love we share in this town of peaceful harmony. In the meantime, I need to show you how much you mean to me and how deeply I love you."

Kaitlin felt stunned by Sierra's passion and understanding. She felt raw and exposed as if she were walking through a shower of emotions and stepping out, free of the demons she had carried for years.

Kaitlin leaned against Sierra's forehead and whispered in a hoarse emotional voice, "I love you so much, Sierra Vaughn, that it scares me. I don't want to lose you like I've lost before."

Sierra held Kaitlin's face in her hands. "Give me the opportunity to take the fear out of your love for me. Don't let your fear push me away and prevent us from sharing something that is already so beautiful. Give me a chance to love you, Kate, with all the love in my heart."

Kaitlin leaned toward Sierra's moist, slightly parted lips and kissed her with astounding, gentle passion. It was a different kiss than the others. It was laced with tenderness and adoration; seeped in unrestrained need and desire.

They held each other close and dried each other's tears as Kaitlin took a deep breath. She reached forward to touch Sierra's heart with her fingertip.

"You move me, Sierra Vaughn."

Sierra touched her fingertip to Kaitlin's heart. "You move me, Kaitlin Bradley. All I ask from you is the opportunity to love you without a barricade every mile down the road. I expect from this moment on you'll give me that opportunity. Understood?"

Kaitlin laughed softly and repeated obediently, "Understood. I can't promise that it's going to be easy to love a rude, ill-mannered, crabby Wizard like me."

Sierra held out her arms with a triumphant smile. "We live in the Emerald City, Dr. Bradley. A place where wishes come true. My wish tonight when I blew out my candle was to share my life with you and everyone at Bradley Bay. Work hard at making that wish come true, would you, my rude, ill-mannered, crabby Wizard?"

They both burst into laughter. Kaitlin pulled Sierra into her arms and kissed her with slow, gentle, caressing kisses. Their tongues barely touched and elicited a gasping moan from deep within their throats. Kaitlin held Sierra's face in her hands and absorbed her deep, passionate want as she guided her to the bench beside her.

Sierra turned and jumped into Kaitlin's arms as they both turned to see Kelly leaning against the railing, smiling from ear to ear.

Kaitlin kissed Sierra's forehead and tried to ease her shattered nerves as she turned to the intruder. "Kelly! I'm going to kill you!"

Sierra turned to Kelly and glared at her beaming smile. "Actually, Kelly, we're both going to kill you. You scared me to death lurking like that."

Kelly laughed and stepped into the gazebo. "I'm sorry, ladies. Really I am. I never meant to scare you like that, Sierra. I came out to tell you guys that the coffee's ready and I saw that you were both rather busy, so I thought I'd wait till you were done." Kelly sat herself down beside Sierra. "Forgive me?"

Sierra smacked her thigh and scowled. "I'll forgive you this time, Kelly, but don't let it happen again, or I'll have to hurt you."

"You'd better watch it, Kelly. I have been forewarned that Sierra is a Scorpio with an unforgiving, stinging tail."

Kelly laughed as they all sat back comfortably on the bench. "A gorgeous stinging tail, I might add," Kelly said.

Kaitlin reached around Sierra and gently smacked the back of Kelly's head.

"Ouch!" Kelly squealed as reached for the back of her head.

Sierra laughed at these two loving women and turned to Kelly. "Thank you for the compliment, Kelly, but I would be ecstatic to have Kate curl into my backside every night."

Kaitlin burst into laughter as Kelly gasped, "You heard me say that back there? Jeez, the woman has bionic hearing and a gorgeous backside."

Sierra reached for Kelly's hand. "I sure did. And I was flattered."

Kelly laughed and looked shyly away. "But that's not fair, Sierra. You never gave any of us a chance to even meet you before you decided who could curl into your backside every night."

Sierra squeezed her hand. "I had no choice in the matter, Kelly. Kate completely captivated my heart and soul before I even knew what was happening."

Sierra turned to Kaitlin's beaming smile and touched her chin. "Do you think I would have chosen to fall in love with such a rude, ill-mannered, emotionally hardened, stubborn, unyielding, insolent ..."

Kaitlin raised her hand and protested, "Hey! Stop while you're ahead. You're killing my ego here."

Sierra leaned toward Kaitlin and softly met her lips. "Just teasing, sweetheart. At least partially teasing."

Kaitlin frowned playfully as Kelly rose to her feet. "Come and get some fresh muffins and coffee before they're all gone and the E.R. fills with the drunks trying to drive home from the bars."

Kaitlin and Sierra rose together and stood beside Kelly.

"Sierra, did Katie tell you about my party tomorrow night?" Kelly asked.

Sierra turned to Kelly with a questioning look. "No, she didn't. We were rather preoccupied talking about other things."

"I could see that. I'm having a barbecue, corn roast, and bonfire at my place on the lake. There will be music and dancing and lots and lots of beautiful lesbians to feast on. There is a good size group of women that live right here in town and a bunch of friends that are driving up from Toronto for the weekend. Kaitlin said she was going to ask you if you would like to go with her. I already called Sabrina and Logan and invited them. I told them to bring Jennifer and any of the other female guests who would be interested."

Sierra gave Kaitlin a joyous smile and turned back to Kelly. "Sounds wonderful, Kelly. I would love to accompany Kate to your party."

Sierra turned to Kaitlin with a mischievous glare. "Imagine that, sweetheart. A barbecue, bonfire, and dancing by the lake with you. It certainly doesn't sound like something we would ever experience in the big city. Mind you, that's just the opinion of a big-city girl."

Kaitlin dropped her face shyly to avoid Sierra's menacing scowl. "All right, smart-ass. You made your point," Kaitlin said.

Sierra's expression softened as she rested her hand on Kaitlin's hip. "Oh, but I have so many more points I want to make."

Kaitlin squished her face playfully as she reached for her milkshake and licorice and followed Kelly and Sierra inside.

"Just tell me one thing, Katie. How does it feel to kiss her?" Kelly said.

Kaitlin laughed as Sierra blushed sweetly. They reached the nurse's station as Kaitlin turned to Kelly. "She's like kissing your wildest fantasy of soft, warm, wet desire."

Kelly dramatically dropped her head against the counter and groaned. "I need to move back to Toronto and find me a woman like Sierra."

They all burst into laughter as Kaitlin guided them both into the staff room.

C3考C3考C3考

Kaitlin guided Sierra into her Honda Passport and closed her door firmly. She watched her start up the engine and glide her window down. Kaitlin easily leaned into the window and kissed Sierra's cheek. "Please drive carefully and call me when you get tucked into your new bed with P.J."

Sierra reached up and touched Kaitlin's face. "I will, sweetheart. I promise."

Kaitlin gently touched Sierra's chin with her thumb, guiding her lips closer. "Thank you for a very emotionally charged and soul searching visit."

Sierra touched a spot over Kaitlin's heart. "Thank you for letting me into your golden heart. I appreciate you granting me the opportunity to love you."

Kaitlin leaned slowly toward Sierra's lips and kissed her with ardent hunger and insatiable desire. Kaitlin hesitantly leaned back and touched her finger to Sierra's heart. "Thank you for touching my heart and allowing our hearts to beat as one."

Sierra leaned forward to kiss Kaitlin softly, letting her tongue linger across her slightly parted lips. "Good night, my golden-hearted girl. I look forward to seeing you around eight o'clock and making you breakfast with our farm fresh eggs."

"Good night, my tower of emotional strength. I hope you enjoy your new bed and the warm fuzzy feeling that P.J. gives you."

Sierra leaned her head back against her seat. "It's your warm, fuzzy feeling that I crave, Dr. Bradley. So hurry and get home so I can hold you in my arms while I watch you drift off to sleep."

Kaitlin smiled beautifully and leaned toward Sierra's moist lips. "Get out of here before I kidnap you and take you into my call room and make mad passionate love to you right now, right here."

Sierra ran her fingertip across Kaitlin's lower lip. "Promises, promises."

Kaitlin groaned with frustration and kissed her one final time. "Drive carefully going home, sweetheart, and be particularly careful of those tarantula's and man eating mice."

Sierra's eyes widened as she quickly raised her window and locked the doors.

Kaitlin burst into laughter as she stepped back and waved. Sierra slowly drove away, watching Kaitlin touch her hand to her heart and blow her a kiss. A kiss that Sierra could feel graze against her lips.

☇ 7

Sierra stepped out onto the front deck of the resort with Licorice at her heels. She checked her watch one more time with a worried frown. Nine o'clock in the morning and Kaitlin had not arrived home from work. She leaned forward against the pine railing and felt the warmth of the early morning sun on her face as a gentle breeze flirted with her sleeveless, bright yellow sundress. A mourning dove squeaked its descent from the nearby maple tree; Licorice instinctively went into huntress mode and bounded toward her prey.

Sabrina and Logan joined Sierra on the deck and stood on either side of her. Logan touched Sierra's arm and saw the concern in her eyes. "Don't worry, Sierra. She probably got tied up with a trauma patient. Gladys is paging her now, so we should find out momentarily what happened to her."

Sierra fought the irrational panic building in her chest. "Thanks, you guys. I appreciate that. I wanted to page Kate after we finished helping the quads with their breakfast, but I kept thinking she would be home any minute."

Logan smiled and squeezed Sierra's arm. "Katie has been late like this before when she gets tied up with a patient, but she usually calls us by now. She knows we will all be worried about her."

Sierra squeezed Logan's hand as Gladys slammed the squeaky screen door behind her. She stepped toward them with concern in her eyes. "Ladies, I just talked to Katie. She's fine. She apologized for not calling sooner. Sierra, she asked if you would meet her at the Rainbow Lodge. It's the nursing home on the way to the hospital. Do you remember seeing it last night?"

Sierra frowned and struggled to understand. "Yes, I remember passing the Rainbow Lodge. What's Kate doing there? Is she seeing a patient?"

Logan and Sabrina sighed with concern as Gladys stuffed her hands into the pockets of her floral dress. "I guess you could say that, but there is someone there that Katie wants you to meet."

Sierra tilted her head sweetly and looked at all the concerned faces around her. "I don't understand."

Gladys took Sierra by the shoulders and guided her to the screen door. "Stop asking so many questions, young lady, and go get your purse and car keys. Katie wants to explain it to you."

Sierra looked back at everyone one final time before she obediently headed to her room.

Gladys turned back to the other two and shook her head.

"What happened, Gladys? Are they both okay?" Sabrina said.

CRROCRROCRRO

Sierra asked for Kaitlin at the reception desk and was told to follow the sweet sound of the piano.

Sierra walked down a long polished hallway and stood in the doorway of a sun-filled community room. She was riveted as she watched Kaitlin's fingers glide across the keys of the piano. The music filled Sierra's soul as she watched Kaitlin sing softly to an elderly lady sitting on the bench beside her.

The woman stared out a huge picture window with a fixed stare. She held a single, black-eyed Susan and continually picked at a fluorescent pink cast on her left arm. Her soft, peach dress fit loosely against her swaying, slender frame. Sierra watched her tap her sandaled foot to the beat of Kaitlin's song.

The old woman suddenly turned as if sensing Sierra's presence and gave her a warm smile. Sierra returned the smile, awestruck by her shimmering emerald eyes.

Kaitlin finished her song and turned to follow the woman's gaze. Her eyes met Sierra's, and she burst into a glorious, exhausted smile. They met halfway and melted into each other's arms.

118

Sierra held Kaitlin tight and caressed her head. She turned her face and kissed Kaitlin's soft cheek. "I was worried sick about you."

Kaitlin leaned back with moist eyes and cleared her throat. "I'm sorry for worrying you, Sierra. It's been a really crazy morning."

The elderly lady slipped from the piano bench and stepped quietly in beside Kaitlin. Her face was aglow with a beautiful smile and those shining emerald eyes.

Kaitlin tenderly placed her hand on the woman's back. "Sierra, I would like you to meet my mother, Mary Bradley. Mom, this is my friend, Sierra, that I was telling you about."

Sierra was stunned as she watched Mary extend the beautiful black and yellow flower to her. "I'm so glad you finally came, Sierra. I picked this flower for you. I've been waiting for you all morning so we can bake those peanut butter cookies for Katie's school lunch."

Sierra graciously accepted the flower and gave Kaitlin a subtle, questioning look.

Kaitlin gently placed her hand on Sierra's lower back. "My mother has Alzheimer's disease, Sierra, and a very vivid imagination." Kaitlin smiled and turned to her mother with tenderness in her eyes. "Mom, I hate peanut butter cookies. If you two are going to bake me cookies could they be chocolate chip?"

Mary tilted her head and leaned toward Sierra. "Oh, dear. I don't know how to bake chocolate chip cookies. Do you, Sierra?"

Sierra laughed at this woman's gentle charm as she leaned closer to her bright emerald eyes. "I sure do. You and I are going to bake Kate the most delicious chocolate chip cookies she has ever tasted."

Mary smiled brightly as Sierra leaned forward and kissed her rosy cheek. "Thank you for the beautiful flower, Mary. I'll press it between the pages of my new journal that Kate gave me and write all about your kindness."

119

Kaitlin smiled at Sierra's warmth and charm as her mother walked away. "Where do you think you're going, Mom?"

Mary turned back to Kaitlin with a look of utter impatience. "Why, to the kitchen of course. I'm going to put a pot of boiling water on the stove for your cookies."

Kaitlin gave her mother a soft smile and reached for her hand. "Oh, no, you're not. You're not allowed anywhere near a kitchen stove unless we're with you."

Mary looked up at her daughter with a frustrated, questioning look. "But why, Katie? If I don't get started on supper, your father will be very cross."

Kaitlin gently fixed the collar on her mother's dress. "You're not allowed in the kitchen because you're a walking fire hazard and secondly, God will make sure Dad gets supper tonight. Why don't you and I take Sierra on a walk through the rose garden so I can explain to her what happened to your arm and why I stood her up for breakfast."

Mary gave them both her glowing smile and stepped towards Sierra. "Is your name Sierra?"

Sierra took Mary's hand and held her close. "Yes it is. My name is Sierra."

Mary looped her arms through Sierra and Kaitlin's. "Let's go then, ladies, or we'll be late for the teddy bear picnic."

Kaitlin and Sierra sat together on a stone bench, keeping a watchful eye on Mary as she walked around the gorgeous pink and yellow blooming roses. Sierra gently slipped her hand into Kaitlin's and felt her heart race with her soft touch.

Kaitlin reached forward and touched Sierra's rosy cheek and marveled at her embracing warmth. "I'm sorry about this morning, Sierra. I should have called you sooner, but I got so caught up with my mother that time escaped me."

Sierra held Kaitlin's hand in her lap and leaned forward to kiss her softly. Their lips lingered and barely touched as Kaitlin released a gasping moan. Sierra gave her a glowing smile and stared into her exhausted eyes. "What happened, darling? What happened to Mary's arm?"

Kaitlin turned her head to watch her animated mother talk to a blue jay lawn ornament. "She got out of bed in the middle of the night to use the bathroom and ended up walking out onto this back patio. She tripped over a garden hose and fractured her left radius and ulna. The staff found her at six o'clock this morning sitting on the back lawn cradling her arm and crying for me."

Tears spilled from Kaitlin's eyes as Sierra leaned closer and held her tight. "Oh, my God, baby! I'm so sorry." Sierra watched Kaitlin wipe away her tears as she reached into her purse and handed her several tissues.

"They brought her into the E.R. and we X-rayed her arm. It's a clean, non-displaced fracture so we casted her arm and she should be good as new in six weeks."

Sierra looked out to see Mary scold a skittish squirrel for shoving too many peanuts in his mouth at once. "She's so adorable."

"You wouldn't have said that ten years ago."

Sierra saw the emotions scramble across Kaitlin's moist eyes.

"When my father died in that mine explosion ten years ago, my mother was devastated and very angry that he'd left her alone. She moved to Toronto after his death and accepted a teaching position at the University. Unfortunately, she never grieved properly and began drinking heavily. I had her admitted into several rehab programs, and every time she walked out halfway through the program. She eventually lost her job and continued to drink herself into oblivion." Kaitlin took a deep, emotional breath and turned to Sierra's compassionate eyes. "She eventually got tired of my interference and completely shut Gladys and me out of her life. Gladys was devastated because she and my mother were very close at one time and my mother is her only sister.

"I got very tired of her abusive crap and backed off for several years, hoping that she would come to her senses and quit drinking on her own before she killed herself.

"Three months before Quinn's accident I got a phone call from the police, telling me that my mother had been found wandering through the grocery store, filthy dirty, dressed in her housecoat, totally confused and causing quite a public disturbance over the price of pickles."

Sierra laughed as they both watched Mary pick the sunflower seeds off a sunflower and leave a neat little pile on a patio stone for the same squirrel she just finished scolding.

Kaitlin shook her head and smiled warmly. "I had her admitted into the hospital where she was diagnosed with Alzheimer's disease. Her alcoholism probably masked a lot of her early symptoms, and I felt sick for not seeing it sooner.

"Quinn and I moved her in with us, and then three months later Quinn became a quadriplegic. We all moved up here together, and I found I just couldn't care for both of them effectively. My mother wandered continuously as you can tell from this morning's escapade. I just couldn't keep up with both of their needs, so I was forced to make a decision."

Tears tumbled from Kaitlin's emerald eyes as she stared down at their entwined hands. "I felt sick about placing my mother in a nursing home, but I had no choice. It was destroying my sanity, and half the time my mother could never remember my name. Quinn and Bradley Bay needed one hundred and fifty percent of my energy and time, and that is where I chose to put it.

"Rainbow Lodge is the nursing home that my grandparents had built and they've been great to Mary here. This is the first accident she's had while wandering. I refuse to let them restrain her. That only makes her extremely agitated and more confused. I don't believe that medicating her and tying her to a bed is any way for her to enjoy her remaining years."

Sierra reached up and wiped away Kaitlin's tears as her own spilled onto her cheeks. "You, my love, have had a hell of a life. You've spent most of your adult life caring for the people you love, with no regard for your own feelings or needs. You've given yourself unselfishly without asking for anything in return.

And now it's your turn, Kate. It's your turn to put the past behind you and let me care for you and love you the way you deserve to be loved."

Kaitlin leaned her teary face into Sierra's soft neck and melted into her arms. Kaitlin's tears fell onto Sierra's slender shoulder as she whispered, "I love you, Sierra."

Sierra held Kaitlin close as she caressed her head. "I love you, Kaitlin. With all my heart."

Mary stepped toward them and reached out to touch Kaitlin's hair. "Don't cry, Katie, we'll find your Barbie dolls."

Sierra laughed softly and reached out for Mary's hand. "Did Katie play with Barbie dolls, Mary?"

"She sure did. She had two of them, and she never wanted to put clothes on them. She always laid them together on her bed."

Sierra burst into laughter as Kaitlin proclaimed, "Even back then, I knew."

Sierra and Kaitlin laughed together as Mary stood before them and gave them a questioning look. Sierra watched Mary continually pick at her cast and reached up to stop her hand. Sierra stood and guided her to sit on the bench beside Kaitlin. She knelt before her and held Mary's cast gingerly in her hand.

"Mary, we don't want you to pick at your cast like that. You have a broken arm and I will only make chocolate chip cookies with you if you promise to stop picking at your cast."

Mary looked down at her cast like it was a foreign object and back up at Sierra. "Can we make peanut butter cookies too, Sierra? I like peanut butter cookies."

Sierra smiled and reached for her purse. "Of course, we can make peanut butter cookies, Mary." Sierra reached inside her purse and pulled out a red and black marker. She rested Mary's cast on her thigh and proceeded to draw a big stop sign on the top of Mary's cast with Kaitlin's name and phone number written below. She held the cast up for Mary to see her artwork.

"What does that say, Mary?"

Mary looked at it carefully and said, "Stop!"

Sierra smiled triumphantly. "That's right, Mary. It means stop picking. I wrote Katie's name and phone number below the stop sign. If you need us for anything, you tell the nurses to call Katie at that number."

Kaitlin was fascinated watching Sierra expertly guide her mother.

"Now tell me again what that means, Mary," Sierra said.

Mary looked down at the stop sign then up to Sierra. "Stop picking, stop picking, and stop picking."

Sierra and Kaitlin burst into laughter and applause. Mary gave them an ecstatic smile.

Sierra rested her hands on Mary's legs. "Mary, would it be okay with you if I took Katie home? She's been up all night. She's very tired, and I can hear her tummy growling at me to feed her breakfast."

Mary reached out to touch Sierra's silky, flowing hair. "Will you make sure she catches the school bus and takes the ham sandwich I made for her lunch?"

Sierra winked at Kaitlin. "Yes, Mary. I promise to give Katie her lunch and get her to school on time."

Kaitlin frowned and crossed her arms across her chest. "Wait a minute. I don't want to go to school today, and I hate ham sandwiches."

Sierra laughed as she guided Kaitlin and Mary to their feet. She turned and gently swatted Kaitlin's behind. "Quit arguing and do as your mother says." They both burst into laughter as they walked back into the lodge.

Kaitlin and Sierra left Mary in the care of the nurses and headed towards the parking lot. Kaitlin pulled her keys out of her pocket, but Sierra gently took them from her and dropped them into her purse. Kaitlin gave her a puzzled look.

Sierra stood intimately close to her exhausted eyes. "I'm driving you home, Kate, and I don't want to hear any argument. It's eleven o'clock in the morning, and you've been up for twenty-nine hours straight! I don't want you driving home when you're that tired. I'll come back later with Sabrina and Logan to get your Explorer while you're sleeping."

Kaitlin didn't dare argue with Sierra and let herself be guided to the passenger door of her Honda Passport. Sierra opened the door and playfully swatted Kaitlin's behind. "Now get in, missy, before I make you walk home for worrying me like that."

Kaitlin stared into Sierra's beautiful blue-gray eyes. "Yes, ma'am." Kaitlin was about to ease herself in when she saw P.J. strapped into the seat. She burst into laughter and unbuckled the seat belt so she and P.J. could share the ride home.

Sierra slipped into her seat and buckled herself in. "P.J. was just as worried about you as I was so she asked to come with me." Sierra put her vehicle in drive as she watched Kaitlin hug the teddy bear tightly to her chest. She marveled at the beautiful smile curling the corners of Kaitlin's sensuous lips, then forced herself to look away and focus on the road.

"You were wonderful with my mother, Sierra. Thank you."

"Your mother is really sweet, Kate. I'm really sorry for what you've been through with her. I do, however, want to thank you for allowing me the opportunity to meet her."

Kaitlin felt a slight edge to Sierra's final words as she stared out the passenger window and watched the scenery race by. Several minutes of silence passed as Kaitlin faced P.J. toward Sierra and continued to stare out the window. She playfully nudged Sierra's thigh with P.J.'s furry little foot.

"Sierra, Kaitlin wants to know if you're upset with her? She said she would be really sad if you are."

Sierra struggled to suppress a smile as she looked down at the adorable little bear speaking on Kaitlin's behalf. "Well, P.J., I have to admit I'm a little sad myself."

Kaitlin quickly turned her face to Sierra and asked softly, "Why, darling?"

Sierra turned to Kaitlin and said sternly, "You just turn your beautiful face to that window and continue staring out at the trees. I'm talking to P.J."

Kaitlin obediently turned away as Sierra gave her a gentle smile. "That's better. Now P.J., I'm sad because it seems that I had to have someone else tell me about Kate's lover, Quinn, and her mother has to fall and break her arm before I'm allowed to meet her. To top it all off, we make our first date for breakfast and Kate stands me up! So you just go back there and tell that Dr. Bradley that I wish it was not so difficult for her to share her life with me. Secondly, you tell my friend over there that I'm sure I could find several other women who would be happy to have breakfast with me and show up on time."

Kaitlin playfully bounced P.J. up to her ear and pretended like she was whispering all of Sierra's comments to her. Sierra tried hard not to laugh at Kaitlin's playfulness as she watched Kaitlin whisper in P.J.'s ear. She watched the bear bounce back toward her and rest against her thigh.

"Sierra, Kaitlin asked me to tell you that she doesn't mean to be so difficult. She's just not used to having someone to share the painful parts of her life."

Sierra jerked her vehicle off the road and into a rest stop among the trees as she slammed it into park. She unclipped her seat belt and turned toward Kaitlin; Kaitlin looked at her in shock. Sierra reached forward and held Kaitlin's face in her hands and looked at her with menacing eyes.

"That's exactly my point, Dr. Bradley. I want to share your entire life with you, good and bad. I don't plan on just being here for the good times, Kate. I plan on being here for all time."

Kaitlin looked deeply into Sierra's, moist emotional eyes, unclipped her seat belt, and set P.J. down. She leaned toward Sierra and guided her into her arms as Sierra's tears moistened their cheeks.

"I know, Sierra. I'm sorry. There are no more surprises. I promise. You know more about me and my life than most people."

Sierra sniffled and gently bit Kaitlin's ear until she yelped, "Ouch! You bit me!"

Sierra laughed and leaned back slightly. "I'm not most people. I'm the woman that loves you and wants to share your life completely."

Kaitlin softly rubbed her ear. "You won't have me completely if you keep chewing on my ear like that." They both burst into laughter as Kaitlin pulled Sierra into her arms and held her close. "No more surprises, Sierra. I promise."

Sierra leaned back and stared at Kaitlin's soft, sensuous lips. "I need you to seal that promise with a kiss, Dr. Bradley."

Kaitlin leaned toward Sierra's slightly parted lips. "You're a needy little woman aren't you, Ms. Vaughn?"

Sierra smiled seductively and leaned closer. "You have no idea, Dr. Bradley. I plan on making you meet my every need like no other woman can."

Kaitlin looked deeply into Sierra's eyes and smiled. "I look forward to that, Ms. Vaughn. I look forward to that very much." Their lips met slowly, seductively, teasingly as a deep gasp slipped from Sierra's lips and sent a surge of burning heat from Kaitlin's chest right down to her thighs. They breathlessly held each other close and gazed into each other's eyes.

Sierra kissed the ear she had bitten and guided Kaitlin back into her seat belt. She got them back on the road as P.J. waddled up to Sierra's thigh one more time. Sierra smiled as she looked down at the bear. "Yes, P.J.?"

Kaitlin struggled to look away from Sierra. "Sierra, Kate wanted me to tell you that she didn't intentionally stand you up for breakfast, and if she ever finds another woman anywhere near your scrambled eggs, she'll personally pack them in one of your fluorescent orange suitcases and send them floating out to sea!"

Sierra burst into laughter as she watched a beautiful smile curl the corners of Kaitlin's sensuous lips. "Well, P.J., you tell my friend Dr. Bradley that she worried me terribly this morning and she'd better find some way to make it up to me." Sierra loved the smile on Kaitlin's face as she forced herself to keep her eyes on the road.

"I look forward to repenting for my sins, Sierra. Very, very much."

Sierra pulled up to the front of Kaitlin's home and let her out on the front deck to an eagerly awaiting Gladys, Sabrina, and Logan. Kaitlin filled them all in on the events of her morning and her mother's new cast.

Gladys, Logan, and Sabrina headed off to attend to the needs of the guests once they felt reassured that Kaitlin and her mother were fine.

Sierra made them both a delicious breakfast of scrambled eggs, tomatoes, toast, and freshly squeezed orange juice. They sat and devoured their meal on the back deck as Licorice curled up under Sierra's chair and enjoyed a midday nap.

Kaitlin finished her breakfast and wiped her mouth on her linen napkin as she looked down at Licorice's content position. "That cat seems to enjoy being around you."

Sierra carefully eased up from her chair and gathered their plates. "I enjoy her company too, and we tell each other everything." Sierra leaned down and kissed the tip of Kaitlin's tiny nose as Kaitlin recoiled in fear of being bitten again.

As Sierra burst into laughter, Kaitlin grabbed her by the waist and pulled her down into her lap. Sierra dropped their plates back down onto the table with a crash. Sierra wrapped her arms securely around Kaitlin and nestled into her lap as she enjoyed her beautiful, exhausted smile.

"Everything?" Kaitlin said.

Sierra combed her fingers through Kaitlin's thick, dark hair. "Yes, my sweet Kate, everything. Maybe you could spend some time watching my open, unconditional relationship with Licorice and learn from her how easy I am to share things with."

Kaitlin growled and buried her face into Sierra's soft neck and luxuriated in her sweet giggles of ecstasy. She buried her face in her thick hair and inhaled her lemon fresh scent. "Ummm, you smell so good." Kaitlin leaned back slightly and stared at Sierra's waiting lips. "Thank you for such a delicious breakfast, my darling. You have made my tummy very happy."

Sierra glided her hand over Kaitlin's strong shoulder. "You're very welcome, my love. I could spend the rest of my life making you happy."

Kaitlin leaned toward Sierra and kissed her with aching, unbridled passion.

Sierra leaned her forehead against Kaitlin's and struggled to catch her breath. She reached up and gently caressed Kaitlin's cheek before reaching to her belt and unclipping her pager. "I'll keep this for you today. I've turned the ringers off on all the phones so you won't be disturbed while you sleep. I thought you might like to have a nice, warm shower while I clean up the kitchen. When I'm done, I'll come up and tuck you in."

Kaitlin kissed Sierra softly. "That sounds wonderful."

They walked into the kitchen together. Sierra set their plates in the sink, and Kaitlin picked P.J. up off the counter. She hugged the bear close and gave Sierra a shy smile.

"I was wondering, Ms. Vaughn, if you would like to join me in that shower?"

Sierra moved intimately close to Kaitlin's shy smile. "I would love to share that shower with you, Kaitlin. However, if I do that, you'll never get any sleep today." Sierra leaned forward and kissed Kaitlin softly before she turned her toward the spiral staircase and gently patted her sexy bottom. "Off to the shower with you, Dr. Bradley, before I can no longer restrain myself and shower you with my kisses."

Kaitlin climbed the staircase with P.J. tucked under her arm. "I'm getting tired of inviting you into my shower, Ms. Vaughn, and continually being denied. I'm sure there are many women out there that would not turn me down as many times as you have."

Sierra stood at the base of the ornate staircase and placed her hands on her hips. "I'm the only woman that you'll ever be inviting into your shower, Dr. Bradley, so it's irrelevant how other women would respond to your seductive invitation."

Kaitlin laughed as she reached her second floor loft and looked back down at Sierra. "P.J. has accepted my invitation to shower with me. What do you say to that?"

Sierra burst into her beautiful laughter and looked up at Kaitlin's playful smile. "She's the only woman that I would allow to join you. Oh, and Dr. Bradley, P.J. asked me to ask you if you don't mind washing her back for her. She seems to have trouble reaching."

Kaitlin leaned against the Mennonite quilt draped elegantly over the railing at the top of the landing. "What if I told you I have trouble reaching?"

Sierra loved the gentle shyness in Kaitlin's smile. "I'm sure P.J. will be happy to scrub your back for you."

Kaitlin gave Sierra a disappointed pout. Sierra blew her a kiss as she watched her walk into the open doorway of her bedroom.

Sierra finished cleaning up the kitchen and climbed the beautiful spiral staircase for the first time. She reached the spacious loft and admired the elegant, circular glass-top table that separated two Santa Fe–style couches. Several huge pillows lay heaped beside the stone fireplace and exuded an invitation to come and play. Sierra ran her hand along the back of the plush couch before stepping quietly into Kaitlin's bedroom.

The exquisite room took her breath away. The blinds had been drawn, and the only light came from a stained glass lamp on the bedside table. The soft glow caressed the pastel pink walls and plush dusty rose carpeting. Sierra stepped around a cozy matching white leather sofa and love seat as she approached Kaitlin's queen size, oak, four-poster bed draped in flowing white crepe. Her breath caught in her chest as she saw Kaitlin peacefully sleeping on her stomach as a soft pink, floral goose down duvet barely covered the gentle contours of her naked back. Sierra took a deep breath and tiptoed toward the bed; she could see P.J. nestled beneath Kaitlin's well-defined arm. Sierra tried to steady her erratic heart as she knelt beside the bed and leaned forward to kiss Kaitlin's soft cheek.

Kaitlin stirred slightly and slowly opened her sleepy eyes. She carefully leaned her head up from the pillow and kissed Sierra softly. "Good night, my darling. I love you."

Sierra loved the way Kaitlin called her darling and watched her bury her beautiful face into her pillow. She reached forward and brushed a damp strand of hair from Kaitlin's long, dark eyelashes and tried unsuccessfully to avert her eyes from the gentle curve of her breast. "Good night, sweetheart. I love you, too."

Sierra ran her fingers through Kaitlin's thick, shiny hair and hesitantly, slowly, grazed her fingertips along her naked back. Sierra could feel the scorching heat of desire mushroom in her belly as she restrained herself from trailing her fingers lower. "I hope you normally sleep naked, Dr. Bradley, because otherwise you're testing my self-control to the max!"

Kaitlin laughed weakly and reached for Sierra's hand and tucked it under her face with childlike innocence. "I don't own any sleepwear, Sierra. I've always slept naked. It makes me feel so feminine and free."

Sierra smiled as her eyes roamed over the gentle contours of Kaitlin's silky back and arms. "You certainly are every inch a woman, my love."

Kaitlin smiled beautifully and opened one eye as she reached toward Sierra and traced her finger seductively along the V-neck of her sundress. "Speaking of feminine, Sierra, you look beautiful in that yellow sundress. It accentuates your eyes and frames your gorgeous body beautifully. I'm thoroughly enjoying your fashion show. Keep up the good work and I might buy your whole collection if it comes with you."

Sierra burst into laughter and nuzzled down against Kaitlin's cheek. "You'll be lucky if I even let you buy my suitcases, let alone the wardrobe, after your comment that first night, Dr. Bradley."

Kaitlin covered her face with Sierra's hand. "Are you ever going to forgive me for that moment of insane anger, Sierra?"

Sierra nestled into her neck and playfully nibbled on her ear. "I think I'll make you work for your forgiveness, Kate. There certainly is something under this beautiful duvet that I'd love to trade for your absolution."

Kaitlin growled erotically as she patted the bed beside her. "Well, come on in, big-city girl, so we can start on that course of absolution."

Sierra groaned with frustration. "You have no idea how much willpower it's taking to stop myself from slipping naked beneath those covers with you."

"If I wasn't so exhausted I'd strip you of your willpower and sexy dress faster than you could blink."

Sierra kissed Kaitlin's warm pink cheek and gently massaged her neck. "That I don't doubt for a minute, sexy lady." Sierra watched Kaitlin sigh with each caress of her fingertips. "If you have some lotion, Kate, I'll massage your back for you to help you get to sleep."

Kaitlin turned her face to kiss the palm of Sierra's hand. "That would be so wonderful, Sierra. The lotion is on the bathroom counter, and Sierra, I can't promise you that I'll let you leave if you start touching me with those soft hands of yours." Sierra began to rise as Kaitlin playfully refused to let go of her hand. Sierra looked into her tired, loving eyes and caressed her face. "You know, Sierra, I've lain awake for hours in this bed fantasizing about having you here with me and now that you're here I can't even keep my eyes open. This is so unfair! Talk about cruel and unusual punishment."

Sierra brushed her lips against Kaitlin's cheek. "That's good, though, because it gives you more Sierra appreciation time. You didn't think I was going to make this easy for you after the way you treated me initially, did you?"

Kaitlin gave Sierra a pouty, forlorn look and quickly grabbed her pillow and buried her head underneath.

Sierra laughed at her frustration and headed into the bathroom. Sierra flipped on the light switch and popped her head back out the doorway. "Kaitlin! There's a huge, whirlpool tub in here."

Kaitlin settled back on her pillow. "Sierra, I'm sorry your room doesn't have a bathtub. If you're nice to me, I might let you share my tub with me."

Sierra returned to the bedroom and settled onto the edge of Kaitlin's bed as she warmed the lotion between her hands. "I'll be real nice. I promise. I'd do anything to join you in that tub, sexy lady."

Kaitlin moaned with ecstasy as Sierra gently glided her hands over Kaitlin's shoulders, neck, and arms. She gently kneaded the tight muscles of her back as Kaitlin purred. "I'm in heaven. P.J. is so jealous," Kaitlin said.

Sierra leaned against Kaitlin's face and kissed her cheek as she slid her hands lower onto her back. Kaitlin moaned and melted to Sierra's touch as Sierra kneaded the muscles along her spine and fantasized about what lay beneath the duvet. Sierra's thumbs slid along her sides and down over her hips as a tingling surge of desire pulsated between her thighs. She lingered her hands along the gentle curves above her hips and along her ribs. Her fingertips brushed the outer softness of her breasts as Sierra had to reign in her self-control.

Sierra worked deeper over Kaitlin's shoulders and whispered against her ear, "You have a gorgeous body, Dr. Bradley, and very talented hands from what I heard coming from that piano today."

Kaitlin nestled deeper into her pillow. "Gladys taught me how to play the piano at a very young age. I owe all my musical talent to her. I have a baby grand piano in the recreation room that I'll play for you sometime."

"I'd like that. I'd like that very much."

Sierra slid her hands along Kaitlin's back as she felt her breathing become deeper. She watched her beautiful dark eyelashes rest softly against her face as she succumbed to a deep, peaceful sleep. Sierra carefully pulled the duvet up to Kaitlin's strong shoulders and kissed her cheek before she headed into the bathroom to wash her hands.

Sierra returned and pulled a chair up beside Kaitlin's bed and tucked the duvet higher up around her shoulders. She leaned against her cheek and whispered softly, "Sweet dreams, my love. I love you." Sierra let her lips linger against Kaitlin's cheek, then leaned back in the chair as she ran her fingers gently through her hair. She tucked a loose strand of hair behind her ear and thought about how much her life had changed in two short days since taking the road into Bradley Bay. The last thing she had ever expected to find here was this incredible woman. She never thought one woman could so irrevocably touch her life. She came here to get some peace of mind and rest and instead she was sent whirling into an emotional tailspin that showed no signs of letting up.

Was she ready for this? Hardly. It's exactly the opposite of what Sierra came to Bradley Bay for. Timing was never Sierra's strong suit. Now this timeless treasure had been placed in her hands.

She spent the last three months trying to understand what went wrong between her and Linda and promising herself never to make those same mistakes again. Was she ready to accept this gift? Hardly. But she was going to take what Kaitlin was ready to offer her and give her back more than what she could have asked for. This was a woman worth fighting for. A woman worth building a life with. She would take that treasure and nurture it and shower it with her love. That was all she knew how to do. She prayed it was enough for Kaitlin and her ravaged heart.

She skimmed her fingertips across Kaitlin's shoulder a she sat and listened to her gentle, rhythmic breathing. "I hope you're ready for this Kaitlin Bradley because I have a feeling our lives will never be the same."

☙ 8

A dozen guests in wheelchairs and at least as many family members and friends stood along the edge of the nature trail at the north rim of Bradley Bay. They overlooked the wide expanse of undisturbed, open field before them and the vast glinting surface of Sturgeon Lake behind them. They burst into wild applause as they watched Logan and Sabrina race down the hill and set the brilliantly colored kite soaring high into the sky. Sabrina walked the ball of string back up to Sierra and handed it over to her as she set off to launch the next kite into flight.

Sierra secured the string to the arm of Jennifer's wheelchair and watched the bright glow in her eyes as she followed the swaying flight pattern of the pink and purple kite.

"When you asked me what I wanted to do today, Sierra, and I said I wanted to fly a kite, I was only kidding, you know!" They both burst into laughter as Sierra knelt down to be at Jennifer's eye level.

"Kate keeps telling me that we make wishes come true in the Emerald City, so when you said you wished to fly a kite, I set out to make it happen."

Jennifer gave Sierra a beautiful smile and awkwardly touched her cheek with the side of her arm. "You're very special, Sierra. Katie should feel blessed to have you."

Sierra leaned her cheek against Jennifer's atrophied arm and smiled. "I'll remind her of that every day, Jennifer. Don't you worry."

Sierra and Jennifer heard sounds of delight and looked up to see Michael expertly guide his kite through a series of looping figure eights and continuous rolls. Everyone applauded his theatrics.

"Show off," Jennifer huffed.

"What did you say, Jen? Did you say how awesome my kite flying skills are?"

"Yeah, something like that, fly boy."

"I bet you did some of these same aerial acrobatics on your motorcycle in your heyday."

"I rode a motorcycle, Michael. I didn't belong to the circus, smarty pants."

Michael burst into laughter and gave Jennifer his devilish grin that he reserved only for her.

"Behave you two," Sierra said.

Sabrina touched Sierra's shoulder and guided her to her feet. "Looks like Sleeping Beauty has awoken from her nap," Sabrina said, as she gestured down the paved trail behind them.

Sierra reached out her arms and squealed with delight as she saw Kaitlin and Gladys walking hand in hand among the towering birch trees. Sierra bounced down the trail with gushing joy and jumped into Kaitlin's arms. Kaitlin spun her in a circle and embraced her with all the love in her heart.

Sierra leaned back with a magnificent smile and reached for Gladys, kissing her cheek.

Gladys rested her hand on Sierra's back. "I'd never know that you two were happy to see each other. My, my, how things have changed from the first time you two met."

Sierra and Kaitlin blushed and held each other close. They watched Gladys walk toward Jennifer and admire her beautiful kite. Kaitlin guided Sierra off the trail and behind a dense group of fir trees.

Sierra smiled knowingly and reached up and caressed Kaitlin's glowing face. "You're up early, sweetheart. It's only four o'clock. I was going to wake you in another hour, but you beat me to it."

Kaitlin turned her face and kissed the palm of Sierra's soft hand. "I woke up with a start about a half hour ago looking for you. The last thing I remember was you massaging my back, and when I woke up you were gone. I thought I had dreamt about you being there; then I remembered Mary's arm, and it all came back to me. The most wonderful thing was waking up to your note and the beautiful yellow rose on the pillow beside me." Kaitlin reached into the pocket of her denim dress and pulled out a small piece of pink paper. She unfolded the note and held Sierra close as she read the message:

My sweet Kate,

> *You have reached the depths of my heart that even I didn't know existed. I ache to be with you. The next time you open your beautiful eyes it will be me you will find on this pillow and not just my note saying: I love you.*

Love always, your Sierra. xoxo

Kaitlin gazed into Sierra's eyes. "That's so beautiful, Sierra. I will always cherish this note from you."

Sierra luxuriated in the feeling of Kaitlin's body firmly against hers as the subtle scent of her perfume awakened each of Sierra's senses. "I would rather you had found me instead of the note on your pillow, but I did promise to let you sleep today." Sierra took Kaitlin's beautiful face in her hands and caressed her cheeks. "You fell sound asleep after I rubbed your back."

Kaitlin tilted her head. "And how long did you sit there and watch me?"

Sierra's eyes burst with surprise. "How did you know I watched you?"

Kaitlin laughed softly and glided her hands across Sierra's lower back. "My chair was not exactly where I usually have it, so I figured my little Peeping Tom must have been sitting in it this morning."

Sierra smiled and ran her hands over the form-fitting contours of Kaitlin's sleeveless denim dress. "You're a beautiful sight to behold, Dr. Bradley. Sleeping and awake. I especially enjoyed pulling the duvet down and viewing your gorgeous naked body in its entirety."

Kaitlin gasped and held Sierra out at arm's length. "Sierra Vaughn, you did not do that!"

Sierra burst into laughter and guided Kaitlin back into her arms. "You have such a gorgeous ass, Dr. Bradley."

Kaitlin looked horrified, then reached for Sierra's waist and tickled her mercilessly till she admitted she was only teasing her. They held each other tight as Sierra caught her breath and dried her tears of laughter.

Kaitlin brushed away a stray strand of hair from Sierra's eyes and said shyly, "I've just been great company for you this morning. First I stand you up for breakfast, then I fall asleep on my masseuse."

Sierra smiled at Kaitlin's sweet shyness and held her face in her hands. "I live for every moment that I can spend in your exhilarating company, Dr. Bradley. The purpose of my massage was to help you sleep, even though my body and mind had other ideas." Sierra reached up to Kaitlin's five-foot-eight-inch height and kissed her softly.

They stared into each other's eyes as Kaitlin gently slid her hands over the subtle curve of Sierra's hips. Sierra felt the intense heat flowing from Kaitlin's hands directly to her tingling breasts and pulsating thighs as she traced her thumb across Kaitlin's moist lower lip.

Sierra ached to consume this passionate woman as she leaned toward her, then suddenly jumped back as she felt Licorice rub herself against their legs. They both looked down at the intrusion from their furry little friend.

Kaitlin bent down to pick her up. She gently rubbed behind her ears and gave her a stern look. "Your timing leaves a lot to be desired, little one."

Sierra laughed and reached out to rub Licorice's chin. They both watched as she went completely limp in Kaitlin's arms and buried her little face in Sierra's hand.

"We both seem to crave your touch, beautiful lady," Kaitlin said.

Sierra leaned toward her to complete the kiss that they had never had the chance to begin.

Sierra leaned back and stared into Kaitlin's smoky eyes and struggled to control her racing heart. She rested her hand on Kaitlin's lower back and guided her back onto the path. "Come join our little circle of kite pilots, sweetheart, before I take you back to your bed and tear that sexy dress off your body and make mad, passionate love to you over and over and over again."

Kaitlin closed her eyes and held Licorice close as she groaned with frustration. "Stop taunting me like that, Ms. Vaughn, and do as you say before I burst into one big puddle right here at your feet!"

They both laughed as Sierra guided Kaitlin up the trail.

Everyone greeted Kaitlin warmly as they watched her set Licorice down beside Jennifer's wheelchair to pursue a buzzing bee. Kaitlin cupped Jennifer's chin in her hand as she marveled at the wondrous smile on her face. "Hello, Ms. Kite pilot."

"Good afternoon, sleeping beauty. I'd rather be behind the controls of my Concorde, but I seem to be temporarily grounded. This kite just won't move as fast as I would like it too and Michael's over there showing off as usual."

Michael executed a perfect figure eight and shouted with glee. "Are you whining over there, Ms. Evel Knievel?"

"Hand me that ball of string, Logan, so I can wrap it around fly boy's neck."

"Play nice, Jen," Logan said, as she handed a soaring kite to Sierra. Sierra watched Jennifer stick her tongue out at Michael as she handed the roll of twine to Kaitlin. She stood beside her and marveled at the look of childlike wonder in her eyes as she watched the multicolored kite dip and soar to its own rhythm. Sierra reached up and gently touched Kaitlin's glowing cheek.

"I haven't flown a kite since I was a kid. Being around you, Sierra, is like walking through a happy childhood."

Sierra turned to see Logan set another kite into flight when she saw a beautiful monarch butterfly perch itself atop Jennifer's wheelchair. "Jennifer, don't move. It looks like you have someone that would like to share your front row seat."

Everyone turned to see the elegant insect perch precariously atop Jennifer's wheelchair. Sierra moved very slowly and grabbed half of an orange from their picnic basket and gently placed it in Jennifer's hands. She knelt beside her chair and captivated everyone's attention as she whispered softly, "Don't move, Jen, and see if our little friend would like to visit for some orange juice."

Everyone stood silently suspended in time as they watched the delicate orange and black butterfly flutter nervously, then drop suddenly onto the orange. Jennifer turned to Sierra with the beaming, ecstatic smile of a child. Everyone smiled in awe as they watched the skittish monarch flutter above their heads and float into the woods.

Jennifer turned to Sierra in utter disbelief. "How did you do that, Sierra? How did you know he would land on this orange?"

Sierra stayed kneeling beside Jennifer's chair. "My grandparents own a fifty-acre farm in Kitchener. Every summer I would spend my vacations with them. They're both very special to me, and they taught me so much about nature. My grandmother would grow what she affectionately called her 'butterfly garden' for the sole purpose of attracting butterflies. It would be filled with marigolds, petunias, blueberry bushes, lilac bushes, and pussy willows. Every morning we would put a plate of sliced oranges in the center of the garden, and I would sit there for hours and watch the different types of butterflies float around my head. They even had a river running through their property that was bordered by the most beautiful wildflowers. I would sit among those flowers and pretend to be a bluebonnet and pray that a butterfly would land on my nose."

Everyone burst into gentle laughter at Sierra's heartwarming story as the monarch butterfly returned to perch on the arm of

Jennifer's wheelchair. They all watched its huge, brilliant wings sway with the gentle breeze as Jennifer marveled at its closeness.

"It's so beautiful," Jennifer said.

Sierra watched it flutter nervously above the orange before landing abruptly. "It sure is but deadly poisonous to birds."

Jennifer turned and looked at Sierra with a questioning frown.

"The butterfly larvae feed off many plants that have cardiac glycosides or heart toxins. As the larvae transform into butterflies, they carry these heart toxins in their wings and abdomen and cause birds to vomit and die if eaten. So therefore, after many nauseating experiences and several emergency meetings around the bird feeder, the bird community has issued a butterfly ban and learned not to eat some monarchs."

Everyone burst into laughter as they watched the monarch flutter away.

Sierra rose to her feet and gently took the orange from Jennifer's hands. She placed it back in the picnic basket as Kaitlin stared at her in amazed disbelief.

Gladys walked toward Michael and his acrobatic kite. She heard a distinctive hum above the rows of flowering rose of Sharon bushes running along the edge of the hill. She pointed to the noisemaker. "Look everyone. A hummingbird."

Everyone looked up to see the tiny, brilliant, metallic green bird hover above a welcoming trumpet flower and expertly guide its beak deep within the succulent flower for the sweet nectar.

Sierra stood before Kaitlin and rested her hand on her arm as she admired the steady, graceful beauty of the tiny bird. "It's called an Anna's Hummingbird. You can tell by its jewel-like metallic green body and beautiful rose cap and throat."

Everyone turned to Sierra with an astonishing look.

Sabrina leaned closer to Sierra's glowing face. "Don't tell me. Your grandparents had a hummingbird garden too, and you pretended to be a rose of Sharon flower and wished that a hummingbird would come and lick the tip of your nose."

Everyone burst into laughter as they watched Sabrina tap the end of Sierra's tiny nose.

Sierra gave her a beautiful pout and stood squarely with her hands on her hips. "Sabrina, are you making fun of me?"

Kaitlin gently swatted Sabrina's shoulder and affectionately rested her hand on Sierra's waist. "She's not making fun of you, sweetheart. She's just jealous of your wonderful childhood and vivid imagination."

Sierra grinned widely and stuck her tongue out at Sabrina.

Sabrina laughed and stepped closer to Sierra and kissed her forehead. "All right, you guys. The butterfly and hummingbird lecture series is over for today. We would like to thank our special guest speaker, Ms. Sierra Vaughn, for her adorable educational stories."

Everyone burst into applause as Sierra turned and curtsied to the crowd. Then she stepped toward Sabrina and wrestled her into a fit of giggles. Sabrina finally begged for Sierra's forgiveness and called a truce. She held Sierra close against her as she said, "All right, everyone, we should gather our stuff and head back to the resort."

They all helped to gather the kites and began to head back down the trail.

Sierra and Kaitlin were the last ones left behind. Sierra stepped in behind Kaitlin, resting her hands on her waist as she watched her slowly reel in her kite.

Kaitlin felt the arousing warmth of Sierra's body against hers as she closed her eyes and melted to her touch. "That was a fascinating lecture from such a big-city girl," Kaitlin said. She felt Sierra's hands slip seductively onto her hips and glide across her belly.

Sierra pulled her back tight against her as she nuzzled into Kaitlin's soft neck and kissed her with slow, moist kisses.

Kaitlin moaned softly and tilted her head to allow Sierra's lips more room to wander. Sierra whispered in a dreamy voice, "This big-city girl has always preferred the peace and tranquility of the farm and at this very second, Dr. Bradley, you are exactly what I prefer." Sierra glided her hands along Kaitlin's hips and down her thighs as they both groaned with desire.

Sabrina stopped at the bend of the trail and looked back. "Will you two please save the foreplay for later and come along. We have a huge lesbian bash to get to. Logan and I are going to bring the van around so we can load Jennifer and some of the other girls. We'll meet you guys out front in about thirty minutes." Sabrina was about to turn and walk away, but she hesitated with a twinkle in her eye. "Thirty minutes, ladies. Just enough time to change into a pair of jeans. Maybe you should come with me, Sierra, so we can escort you to your room without any major distraction tagging along."

Sierra shuffled her feet as she walked down to Sabrina and took her hand like an obedient child. She turned to watch Kaitlin gather her kite and extended her hand to her. "You can come too, baby. Just promise Bri you won't be a distraction while I'm getting dressed."

Kaitlin burst into laughter and took Sierra's hand. "You let me be there while you're getting dressed, and I can promise you I'll be a major distraction." They all burst into a warm laughter as they headed down the trail together.

CRITICAL

Sierra stood before her tiny bathroom mirror and finished pulling back her chestnut brown, flowing hair into a ponytail. She heard a soft knock at the door. She quickly straightened the collar of her red silk shirt and smoothed her hands over her jeans. She caught a final glimpse in the mirror and said, "Who is it?"

A deep, sexy voice that melted Sierra's soul resounded through the closed door. "It's the Wicked Witch of the West, my sweet little Dorothy, and I want you to open this door before I cast a spell on you with my fire-breathing broom."

Sierra leaned against the inside of the door. "What is it that you want from me, Wicked Witch?"

Kaitlin smiled, as she smelled the sweet red rose she picked from her garden for Sierra. "What I want from you, my sweet little Dorothy, is your magical ruby red slippers, your friendship, your loving heart, your fascinating mind, and your gorgeous body. And not necessarily in that order."

Sierra whipped her door open and spread her arms out wide. "Take me, you big bad witch, and make me squirm."

Kaitlin held the delicate rose to her lips and gave Sierra a smoldering, seductive look as Sierra slowly backed into the room. Kaitlin eagerly followed and swiftly closed the door with her cowboy boot.

Sierra was awestruck by the intense chemistry flowing between them as Kaitlin tossed the rose onto Sierra's pillow. She stepped toward her and took her by the shoulders, dramatically laying her across the bed and easing herself above her.

Their eyes met with jolting intensity as Sierra slowly glided her hands over Kaitlin's slender body in a white, ribbed turtleneck and faded Levis. Sierra slowly cleared her dry throat and stared at Kaitlin's moist, hungry lips, positioned only aching inches above her. "Thank you for the beautiful rose. Do you always enter a girl's room with such dramatic flair, my beautiful Wicked Witch of the West?"

Kaitlin swam in Sierra's torrid blue-gray eyes. "Only your room, my sweet little Dorothy. Only when I need to show you how badly I want you and need you."

Sierra's heart overflowed with emotional intensity as she felt a liquid heat fill her belly. She slowly entwined her fingers into Kaitlin's hair and guided her closer. Their lips meet softly, tenderly.

Sierra breathed a gasping moan that ignited a raging fire deep within Kaitlin's soul. Kaitlin watched her slowly open her heavy-lidded, moist eyes and leaned close to lay soft, nibbling kisses across her lips, jaw, and cheeks. Her lips suckled their way to the bounding pulse on her arched neck. She luxuriated in Sierra's uninhibited moans of delight. She lazily kissed her way back to Sierra's moist, pillowy lips, gently easing them apart with her hungry tongue before plunging deeply to taste Sierra's sweet nectar.

Sierra brazenly caressed Kaitlin's tongue with her own as she trailed her hands along Kaitlin's back and shapely bottom, basking in her lusty, aching groan.

Kaitlin sucked Sierra's lower lip deep into her mouth and ran her tongue along the edge of her teeth before plundering her with a sensual, intimate rhythm.

Sierra arched her heated body beneath Kaitlin's and swayed intimately against her as she heard Kaitlin gasp against her lips.

Kaitlin felt her world sway in blissful ecstasy as their bodies danced in heated passion.

Sierra leaned her cheek against Kaitlin's and held her close as she struggled to catch her breath. "I have never in my life been kissed like that. You, Dr. Bradley, turn my insides into Jell-O with one kiss from those sexy, sweet lips."

Kaitlin nuzzled into Sierra's neck and playfully freed the top button of her silk shirt. "What do you say we skip the party and carry out that quality assurance test on this new bed of yours?"

Sierra sighed as Kaitlin nibbled on her neck and teased her earlobe with her tongue. "No way, Dr. Bradley. I need to prove to you that all the action and excitement that I need is right here with you in this bustling northern town."

Kaitlin groaned with frustration and rolled onto her back to lay beside Sierra. Sierra rolled onto her side and rested her leg across Kaitlin's thighs, admiring her feminine curves. She traced her finger along Kaitlin's chin and seductively between her breasts to her slender belly. Kaitlin basked in Sierra's sensuous touch and dropped her arms above her head,

"That quality assurance test must be done in the next twenty-four hours, Ms. Vaughn, or this bed will turn into a pumpkin and you will be transformed from Dorothy to Cinderella and spend the rest of your life scrubbing the castle floors for your wicked stepsisters, Sabrina and Logan."

Sierra burst into laughter and brushed her fingertip across Kaitlin's jaw. "I'm not worried. I know that my charming

Wizard will lay me naked atop this new bed before the final hour and save me from the depths of slavery to my stepsisters and wicked stepmother, Gladys."

Kaitlin burst into laughter and ran her fingers through Sierra's ponytail. "The three musketeers would kill us if they heard us talking about them this way."

Sierra leaned toward Kaitlin and kissed her softly, slowly, stunned by the shock waves that rippled through her soul with each kiss.

Kaitlin reached up and held Sierra's face in her hands. "Speaking of the three musketeers, they were loading everyone into the van when I told them I was coming up here to get you. We'd better get going before they come up here with a battering ram and break down your door." Kaitlin stared deeply into Sierra's playful eyes and ran her fingertip across her moist lower lip as Sierra met it with her warm, wet tongue. Kaitlin gasped with passionate desire and raised her head to kiss those incredible lips. Kaitlin brushed her lips softly across Sierra's and whispered in a hoarse, sultry voice, "I love you, Sierra Vaughn."

Sierra touched her fingertip to Kaitlin's heart. "I love you, Kaitlin Bradley. More than words can say." Sierra leaned down and kissed Kaitlin deeply, fiercely, with all the love in her heart.

Sierra covered Kaitlin's face with kisses before she eased her to her feet and openly admired the way her turtleneck hugged her breasts. Sierra gave her a seductive smile as she stepped toward her tiny closet and reached in for an elegant black cardigan.

Kaitlin stepped toward Sierra's secretary's desk and ran her fingers across the velvety cover of her closed journal.

Sierra slipped into her sweater and watched the beautiful smile radiate from Kaitlin's eyes. Sierra adjusted the sweater and stepped toward Kaitlin. She picked up the journal and handed it to her with pride. "Have a look and see how many wonderful memories have found their way into my journal."

Kaitlin ran her thumb along the edge of the journal as she timidly looked up at Sierra. "Have you shared any of those wonderful memories with your parents?"

"I sure did. I called them and told them about Springfield and how beautiful it is here at Bradley Bay. We talked about the guests, Licorice, Gladys, Sabrina and Logan. Then they filled me in on their plans for the week and we said good-bye." Sierra watched Kaitlin for several seconds then burst into laughter at the look of utter shock in those wide emerald eyes.

"I guess I deserved that."

"You sure did, Dr. Bradley. However, now that I think back to that conversation with my parents, I may have mentioned your name once or twice. Maybe just once when I told them about being thrown in the lake."

Kaitlin grimaced as she hugged the journal to her chest. "If you were gong to mention me once you could have thought of a more favorable memory to share with them."

"I guess you're just going to have to meet them, Kate, and have them formulate their own opinion of you."

Kaitlin swallowed hard as Sierra tapped the journal in her hands. "Why don't you flip through my journal and read what this place and its people have come to mean to me."

Kaitlin held the journal tenderly and watched Sierra step into her tiny washroom and brush through her ponytail. Kaitlin looked down at the journal with the eager anticipation of a child on Christmas Eve as she opened the front cover and saw her mother's daisy pressed between the pages. Kaitlin held the flower gently as she flipped through the journal and found half the book filled with Sierra's flowing penmanship.

Sierra watched Kaitlin's reflection in the mirror as she began to read softly, "... her tongue tastes like honey on hot toast and fills me with a warmth that caresses my soul. Her hands touch me with soft, warm strokes that leave the imprint of her fingers for hours. Her eyes, like no other emerald that could ever be found or created, look at me with an intensity that shakes my foundation and makes me feel so special."

Kaitlin slowly looked up from the journal with intense eyes. "You are very special to me, Sierra. I have never felt love so profound as I do when I look at you."

Sierra reached up and caressed Kaitlin's soft cheek. "You're very special to me, Kaitlin Bradley. I love you with a depth that I never knew existed."

Sierra tenderly took the journal from her hands and placed it in her drawer. She reached for Kaitlin's waist and guided her to sit on the edge of the desk as she stood between her thighs. Their eyes danced with fierce love as Sierra pressed herself intimately between Kaitlin's thighs and reached for her face. She slowly leaned closer and united their lips in a kiss of thunderous sensuality.

Sierra felt Kaitlin's hands glide over her back and hips as she leaned her forehead against her cheek and struggled to slow her breathing.

Kaitlin held Sierra's warm, slender body tightly against her. They both jumped at the sound of loud knocking at the door. Sierra nuzzled her lips against Kaitlin's ear and whispered, "Sounds like the wicked stepsisters have arrived with their battering ram."

Kaitlin tilted her head slightly to allow Sierra's lips to linger as they heard Sabrina's animated, booming voice. "This is the police! Open this door immediately! We have reason to believe that we have two fugitives of love hiding out behind this door. We have warrants out for the arrest of one Wizard of Oz and one Audubon Society bird and butterfly nut."

Sierra and Kaitlin huddled close and laughed. "What do you think, my beautiful Wizard? Should we open the door and turn ourselves in?"

Kaitlin tenderly touched Sierra's chin and guided her face closer. "No way. I need you to kiss me again, my little Audubon Society bird and butterfly nut."

Sierra leaned closer and whispered against Kaitlin's moist, waiting lips, "Your a needy woman, my sweet Wizard."

Kaitlin held Sierra's face in her hands. "You have no idea, Ms. Vaughn. I plan on making you meet my every need like no other woman can."

Sierra leaned into Kaitlin's lips and probed her deeply with her tongue. "I look forward to that very much, Katie. Very, very much." Sierra took Kaitlin's lips with an astonishing fierceness that sent a wave of heat crashing into Kaitlin's chest and thighs.

The door burst open with a loud bang as three smiling faces walked slowly into the room and absorbed the cloud of passion before them.

"Well, well, well! I'm glad to see that you're not still struggling with your decision to be at Bradley Bay, Sierra."

Sierra spun her head around and squealed with delight, "Sydney!"

Kaitlin rubbed her fingers across her swollen lips as she watched Sierra bounce into Sydney's arms.

"What are you doing here? What a lovely surprise," Sierra said.

Sydney held Sierra at arm's length as Sabrina and Logan stood beside a glowing Kaitlin. "Kelly and Katie called me and invited me to Kelly's party. I'm off this weekend, so I thought it would be a great opportunity to come visit with my dear friends and make sure that they were treating you right." Sydney gave Kaitlin a suspicious smile and was filled with the depth of her happiness. "From that kiss we all witnessed, I can see that at least part of you is being well watered."

Sydney stepped into Kaitlin's arms and hugged her tight. "Hello, beautiful," Sydney said.

Kaitlin kissed Sydney softly and held her close. "Hello, Sydney. It's so wonderful to see you. We're thrilled you could come for the weekend."

Sydney smiled and stepped back to admire the bursting happiness in Kaitlin's eyes, a rapturous glow that she had not seen in her dear friend in the five years that she had known her.

"I'm thrilled to see you guys too, Katie. It's been at least two months since I've been up to Bradley Bay. You guys all look terrific as always."

Sydney reached for Sierra's hand and squeezed it warmly as Sierra gave her a beautiful smile. "It looks like a few things have happened since I sent my friend Sierra up here to help you guys out. You're absolutely glowing, Sierra. I don't think I've ever seen you look this happy."

Sierra blushed and looked into Kaitlin's glowing eyes. "A few things certainly have happened since I arrived at the Emerald City, Sydney. It's been the experience of a lifetime."

Logan and Sabrina laughed discreetly behind their hands.

Sierra turned to Sydney. "Sydney, I would love to know how you and Kaitlin met and why it took you this long to introduce me to these three nut cases."

Sydney smiled and reached for Kaitlin's hand. "Remember when I used to moonlight at St. Mike's to pick up some extra shifts?" Sierra nodded her head yes as Sydney continued. "Katie was doing her residency there, and that's how I met her and Sabrina and Logan. Then when Quinn had her horrible accident, she was admitted to St. Mike's, and the three of us worked every shift we could to take care of her and Katie. It was a tragic time, and it certainly brought the four of us closer."

Sabrina tenderly touched Sierra's back. "We wish you'd been there with us at the time, Sierra. We really could have used your bubbly spirit. Quinn would have really enjoyed your company."

Sierra rested her hand on Kaitlin's arm. "I really wish I could have been there too."

Kaitlin reached for Sierra's hand and squeezed it gently. "I don't know what I would have done without these guys being there for Quinn and me. They blessed me with their love and friendship, and now they have blessed me with you." Kaitlin leaned toward Sierra and kissed her softly as the other three gushed over their newfound love.

Sydney beamed with happiness for her friends as she turned to Sierra. "You see, Sierra, there was no reason for you to fight me tooth and nail about coming up to Bradley Bay. I told you it would be wonderful for you to get away and bask on the shores of Sturgeon Lake with my special friends."

Sabrina, Logan, and Kaitlin abruptly cleared their throats. Sierra threw them all a menacing stare and stepped to within inches of Sydney's questioning chocolate brown eyes. "Let me tell you, Ms. Sydney, about basking on the shores of Sturgeon Lake with your special friends. First of all, Dr. Kaitlin Bradley treated me like shit the moment we met! She made me feel like I am more of a spoiled, big-city inconvenience, like I was incapable of being any help at all."

Sydney turned in shock and stared at Kaitlin, who turned her guilty face to the window.

"Logan, Bri, and Gladys had to threaten her with a near-drowning experience before she would even think of apologizing for her appalling behavior."

Kaitlin gave Sydney a sidelong look. Sydney was stunned to see the mischievous guilt gleaming in those emerald eyes.

"And, as if that wasn't bad enough, Logan and Sabrina have worked me to the bone. To show their appreciation, these two thugs threw me in the freezing cold lake among all the slimy fish and fabled Loch Ness monster while Kate stood back and watched them do it!"

Sydney turned and glared at Sabrina and Logan as they quickly turned their backs and joined Kaitlin at the window.

"Gladys has truly been my saving grace. If it wasn't for her and the simple fact that I love these three nutcases and what they do here, then I would have packed my bags and driven back to Toronto long before now and come looking to skin your hide for introducing me to this constant mayhem and emotional whirlwind!"

Sydney took one cautious step away from Sierra and swatted Sabrina, Logan, and Kaitlin's behinds as they all protested loudly. "Is this true, ladies? I send you my dear friend to help you guys out and you treat her this way? What's gotten into you guys? Is all this northern fresh air fermenting your usually wonderful hospitality?"

Sierra stood behind Sydney and beamed a joyous smile, then stuck her tongue out at all three guilty faces.

"Get your sorry behinds out that door, and I expect that from this moment on, you three will show Sierra how wonderful you really are and treat her like the special guest she is."

Sierra placed her hands on her hips and mimicked Sydney's stern tone. "Yeah! Treat me like the special guest I really am."

Kaitlin dropped her head in shame and walked by Sierra's bed, picked up her pillows, and handed one each to Logan and Sabrina. She slowly reached for Sierra and guided her into her arms as she commanded, "Get her!"

Logan and Sabrina shrieked with glee and raised their pillows high as they begin pummeling Sierra relentlessly.

Sydney watched the chaos in shock as Sierra buried her face in Kaitlin's neck and squealed, "Sydney, don't just stand there like an imbecile, help me!"

Sydney foolishly reached for Sierra as Kaitlin pulled her in and threw them both on the bed as pillows, pillowcases, and feathers floated throughout the room on their ticklish, youthful laughter.

⟲ 9

The soothing melody of the Indigo Girls floated above the excited, noisy crowd of women as Sierra turned slightly in Kaitlin's arms and fed her a roasted marshmallow. Kaitlin seductively licked the remaining soft, sticky goo from Sierra's fingers as she basked in the sizzling lust blazing in Sierra's eyes. They stared intently as the smell of burning wood permeated their senses and sparks flew like fireworks from the crackling logs.

Loons called to their diving mates across the calm, glistening lake. The cool night air invited Kaitlin to wrap her arms snuggly around Sierra. They sat on a flannel blanket, surrounded by a circle of friends, as the excitement in the air fanned the caressing flames. Sabrina and Logan sat close beside them as they watched Jennifer wheel by and wave.

"See ya, ladies. I'm off to cruise some chicks."

"Be careful, Jennifer, there are some wild women at this party," Sabrina said.

Jennifer stopped her wheelchair and turned her head to look back at their smiling faces. "I know. I already met Sydney."

They all burst into laughter as they watched Jennifer head for the crowded dock, where they could see Sydney greet her with a huge smile.

Logan shook her head as she passed Sierra another marshmallow. Sierra hesitantly looked away from Kaitlin's mesmerizing eyes and thanked Logan as she speared the marshmallow and guided it toward the flames.

Kaitlin took a sip of their ice-cold beer and handed the bottle to Sierra, watching her sensuous lips meet the glass. Kaitlin looked up when two tall, sinewy, brunettes's plunked themselves down beside her and leaned in to give her a kiss.

"Hey, you two. I'm so glad you guys could make Kelly's party. She told me she had invited you both but wasn't sure if you were on duty or not." Kaitlin turned to Sierra and gestured to the women beside her. "Sweetheart, this is Liz and Darcy. Liz is a police officer with the marine patrol unit and Darcy is a firefighter in town. Imagine the pillow talk they must have. Ladies, this is Sierra Vaughn."

Sierra reached over and shook both their hands. "Hello, ladies. It's a pleasure to meet you both."

"It's a pleasure to meet you, Sierra. We've heard some juicy gossip over the past few days and just had to come and see if it was true that our darling Dr. Bradley actually fell out of her self imposed exile and into the arms of a beautiful woman. Looks like it's true on both counts," Liz said.

"What do you mean self imposed exile? I've hardly led the life of a hermit."

"No you're right, Kate. You have not lived the life of a hermit. Since Quinn's death you have lived the life of a cloistered nun," Darcy teased.

"Sierra, Kate has left a few women banging their heads against a tree trying to get her attention over the past year. Now we hear about a stranger coming into our town and sweeping her off her feet. That has made those same women bang their heads so hard you would think they were woodpeckers," Liz teased.

Sierra beamed Kaitlin her ravishing smile. "I feel blessed not to have become one of those woodpeckers but I think I know exactly how those women feel. It takes a tank to sweep Kate off her feet."

Everyone burst into laughter as Liz squeezed Kaitlin's shoulder. "You certainly have met your match, Kate."

Kaitlin held Sierra tight as she kissed her temple. "Yes, I certainly have met my match."

Sabrina reached past Sierra and handed Liz two bottles of beer. "Do we have anything nonalcoholic around here?"

Darcy twisted the tab off both bottles and handed one to Liz. "Oh, shut up and take a swig, darling. We're off duty, remember."

"I'm an officer of the law, darling. That never stops whether I'm in uniform or not. I must uphold justice and maintain the safety of the citizens of Springfield at all times."

Logan quickly tossed Darcy a bag of jumbo marshmallows and watched her tear the bag open, reach inside and pop one into Liz's mouth. "That should ensure the safety of the citizens of Springfield for the next five minutes at least."

Everyone burst into laughter as they watched Sydney walk by with a tray laden with steaks, ribs and hamburgers for the barbecue.

"Hey, Sydney, is that all we're going to be offered tonight is meat. Some of us are vegetarians you know," Liz said with a full mouth.

"God. There has to be one in every crowd. I'm sure Kelly has some tofu burgers in her freezer with your name on them, Liz. I just don't know how you can eat those disgusting sawdust burgers and claim to be eating healthy."

"I'm an officer of the law, don't you know. I have to stay healthy so I can uphold justice and maintain the safety of the citizens of Springfield at all times."

Everyone groaned as Darcy reached inside the bag and grabbed two marshmallows and shoved them both in Liz's mouth to uproarious laughter.

Sabrina leaned toward Logan's ear and whispered softly, "I'll go get us all some more beer, sweet pea. Keep my spot warm for me."

Logan turned her face to brush her lips lightly against Sabrina's. "Always, babe. This spot will always be warm for you."

Sabrina kissed Logan deeply before rising to head toward their cooler on the back deck. Sabrina wove her way through the crowd before climbing the back steps. She stopped as she saw Kelly leaning against the back railing watching Sydney flirt with all the women around the barbecue. Sabrina felt saddened as she saw the undisguised pain and frustration etched in Kelly's crystal blue eyes. Sabrina laid her hand warmly on Kelly's shoulder. "Why don't you go ask the big flirt to dance with you?"

Kelly turned to Sabrina as she struggled to disguise the anguish in her eyes. "I already did ask Sydney to dance with me, Bri. She told me that I was about number thirty on her dance card and that I was to be patient till it was my turn."

Sabrina openly gaped at Kelly as a burning anger and disbelief left her staggering to speak. "She did not say that!"

Kelly leaned back against the railing and rubbed the back of her neck to relieve the tension that had started building there since the moment she saw Sydney again. "I've never lied to you before, Bri. Why would I start now? I couldn't even make up something as outrageous as that. That is a line that could only come out of Sydney's mouth."

Sabrina watched Kelly squeeze her eyes tight and attempt to rub out the emotional stress etched on her face. "I don't know why I always set myself up to be hurt by Sydney. You'd think I would learn by now and just stop trying to get her attention. Sydney just naturally attracts a crowd of women, so why would I ever think she would stop to notice how much I care about her?"

Sabrina looked back out at the barbecue and watched the women surrounding Sydney laugh outrageously at something she had said. "It's her loss, Kelly. I know this is hard for you, but why don't you come right out and tell her how you feel about her. Why do you permit yourself to sit back in the wings and allow this love for her to fester instead of doing something about it and seeing what could happen? Sydney might just surprise you, you know."

Kelly shook her head of blonde curls and laughed halfheartedly. "She never ceases to surprise me, Sabrina, but unfortunately those surprises always leave me feeling hurt and empty." Kelly pushed herself off from the railing and took in a deep breath, glancing back at the barbecue once again.

Sabrina reached out and took her hand. "Come on, Kelly. Don't do this to yourself. You deserve to be treated better. Come grab a bunch of beers with me and join us by the fire. You've thrown a hell of a party tonight, Kelly. Don't let Sydney fill you with aggravation and grief. It's not worth it."

Kelly looked back at the dock as she started to follow Sabrina. "Unfortunately, my heart feels she is worth it, Sabrina, and I can't convince it otherwise. Trust me, I've spent years trying."

Minutes later Sabrina handed the girls each a beer and took the remaining beers from Kelly's hands. The music abruptly changed to a faster, pulsating beat as Kelly extended her hand down to Sierra. "Come dance with me, Sierra? It's the least you can do since you won't let me curl into your backside at night."

Sierra laughed and handed Kaitlin their roasting stick and beer as she watched a frown crease her beautiful face. Sierra kissed Kaitlin's cheek and took Kelly's hand as she rose to her feet. "I'll be back soon, baby," Sierra said.

Kaitlin glared at Kelly's beaming face and pointed their roasting stick dangerously at her. "Keep your hands where I can see them, Kelly, or the next shift we work together, I'll make sure you'll be the enema queen of your worst nightmares!"

Kelly brushed the roasting stick aside and leaned closer to Kaitlin's pouty scowl. "Your jealousy is so heartwarming, Dr. Bradley. It's so wonderful to see you in love again." Kelly kissed Kaitlin softly and winked playfully as she guided Sierra to the raised deck.

Everyone watched them walk away as Kelly impishly slipped her hand onto Sierra's curvaceous behind. Sierra didn't miss a step as she reached back and smacked Kelly's hand and guided it to rest on her lower back. Everyone burst into laughter as they watched them climb the steps and join the crowd rocking and swaying seductively on the deck.

Kaitlin smiled and set down the roasting stick. The sensual movements of Sierra's slender frame mesmerized her as she thought of how quickly she had fallen in love. She had promised herself she would not let this happen again, but it seemed like someone wasn't listening. She had been so happy with her simple life till Sierra came in like an unrelenting monsoon and blew open doors and windows that Kaitlin thought were locked forever.

Her need for Sierra staggered and frightened her till she realized she had no control over the love she felt for her. No more control than she had over an unrelenting monsoon. She could either board up her windows and pray for the return of calm weather or she could go out in the elements and feel the power and energy surrounding her. Sierra's energy drew her like a bee to honey. It was innate. It was right. There was no way of fighting it or trying to protect herself from being hurt. It was just meant to be. Sierra was meant to be.

Sabrina and Logan felt warmed by the depth of love in Kaitlin's eyes. They all turned and watched Sierra and Kelly dance among the throng of gyrating women.

The music changed to a seductive swagger as Kaitlin rose to her feet. "Come on, ladies. Let's go dance so I can save Sierra from Kelly's wanderlust hands." Everyone rose to their feet to follow Kaitlin onto the dance floor.

Kaitlin watched Sierra kiss Kelly's cheek and thank her for the dance as Kelly saw Kaitlin standing against the railing. Kelly graciously bowed out to Kaitlin and walked away to stalk her next prey.

Sierra moved to the center of the dance floor and seductively crooked her finger at Kaitlin to come join her as she sensuously began to sway her hips and move to the intrinsic beat of the music.

Kaitlin was filled with intense desire as she slowly walked toward Sierra and enjoyed her fluid, graceful movements. Sierra slowly twirled as Kaitlin glided her hands onto her hips and pulled her tightly back against her. Sierra gasped at Kaitlin's arousing touch as Kaitlin pressed herself firmly against Sierra's back and allowed her hands to float across her waist and tauntingly down the front of her thighs.

A swell of excitement and anticipation splashed against Sierra's chest as she struggled to catch her next breath. Sierra reached up and entwined her fingers into Kaitlin's hair as they slowly swayed to a rhythm created from their intense passion. Sierra tilted her head and held Kaitlin tight as she felt her lean closer and mold her lips into the shallow, warm curve of Sierra's neck. Sierra gasped with escalating desire as Kaitlin's kisses burned a path directly to her aching, throbbing thighs.

Kaitlin brushed her hands along Sierra's shapely thighs and up over the cool silk draped over her slender belly. She held Sierra firmly against her wanton body as one hand gingerly glided higher and grazed intimately over Sierra's erect nipple. Sierra released a deep, throaty gasp as she turned quickly to face Kaitlin. She grabbed her firmly by her waist and pulled her intimately against her as they stared into each other's hungry eyes.

Kaitlin slowly released Sierra's hair band and freed her ponytail. She entwined her fingers into her thick hair and pulled her face closer. "I want you, Sierra. I want to make love to you now and forever."

Tears welled in Sierra's blue-gray eyes as she kissed Kaitlin softly and whispered against her moist lips, "I want you, Kaitlin. More than I've ever wanted any woman before." Kaitlin beamed Sierra her magnificent smile and kissed her with uninhibited passion.

Everyone on the dance floor couldn't help but see their ravishing, unrestrained desire.

Sierra leaned back and rested her forehead against Kaitlin's as she slowly caught her breath. She reached up and touched Kaitlin's flushed cheeks. "Take me home and make love to me, Kate."

Kaitlin took Sierra by the hand as they walked around and kissed everyone good night before climbing into Kaitlin's Explorer.

છબળછબળછબળ

The full moon shone bright above them as Kaitlin unlocked her front door and followed Sierra and Licorice inside, locking the door behind them. They slipped out of their shoes and cowboy boots as Licorice wove her way around their feet. The glowing moon dimly lit the house as Sierra reached for Kaitlin's hand and guided her toward the spiral staircase.

"Are you sure you don't want something to drink, Sierra, or even something to eat? You didn't eat much at the party. I can whip us up something to eat in no time and ..."

Sierra stopped halfway up the stairs. She guided Kaitlin to sit on the step and carefully knelt between her thighs. The moon cast long beams of smoky light around Kaitlin as Sierra held her apprehensive face in her hands and smiled at her unease. "Are you okay, sweetheart? You seem to be uncomfortable all of a sudden."

Kaitlin dropped her face and toyed with a button on Sierra's elegant silk blouse. Tightly coiled tension swirled in Kaitlin's gut as she struggled with the excitement of taking that final step to completely surrendering her heart and soul to Sierra—a risk that terrified her and yet filled her with the knowing that Sierra was the woman she had needed for a very long time.

"I'm really not uncomfortable, Sierra, it's just that ...," Kaitlin hesitated as Sierra tenderly touched her chin and raised her face to meet her frightened eyes. She saw an insecurity and vulnerability that moved her deeply.

"It's just what, sweetheart? Don't be afraid to tell me."

Kaitlin felt embraced by the warmth in Sierra's eyes as she leaned her forehead against hers and whispered softly, "It's just that I haven't done this in a very long time."

Sierra smiled at Kaitlin's sweet shyness and gently caressed her face, knowing that her meaning went deeper than just the physical sense. "I understand, sweetheart. Neither have I."

Kaitlin quickly sat up with a shocked look and held Sierra close. Sierra leaned intimately between Kaitlin's thighs and wrapped her arms around her. "Linda and I had not been intimate for the last year of our relationship, so I understand your apprehension."

Kaitlin frowned and tilted her head sweetly. "Linda should have her head examined for wasting such precious time with you. She has no idea what she has lost."

Sierra kissed Kaitlin's furrowed brow. "I guess I should be grateful that she didn't want to make love to me in that last year since she seemed to be screwing everyone else."

They both shook their heads in disbelief. Sierra gently touched Kaitlin's chin. "This is overwhelming for both of us, Kate. The intensity and chemistry between us both frightens and amazes me. We are just going to have to deal with those emotions together and hope that we never lose the essence of both." Sierra skimmed the soft pad of her thumbs under Kaitlin's brilliant green eyes and saw vulnerability, kindness, warmth, and undying love.

"All I know, Kate, is that I love you very deeply and you make me squirm with one smile of your beautiful face. I can't imagine how my body is going to respond when you reach for my naked skin."

Kaitlin leaned toward Sierra and kissed her with gentle warmth. She felt Sierra wrap her arms around her and arch toward her in complete surrender. Sierra's lips parted slowly as Kaitlin tasted the heady need in her kiss. Kaitlin touched her tongue to the tip of Sierra's as her mind reeled with their scorching desire.

"I ache to feel you squirm beneath my touch," Kaitlin breathed against Sierra's eager lips.

Sierra sighed deeply with lustful desire as Kaitlin brushed soft, moist kisses across her closed eyelids and down to her wanton lips. She slanted her mouth firmly against Sierra's and took her mouth with ravenous need.

Sierra's mind teetered on the edge of ecstasy as she leaned her cheek against Kaitlin's. She basked in the sensation of her tingling lips as she felt Kaitlin gracefully release each button on her blouse. Sierra leaned back and watched the look of intense need brimming in Kaitlin's eyes as Kaitlin gently eased Sierra's blouse over her delicate shoulders and watched it float like a butterfly to the bottom of the stairs.

Kaitlin smoothed her hands over Sierra's slender belly and up over her ribs. She slipped her fingers beneath Sierra's fitted sports bra and guided it over her head and tossed it carelessly toward the discarded silk.

Sierra remained kneeling before Kaitlin and luxuriated in the look of excitement and wonder in her eyes. Her heart thudded wildly in her chest as the look in Kaitlin's eyes caressed her with more tenderness and passion than she could ever wish for.

Kaitlin slowly reached forward, like she was about to touch a rare object of art, and gently cupped each of Sierra's firm breasts in her hands. She slowly skimmed the soft pads of her thumbs over each erect nipple before leaning forward to take the straining buds in her mouth. She felt Sierra tremble against her before she heard her gasp of surrender.

Kaitlin looked up into Sierra's smoky eyes and slid her thumbs over her responsive nipples. "You're so beautiful, Sierra. I want you so badly."

Sierra took Kaitlin's hands and glided them down her belly to the button on her jeans. Their eyes locked in astounding intensity as Sierra slowly released Kaitlin's hands. "Please undress me, Kate."

Kaitlin swallowed hard and slowly unzipped Sierra's jeans. Her request was as seductive as a candlelight dinner on a moonlit night. Kaitlin felt a surge of liquid fire course through her belly and mushroom in her chest as she hooked her thumbs into the waistband and leisurely lowered the denim over Sierra's slender hips. Kaitlin ached to savor this moment, unsure of how much control she would have once she had Sierra arching beneath her.

Sierra rested her hands on Kaitlin's shoulders and stepped out of her jeans as she watched Kaitlin shamelessly toss them down the stairs.

Kaitlin placed her hands on Sierra's well-shaped calves and slowly molded her hands up over her knees and warm thighs.

She never knew she could want a woman with such intensity as she wanted Sierra. Her fingertips traced the edges of Sierra's midnight black, French-cut Jockeys as Sierra arched her neck and moaned expectantly. Kaitlin hooked her thumbs into the waistband of Sierra's sexy panties and lowered them to Sierra's feet, adding them to the discarded pile at the bottom of the stairs.

Sierra stood before Kaitlin and closed her eyes as Kaitlin floated her hands along the outside of Sierra's thighs and over her sexy bottom. Kaitlin felt her own desire swelling between her thighs as she guided Sierra closer by her bottom and tenderly kissed the inside of her thighs.

Sierra rested her hands on Kaitlin's shoulders and moaned with incredible pleasure as Kaitlin nuzzled her forehead against Sierra's soft, dark mound and inhaled her intoxicating, womanly scent. "God, Sierra, you smell wonderful."

Sierra smiled and guided Kaitlin to her feet. She wordlessly eased Kaitlin out of her white turtleneck and playfully tossed it over her shoulder and watched it sail below to land on Kaitlin's computer. They both laughed with bursting excitement as Sierra reached behind Kaitlin and freed her of her lacy white bra. The bra landed across the computer keyboard; Kaitlin's jeans tumbled down the stairs and entwined with Sierra's.

Sierra was overcome with excitement as she hooked her thumbs into Kaitlin's lacy white panties and guided them slowly over her slender hips. Kaitlin closed her eyes and rested her hands on Sierra's shoulders as Sierra knelt before her and seductively eased the white lace lower, exposing her sensuous, v-shaped mound of dark hair. Sierra leaned forward and kissed the dark patch and basked in Kaitlin's sweet scent. She was consumed by her desire for this woman as she leaned closer and dipped her tongue into Kaitlin's glistening wet hair. Kaitlin dropped her head back and moaned with ecstasy as Sierra guided the alluring lace panties down Kaitlin's thighs and dropped them on the step below.

Sierra slowly guided Kaitlin up the rest of the stairs and grabbed several of the huge pillows beside the fireplace and laid them down on the landing. She rested her hands tenderly on Kaitlin's waist and guided her down onto the pillows.

Kaitlin watched Sierra with burning desire as Sierra eased herself gently between Kaitlin's parted thighs. They both moaned as their soft skin met as one for the first time. The heat of their contact emanated from their joined bellies to the hypersensitive touch of their straining breasts. Sierra felt Kaitlin open herself to her completely as her heart surged with love and want. Sierra kissed Kaitlin softly, tenderly, tasting her restraint and probing to unleash the fountain of passion she knew was aching to erupt. Their tongues met and plunged, fueling their hungry, aching need.

They both groaned and swayed against each other's hot bodies as Sierra lowered herself and took Kaitlin's erect nipple in her mouth and bathed it with her warm, wet tongue. She left each nipple tingling and aching for more as she eased herself lower and felt Kaitlin's fingers glide through her hair and massage her scalp. Sierra kissed Kaitlin's slender belly with wet, sucking kisses as Kaitlin arched her neck and groaned with exhilarating ecstasy. Sierra moved lower and kissed the inside of Kaitlin's warm thighs and felt her eagerly spread her legs.

Kaitlin writhed and swayed beneath Sierra's soft, enticing lips as she felt herself floating on a euphoric wave beyond anything she had ever experienced before. "Oh God, Sierra. You feel so wonderful."

Sierra struggled to keep her hands gentle as she ached to take Kaitlin with a ferocious hunger that startled her. Sierra eased herself back up to Kaitlin's flushed face and suckled on the bounding pulse in her lean neck. "You are wonderful, my dear, sweet, Kaitlin."

Kaitlin's thick eyelashes battled back her joyous tears as she took Sierra's face in her hands and kissed her with fierce longing. Kaitlin arched her hips to feel Sierra intimately as Sierra was consumed by her urgent need.

Sierra trailed soft, wet kisses across Kaitlin's face as she ran her fingertip across her full lower lip. Her eyes were filled with awe as she glided both hands over Kaitlin's shapely breasts and toyed with each erect nipple. "You're so beautiful, sweetheart."

Kaitlin's eyes floated closed as she succumbed to the sizzling rapture begging to be granted release.

Sierra struggled to make this moment last as she leaned toward her breasts and took each straining nipple into her mouth, sucking them deeply.

Kaitlin gasped as she combed her fingers through Sierra's hair and guided her closer and her breast deeper.

Sierra floated her fingertips over Kaitlin's hips and down inside her thighs as she eased herself down lower. She left a warm, moist trail of kisses along the inside of Kaitlin's thighs as she eased herself forward and inhaled Kaitlin's sweet scent before plunging her tongue deeply into her pool of wetness.

Kaitlin felt like she was floating in a sea of unfathomable ecstasy as she rhythmically swayed her hips to meet Sierra's gentle strokes. Kaitlin gently rested her hands on Sierra's head as Sierra floated her tongue higher and swirled around Kaitlin's hardness. Kaitlin arched her neck and writhed in agonized pleasure as Sierra's fingers explored her intimately. They both rode on a wave of searing bliss as Sierra marveled in Kaitlin's responsiveness and erotic taste.

Kaitlin struggled to breathe as her thighs tensed and she held Sierra's head tight in her hands. She suddenly stopped swaying and groaned, "Oh God, Sierra! Oh God, yes ..."

Sierra rhythmically entered Kaitlin and swirled her tongue lighter and lighter as she felt a pulsating shudder beneath her tongue. Kaitlin arched her back higher and groaned erotically, "Oh God, Sierra! Oh God, Sierra, I'm coming ..." as a burst of wetness bathed Sierra's tongue and a wave of undulating spasms gripped Sierra's fingers and pulled her in deeper. Kaitlin released a final gasping scream and collapsed back onto the pillows as a kaleidoscope of brilliant blues and greens exploded before her eyes.

Sierra nuzzled her damp chin into Kaitlin's soft, dark mound and rested her head against the inside of her thigh. Moments later she gently removed her fingers and basked in their passionate afterglow. Sierra sighed deeply as she glided her wet fingers along the inside of Kaitlin's thigh and eased herself up to lie in her loving, spent arms. A place where Sierra could lie forever.

Minutes later, Sierra nuzzled into her warm neck and kissed her cheek softly before she began to rise. Kaitlin opened her heavy eyes and reached for Sierra's radiant face.

"I'll just go wash my face, baby. I'll be right back."

Kaitlin gently wiped Sierra's moist chin, feeling her sudden unease. "Why, my darling? I want to kiss you. I want to taste our intimacy on your beautiful lips."

Sierra's eyes filled with surprised shyness as she slowly eased back into Kaitlin's arms. She leaned up on one arm and slowly traced her fingertip over Kaitlin's warm, soft breasts.

Kaitlin tilted her chin to meet her eyes. She saw years of discomfort and disappointment shadowed in those shining blue-gray eyes. "What is it, my darling? What's bothering you?"

Sierra felt embarrassed as she tilted her head to kiss Kaitlin's hand. "It's just that Linda would never let me kiss her after unless I washed my face."

Kaitlin touched Sierra's damp chin and fought to maintain a swell of anger. "Look at me, my darling. I'm not Linda. You ended that relationship months ago, and with it you have ended Linda's quirks. It's me you're making love to, and I ache to kiss you and taste myself on your lips."

Sierra felt her heart swell with Kaitlin's compassion and kindness as she slowly lowered herself closer to Kaitlin and cautiously brushed her lips against hers. She closed her eyes and indulged in Kaitlin's gentle sigh as Kaitlin held her face close and kissed her with insatiable hunger, melting away years of caution and restraint.

Sierra eased herself on top of her and timidly responded to her probing tongue. Sierra's eyes filled with a newfound pleasure at Kaitlin's comfort with their intimacy as she ran her tongue along Kaitlin's upper lip and delved deeply into her mouth.

Kaitlin glided her hands along Sierra's silky back and down over her sexy bottom as she smiled at the beautiful look of delight in Sierra's eyes. "Ummm. Delicious. Especially on your tongue, my darling Sierra."

Sierra brushed a loose strand of hair away from Kaitlin's eyes. "You're delicious, sweetheart. Thank you for sharing yourself so openly."

Kaitlin easily rolled Sierra onto her back. She adjusted the pillows beneath her and gracefully eased herself on top of her. Kaitlin stopped to look around them and realized they were still at the top of the spiral staircase. "Sierra, I have never made love to a woman anywhere besides a bed."

Sierra glided her hands over the shallow curves of Kaitlin's back and down over her tight ass. "Well then, Dr. Bradley, I'm touched to be a virginal experience for you. I'd love to show you that a bed is not always a necessity."

They both laughed as Kaitlin looked back down the stairs at the disarray of strewn clothing, then back at Sierra. "I'm never going to be able to walk up these stairs again without smiling from ear to ear."

Sierra separated her thighs and guided Kaitlin to rest intimately against her. "Come here, my sweet Kaitlin, and make me smile from ear to ear."

Kaitlin needed no further encouragement as she kissed Sierra with a yearning that heated their desire to an instant boiling point. Kaitlin felt Sierra's desire flow around and completely through her, igniting places she had not yet discovered. Kaitlin craved the sweet cavern of Sierra's mouth as she kissed her softly with a tender, lingering kiss. She leaned back slightly and whispered against her moist lips, "I plan on doing more than just making you smile, my darling Sierra. I plan on making you squirm as I acquaint myself with your beautiful, naked body."

Sierra's eyes darkened with desire as she leaned toward Kaitlin and kissed her with a deep awakening hunger that Kaitlin happily fed. Kaitlin's hands explored and claimed every gentle curve of Sierra's soft, warm skin as their kisses became more urgent and bold. Sierra rocked her body against Kaitlin's and eagerly spread her thighs as Kaitlin's inquisitive, probing fingers glided through her soft mound of curls and plunged into her intimate depths of wetness. Sierra gasped and arched her neck as Kaitlin caressed and explored her wet, velvety folds. Kaitlin kissed Sierra's neck and teased her ear with her tongue as she whispered hoarsely, "God, Sierra, you're so wet. You feel so wonderful and I ache to taste you."

Sierra tilted her flushed face to Kaitlin's and kissed her softly. A kiss that lingered and fluttered across Sierra's heart as she realized she was looking into the eyes of the woman she belonged to. "Only if you promise to kiss me after."

Kaitlin beamed with happiness as she ran her tongue between Sierra's soft lips. "That's one promise I will keep forever." Kaitlin kissed Sierra firmly, then lowered herself to each budding nipple. Sierra moaned and squirmed as Kaitlin teased and tantalized them and left them engorged and throbbing for more. Kaitlin's hungry, impatient kisses descended to Sierra's hips and thighs as she lowered herself between her legs and gently separated Sierra's legs. Sierra arched her back and grabbed the pillow beneath her head as Kaitlin slipped her hands beneath Sierra's shapely bottom. Her fingers floated between her shapely curves and teasingly through Sierra's damp curls.

Sierra gripped the pillow tighter and arched her neck as she felt Kaitlin's warm breath along her thighs.

Kaitlin glided her fingers into Sierra's pool of wetness as she gently touched her tongue to her sensitive tissue. They both groaned with ecstasy as Sierra squirmed to Kaitlin's gentle strokes. Kaitlin basked in Sierra's spicy, heady scent as her tongue floated over Sierra's erect tissue and her fingers explored her deeply.

Sierra swayed against Kaitlin's flickering tongue as a swell of longing passion quickly built between her thighs. Sierra moaned with aching ecstasy as she completely surrendered herself to this incredible woman.

The swell of desire continued to surge and build as Kaitlin continued to drive Sierra's ecstasy higher and higher. Kaitlin's tongue swam in Sierra's flowing passion as she felt a gentle quiver beneath her tongue.

Sierra's thighs clamped around Kaitlin's shoulders and held her still as Sierra's entire body shivered with ecstasy. She suddenly arched her neck and screamed Kaitlin's name as a thunderous explosion sent a shower of millions of sparkling crystals soaring before Sierra's eyes.

Kaitlin watched Sierra gasp for air as she gently rubbed her wet chin in Sierra's soft mound of hair. She gently withdrew her fingers and saw Sierra wince from the heightened sensitivity. Kaitlin floated over Sierra and allowed Sierra to guide her into her arms. They held each other tight as Sierra's breathing slowly returned to a gentle rhythm.

Sierra slowly opened her eyes and turned to Kaitlin's beaming face. She laughed and kissed the tip of Kaitlin's nose. "You should be proud of yourself, Dr. Bradley. That was the most incredible experience I've ever shared."

Kaitlin smiled triumphantly and leaned up on one elbow. She stared down at Sierra's glistening body and slid her fingertips over her warm, soft nipples. "That was so beautiful, Sierra, and you taste absolutely delicious. I swear I tasted a hint of cinnamon."

Sierra released a shocked laugh as she held Kaitlin close. "How can that be? I don't even like cinnamon."

Kaitlin burst into laughter and gently caressed Sierra's firm breasts as she leaned closer to her waiting lips. "Well, you're certainly going to grow to love it."

Sierra giggled sweetly as Kaitlin leaned closer and allowed her to slowly taste herself on Kaitlin's lips. Sierra's eyes burned with renewed passion. "I don't taste cinnamon, Kate, you're just teasing me. However, I do love the taste of our loving on your tongue."

Kaitlin laughed softly and gently probed Sierra with her tongue as she whispered provocatively, "Good, because I plan on loving you forever."

Sierra held Kaitlin's face in her hands and guided her closer as she eagerly chased her tongue and reveled in the taste of their intimacy.

Kaitlin leaned back slightly and grinned mischievously. "Hey, you. Don't take all my cinnamon from me."

Sierra gave her a coy, seductive grin. She reached for her hand and guided it down to her thighs. "There's lots more where that came from. My cinnamon spring awaits you, Dr. Bradley."

Kaitlin's arousal surged in her belly as she allowed Sierra to guide their fingers between her thighs. Kaitlin stared deeply into Sierra's smoldering eyes and rested her hand on top of Sierra's. Sierra closed her eyes and gasped as Kaitlin felt her fingers move away and disappear into her intimate depths. Kaitlin's desire erupted in her chest as she lowered herself to Sierra's fingers and replaced them with her tongue. Kaitlin rubbed her cheek against Sierra's soft mound and inhaled her heavenly scent as Sierra glided her hand onto the back of Kaitlin's head and gently guided her mouth closer. Kaitlin's warm breath lingered along the inside of Sierra's thighs just before she dipped her tongue into her glistening pool.

CRACRACRA

An hour later Sierra grazed her fingers across Kaitlin's slender belly as she watched her slowly catch her breath. Kaitlin dramatically dropped her arms to her sides and took a deep breath. "Wow! You melt me, Sierra Vaughn."

Sierra rested her hand on Kaitlin's dark, damp curls. "You're wonderful to love, Kaitlin Bradley, and you're an unbelievable lover."

Kaitlin brushed a strand of hair off of Sierra's shoulder. "Would you like to have a bath with me, Ms. Vaughn?"

Sierra's eyes lit up like a child's on Christmas morning. "A real bath? Like in a real bathtub and not just a toss into Sturgeon Lake?"

Kaitlin laughed at Sierra's childlike exuberance. "I love you, Sierra, and yes, a bath in a real bathtub. I promise to protect you from those two thugs from now on."

Sierra frowned and sat up beside Kaitlin. "Promises, promises." They both laughed as Sierra got to her knees and helped Kaitlin to slowly sit up.

Kaitlin looked down the stairs and back up at the multitude of pillows covering the landing. "I like how you've decorated the house, Ms. Vaughn. Lovely personal touch."

Sierra burst into laughter and helped Kaitlin to her feet. "Imagine what I could do if you actually asked me to live with you."

Kaitlin stepped toward Sierra with serious tenderness in her eyes. She reached for Sierra and held her intimately against her. "I want you to live with me, Sierra. I want you to leave your life and your work in Toronto for me." Kaitlin stared into Sierra's moist, sensitive eyes and took a deep breath. "I want to be your partner, your lover, your wife, your whatever you want to call me. I just want to be yours. I want to wake up beside you every morning and see that look of pure love in your beautiful blue eyes and know that our day will begin and end in each other's arms."

Tears filled Sierra's eyes as she reached up and caressed Kaitlin's soft cheek. "It took a lot for you to say that, sweetheart. Especially for a woman who told me that she's not very good at expressing herself when it comes to this emotional stuff."

Kaitlin's own tears flowed across Sierra's hand. "Yes, it did because I promised myself I would never ask those things of you until you were absolutely sure you could make those huge sacrifices for me. Well, let me tell you something, Sierra Vaughn. I have spent three days watching you make me feel alive again. You make me blow bubbles and fly kites and watch butterflies and hummingbirds. You make me smile and laugh and dance and eat toasted marshmallows. You fill me with a youthfulness and excitement that I have not felt in many years. Last night when you went home after visiting me at the hospital, I knew you were a special gift. A gift I realized I could never turn away if you graciously allowed me to have you."

Sierra's tears flowed to her cheeks as she leaned forward and rested her forehead against Kaitlin's. "I would love to move in here with you, Kate. I want so badly to be your wife. I was so afraid you were never going to let me be this close to your heart."

Kaitlin held Sierra close and tenderly caressed her head. "I told you it wouldn't be easy to love this rude, ill-mannered, crabby Wizard."

Sierra leaned back and wiped at her tears. "No, Kaitlin. You're wrong. It's very easy for me to love you. You just have to let go of your painful past and believe that our love is real and not fear that another tragedy will take me away from you."

Kaitlin looked away from Sierra's loving eyes. Sierra gently touched Kaitlin's chin and guided her eyes back to her. "I'll help you let go, baby. Please give me the chance to love you completely, Kaitlin. I promise never to be a burden to you. I only want to be the woman that holds you every night and whispers, 'I love you.'"

Kaitlin melted into Sierra's arms and allowed their bodies to unite like two pieces of a puzzle. "You could never be a burden, Sierra. So don't ever say that. I just don't think I could live through another experience like I did with Quinn. It was so awful to watch such a talented, beautiful woman's life wasted like that."

Sierra held Kaitlin tight and felt her sobbing tears of years of suppressed pain and desperation. Sierra caressed her naked back and felt Kaitlin's tears tumble onto her shoulder. She held her tight and felt her emotional floodgates freely swing open as Kaitlin slowly caught her breath. Kaitlin leaned back and allowed Sierra to dry her tears.

"Just promise me, Dr. Bradley, that you won't allow anyone to throw me in a pool or freezing cold lake so that we can bury your nightmare forever."

Kaitlin glided her hands over Sierra's smooth hips. "Pool parties are taboo on my list of things to do, and I promise to protect you from your wicked stepsisters."

Kaitlin took a deep breath and took Sierra's hands in her own. She looked down at their entwined hands and felt blessed to be given a chance to start a life with Sierra. She looked up to see a blanket of joy dancing in that incredible depth of blue-gray that she promised herself she would work hard to keep there from this day forth. "I have something I would like to give you, Sierra."

Sierra's eyes brimmed with excitement as she reached up and touched Kaitlin's damp cheek. "What more could you give me, Kate, after you just gave me yourself completely?"

Kaitlin kissed the palm of Sierra's hand. "This gift comes in a small gift-wrapped package."

Sierra smiled mischievously and held Kaitlin's arms out at her sides as she seductively looked her up and down. "I know exactly where I would put a bow on you, my beautiful Kate, but you wouldn't remain wrapped for long."

Kaitlin took Sierra by the hand and guided her toward the bedroom. "Come on, you. I'll get you into your bubble bath and bring your gift to you."

CROSOCROSOCROSO

Sierra leaned her head back against the edge of the jade green, sunken whirlpool tub and closed her eyes as the warm, effervescent water caressed her tingling skin. Her mind was replaying Kaitlin's words; she had never imagined she could be so swathed in one woman's love. Sierra was thrilled to embark on this journey with Kaitlin and knew in her heart that this was a commitment for all time. Sierra vowed to slowly put her painful past to rest and build a future with Kaitlin that would fill her with a joyfulness she could never have imagined in her wildest dreams.

Kaitlin stood in the doorway holding a tray adorned with fresh strawberries, green grapes, cheese, crackers, and two glasses of white wine. She was mesmerized by the flickering candlelight casting a soft glow across Sierra's beautiful, satiated smile. Her firm breasts were embraced by the foamy, white bubbles; her slender shoulders bobbed gently above the water line. Kaitlin was filled with a deep sense of peace and oneness as she gently laid the tray down behind Sierra and watched her slowly open her glistening eyes. Kaitlin sat on the ledge surrounding the tub and leaned toward Sierra, kissing her softly. "You're such a beautiful woman, my darling. Especially when all you're wearing are bubbles."

Kaitlin reached for a strawberry and slipped it between Sierra's sensuous lips. Sierra sighed contently as she consumed the succulent fruit. Kaitlin handed Sierra a glass of white wine as she sat up.

"Thank you, sweetheart. The strawberry's delicious." Sierra clinked her glass against Kaitlin's and toasted, "To us. Now and forever."

Kaitlin leaned forward to taste the strawberry on Sierra's tongue. "To us. Now and forever," Kaitlin whispered against Sierra's moist slightly parted lips.

Sierra took Kaitlin's lips with urgent need and aching desire as she reached forward and tugged on the belt of her white terry cloth robe. "I miss you, Dr. Bradley. Please come in and join me."

Kaitlin leaned back as she reached inside her robe pocket and pulled out a beautifully wrapped, flat gift.

Sierra squealed with delight and set down her wine glass. She reached for the towel draped over the edge of the tub and dried her hands.

Kaitlin gently placed the gift in Sierra's hands and kissed her softly. "This is from me to you."

Sierra stared down at the shiny pink-wrapped gift then looked up to watch Kaitlin seductively slip out of her robe and gingerly step into the sunken tub behind her.

Kaitlin guided her back into her arms and held her close. "Go ahead, my darling. Open your gift." Kaitlin reached for her wine glass and took a sip as she watched Sierra rip open the gift. She watched with equal enthusiasm as Sierra carefully lifted the lid on the gift box and gasped.

Sierra gently reached in the velvet box and dangled a beautiful gold necklace before them. Tears spilled from Sierra's eyes as she saw the shiny, gold dolphin pendant swinging from the chain. Sierra rested the pendant in the palm of her hand and looked closer to see two gold dolphins swimming side by side. She turned and looked up at Kaitlin with huge, teary eyes. "That's you and me."

Kaitlin brushed a strand of damp hair from Sierra's eyes. "That's right, my darling. You said you once felt like a trapped dolphin that needed to be set free. I only pray that my love sets you free as your love has done for me."

Sierra was awestruck by Kaitlin's words as she turned and floated into her arms. Kaitlin guided Sierra to sit in her lap as Sierra wrapped her legs and arms securely around Kaitlin and hugged her tight.

"You have set me free, sweetheart. You've pushed me to find myself and along the way I was blessed with your incredible love. I've always searched for the missing light to my train, and I've finally found you."

Sierra leaned toward Kaitlin and wiped away her tears as she kissed her with intense, burning passion. Sierra leaned back and caught her breath as Kaitlin took the necklace and secured it behind Sierra's neck. They both watched the dolphins dangle gracefully between Sierra's breasts and bob into the water.

Sierra looked up into Kaitlin's shimmering eyes and kissed her softly. "Thank you, baby. It's beautiful."

Kaitlin reached forward and held the dolphins between her fingers as she smiled at the way Sierra called her baby. "You're very welcome, my beautiful Sierra. May these dolphins and our love always show you the way."

Sierra guided Kaitlin into her arms and hugged her tight. "I love you, Kaitlin Bradley, with all my heart."

Kaitlin held Sierra tight. "I could not ask for any greater love than yours, Sierra Vaughn."

Sierra leaned toward Kaitlin's moist lips and kissed her with gentle tenderness. She leaned back and dropped a strawberry into each glass of wine and handed one to Kaitlin. They both took a sip of the sweet, cool liquid as Sierra sat comfortably in Kaitlin's lap and reached to feed her a sweet, juicy grape. They sat close among the jetting, warm bubbles and fed each other delicious treats as they talked about their future, their dreams, and their goals.

Sierra popped the last strawberry into Kaitlin's mouth and sighed. "Unfortunately I have to go back to Toronto at the end of my two weeks here and give them two weeks' notice at work. Sydney would probably love to rent my house while you and I decide what we want to do with it."

Kaitlin sipped on her wine and listened intently. "I understand, sweetheart, but I would really like you to take some time off from nursing after that and just help me run Bradley Bay. I would love us to run the resort together. I don't expect you to take a nursing position here in town unless it's important to you to do that. I would support your career decision one hundred percent. But you know what it takes to run this place, and I would love the opportunity to do it together."

Sierra sat up tall and beamed with excitement. "Are you offering me a job, Dr. Bradley?"

Kaitlin laughed and set down their wine glasses. She glided her hands onto Sierra's sexy bottom and guided her even closer. "Yes, my darling. I'm offering you a full-time, full benefits, paid position to be the coproprietor of Bradley Bay."

Sierra shrieked with delight and clapped her hands with excitement. Kaitlin caressed her back and hips as she laughed at her blissful glee. "Does that mean you accept the position, Ms. Vaughn?"

Sierra leaned back and coyly crossed her arms across her perky breasts. "Just one question, Dr. Bradley. How much are you paying me?"

Kaitlin laughed as her hands seductively followed the curves of Sierra's bottom. "What! Isn't sleeping with me enough?"

Sierra leaned forward and tickled Kaitlin mercilessly. "All right! All right! I give up. What would you say if I doubled your nursing salary?"

Sierra stopped frozen in time and stared at Kaitlin in shock. "What?"

Kaitlin glided her wet hands along Sierra's arms. "I thought that might get your attention. That's what I pay Sabrina and Logan."

Sierra swallowed against her dry mouth and regained her composure. "Sweetheart, I was just kidding. I would never expect you to pay me. I would be more than happy to find a full-time nursing job and help you run Bradley Bay."

"Then you'll have no time for yourself, me, or us. Forget it. Let's try plan B. How about you take some time off from nursing and see what it entails to help me run this massive place. If and when you decide you want to keep your foot in hospital nursing, then maybe we could research a casual or part-time position that would suit your needs and time requirements. I'm sure the hospital would love to have you in their intensive care unit or the emergency department if those are the areas that still interest you."

Sierra attempted to speak as Kaitlin gently pressed her finger to her lips. "Ah, please let me finish. When my father and grandparents passed away they left me a huge inheritance. More money than I can spend in a lifetime, Sierra. Bradley Bay also makes a very healthy profit every year. You and I could leave medicine tomorrow and live off the interest of what I have accumulated for the rest of our lives. That's why I pay Sabrina, Logan, Gladys, and all my staff very well. They deserve to reap the rewards of all their hard work. Now, I'm offering you the same salary as Sabrina and Logan to help me keep the Emerald City alive. You've already proven your value tenfold as a dedicated hard worker, Sierra. It would be a dream come true for me to have you at my side. You're the very special woman that I want to share my life with. Now, do you accept the position and its salary, Ms. Vaughn?"

Sierra sat in stunned disbelief as she slowly replied, "Yes. I accept the position of coproprietor of Bradley Bay with you, Dr. Kaitlin Bradley."

It was Kaitlin's turn to shout with glee as she clapped her hands in celebration.

Sierra beamed with joy as she seductively ran her finger down Kaitlin's throat and between her flushed breasts. "Are you open to negotiating certain terms of my contract, Dr. Bradley?"

Kaitlin rolled her eyes and wrapped her arms around Sierra's slender waist. "What terms might those be, my spirited new partner?"

Sierra molded a handful of bubbles around Kaitlin's breasts. "First term is that as your coproprietor, I will never get thrown in the lake again."

Kaitlin laughed and quickly put on a serious business face. "First term agreed." Kaitlin loved the girlish charm in Sierra's smile as she watched her confidence grow.

"Good. Second term is that I no longer have to milk the cows, round up the sheep, groom the horses, or gather the chicken eggs."

Kaitlin unsuccessfully tried to suppress a giggle as she quickly covered her mouth. "Second term agreed."

Sierra enjoyed their playful banter as she leaned closer to Kaitlin and grazed her fingertips across her soft nipples. "Good. Third term is that you, Dr. Kaitlin Bradley, promise to share your life completely and unconditionally with me, Sierra Vaughn."

Kaitlin stared into Sierra's glowing blue-gray eyes and leaned forward to kiss her softly. "Third term agreed completely and unconditionally."

Sierra's heart burst with joy as she slid closer against Kaitlin and allowed their breasts to unite playfully. "My fourth and final term would be that you understand that my salary belongs to both of us."

Kaitlin was overwhelmed by Sierra's tenderness and charm as she touched Sierra's chin. "I'm so glad you feel that way because I plan on having you support me for the rest of my life."

Sierra scowled playfully and tickled Kaitlin till she begged for mercy.

Kaitlin sank lower into the water and gently rocked against Sierra, trailing her fingers along the inside of Sierra's thighs. Sierra ran her fingers over Kaitlin's beautiful breasts as she smiled sheepishly. "Tell me, Dr. Bradley, is this how you interview all of your prospective employees?"

Kaitlin leaned toward Sierra's soft nipple and gently peaked it with her caressing tongue. She looked up into Sierra's wanton eyes and smiled coyly. "Only the ones who taste like cinnamon."

Sierra burst into laughter as Kaitlin leaned forward and slowly caressed her nipple with her tongue till it budded hard and erect in her mouth. Sierra basked in Kaitlin's moist caresses as she arched her neck and moaned with delight.

Kaitlin gently floated her hands over Sierra's silky back and down across her sexy bottom. Her hands glided teasingly along the inside of Sierra's thighs as she watched Sierra rock gently against her.

Sierra reached for Kaitlin's face and leaned against her lips. "Please, baby, I want to feel you deep inside me."

Kaitlin stared at Sierra's pillowy lips and gently glided her fingers across her wet curls and deep inside her. Sierra gasped with incredible pleasure as she rocked hard against Kaitlin's fingers. Kaitlin's desire burned hot through her veins as she watched their passion darken Sierra's eyes to a deep aqua blue. Those heavy-lidded eyes burned deep into Kaitlin's soul as she watched Sierra sway and surrender to their rhythm. Kaitlin leaned toward Sierra and outlined her full lower lip with her tongue, leaving her impatient for more. She planted moist kisses along the edge of her mouth before probing between her awaiting lips and plundering her recklessly.

Sierra matched her thrusts and drove her to the brink of insanity as she molded Kaitlin's breasts to the palms of her hands. She grazed over her taut nipples and luxuriated in their responsiveness. Her fingertips traced the outer edges of her breasts and skimmed the soft underside before recapturing those raised peaks.

Kaitlin heaved and arched higher toward her exploring hands. "God, Sierra, I want you again. I want to make love to you forever."

Sierra looked into Kaitlin's glowing eyes and swiftly reached for a bath towel. She guided Kaitlin to her feet and out of the bathtub.

Wordlessly, they dried each other off. Kaitlin reached for another towel and laid it down on the plush carpeting and guided Sierra down onto her back. She gracefully eased herself over Sierra and impatiently removed her necklace. Sierra held Kaitlin's face in her hands and guided her closer as their damp skin united with tiny, sucking noises. Kaitlin eased herself into Sierra's warm neck and chased several water droplets with the tip of her tongue.

Sierra moaned and writhed beneath her playful tongue as she glided her hands onto Kaitlin's sexy ass and pulled her tightly against her. Their lips met in a hungry, aching kiss as their desire soared and their tongues danced to their own passionate rhythm. Sierra arched her neck and gasped in lustful pleasure as she ascended to a higher level under Kaitlin's artful touch.

Kaitlin's burning need drove her to take as much as Sierra could give. Her mind wanted to take her slow and make the moment last, but her hunger fought her control and spurred her to propel Sierra mindlessly to the pinnacle of ecstasy.

Kaitlin's hand molded to Sierra's hip, then floated to the inside of her open thighs before gliding into her pool of wetness. Kaitlin floated her fingers higher and rhythmically caressed Sierra's erect center as she felt her dig her fingers into her back.

Sierra buried her face into Kaitlin's damp hair and barely whispered, "Yes, baby! Yes ..." as her body shivered and bucked against Kaitlin's hand. Sierra's body suddenly stopped moving and tensed in Kaitlin's arms as she dropped her head back and screamed Kaitlin's name.

Sierra felt Kaitlin's fingers slip deep inside as she tumbled through a buoyant space of exploding lights, color, and her own screaming ecstasy.

Kaitlin shifted her weight slightly off Sierra as she wallowed in the heady aftermath of her exhilarating release. Slowly, she leaned above Sierra and gently caressed her beautiful, glowing face, watching her slowly return to earth. Her thick, dark eyelashes rested peacefully against her flawless olive skin; Kaitlin was overwhelmed by the love she felt.

Sierra sighed deeply as she opened her dreamy eyes. She reached up and traced her finger across Kaitlin's joyous smile. "Wow, baby! That was incredible."

Kaitlin kissed the tip of her finger and smiled. "I love how you call me baby, and I absolutely love to make you shiver."

Sierra smiled beautifully as she rolled Kaitlin onto her back. She lowered herself to her awaiting breasts and devoured her body with an aching, burning need till Kaitlin arched her neck and screamed the arrival of her exultant release.

Sierra stepped out of the bathroom wrapped snuggly in Kaitlin's white terry cloth robe and set their tray on the coffee table. She reached inside the pocket of the robe and gently pulled out her new necklace and laid the dolphins out on the tray. She heard the crackling of dry firewood and turned to see the blazing fire behind her. She smiled at this romantic sight as she took two steps closer. She laughed softly, seeing that Licorice had already found the makeshift bed laid out invitingly before the romantic glow.

Kaitlin turned the lights out in the bathroom and came to stand behind Sierra. She wrapped her arms snuggly around her and held her close. "I thought you might like to sleep before the fire since we don't seem to have any intention of making love in a bed tonight."

Sierra smiled beautifully as they both looked over at the four-poster bed draped in flowing white crepe. "It looks like P.J has the bed to herself tonight."

Kaitlin kissed Sierra's warm cheek. Sierra turned and melted into her arms, luxuriating in the sight of her beautiful naked body. "It's beautiful, sweetheart. It looks so romantic."

Kaitlin slowly loosened the belt on Sierra's robe. "It's a futon mattress. I use it to sit on when I read in front of the fire. I have never used it for this purpose, but it certainly seems very handy at this moment." Kaitlin slipped the belt from Sierra's waist and draped it across the back of the white leather couch as she stared into Sierra's loving eyes. She gently ran her fingers beneath the collar of the plush material and eased the robe over Sierra's slender shoulders. She watched the robe fall to Sierra's feet as she took her by the hand and guided her before the fire and beneath the goose down duvet.

Licorice protested with an annoyed squeak at having to share her warm haven as she uncoiled and gingerly stepped to the foot of the futon. She kneaded her claws into the billowy duvet and molded a small hollow for herself before curling up once again into a midnight black ball of fur. She gave Sierra and Kaitlin a *do not disturb me like that again or I'll be really cross* look. Sierra and Kaitlin burst into laughter at her annoyance as Sierra lay on her back and guided Kaitlin to lie on top of her.

Their eyes burst with satiated happiness as Kaitlin reached beneath their pillows and sheepishly positioned herself along Sierra's side. Sierra watched her playful grin as Kaitlin pulled back the duvet and ceremoniously held up a bright yellow, happy face sticker. Sierra burst into laughter as Kaitlin removed the adhesive backing and placed the sticker directly below Sierra's belly button. "That, my darling Sierra, is for being such a good girl."

Sierra raised her head and looked down at her new sticker and beamed Kaitlin a beautiful smile. "Thank you, nice lady doctor. I was really working hard to earn that sticker." Sierra pulled Kaitlin into her arms and playfully rolled her onto her back.

Sierra rested her head on Kaitlin's chest. Kaitlin tenderly tucked the duvet around Sierra's shoulders and held her tight as a sense of peace and happiness embraced them both. Kaitlin ran her fingers through Sierra's thick, dark brown hair and heard the soft chime of her mantel clock. She looked up and saw that it was four o'clock in the morning. She tilted her head back to Sierra and kissed the top of her head. "Did I ever tell you how honored I am to be chosen as the one to curl into your gorgeous backside and fulfill your every whim and desire?"

Sierra tilted her face up to Kaitlin's. "You should be honored, Dr. Bradley. That's a privilege that I've bestowed upon very few women."

Kaitlin growled playfully and attempted to bite the tip of Sierra's tiny nose as Sierra shrieked with fright and buried her face in Kaitlin's warm neck.

Sierra trailed soft kisses along Kaitlin's neck to her ear and down her throat. Kaitlin sighed deeply as an arousing exhaustion shook her entire being. Sierra raised her face above Kaitlin's and looked into her loving eyes. "I love you so much, my baby."

Kaitlin reached up and caressed Sierra's glowing face. "I love you, my darling." They stared into each other's emotional eyes and communicated an intense love. Sierra slowly, softly kissed Kaitlin's face as they made love with an unhurried, profound gentleness.

⚙ **10**

Sydney reached for the spare key beneath the potted mums on Kaitlin's front deck and slipped it into the door. Logan shook her head as Sabrina crossed her arms across her chest.

"Sydney! Katie and Sierra are going to kill us if we walk in on them in a most compromising position."

Sydney unlocked the door and opened it wide as she turned to Sabrina with a ghoulish grin. "Relax, Bri. It's already eleven o'clock in the morning. We've let those two lovebirds sleep in long enough. After all, they can't survive on love alone. It's time they got up and joined us for lunch and enjoyed this beautiful day and my invigorating company."

Sabrina and Logan rolled their eyes and hesitantly followed Sydney inside as Sabrina gently closed the door behind them. They both bumped right into her as she stopped dead in her tracks. All three of them burst into laughter as they took in the scene of discarded clothing before them.

Sydney walked to the bottom of the spiral staircase and spun Sierra's Jockeys on the tip of her finger. "Looks like our resident lovebirds were in a bit of a hurry."

Logan lifted Kaitlin's bra off the computer keyboard and looked toward Sabrina. "Look, babe. What a great idea for a keyboard cover. However, if we used your bra it wouldn't cover half the alphabet."

Sydney burst into laughter as Sabrina walked menacingly toward Logan and playfully backed her up against a wall. Logan quickly tossed Kaitlin's bra back on the computer as Sabrina entwined their hands and pinned Logan's hands above her head. "Are you complaining, my little sweet pea?"

Logan kissed Sabrina softly. "Absolutely not, sweetheart. More than a mouthful is a waste anyway." They smiled lovingly with years of tender passion. Sabrina leaned forward and kissed Logan deeply.

Sydney threw Sierra's silk shirt at them both. "Will you two cut that out and come help me disturb the honeymooners?"

They all grabbed the discarded clothing and headed up the spiral staircase. They carefully stepped over the pile of pillows at the top of the landing.

Sabrina picked up the pillows and leaned them against the couch. "It looks like they didn't even make it to the bedroom."

Sydney peeked into Kaitlin's bedroom and signaled back for Sabrina and Logan to be very quiet as she tiptoed into the room carrying Sierra and Kaitlin's panties. They all stood huddled close together by the white leather couch as they saw Sierra peacefully cocooned in Kaitlin's arms. A soft, white cotton sheet barely covered their naked bodies, as they lay entwined in each other's arms before the dying embers of the fire.

Sydney carefully knelt beside the futon. She tried hard to suppress a giggle as she brushed Kaitlin's lacy white panties across Sierra's flushed cheek.

Sierra sighed softly and partially opened one eye. "Ummmm. Smells familiar. Thank you, Sydney. I believe those belong to me." Sierra moved her hand out from under the sheet and squealed with delight as she relentlessly squirted Sydney with a toy water gun.

Sydney screamed with fright and dove behind the leather couch as Sabrina, Logan, and Kaitlin laughed hilariously.

Licorice saw the first squirt of water escape from that water gun and immediately dove under the four-poster bed for cover. Sierra's supply of ammunition finally dried up as Sydney peeked out from behind the couch.

"You shit, Sierra. You knew we were coming."

Sierra shook her head as she positioned herself gently above Kaitlin. "How could we not, Syd. You guys sounded like a herd of stampeding buffalo coming up those stairs."

They all burst into laughter as Sydney cautiously came out from behind the couch. Logan and Sabrina kissed Kaitlin and Sierra good morning and joined them on the futon.

Sydney sat with her back against the couch and tossed the discarded panties at a beaming Sierra. "I'm so glad all you guys had wonderful sexual experiences last night. I offered myself to three different women at that party, and do you know what they said?"

Kaitlin ran her fingers through Sierra's slightly disheveled hair. "No," she offered.

Sydney stuck her tongue out at Kaitlin. "You're right, smart ass. Two said no, and one said kiss my ass. I told her that's what I was trying to do and she laughed and walked away." They all burst into laughter as Sydney frowned at her own lack of success.

Sabrina held Logan close in her arms as she turned to Sydney. "Syd, why do act like such a jerk when you're around Kelly?"

Sydney tilted her head and looked stung by Sabrina's words. "What are you talking about? I'm not a jerk around Kelly. She's one of my dearest friends."

Logan lifted her head off Sabrina's warm chest and looked thoughtfully at Sydney. "Come on, Sydney. We all know how much you care about her, yet every time you two are together you go into this female Casanova routine. She acts like she doesn't give a shit even though it's killing her inside to see you behave like such a flirt. You've always been a big flirt, Sydney, but around Kelly you act like you want every other woman but her."

Sydney looked stunned and hurt as she turned away from the concerned faces before her and stared down at her hands. "Why would Kelly care who I was with anyway? She doesn't feel that way about me. We're only friends in her eyes."

Kaitlin held Sierra close and frowned at Sydney's discomfort. "Sydney, when Kelly first told me about her party, you were the first one she had called and invited. You should have seen how excited she was when she was telling me that you were coming up for the weekend. You'd think that a member of the royal family was about to grace us with their presence the way she was bursting with excitement."

Sydney dropped her head back against the couch and closed her eyes. She thought of all the times she wanted to reach out to Kelly and tell her how often she thought of her. How she drove for three hours just to see that sweet smile. How she dove for the phone every time she heard that engaging voice on her answering machine. Her own feelings of inadequacy always held her back. It was easier to throw herself at a complete stranger for a night and walk away then lay herself open to rejection from a woman she had grown to adore.

Sydney slowly opened her eyes and stared off at a point beyond the picture window. "I have loved Kelly for years. I've never sensed that she felt the same way."

Everyone smiled at Sydney's innocence. Sabrina reached for her hand. "That's because you've been terrified to tell her. Instead, you both pretend like your deep feelings don't exist and continue being friends. She cares very deeply for you, Syd. She's been so afraid to share her feelings with you because you always chase after some other skirt when she's around. She feels like you could never be interested in her, so you both continue loving each other as friends and stand back and watch as you both pursue empty relationships."

Tears welled in Sydney's eyes as she stared down at her own hands. Feelings of shame and shock squeezed around her heart. Her love for Kelly was something she cherished and protected fiercely, so fiercely that she shielded her eyes from the love that was there for her.

"Why didn't you guys tell me about this sooner?" Sydney whispered.

Logan handed Sydney a tissue as they watched her catch her tears. Sabrina rested her hand on Sydney's knee and squeezed it gently. "Because Kelly begged us not to. She hoped and prayed that over time you would feel the same way about her as she feels about you. She wanted to earn your love and not just have you shower her with your fleeting passion."

Sydney shook her head and ran her fingers through her hair in frustration. "She earned my love years ago. She's such a twit for feeling she could be just a simple affair in my life."

Logan reached for Sydney's hand. "Maybe it's about time you told that twit how you really feel about her. We've seen enough of these childish games between you two. So much precious time has been wasted."

Sydney stared at Logan with determination in her eyes. "You're right, Logan. Kelly is coming to join us for dinner tonight, and I think there are a few things that I would like to say to that beautiful little twit. Hopefully by then I can come up with some plausible excuse as to why I've never told her how much I really love her."

Everyone smiled at Sydney as they felt her emotional turmoil.

Sabrina held Logan close in her arms and kissed her softly. She turned to face Sierra and Kaitlin and smiled into their beaming faces. "Okay, ladies. Let's hear it. Describe your honeymoon in one sentence or less."

Sierra brushed a stray strand of hair from Kaitlin's shimmering eyes as she said softly, "Just the beginning."

Kaitlin gently caressed Sierra's silky back. "God, Sierra. If that's only the beginning, I may not live to see the end."

They all burst into laughter as Sierra bent down and kissed Kaitlin's smiling lips. Kaitlin's hands glided over Sierra's firm bottom and warm thighs as she smiled beautifully. "I would say that last night was an unforgettable beginning."

They all smiled warmly at the love that permeated the room.

Sydney rose to her knees. "All right, you two lovebirds. It's time to get out of your love nest and come outside and play. It's a gorgeous day, and you two are nestled here in each other's feathers."

Sierra scoffed at Sydney. "I'm sure if someone let you kiss her ass, Sydney, you would be lip-deep in feathers."

188

Sydney crawled toward a shrieking Sierra and Kaitlin and nuzzled playfully into their warm necks. Kaitlin finally grabbed her pillow and swatted Sydney.

"Would you guys please get out of here so Sierra and I can climb out of our love nest and shower?"

Sabrina helped Logan and Sydney to their feet and guided them to the door.

Sydney stopped in the doorway and turned back to the girls with a loving look in her warm, chocolate brown eyes. "Ladies, I'm thrilled to see you two so in love. You both deserve the best, and I do believe that I deserve the credit for this newfound union. Especially since you, Dr. Bradley, swore you would never fall in love again and you, Sierra, had to be coaxed and shoved to come up here to Bradley Bay."

Kaitlin kissed Sierra's beautiful face and turned to Sydney. "Thank you, Sydney. Sierra is the greatest gift you could ever have given me."

Sydney blew them both a kiss just as Logan reached toward her and yanked her out of the room.

Kaitlin listened for their thunderous footsteps running down the staircase before she helped Sierra to her feet and openly admired her slender body. They headed into the bathroom together beaming with happiness.

Kaitlin reached into the huge glassed-in double shower and turned on both jets of water. She reached for a towel and dried her arm as Sierra seductively took her into her arms. Kaitlin smiled beautifully and kissed her softly.

"Sydney is a special woman. I'm glad she's our friend."

Sierra glided her hands along Kaitlin's strong arms. "She almost became more than that. One night at a party she offered to kiss my ass. I just laughed and walked away."

Kaitlin's laughter vibrated off the Italian tiled walls as Sierra took her by the hand and guided her into the steaming mist. They both stepped beneath a hot flow of water and let it cascade over their bodies.

Sierra turned and watched Kaitlin. She stood with her back to the spray of water and finger-combed it through her lush hair. Her face shone with an ethereal peacefulness as she swayed gently to the rhythm of the water. Sierra watched the water stream over her well-defined shoulders and hug the gentle planes and curves of Kaitlin's trim figure. A desire so wanton surged in Sierra's belly as she stepped toward Kaitlin and rested her hands on her slender waist and united their hips intimately.

Kaitlin brushed the water from her eyes and felt overwhelmed by the love and yearning in those blue-gray eyes. Kaitlin wordlessly took Sierra by the shoulders and slowly backed her up against the cool mosaic tiles. Their eyes never wavered as Kaitlin met her lips with soft, gentle, unhurried kisses. Her hands slipped over Sierra's wet shoulders and down over her silky breasts. Her hands molded to the curve of her waist as Kaitlin slowly went to her knees. Their eyes locked with profound need as Kaitlin tilted Sierra's hips toward her and leaned forward and tasted her essence.

Sierra gripped Kaitlin's shoulders and gasped with delirious delight. The heat of her caressing tongue enflamed Sierra's burning need as she arched her head back and soared with each fierce stroke.

Sierra crested higher and higher, achingly close to the pinnacle of release, only to have Kaitlin ease her back down to wallow in her ecstasy. Sierra could wait no longer as she thrust faster and harder against Kaitlin's scintillating strokes. She gripped Kaitlin tighter and arched back against the cool tile as a spellbinding orgasm ripped through her center and exploded in her mind like a thousand shattered shards of colored glass.

Kaitlin rose to her feet and held Sierra tight in her arms. She brushed the wet hair away from her eyes and kissed her flushed cheek. "You're right, babe, who needs a bed anyway."

Sierra burst into a bubbling laughter as she happily let Kaitlin guide her beneath the cascading warm droplets. Sierra reached for the bar of soap and gently skimmed it over Kaitlin's flat belly and around each firm breast as if smoothing the surface of an exquisite sculpture. She lathered each nipple till it was consumed by frothy bubbles, then worked her way back down Kaitlin's belly. Kaitlin leaned back against the cool frosted glass and surrendered to the ethereal bliss. "I can see that this is going to be a very long shower," Kaitlin said, on a very shaky breath.

☙☙☙☙☙☙

Kaitlin, Sierra, Sabrina, Logan and Sydney leaned comfortably against the cedar railing surrounding the front deck of the resort after enjoying a delicious lunch of Caesar salad and chicken parmesan. The billowy white sails of the boats fluttered in the dying wind as the guests persevered through their sailing lessons.

Sierra sighed happily and leaned back in Kaitlin's arms. Sydney reached into the pocket of her denim shorts. "Sierra, I almost forgot. I collected your mail at your house before I came up here, and there was a letter from the ex, Linda. I thought you might like to read it before I fed it to my paper shredder."

Sydney handed Sierra the white envelope and watched sadness and anger mist her eyes. She hated to see what Linda could do to Sierra even after their relationship had finally ended. She cursed herself for not giving Sierra the letter later instead of spoiling this beautiful time together.

Sierra stared at Linda's familiar writing on the envelope and felt instantly irritated by her intrusion on her new life. This was the first letter she had written in three months. She refused to allow one thought of Linda to affect this moment with the ones she loved. She would deal with the letter later. Sierra quickly folded the envelope in half and shoved it into the pocket of her white pleated shorts.

Kaitlin was surprised and irritated by Sierra's need to conceal the letter. She knew she had no right to feel irritated. Sierra needed to deal with Linda in her own way. Kaitlin did not like feeling shut out. She desperately wanted to help. An uneasy silence prevailed as Kaitlin touched Sierra's chin and guided her anguished eyes back to her. The screen door squeaked open with a jerk as Gladys appeared in the doorway.

"Katie, the insurance company is on the phone. They want to discuss our current property insurance policy with you."

Kaitlin sighed with impatience and cursed under her breath. "I'll be right there, Gladys." She gently held Sierra's face in her hand, studying the annoyance and distress etched in her eyes. "Are you okay, darling?"

Sierra wished Sydney had shred the letter; she found it difficult to meet Kaitlin's concerned eyes. "Yes, I'm fine, sweetheart." Sierra saw the questions swimming in Kaitlin's eyes and reached up to touch her face. "Honest."

"We'll talk later, if you like," Kaitlin said. She leaned forward and kissed her forehead, then hesitantly headed indoors.

Sierra watched the screen door slam behind her as Sabrina began to list the afternoon activities planned for the guests. Sierra's conflicting emotions blocked out her voice as her heart shuddered over the questions in Kaitlin's eyes.

ৎৡৡৎৡৡৎৡৡ

Kaitlin dealt with the insurance company and spent several hours in the main office returning phone calls and sorting through the day's mail. She finally signed the last check, sealed the envelope, and gathered the stack of mail. She tossed them into the tray of outgoing mail on the corner of her desk. She picked up the file on their current advertising plans and flipped open the file folder. She tried to focus on the proposal and found her mind drifting to Sierra as it had for the millionth time since she sat at her desk.

Her burgundy leather chair squeaked as she leaned back and swiveled to look out the bay window facing the woods. Sierra's smile swam before her eyes as those tear drop blue-gray eyes lit Kaitlin from the inside out. Her warmth and intensity continually intrigued Kaitlin as did her intelligence and vibrancy. Kaitlin had been happy with her life and its simplicity till Sierra came along

192

and filled it with color and depth. Kaitlin had no idea the beauty of color till Sierra filled it with rainbows.

Sierra's reaction to Linda's letter troubled Kaitlin. But she knew she had to respect Sierra's privacy. It was her own fears of what that letter contained that really troubled Kaitlin. Did Linda still have a pull on Sierra's heart? Could she possibly be asking Sierra to come back to her? These were questions Kaitlin needed to stop dwelling on before they made her crazy. She could have easily gone to find Sierra after she dealt with the insurance agent, but she felt Sierra needed some time. Time, Kaitlin prayed, that did not pull her farther away than that letter already had.

Kaitlin swung herself back to her desk and picked up her pencil, forcing herself to focus on business and take care of the matters at hand.

Gladys stopped in the office doorway and watched Kaitlin pick up her pencil and chew on the eraser, a habit she had not been able to break her of since she was a little girl laboring over her multiplication tables. Her heart swelled with love and pride as it always did when she was able to watch Kaitlin unnoticed. Her eyes naturally flowed across the multitude of pictures of Kaitlin across her own desk from her first day in kindergarten to her graduation from med school.

Since the day that Kaitlin had come to live with Gladys, she had treasured her as a rare gem and vowed to give her the life and love she deserved, not the unattended vagabond dreams her sister thoughtlessly thrust on her precious daughter. She never understood how her sister could see her own daughter as an imposition rather than the gem that Kaitlin was. Even as a child she was filled with love and wonder. Gladys thanked the day she was gifted with the child she could never have.

Gladys stepped into the office and wrapped her arms around Kaitlin in her usual affectionate way.

Kaitlin closed her eyes and inhaled Gladys's fresh citrus scent as she hugged her arms tight to her chest. She marveled at how she always felt so safe in Gladys's arms.

Gladys kissed the top of her chestnut head and looked over her shoulder at the open file on her desk. "What are you concentrating so hard on in here when it is such a gorgeous day outside?"

"I was just reviewing the advertising plans and budget. I just finished paying all our bills and I double checked the payroll and returned the phone messages from this morning."

Gladys smiled and squeezed Kaitlin tight against her chest. "Well, after all that hard work you deserve a treat, my dear girl. And I believe the treat of your choice has finally had a chance to take a break herself. I just saw Sierra walking to the west bank of the lake with Jennifer at her side."

Kaitlin closed the file and rose to her feet. She kissed Gladys's rosy cheek and hugged her tight. "I love you, Gladys."

Gladys took Kaitlin's hands and squeezed them tight as she fought the tears filling her eyes. "I love you, my sweet girl. Now get down to the lake and share some of that tremendous love with your soul mate."

Kaitlin gave her one final quick kiss on the cheek before dashing for the front door. Gladys moved to the bay window above her desk. She could see Kaitlin dash down the front steps with a whistling song floating in her wake, just as she once did with a golden retriever puppy nipping at her heels.

Kaitlin strolled across the front lawn and saw Sydney tossing a baseball back and forth with Michael. Sydney tossed a perfect strike right into Michael's glove as she saw Kaitlin walk towards her.

"Katie, are you going to meet Sierra and Jennifer?"

"That I am. Why do you ask, Syd?"

"Just because I told Sierra that there is a lot of ragweed growing wild on the west side of the lake and ragweed usually sets off her asthma. I told her to take her puffer but she said she will be fine and won't need it. Stubborn pain in the ass. What would it have hurt to take it along? She said she has it sitting in the drawer of her desk in her room. I thought I would get it and meet them there but since you are going you could save me the trip and I could show this boy how to really throw a ball."

"You just fantasize about being a boy, Sydney. Isn't that the problem with most lesbians?" Michael threw a solid pitch right into the palm of Sydney's glove causing her to wince with the stinging contact. She inhaled sharply and whipped the ball right back at him. "Take that you opinionated, narrow minded boy. What do you know about what a lesbian fantasizes about anyway?"

Sydney removed her glove and slowly massaged her burning palm.

"I never knew Sierra had asthma, Sydney."

Sydney watched the concern and anger shadow Kaitlin's eyes. "I'm sure she's fine, Katie. I didn't mean to worry you. Sierra's had it since she was a kid but it rarely bothers her. However, whenever she's at her grandparent's farm she keeps it on her because it's usually triggered by environmental allergies. I told her it would be the same here at Bradley Bay so she should always have her puffer with her when she wanders off like that. She's not used to the trees and weeds out here and who knows what may trigger her asthma."

Kaitlin combed her fingers through her hair in frustration. "I'm going to kill her. I'll take her puffer to her and then I'm going to kill her. Thanks, Sydney." Kaitlin squeezed Sydney's shoulder and quickly headed back to the resort.

Sydney watched Kaitlin's tensed, rigid back as she took the front steps two at a time and bounded through the main doors of the estate. She slipped her glove back onto her hand and smiled. "That'll teach you to listen to me next time, Sierra."

Sydney looked up just in time as she leaped high into the air and caught the ball before it sailed clear over her head. "What the hell was that, Michael? Do I look like an Amazon woman to you?"

"You sure do from where I'm sitting."

"Watch it, mister, or I'll strap a pair of water ski's to your wheelchair and drag you around this lake like a bunch of cans behind a newlyweds car."

CRITIC: ᏮᎦᏋᎳᏮᎦᏋᎳᏮᎦᏋᎳ

Kaitlin stormed up the grand staircase two steps at a time as she tried to expend the burning anger searing her belly. She refused to acknowledge the sharp, cutting edges of jealousy and hurt slicing at her heart. Why didn't Sierra tell me about her asthma? Why did she feel she had to hide Linda's letter? Doesn't she trust me? What kind of a relationship will we have if she can't trust me? Kaitlin jammed her master key into Sierra's door. She should knock but she didn't care. If by chance Sierra were in her room she would be answering her questions even sooner.

Kaitlin whipped the door open and quickly scanned the empty room. Sierra's room. She had filled an antique milk jug with daisy's, peonies and tiger lilies and placed it beside her desk. Kaitlin exhaled deeply as her anger fizzled like a deflating balloon. She traced the petals of an orange and black speckled tiger lily and felt embraced by Sierra's warmth. She stepped towards the secretaries' desk beneath the picture window and picked up Sierra's black cardigan sweater neatly draped behind the chair. She brought the sweater to her face and inhaled deeply. She was surrounded by the subtle scent of Sierra's lemon shampoo and vanilla hand cream. Scents that were now as much a part of her as the air she breathed. Scents she could not live without. Damn you, Sierra. I never imagined wanting and needing someone like I need you. I never imagined loving someone like I love you. Kaitlin draped the sweater back on the chair and knew this was something she was willing to fight for. Regardless of what Linda wrote in that letter, she was determined to let Sierra know she was willing to fight for her and what they have already built together.

Kaitlin jerked open the top drawer of Sierra's desk and saw her closed journal sitting beside Linda's unfolded letter. Her eyes automatically scanned the opening lines:

My dear Sierra,
I know you don't want to hear from me but
there are things that I need to say. Things I need
for you to hear.

Kaitlin grabbed the letter, quickly folded it, and slipped it into Sierra's journal. She ran her fingers anxiously through her hair and whispered, "I can't do this." She grabbed the edges of the drawer and yanked it out of the desk as Sierra's puffer rolled toward her. She tossed the drawer on top of the desk and ran out of Sierra's room.

Kaitlin followed the path along the lake and arrived at a large clearing. She stopped suddenly as she saw Jennifer's electric wheelchair sitting strangely alone in the field. Fear squeezed the air in her chest till she could barely breathe. What happened to Jennifer? Where was Sierra? Her heart raced wildly as she started walking faster. She saw Sierra and Jennifer lying in the tall grass head to head, staring up at the blue sky, and heard the sweet sound of Sierra's laughter. Kaitlin felt instantly soothed as she finally reached them and looked down with a questioning frown.

Sierra reached her arms up to her lover and shouted with glee as Kaitlin instantly succumbed to Sierra's childlike exuberance. A smile burst across Kaitlin's face at Sierra's loving reception. She got down to her knees and kissed her softly. Relieved to know they were both all right.

Sierra saw that Kaitlin's smile never reached her eyes; those emerald eyes were dark with concern and irritation. Her kiss never reached her heart.

Jennifer smiled at their intensity and said, "Hey! I want one of those too."

Kaitlin leaned toward Jennifer and kissed her puckered lips. Kaitlin sat back on her heels and looked down at both of their smiling faces. "May I ask you two lovely ladies what you're doing lying in the grass, besides scaring me half to death?"

Sierra studied Kaitlin's tense jaw and furrowed brow, trying to unravel what could have made her so angry. She slowly reached for her hand. "Isn't it obvious, sweetheart? We're making angels in the grass. Just like you made angels in the snow when you were a kid."

Kaitlin laughed in amazement as she looked into Sierra's stunning eyes. "You're incredible, Sierra Vaughn. Now I hope you two realize that Gladys is going to kill you both for getting your clothes covered in grass stains."

Jennifer slowly rolled her arms in the cool grass. "Oh, stop bitching at us, Dr. Bradley, and lay your gorgeous body on this lovely grass."

Kaitlin smiled and lowered herself in the grass and joined her head with Sierra and Jennifer's. Kaitlin stared at the beautiful, fluffy white clouds floating effortlessly in the baby blue sky as she felt Sierra's fingers gently entwine in hers. Her soft hand squeezed gently as Kaitlin felt profoundly warmed by her touch.

Jennifer watched the flock of squawky Canada geese as they flew overhead in a perfect v-formation. She wished she could be the lead goose so she could guide those followers into a dizzying set of spiral loops and aerial acrobatics that would make them puke till they were ready to pull out their feathers.

She wondered if they knew she envied their freedom. She could feel the exhilaration of their flight as she once did on her Harley. She may have been robbed of her legs but nothing will ever steal her memories.

Jennifer turned her face to the side and felt the cool sharpness of each blade of grass as it brushed against her cheek. She closed her eyes and inhaled the heady scent as she rolled her arms along the soft bed of grass.

"This is the first time since they scraped me off the road with a spatula that I've felt the earth beneath my skin. This is also the first time since my accident that I've felt equal to any human being out of my wheelchair."

Sierra and Kaitlin both reached for one of Jennifer's tiny, contorted hands and created a circle of life and love as they lay in the safety of nature's arms.

෮෨෮෨෮෨

Kaitlin and Sierra easily lifted Jennifer into her electric wheelchair and adjusted her footrests as she held Licorice close in her arms. Kaitlin secured her lap belt, and Sierra stepped back to brush the grass off her shorts.

Sierra stood tall and took a deep breath as she emitted a high-pitched wheeze. Kaitlin looked at her and reached for her arm. "Sierra, are you okay? Are you wheezing?"

Sierra took another deep breath and felt a familiar, frustrating tightness in her chest as another wheeze escaped when she inhaled. Sierra frowned and looked into Kaitlin's concerned eyes. "I'm okay, baby. You're right about what you heard, Kate. I have asthma. I've had it since I was a kid, but it rarely bothers me. It must have been triggered by lying in the grass."

Kaitlin dug into her pocket and handed Sierra her puffer. "Here, you might want to take a puff. Sydney told me about your asthma."

Sierra looked down at her puffer like it was something she had never seen before. She slowly looked up at Kaitlin and saw the hurt and anger battling to stay contained.

"You should have brought your puffer with you and you should have told me about your asthma, Sierra. Please, take a puff. I can't stand to hear you wheeze."

Sierra frowned, frustrated with her inability to breathe deeply and Kaitlin's scolding tone. Sierra put the puffer to her mouth and took a deep inhaling breath of the medication. She instinctively placed her hand over her chest and breathed slowly as she felt the air fill her lungs more completely and comfortably.

Kaitlin watched her with piercing intensity as she made the final adjustments on Jennifer's leg straps. She stood tall and placed her hand on Sierra's back. "Better?"

"Much, thank you. Now, can we please go, Dr. Bradley, before you feel the need to spank me for concealing my medical history from you?" Sierra shoved the puffer in her pocket. She was stung by Kaitlin's harsh tone and icy stare. She never wanted Kaitlin to learn about her asthma like this. She never meant to be devious or secretive. She never meant to disappoint her.

Sierra stubbornly headed down the path as Jennifer and Kaitlin exchanged concerned glances.

"Gee, Kate. Why don't you just kick her while she's down." Kaitlin cursed under her breath as Jennifer quickly set her wheelchair in motion and caught up with Sierra.

Jennifer reduced her speed to Sierra's gait and looked up at her teary eyes. "Want a ride, good looking?"

Sierra failed miserably at holding back her laughter as Jennifer enjoyed her smile.

"I would even give you a lollipop if you sit in my lap, little girl."

Sierra stopped walking and playfully swatted at Jennifer's shoulder. Jennifer sped up to avoid the next assault. "You'd better move that chair out of my way, missy, or I'll stick a bunch of lollipops in your spokes!"

Jennifer's laughter could be heard down the trail as she headed toward the resort.

Kaitlin quickly caught up with Sierra and stepped in beside her. She bravely took Sierra's hand and guided her along. Their fingers naturally entwined as Kaitlin gripped her tight. They walked briskly as the tension crackled between them; neither one feeling brave enough to look at the other.

Minutes later, Kaitlin looked cautiously over at Sierra and watched her brush away a tear. Nothing crumbled her anger or swelled her with compassion like Sierra's tears. Kaitlin looked straight ahead and listened intently to Sierra's breathing. "I'm sorry, darling. I didn't mean to hurt your feelings. I just would like to have known about your asthma so that if this ever happens I would know where your puffer is and be able to treat you immediately. I didn't like having to hear about your asthma from Sydney."

Sierra squeezed Kaitlin's hand firmly and looked away as her tears spilled onto her cheeks.

Sierra's distress gripped at Kaitlin's chest. Kaitlin stopped her and pulled her into her arms and held her close. "Please don't cry, Sierra. I can't stand to see you cry."

Sierra sniffled against Kaitlin's soft cheek and struggled to breathe deeply. "I'm sorry, baby. I was going to tell you about my asthma, but I was afraid you would feel it was just something else you would have to take care of. I never want to be a burden to you."

Kaitlin reached for Sierra's face and held her tightly before her as anger flashed in her emerald eyes. She struggled to contain that swell of enraged disbelief as she swiftly turned Sierra toward the resort and pulled her along roughly by the hand. "We'll deal with this garbage later. I need to get you home."

Sierra tugged on her hand and brought her to a screeching halt. "We will deal with this right now, Kaitlin Bradley. My breathing is fine, and I want to know why you're so angry with me."

Kaitlin stood nose-to-nose with Sierra and towered above her as her anger inflamed her resolve. "I'll tell you why I'm so angry, Sierra. That is such crap about you ever being a burden to me and you know it. I wish you would just stop with that shit! I would never feel that way about your asthma or anything else that concerns you. There isn't anything we couldn't take care of together, and you could never be a burden to me. I've made a commitment to being your life partner, and to me that means we walk through each day together whether it rains or shines. You're the one that keeps giving me that lecture on sharing everything unconditionally and you go and pull a stunt like this. How fair is that? I accept everything that comes to us in our life together, Sierra. What I don't accept is you hiding things from me that I should know about."

"I wasn't hiding anything from you, Kaitlin. I was going to tell you about my asthma. I did not set out to intentionally hurt you by not telling you. I was just waiting for the right time. And why do I feel this has to do with more than just my asthma?"

Kaitlin took a step back and combed her fingers through her hair. She inhaled deeply before turning back to Sierra. "It hurt that you felt you had to hide that damn letter from me, Sierra. It terrifies me to ask what that means."

Kaitlin shoved her hands in her pockets and took one step back from Sierra. "There, that's all I have to say."

"Well, that's pretty impressive for a woman that once told me she's not very good at expressing herself when it comes to this emotional stuff." Sierra slowly stepped before Kaitlin and rested her hands on her elbows. Fire and vulnerability spewed from those emerald eyes. Sierra could feel the tightly coiled tension ready to spring as she slid her hands down slowly and guided Kaitlin's hands out of her pockets, holding them in her own.

"I never intended for you to find out about my asthma this way, Kate. I'm sorry about that. I would have told you myself. I never intended to hurt you. You have to believe me. I know I made you feel uneasy this morning the way I shoved the letter in my pocket. I just didn't want Linda's negativity and manipulative behavior to touch our day. I read her letter earlier and laid it out in my drawer so I would remember to have you read it. There's nothing that you have to fear from Linda. I have nothing to hide from you, Kate. There is nothing that I would not share with you completely."

Kaitlin leaned her cheek against Sierra's and kissed her neck. She nuzzled in deeper and whispered against her ear, "Nothing except your asthma." Kaitlin took Sierra's tiny earlobe between her teeth and playfully clamped down.

"Ouch!" Sierra tugged her ear away from Kaitlin's teeth and grimaced as she reached for her earlobe. "You bit me!"

Kaitlin beamed Sierra her magnificent smile and proclaimed, "Touché, my darling. Touché."

Sierra giggled sweetly and pulled Kaitlin into her arms and hugged her tight. "Are you saying we're even now, my special lady?"

Kaitlin slowly caressed Sierra's silky back beneath her T-shirt. "You can now wipe the slate clean, my darling."

Sierra nuzzled her face into Kaitlin's warm neck as Kaitlin easily slipped her fingers beneath Sierra's sports bra. She kneaded the muscles of her back as she luxuriated in her subtle moans. Kaitlin surrendered to Sierra's seductive eyes and leaned closer as she basked in her soft, sensuous kisses.

Sierra leaned back and slid her hands into Kaitlin's and held them tight against her chest. "Can you find it in your heart to forgive me, baby?"

Kaitlin slid her thumbs along Sierra's palms and pulled her closer. "Apology accepted. Don't do that to me again, Sierra. Have more faith in me. I want you to know that you can share yourself completely, good and bad, and know that nothing will ever change my love for you."

Sierra glided her hands onto Kaitlin's waist and pulled her intimately against her. "That's what I've been trying to tell you for days, knucklehead."

"Oh, so now we're going to resort to name calling."

"If the shoe fits, lace up."

Kaitlin slid her hands up Sierra's back and entwined her fingers in her hair, holding her tight before her. "I find that you fit quite nicely, Ms. Vaughn, and I would much rather unlace you at this very moment." Kaitlin crushed her lips to Sierra's, smothering her gasping moan and infusing her with her scorching desire.

Sierra arched against her and clutched at her back as she soared with each ardent thrust of her ravenous tongue. Her punishing lips drove Sierra to near madness as she pushed her to unleash all her tortured emotions.

Kaitlin struggled to rein herself in as she held Sierra's face in her hands and floated in the unquenched hunger in her brilliant blue-gray eyes. No one drove her to such unimaginable heights of passion as Sierra did. She slid her tongue along Sierra's swollen lower lip and nipped it with gentle, caressing kisses.

"If this is how we're going to make up, Dr. Bradley, then I would really like it if we could fight ever day." Sierra moaned softly into Kaitlin's moist lips as she felt Kaitlin's hand glide down her back and firmly smack her behind.

"Ouch," Sierra squealed in shock as she reached back to cover her behind.

Kaitlin glared at Sierra and tenderly rubbed the punished cheek. "You deserved that, Ms. Vaughn, for not telling me and feeling that you could ever be a burden to me!"

Sierra pouted and looked up with huge, teary eyes. "Have I not been forgiven yet, baby?"

Kaitlin emitted a low growl as she leaned menacingly close to Sierra's moist, pouty lip. "Absolutely not, little lady. However, I'm willing to discuss your forgiveness over a glass of wine and a tub full of bubbles."

Sierra's face lit up with her memories of their night of endless passion as Kaitlin wallowed in her mischievous smile. Kaitlin kissed her softly and took her by the hand. "Come on, my little cinnamon lover. Let me get you home before you start wheezing again and pop a lung."

Sierra entwined her fingers into Kaitlin's and gave her a seductive smile. "If our lovemaking last night didn't make me pop a lung, then nothing will."

Kaitlin gazed into Sierra's beaming eyes. "I look forward to spending the rest of my life making you shiver the way you did last night."

Sierra squeezed Kaitlin's hand. "I love you, baby. And I love the way you make me shiver."

Kaitlin gently touched Sierra's chin. "I love you too, my darling. Very, very much. In sickness and in health. Till death do us part."

Sierra's eyes welled with joyous tears as they shared a smile of undying love. Kaitlin kissed her damp cheek and caressed her face before guiding her down the trail.

They finally reached Kaitlin's home where a very concerned Sabrina, Logan, and Sydney met them. Kaitlin settled Sierra into a lounge chair and disappeared inside while Sierra explained what happened.

Kaitlin returned with her stethoscope dangling from her ears. She kneeled before Sierra and gently placed the bell of the stethoscope under Sierra's teal and white striped T-shirt and listened to her clear breath sounds. "Lean forward a bit, babe, so I can listen to your back."

Sydney admired Kaitlin's meticulous professionalism as she watched her calmly attend to Sierra. "You know, Dr. Bradley, that's an excellent idea. I never thought of that one to get inside a woman's shirt. Why can't I fall in love with a woman with asthma?"

"Now that your attention-seeking gimmick seems to have subsided, Sierra, I think we'll leave you in Katie's capable hands and go help the quads with their dinner," Logan said.

"Sorry for scaring you like that, ladies. I feel one hundred percent better now. I'll come and help in the dinning room in a minute."

"Forget it, Sierra. Stay here with Katie and rest for a while. Give your lungs a break. Sydney will help us in the dinning room. It won't be the same as you, but we'll manage just this one time," Sabrina teased.

205

They all waved good-bye and headed toward the main resort. Sydney whined at Sabrina, “What do you mean, it won’t be like Sierra? I’ll have you thankless women know, I’ve been helping out at this resort a lot longer than Sierra has.”

Logan patted her on the back playfully. “Shut up and keep moving, Syd. We were trying to make Sierra feel better.”

“Make Sierra feel better! The woman comes up here for the first time in her life, and it takes her three days to end up in Katie’s bed! How much better can that woman feel?”

Logan and Sabrina stopped as they studied the serious expression of frustration and disappointment on Sydney’s face.

Sydney felt the concern emanating from her dear friends as she shyly looked away to the paddleboats skimming across the lake. She took a minute to collect her thoughts. “Don’t get me wrong. I’m thrilled for Katie and Sierra. They make such a perfect couple. I love them both so much, and I think they were made for each other.”

Sabrina squeezed Sydney’s shoulder as she stood before her. “You’re human, Sydney. I can’t imagine how hard that would be to watch a woman you have loved for five years fall into the arms of another friend after meeting just four days ago. Regardless of how mature you’re trying to be about this, it still has to hurt a little.”

Sydney stared off across the lake to an aimless point as she sighed deeply. “I guess I can’t be fortunate enough to have every woman who crosses my path think I’m the goddess of love.”

Sabrina and Logan burst into laughter as they hooked their arms in Sydney’s and walked together up the wheelchair ramp to the front deck.

“Come on, goddess of love. Lets go help in the dining room so you can practice your magic on Kelly when she gets here,” Logan teased.

Kaitlin slung her black Littmann stethoscope around her neck and knelt before Sierra. She watched her take several effortless breaths and felt completely relieved. "I give you a clean bill of health, my love. You're now discharged from my home clinic."

Sierra reached for the ends of the stethoscope and pulled Kaitlin closer. "Thank you for taking such good care of me, Dr. Bradley. Please send me your bill for this house call as soon as possible."

Kaitlin kissed Sierra softly, teasingly, and slowly pulled away. "Oh, you'll get my bill for scaring me to death. Don't you worry. And the payment will not be of a monetary value. I can guarantee you that."

Sierra smiled mischievously and ran her tongue along Kaitlin's lower lip. "Does that mean I don't get another happy face sticker, nice lady doctor?"

Kaitlin gently probed Sierra with her tongue. "My stickers are reserved for good girls, Ms. Vaughn. You seem to have failed to fulfill that criteria with this little wheezing episode of yours."

Sierra pouted and gently caressed Kaitlin's face. "Stop being so stern, Dr. Bradley, because you're really turning me on."

Kaitlin surrendered to Sierra's seductive eyes and leaned closer as she basked in her soft, sensuous kisses.

Kaitlin leaned her forehead against Sierra's and slowly opened her eyes. As her loving warmth embraced her, Sierra saw the apprehension in Kaitlin's eyes. Sierra held her lover's face in her hands and brushed away a stray strand of hair from her emerald eyes. "What's wrong, sweetheart? I'm okay now. Don't be frightened."

Kaitlin rested her hands on Sierra's thighs. "I can't tell you how relieved I am that your breathing is back to normal."

Sierra scanned Kaitlin's expressive, emotional eyes and held her face close. "Talk to me, Kate. Tell me what's brewing behind those beautiful eyes."

Kaitlin looked away and took a deep breath. "When I opened your drawer for your puffer, I saw Linda's letter." Kaitlin's eyes were consumed with guilt as Sierra reached for her hands and pulled her closer. "I started to read it, then I stopped myself and tucked it into your journal. I'm sorry, Sierra. I should never have done that without your permission. I only read the first few lines, but I feel so bad about reading your personal things like that."

Sierra watched the fear and shame tumble across Kaitlin's eyes. She reached for her face and kissed her forehead. "You're such an incredibly honest woman, Kaitlin Bradley. Now look at me, baby."

Kaitlin slowly raised her eyes to Sierra's. "It's okay, Kate. Everything that belongs to me belongs to you. Everything that touches my life now touches yours. There would never be any letter that I would not share with you. I will never shove a letter away like that again and cause you such pain. I can promise you that."

Sierra kissed each of her eyes before hugging her tight. "I'm so sorry for causing you this pain, Kate. Please tell me you forgive me."

"I forgive you if you forgive me for prying without your permission."

Sierra leaned back and looked into the face of the woman that touched her soul. "You are forgiven, Kate." Sierra held Kaitlin's face in her hands and glided the soft pads of her thumbs over her cheeks. She guided her closer and brushed her lips softly, slowly, dissolving away her pain and worry.

Kaitlin glided her tongue across Sierra's pillowy lower lip and whispered in a deep, husky voice, "So tell me, my precious Sierra. Is Linda begging to take you back from me now that she realizes what a precious gem she has lost?"

Sierra jerked her head up and looked directly into Kaitlin's eyes. "That will never happen, Kate. How could you possibly even think that?"

Kaitlin slid her hands onto Sierra's lower back and stared intently into her anguished eyes. "The thought crossed my mind when I saw the way you needed to hide Linda's letter."

Sierra struggled to maintain calm as her anger battled to gain control. "I wasn't trying to hide the letter, Kate. I was trying to remove any evidence of Linda from my new life with you." Sierra reached up and took Kaitlin's face in her hands, gently caressing the contours of her cheeks with her thumbs. She was startled and moved by the jealousy and fear lurking in those emerald depths. "I obviously need to show you how serious I am about you and me."

Sierra quickly guided Kaitlin to her feet and took her by the hand to march her toward the resort.

They rushed past Sabrina and Gladys at the reception desk. Sabrina saw the look on Kaitlin's face. "Uh-oh! Somebody's in trouble."

Gladys watched them storm up the stairs. "That's the kind of trouble that I think Katie will thoroughly enjoy."

Sierra unlocked her door and wordlessly guided Kaitlin to sit on the edge of her new bed. She marched back to the door and locked and bolted it shut.

Kaitlin watched intently as Sierra took the drawer off the desk and reinserted it after handing Kaitlin her journal.

Kaitlin brushed her open palm across the crushed velvet and opened the front cover. She smiled as she found her mother's black-eyed Susan and the single rose she had tossed onto Sierra's pillow the day before pressed together between the pages.

Sierra reached for Linda's letter poking out from the journal and handed it to Kaitlin. She eased the journal from Kaitlin's hands and placed it on her desk. She turned back to Kaitlin and gently ran her finger along her chin. "Please read the letter, Kate. It would mean a lot to me to share it with you."

Kaitlin watched the warmth flow from Sierra's eyes as she slowly unfolded the letter and began reading where she had left off.

... things I need for you to hear. I love you so much, Sierra, and I realize I have hurt you very badly. You didn't deserve to be treated the way I treated you and I realize your love for me was purely unconditional.

Kaitlin looked up from the letter to watch Sierra slowly remove her T-shirt and teasingly slip her sports bra over her head.

"Excuse me, ma'am, but you're making it very difficult for me to concentrate on this letter."

Sierra smiled seductively, turned her back on Kaitlin and flirtatiously wiggled her white shorts over her Jockeys. "Is that better, my lover?"

Kaitlin sighed at the sight of Sierra's curvaceous, sexy ass, dropped the letter onto her lap, and leaned back on her elbows. "Oh, yeah. That makes it so much easier for me to concentrate on anything other than what your gorgeous body is doing to me right now."

Sierra giggled sweetly and tossed her shorts onto her desk.

"Forget the letter, Sierra, let's pull the blinds."

Sierra stepped toward Kaitlin, eased her down onto the bed, and handed her back the letter. "Why, my love? The only person I know with a peeping telescope is you, my sexy lady." Sierra leaned closer and brushed her lips lightly against Kaitlin's. "Continue reading please, my precious Kate."

Kaitlin held the letter over her face and peeked toward Sierra as she watched her enticingly slip her Jockeys over her slender hips. Kaitlin swallowed hard as she felt her desire blaze in her belly and mushroom between her thighs.

Sierra smiled at the unbridled desire clouding Kaitlin's eyes. She knelt onto the bed and lowered the letter to obscure Kaitlin's view.

Kaitlin dropped her arms to her sides and exhaled a deep breath. "Sierra! This letter is far less interesting than the sight of your gorgeous naked body before me."

Sierra leaned intimately over Kaitlin and as she felt her hand glide over her smooth thigh. "Please finish reading the letter, baby. It would mean a lot to me. There will be a treat waiting for you on completion of your task."

Kaitlin quickly brought the letter back up to her face and began speed-reading as she kept one eye on Sierra's elegant naked frame.

... nobody will ever love me the way you did, Sierra, and I know that now.

Kaitlin heard the unmistakable sound of her zipper descending on her peach shorts as she looked down at Sierra's busy fingers. She obediently raised her hips as Sierra quickly disposed of her shorts and white bikini Calvin Klein's.

Sierra looked up at Kaitlin's glistening eyes and signaled for her to continue reading. Kaitlin flushed with bursting anticipation and quickly returned to the letter.

However, now is too late. You deserve much better than me, Sierra. I heard you have taken your two-week vacation and gone up north. I hope you have a fabulous time and meet someone that will treat you with the love and respect you deserve.

Sierra planted moist, soft kisses along Kaitlin's thighs as she watched her close her eyes and sigh deeply. Sierra smiled at Kaitlin's pleasure as she took the bottom of the letter and jiggled it in Kaitlin's hand.

Kaitlin slowly opened her smoky eyes and gave Sierra a frustrated scowl. "Sierra Vaughn, you're torturing me!"

Sierra nuzzled her nose into Kaitlin's soft mound and inhaled deeply. "That's what you get for being so mean to me about my asthma. You'll think twice next time about being so stern won't you, my sweet Kate?"

Kaitlin squinted her eyes and glared at Sierra. "There won't be a next time, my darling, because someone has promised me that she has nothing to hide."

Sierra nibbled below Kaitlin's belly button and smiled shyly. "Oh, yeah. That's right." Sierra guided the letter over Kaitlin's face as her lips found their way to her ticklish hips.

I want to thank you for the love and time you gave me. I wish that you will find the true happiness that you deserve. Good-bye, Sierra. I love you.

Love always, Linda

Kaitlin dropped the letter onto the bed and sat up as Sierra eased her out of her T-shirt and bra. She lay back down on the bed as Sierra eased herself intimately on top of her. "Hello, true happiness. Ready to do that quality assurance test on my new bed?"

Kaitlin reached for Sierra's face and kissed her softly. "I've been ready since the moment I had this bed delivered to your room."

Sierra positioned herself between Kaitlin's parted thighs and kissed her softly, slowly, escalating the desire burning between their gyrating hips.

Kaitlin ran her finger across Sierra's full lower lip as tears brimmed in her emerald eyes. "Thank you, darling, for letting me read your letter. That means a lot to me that you feel comfortable enough with me to do that."

Sierra slowly entwined her fingers into Kaitlin's shiny brown hair. "You're welcome, sweetheart. I do feel completely comfortable around you. I just wanted you to read that Linda is finally letting me go and finally appreciates me after all those painful years."

Kaitlin trailed her fingertips across Sierra's sexy ass. "I'm so glad to hear that, sweetheart, and I would really appreciate you if you would kiss me again."

Sierra leaned into Kaitlin's lips and whispered seductively, "You're such a needy girl, my precious Kaitlin." Sierra's hand glided over Kaitlin's subtle curves. Their lips met slowly, tenderly as their tongues connected in a kiss of explosive desire and need.

Sierra trailed soft, wet kisses across Kaitlin's cheek and across her eyes. "Tell me, Dr. Bradley, were you jealous of

Linda's letter by any chance? Because I find that very arousing if you were."

Kaitlin slowly opened her eyes and stared into Sierra's mischievous smile. She curled her fingers into Sierra's hair and pulled her closer. "I was terrified that letter could have taken you away from me. I don't ever want to lose you to anyone or anything, Sierra. I would fight for you and our love till my dying day."

Sierra knew that she had felt love before but she had never felt love as she did at that moment for Kaitlin. She was awed and overwhelmed as she rested her forehead against Kaitlin's and let her tears fall unchecked. "I love you so much, Kate. I too would fight for you and our love till my dying day. Please trust me to share everything with you and know that where I want to be is here in your arms."

Kaitlin gently guided Sierra's face closer as she kissed her with a tenderness that embraced her heart with the same warmth that encased her lips.

Sierra gently trailed her tongue between Kaitlin's slightly parted lips and plunged deeper. Their yearning exploded with each thrust as Sierra skimmed her hand over Kaitlin's breast and straining nipple. Her thumb toyed with the erect nipple as Kaitlin swayed and writhed beneath her.

Sierra's fingers floated over Kaitlin's sensitive hip and burrowed into her soft curls and deep inside her passionate center. Kaitlin arched her neck and gasped with ecstasy as Sierra sighed against her cheek. "You're so wet, sweetheart."

Kaitlin arched her hips to bury Sierra's fingers deeper and turned her face to join their lips. "That's all your fault, my little sexual imp."

Sierra kissed Kaitlin with burning passion as she caressed her into a frenzied rhythm of explosive, cascading ecstasy.

Sierra slowly withdrew her fingers, eased herself above Kaitlin, and watched her slowly open her eyes. Her smile illuminated the dim room as Sierra showered her face with soft kisses.

They held each other close as Kaitlin rolled Sierra onto her back and pinned her arms above her head. Kaitlin smiled seductively as she used her knee to ease Sierra's thighs apart and rested herself intimately against her. Kaitlin stared deeply into Sierra's passionate eyes and was filled with a sense of peace and unity. Their entwined hands clung desperately as Kaitlin swayed against her and sent her soaring to that place that was solely theirs.

Sierra moaned in wanton, aching need as the walls of the room melted into abstract light and filled her with a sense of floating on a gentle breeze.

Kaitlin kissed her neck and nibbled on her tiny ear. She flicked her tongue against her earlobe and whispered in a deep, sultry voice, "I smell cinnamon."

Sierra burst into laughter and took Kaitlin's face in her hands. "What are you waiting for, Dr Bradley? Your cinnamon spring awaits you."

Kaitlin's smile burst across her beautiful face as she lowered herself to Sierra's breasts and began a trail of warm, moist kisses that ended with Sierra's explosive, mind-shattering ecstasy.

Kaitlin held Sierra close in her arms and caressed her flushed, warm face as she allowed her to come back down. She kissed Sierra's forehead and allowed her lips to linger as she whispered, "How about I help you pack those fluorescent orange suitcases of yours and we'll have the boys deliver them to our house. This bed certainly meets my quality assurance standards, but there is another bed that eagerly awaits your gorgeous body."

Sierra ran her hands over Kaitlin's silky back and shapely bottom. "After what you just did to me, Dr. Bradley, I would follow you anywhere."

↺ 11

Kelly parked her midnight black Jeep Cherokee in front of Kaitlin's home and jumped out to hug Sabrina, Logan, Kaitlin, and Sierra. She looked so chic in her pastel blue sundress.

She held Kaitlin's hands softly and looked beyond the girls with a puzzled frown. "Where's Sydney?"

Kaitlin squeezed Kelly's hands. "She's waiting for you on the back deck."

Kelly's frown deepened as she looked at the expectant, excited faces before her. "What's up, guys? You guys all look like you're ready to burst with some juicy secret."

They all grinned like impish brats as Kaitlin guided Kelly up the steps to the front deck. She released her hand and signaled for her to go on to the back deck.

Kelly hesitantly moved two steps away and stopped to look back at the girls. "Wait a minute. Sydney's not going to jump out in a gorilla costume and scare me half to death, is she?"

Kaitlin turned her toward the back deck and rested her hands on her shoulders. "Don't be silly, Kelly. If we were going to dress Sydney up, we would put her in a pair of angel's wings because that would be the ultimate scare."

Kaitlin gently turned Kelly around and pointed to the back deck. "Go ahead, Kelly. Trust us. Everything's going to be fine. We'll see you guys a little later."

Kelly frowned with frustrated confusion as she looked at the expectant crowd behind her. Kaitlin signaled for her to take a peek.

Kelly took a deep breath and slowly stepped around the corner. Her breath caught in her throat as her heart pounded wildly in her chest. An elegant, romantic, candlelit table for two had been set in the far corner of the deck. Kelly's crystal blue eyes trailed from the flickering candlelight to Sydney. She

215

looked so uncharacteristically nervous as she leaned against the cedar railing. The edginess added an air of alluring danger to Sydney's magnetic appeal.

Kelly admired her pleated khaki pants and black blouse that accentuated her tall, sleek frame and short, dark brown hair. She had always craved the opportunity to run her fingers through that perpetually mussed hair. She was bewildered and filled with pounding excitement as Sydney cautiously stood before her holding three delicate red roses.

Sydney's breath struggled to fill her lungs as her eyes trailed over Kelly's pastel blue sundress that seemed to float over each subtle curve as if guided by a gently blowing breeze. Sydney ached to reach out and feel those big, bouncy blonde curls entwine around her fingers, and to taste those sensuous lips. Her eyes locked onto Kelly's as those expressive crystal blue depths blazed with shadowed desire and vulnerable confusion.

Sydney extended the roses to Kelly and nervously cleared her throat. "These are for you. One rose for each year that I've loved you."

Kelly's eyes filled with tears as she quickly looked down at the delicate roses in her hands. Sydney reached for Kelly's chin and guided her eyes back to her as she wiped away her tears. "Please say something. I'm just dying here."

"If this is your idea of a joke, Sydney, I'm not laughing."

Sydney took Kelly's anguished face in her hands and held her firmly. "The last thing in the world I would joke about is how much I love you."

"I don't understand, Sydney. Why the sudden change?"

"The girls shared your true feelings with me and there is nothing sudden about how I feel about you, Kelly. I just never thought you could feel anything more than friendship for me so I never talked to you about how I feel."

Kelly took a deep breath as she looked into Sydney's chocolate brown eyes. "I fell in love with you the first day I met you when you came up here to visit Quinn and Katie. You were wearing a neon yellow bathing suit and trying to convince Quinn that she needed to turn Bradley Bay into a nudist colony for lesbians."

Sydney reached forward and gently touched one of the partially opened roses. "I still think the nudist colony would be a great idea."

Kelly laughed softly and gently reached for the hand caressing the rose. Their fingers slowly entwined and joined as one as Kelly looked deeply into Sydney's sensitive eyes. Anger and disbelief swirled in her chest as she thought of all the times she needed this from Sydney, only to be turned away for another. "I have loved you for three years, Sydney. I prayed that someday you would feel the same way. Now, all of a sudden you're telling me that you love me. Excuse me if I seem a little skeptical. It's just that I never sensed you felt anything more than friendship. I don't mean to destroy the ambiance but I'm finding this all a little difficult to swallow at this moment."

Sydney shook her head and hesitated to find the right words. "I don't blame you for not believing me, Kelly. I have wanted you so badly these past three years. Instead of showing you or telling you I have been so terrified of what your reaction would be that I did the exact opposite and acted like a total idiot around you and tried to prove to myself that I didn't need you. Well that failed miserably. It only made all the women I did spend time with pale in comparison to you. It only made me realize how much I really needed you.

"Your friendship is so precious to me, Kelly. I never wanted to do anything stupid to affect that. I always felt that you saw me as a big kid who would never grow up. I convinced myself that you deserved better than me. I love you, Kelly, and it saddens me that you never realized what a special place you have in my heart."

Kelly placed her roses on the railing and reached for Sydney, guiding her into her arms. They held each other tight as Kelly gently kissed Sydney's cheek. "You are just a big kid who will never grow up, and that's just one of the millions of things I love about you. I have stood back and watched you flirt with a

217

thousand women and each time I wished that it was me you were flirting with."

Sydney leaned back and stared into Kelly's moist blue eyes as Kelly reached for her face. "I love you, Sydney, like I have never loved any other woman on the face of this earth. You're so silly for thinking I deserved better than you when it's you I've always wanted."

Sydney's smile danced in her emotional eyes as Kelly guided her face closer, slowly, hesitantly. They stared into each other's eyes as years of hidden love exploded between them. Kelly slowly leaned closer and tenderly brushed her lips against Sydney's, emitting a soft moan of desire. Sydney glided her hands into Kelly's hair and held her close as they shared a kiss of fiery, unbridled passion.

Smiles beamed from all the girls' faces as Sierra slowly stood tall and moved back around the corner to allow Sydney and Kelly their privacy. Sabrina, Logan and Kaitlin were still glued to their hiding spots as Sierra smacked each of their bottoms and signaled for them to move away. They all quietly squished their faces at her like disobedient children and turned back to watch the passionate scene before them. Sierra reached for each of them and pulled them away like unyielding mannequins.

They reached the front deck as Sabrina turned to Logan. "I think this woman is much too bossy for her britches. What do you say we teach her another lesson, sweet pea?"

Sierra shrieked with fright and reached for Kaitlin's hand as they dashed down the steps with Sabrina and Logan close on their heels.

CRUCRUCRU

After dinner, Kaitlin spent two hours in the main office with Sierra, answering the phone, booking reservations and explaining the billing and business end of running the resort. Sierra was fascinated by the organization involved and proved to be a quick learner. Kaitlin was amazed by her astuteness and intelligent questions as she eagerly explained the responsibilities behind making Bradley Bay a success.

Sierra sat snuggly in Kaitlin's lap as Kaitlin pointed to the advertising ideas on the computer screen.

Sabrina poked her head in the office and smiled at the loving sight before her. "Does this mean when Sierra completes her coproprietor orientation we're going to have to treat her like our boss too?"

Sierra balled up a piece of paper and threw it at Sabrina, narrowly missing her head. "You'd better not treat me any differently, Bri, except for maybe the threats of revisiting the Loch Ness monster."

Kaitlin swiveled her executive chair to face Sabrina. "You guys never treat me like a boss, so why should it be any different for Sierra?"

Sabrina sat on the corner of the desk and touched Sierra's soft cheek. "Because she's much bossier than you, Kate, and she's damn lucky you were there to protect her from revisiting the Loch Ness monster earlier. We need to find some way to keep this woman in her place, so stop interfering, would you?"

Sabrina smiled warmly at Sierra. "Welcome aboard, Sierra. Logan and I are thrilled to have you as part of our family."

Sierra reached for Sabrina's hand and squeezed it softly. "Thank you, Sabrina. That means a lot to me."

Sabrina gently tugged on Sierra's hand. "The reason I came looking for you two was to tell you that we lit a bonfire down by our place if you want to come and join us. We helped all the guests that needed assistance into bed but a few of the new guests who arrived today are itching for a wiener roast, so Logan, Gladys, Sydney, and Kelly are busy down there spearing the poor little dogs. I'd really like you two to come and save us from Sydney's sick wiener jokes."

Kaitlin saved her files and shut down the computer as Sierra eased herself to her feet.

"I'm surprised that Sydney and Kelly have hung around as long as they have this evening," Sierra said.

Sabrina watched Sierra help Kaitlin to her feet. "Me too. Those two are like a hurricane of hormonal intensity about to touch down. They're even worse than you two, and that's tough to beat."

Sierra and Kaitlin laughed shyly as they took Sabrina by the hand and strolled out of the office. "You should talk, Bri. I've watched the way you and Logan look at each other and sneak in an occasional kiss. Don't tell me that when everyone is tucked in and you two finally get a chance to slip beneath your sheets that you don't create a whirlwind of hormonal intensity yourselves," Sierra said.

Sabrina blushed beautifully as Kaitlin smacked the palm of her hand against her forehead. "And all these years I thought that was just a northerly wind gusting across the lake every night."

Sabrina playfully smacked Kaitlin's arm as she guided them both toward the roaring fire to join in the festivities with their new guests.

CRITICAL CRITICAL CRITICAL

The onyx black water lapped gently at the edge of the bay as the girls sat in their lounge chairs listening to the melodic hooting of a barn owl. The half-moon glistened off the glassy surface of the lake as the blazing lights from Sabrina and Logan's home shone from behind.

Hours later Gladys gathered their supplies and kissed the girls goodnight. "I'll check on the quads and para's and make sure they are all settled in for the night. You girls stay here and enjoy yourselves."

"Thanks, Gladys. That would be great. Page us if you need a hand with anything," Logan said, as she expertly extinguished the smoldering bonfire at the lake's edge.

Kelly and Sydney bent down to their friends in their lounge chairs and kissed and hugged them good night. They waved as they started walking toward Kelly's Cherokee hand in hand.

Sabrina rose from her chair and called after them, "Where do you think you're going, Syd? I thought you came up here to spend the weekend with us."

Sydney and Kelly stopped and shared a sweet smile. Sydney turned back to the girls' smiling faces and said, "Kelly bought a new pillow that she needs someone to break in with her. I volunteered to be her little helper. It's a tough job but someone has to do it."

Sydney waved good-bye and guided Kelly to her vehicle.

Logan stepped up to Sabrina and wrapped her arms around her waist. "It looks like Sydney has finally found the right ass to kiss."

"It sure does, sweet pea. I just wonder if we should have interfered sooner and clued them in to the real picture years ago."

"The timing is right now, Sabrina. They both needed to chart their own course and have the experiences that they did before they could commit to each other."

"I guess. I personally couldn't deal with that emotional stress for three years," Sabrina said, as she let her lips linger across Logan's forehead. "It's a good thing you knew I was the one for you the moment you met me."

"Oh, yeah! It's also a good thing I'm a very patient woman, darling. It only took me three months and several hints on Sydney's part to clue you in to the fact that I was madly in love with you." Logan rolled her eyes as Kaitlin and Sierra smiled at their playfulness. "At first I just thought you had no interest in blondes till Sydney explained that you aren't exactly the sharpest pencil in the cup when it comes to women's attraction to you."

Sabrina blushed shyly. "Well, you certainly realized how attracted I was to you when you asked me out to dinner and showed up at my house wearing that sexy, slinky, strapless black dress. A dress that looked gorgeous on you and even more beautiful when it was piled at your feet hours later."

"You certainly were the sharpest pencil after that date my gorgeous, Bri." Logan tilted her head up and briefly brushed her lips against Sabrina's. "What do you say we go inside and I put that dress on for you again?"

"Let's just skip the dress and wrap ourselves in our bedsheets instead."

Logan glowed with sexual tension as she turned and blew Sierra and Kaitlin a kiss. "Good night, ladies. Love each other well."

They watched them head toward their cottage hand in hand. "We certainly will, Logan. Don't you worry about that," Kaitlin said in their wake. Kaitlin squeezed Sierra's hand and slid from her lounge chair, guiding her to her feet. "I was wondering, my little fashion plate, if you have a sexy, slinky, strapless black dress in one of those orange fluorescent suitcases of yours that you would wear for me?"

Sierra leaned intimately against Kaitlin and slid her hands along her waist and onto her tight bottom. "I didn't think that I would need my black dress up here to seduce you, Kaitlin, however, when I do get you into my home, I would love to put it on for you and see how quickly you can pool it at my feet."

Kaitlin sighed happily as she swayed with Sierra in the moonlight. "Since there is no black dress in that expansive wardrobe of yours, how about I just wrap you in my bedsheets?"

"I would rather be totally wrapped up in you, Dr. Bradley, than your bedsheets."

Kaitlin groaned erotically before leaning toward Sierra and nibbling at her lower lip. She took her lower lip into her mouth and caressed it with her tongue as she luxuriated in Sierra's unrestrained gasp. Kaitlin crushed her lips to Sierra's and eased her tongue between her moist, parted lips, tasting the sweetness that awaited her.

Kaitlin held Sierra tight and kissed her closed eyelids. "Let's go home, darling," Kaitlin whispered hoarsely. Kaitlin entwined her hand in Sierra's and guided her across the well-manicured lawn.

Licorice sprinted out from behind a lilac bush and stepped in beside Sierra. Kaitlin rolled her eyes at Sierra's little companion as they happily took their little family home.

CRWGRWGRW

Kaitlin tilted her telescope slightly and pointed to the right as she held Sierra close in her arms. "Do you see the Big Dipper?"

Sierra squinted her left eye closed and strained to focus her right eye through the telescope. The excitement in her voice was contagious as she bounced in Kaitlin's lap in the lounge chair. "I see it! I see the Big Dipper!"

Kaitlin smiled proudly and gently slid her hand over Sierra's teal shorts and under her T-shirt to caress her back. "Good girl. That is indeed the Big Dipper. It's also known as Ursa Major or the Great Bear. The Big Dipper is made up of seven bright stars and it only makes up the tail and hindquarters of the bear, so you really have to stretch your vivid imagination to see the bear in its entirety."

Sierra turned back to Kaitlin. "Why do they call it the Great Bear?"

Kaitlin handed Sierra their glass of white wine and watched her take a sip. "From Greek mythology, apparently Zeus made some huntress named Callisto pregnant. This Callisto chick bore Zeus a son and that did not in any way impress Zeus's wife, Hera. Now Hera got her knickers in a knot over Zeus's little indiscretion and turned Callisto into a bear. It also turns out that their son, Arcas, was a hunter. Hera, the evil witch, schemed to bring Callisto before her unsuspecting son, and have him kill her. Zeus, the big bad boy, was devastated, so he placed Callisto in the heavens as the Great Bear. Their son, Arcas, was placed beside her as the lesser bear. This in no means pleased the ever spiteful, Hera."

Sierra was mesmerized by Kaitlin's story as she stared at her with her huge blue-gray eyes. "What an amazing story. That Zeus better behave himself, or his wife will create a zoo out of all his little indiscretions."

Kaitlin burst into laughter and set down their wine glass. She tilted the telescope down slightly and turned to kiss Sierra's awaiting, wine-flavored lips. She hesitantly leaned back and whispered against her sensuous lips, "See if you can find the Little Dipper."

Sierra refocused beneath the telescope and smiled impishly. "This is just about as much fun as a game of 'Where's Waldo.'"

Kaitlin burst into laughter and teased Sierra's tiny earlobe with her tongue till she giggled with girlish charm. "I do believe that my astronomy lesson is a little more educational than a game of 'Where's Waldo.'"

Sierra burst into her sweet laughter as she tried to focus on the majestic night sky before her and not the warm sensuous body beneath her, dressed only in a white tank top and white, spandex knit, drawstring pants. "I have already told you what that stern voice does to me, Dr. Bradley, so you'd better get on with the lesson before I tear your sexy clothes off you here and now and make mad, passionate love to you beneath this gorgeous northern sky."

Kaitlin glided her hand beneath Sierra's teal and white striped T-shirt and traced her fingertips along her spine. "Promises, promises."

Sierra tilted her eyes away from the telescope and gave Kaitlin a coy smile. "Promises I intend to keep, my delicious lover."

Kaitlin stared at her in lustful, aching need as Sierra blew her a kiss and returned to the telescope. Kaitlin dropped her head back against the lounge chair and groaned with insatiable desire.

Sierra smiled at Kaitlin's passion as she stared intently into the telescope and pointed up to the left. "Look, baby. There it is. The Little Dipper."

Kaitlin smiled deeply and gently caressed Sierra's hair. "Good girl! The Little Dipper is also known as Ursa Minor or the little bear. If you look closely you can pick out the single, brightest star in the Little Dipper. It's called Polaris because it is only one degree away from the North Pole."

Sierra looked away from the telescope and back at Kaitlin in pure amazement. "That's like you, baby. You're my Polaris. My brightest star."

Kaitlin kissed Sierra's soft lips and guided her ravishing eyes back to the telescope. "Your astronomy lesson's not quite over, my sweet darling, so stop seducing me with those beautiful blue eyes of yours. There is just one more that I would like to show you, my little Scorpio with the stinging tail, before I beg you to make mad, passionate love to me, here and now." Sierra hesitantly turned back to the telescope as Kaitlin held it still for her. "Look down below the Little Dipper and see if you can see eight stars that make a u-shape."

Seconds passed before Sierra bounced with glee. "I see the u-shape, babe!"

Kaitlin gently ran her fingers along Sierra's spine. "Good girl. Those eight stars make up the tail of the scorpion. Now look directly above the tail and see if you can see seven stars that look like an arrow pointing up into the sky."

Again, Sierra bounced in Kaitlin's lap. "I see it, I see it!"

"The u-shape is the scorpion's tail, and the arrow is his body and claws."

Sierra attempted to piece together the picture as she felt the caressing heat from Kaitlin's hand.

"The story goes that Scorpuis, the Scorpion, was the creature that stung Orion, the mighty hunter, to death. The gods that be were pissed enough to place Orion and Scorpuis on opposite sides of the heavens so that Orion disappears when Scorpuis rises." Sierra looked at Kaitlin with intrigue and wonder as Kaitlin ran the soft pad of her thumb across her full, pillowy lower lip. "So the moral to that story, my precious little scorpion girl, is you'd better not sting this crabby Wizard to death or the gods that be might put us on opposite sides of the heavens, and we might never see each other again."

Sierra swung the high-powered telescope away and swiftly turned to straddle Kaitlin's thighs. She wrapped her arms around her and slowly threaded her fingers through her thick chestnut hair. "That goes without saying that maybe the crabby Wizard should do her best not to be so crabby as to provoke the whip of the scorpions tail."

Kaitlin slid her hands along Sierra's bare thighs and onto her tight bottom. "That goes without saying that maybe the scorpion girl needs to have her gorgeous tail whipped once in a while to keep her in line."

Sierra slid her hands along Kaitlin's jaw and guided her face intimately close. "You're really turning me on now, my crabby Wizard." She stared into Kaitlin's smoky, wild eyes before taking her lips ferociously; stunning them both.

Kaitlin gripped her hips and arched against her with intense zealousness. Her body felt like an eruption of liquid fire, ignited hotter and faster with each caress of Sierra's masterful lips.

Minutes later Sierra rested her forehead against Kaitlin's and heaved to catch her next breath. "Fascinating astronomy lesson, baby. What else do you plan to teach me tonight?" Sierra leaned back, kissed Kaitlin gently, and stared into her beautiful eyes.

Kaitlin slipped her hands beneath sierra's t-shirt and ran her fingertips along her spine. "I plan to teach you to soar higher than the Polaris star."

Sierra gazed deeply into Kaitlin's heavy-lidded eyes. She held her face in her hands and caressed her cheeks with the soft pad of her thumbs. She watched Kaitlin's eyes drift closed as she leaned forward to take her lips with aggressive urgency.

Kaitlin was consumed by her scintillating passion and desperate need. She molded her hands tightly over Sierra's sexy ass and down along her thighs. Her hands slid beneath her shorts and dipped beneath her white cotton Jockeys.

Sierra arched her hips and gasped with burning desire. She wove her fingers into Kaitlin's thick hair and tilted her head back as she ravished her neck with moist, suckling kisses.

Kaitlin ground her hips against Sierra's parted thighs before slipping her thumb across Sierra's dark mound and between her wet, velvet folds. The soft pad of her thumb found her erect, swollen tissue as she swirled her in her own wetness.

Sierra cried out with intense euphoric pleasure as she arched her back and raised herself higher on her knees.

Kaitlin tilted her head up and grazed her tongue along Sierra's chin till their lips met with fierce, insatiable hunger. "Let's go inside, sweetheart, before we put on quite a show for all the guests," Kaitlin whispered hoarsely.

Sierra ground her hips into Kaitlin's fingers and moaned against her moist lips. "I can't wait, baby. Please, I want to feel you deep inside me."

Kaitlin's yearning burned with an intensity she'd never known as she twisted to the edge of the lounge chair and easily carried Sierra into the kitchen. She laid her down across the kitchen island and impatiently stripped her of her shorts and Jockeys. Sierra sat up quickly to allow Kaitlin to tear off her T-shirt and bra. "You're never going to be able to look at this kitchen the same way, Dr. Bradley."

"I'm never going to be able to look at my life the same again, Ms. Vaughn, let alone this kitchen, the stairs, the bathroom, or my futon."

Sierra reached for Kaitlin's white tank top and tossed it to the floor as she swiftly removed her bra. She impatiently reached for her face and guided her closer as she kissed her with astounding desire. Sierra's tongue invaded Kaitlin's mouth with force and ownership as she basked in the sensation of Kaitlin's hands molding to her breasts and taunting her nipples. "It looks like you have some wonderful ideas of where to make love, my sweet Kate, besides your bed. I told you a bed would not be a necessity."

Kaitlin gripped Sierra's waist and guided her down off the island. "You're my fantasy lover, Sierra. I'm going to play out all of my fantasies with you and this kitchen island is just not big enough for what I have in mind." Kaitlin guided Sierra toward the huge bay window seat and laid her among the thick fluffy pillows.

Sierra snuggled down into the pillows as Kaitlin eased herself between her parted thighs "I love the sounds of that, Dr. Bradley." Sierra closed her eyes and gripped the pillow behind her head as she felt Kaitlin rest her hands on the insides of her thighs and part her legs wider. Sierra arched her hips toward her as Kaitlin greedily plunged her tongue deeply into her glistening, wet pool of passion.

Sierra arched her neck and reached for Kaitlin's head as she gasped for her next breath. She thrust to the rhythm of Kaitlin's tongue as her mind surrendered to the motion of Kaitlin's caress.

Sierra's thighs clamped tighter to Kaitlin's shoulders as her body suddenly stilled. Her thighs quivered as a wave of liquid heat embraced her entire body from the tip of Kaitlin's tongue. She arched one final time as a scream of blissful rapture reverberated off the ceramic tiles like a handful of ice cubes tossed into an empty glass.

☌ **12**

The midmorning sun glistened off Logan's blonde, thick curls as she and Sabrina finished dressing Michael's knees. Sabrina gathered up their remaining supplies while Logan readjusted Michael's footrests. "That should do you till this evening, Mike. Those scrapes on your knees are healing really well," Sabrina said.

"Thanks, ladies. I really appreciate what you've done."

Logan squeezed his shoulder. "Our pleasure. Just make sure you hang on to your fishing pole on this trip, otherwise you'll end up kissing a carp instead of the deck."

They all burst into laughter as they watched the recreation crew wheel Michael onto a ramp and carefully ease him into a fishing boat.

"Thanks again, ladies. I'll see you guys later," Michael said, as the boat headed off for a morning of fishing on the north shores of Sturgeon Lake.

Sabrina turned and saw Sierra approach. "Hey, ladies. I've been looking everywhere for you two. Jennifer's wheelchair has died out front of Kaitlin's place and I don't know how to get it started again."

Logan picked up the first aid kit and looked concerned. Sabrina tilted her head slightly and looked at Sierra suspiciously. "That's strange, Sierra. It's a brand new chair, and nobody knows how to run that thing better than Jennifer. After all, we're talking about a girl that used to dismantle her motorcycle and put it all back together again for fun."

"What a lesbian," Sierra teased, as she sheepishly averted her eyes. "Come with me, you guys, so you can see if you can help Jennifer."

Sabrina and Logan shared a questioning look as they stepped in beside Sierra and headed toward Kaitlin's home. Sabrina knew something was up, but her concern for Jennifer was foremost in her mind.

"How's your asthma today, Sierra?" Sabrina said.

"No problems. My breathing's great this morning. I'm sure it was lying in the grass with Jennifer that set me off. I haven't done that in a long time. But it was well worth it for Jennifer's sake."

"Jennifer will never forget that time with you and Katie as long as she lives. She hasn't stopped talking about it. She loved lying on the grass with you guys even though it cost you some precious oxygen and a tongue lashing from Katie," Logan said.

"We all know that Katie's bark is worse than her bite. Well, at least this time it was," Sierra said shyly as she quickly guided them along the trail of towering spruce and elm trees along the edge of Kaitlin's backyard.

Sabrina looked ahead and spotted Jennifer sitting in her idle wheelchair and waved. Jennifer smiled, waved back, and waited till the three were ten feet away from her. She grinned from ear to ear and slowly maneuvered her wheelchair away.

Sabrina and Logan stopped dead in their tracks as Jennifer shouted, "Hello, ladies. Enjoy Sierra's sweet revenge."

Sierra turned and gave them a devilish grin and shouted, "Get them!"

A chorus of cheers erupted from Kaitlin's front deck just as a bewildered Sabrina and Logan were bombarded with water balloons and endless high-powered streams of water from Star Wars-like water guns.

Kaitlin, Kelly, and Sydney continually resupplied the wheelchair-bound guests with bulging water balloons as Sabrina and Logan clung to each other and tried to find a way off this battleground.

Sierra giggled with pure delight as she crouched behind the nearest tree and relentlessly drenched Sabrina and Logan with her neon orange water gun.

Sabrina saw her out of the corner of her eye and signaled her position to Logan. They both counted to three and dashed toward

Sierra, who squealed with fright and continually squirted them till they tackled her to the ground and rolled together in a heap of laughter. Sabrina and Logan hauled Sierra to her feet and marched her toward the battlefield, using her as a human shield. Sabrina intelligently used Sierra as a hostage and quickly put an end to the siege.

Sierra led everyone on the deck in thunderous laughter and applause of their triumphant battle as Sabrina gently tapped her shoulder. "What? Do you think you won?"

Sierra looked into Sabrina's mischievous eyes and slowly started to back away. "I'll show you who gets the last laugh," Sabrina said, as she swiftly tossed a squealing Sierra over her shoulder in a fireman's lift and headed toward the lake.

"Katieeeeee, save me!" Sierra screamed in panic.

Logan intercepted Kaitlin at the bottom of the deck steps and easily tossed her over her shoulder and followed Sabrina's path. Everyone watched with amused excitement as Sierra and Kaitlin's pleas for leniency fell on deaf ears. A large crowd on the dock wisely moved aside as they watched Sabrina and Logan ceremoniously toss them both into the icy cold lake amidst cheers and laughter.

Kelly and Sydney peered over the edge of the dock in shock and burst into laughter as Sierra and Kaitlin clung to each other in the freezing water.

Sabrina and Logan tiptoed behind them and tapped them both on the shoulder as they smiled into their apprehensive faces and added them to the Loch Ness monster's dinner menu.

Everyone was stunned by Sabrina and Logan's playfulness as they applauded their jubilant revenge.

Sabrina and Logan stood side by side at the edge of the dock and laughed as they stared down at the barrage of verbal threats and profanity spewing from the chilled guests of Sturgeon Lake. Sabrina scoffed at their dear friends and laughed. "Serves you guys right for banding together against us and thinking you would get away with it. Next time Sierra comes up with a plan of attack, you guys will think twice about getting involved."

Sabrina and Logan laughed together as they both felt something hard tap against their shoulders. A hush fell over the large crowd as they both turned slowly to face a stern Gladys slapping a huge wooden spoon against the palm of her hand.

"I strongly suggest that you two lovely ladies voluntarily join your precious friends, or neither one of you will be able to sit for a week!"

Sabrina and Logan shrieked with fright and dove head first into the deep, clear, ice water to uproarious laughter and applause.

⟳ **13**

The girls all showered after their icy adventure and completed their afternoon chores. They sat comfortably together on the dock bench and watched the guests go through their water aerobics.

Kaitlin watched a paddleboat return and turned to Sydney. "Your yacht awaits you, Syd. Take that new paddleboat out for a spin."

Sydney kissed Kelly's temple and nuzzled her lips against her warm cheek. "Come for a ride with me, Kelly."

Kelly turned her face to Sydney and leaned her head back against her strong shoulder. "My legs are incapable of powering that vessel, Sydney, after what you did to me last night."

Sydney blushed sweetly and buried her face against Kelly's.

Sierra bounded off the bench and took her by the hand. "Come on, Sydney. I'll take you for a ride while your lover stays behind and recovers from your passionate honeymoon."

Sydney kissed Kelly's cheek and followed Sierra down the steps. Kelly slid along the bench and took Sierra's place beside Kaitlin.

Sierra turned back to Kaitlin with a dramatic wave of her hand. "Good bye, lover. Parting is such sweet sorrow."

Kaitlin blew Sierra a big kiss as Sydney rolled her eyes and roughly placed her in the paddleboat. Licorice watched Sierra intently from her perch on the redwood railing and decided that she was much happier on dry land than joining Sierra on this adventure.

The girls rested back in the cushioned bench and watched the water churn chaotically behind the departing paddleboat.

Kaitlin ran her fingers through Kelly's unruly blonde curls. "Are you happily satiated, my little friend?"

Kelly turned to Kaitlin with a beaming smile. "I've never been so happy. And how about you, Katie? Are you happily satiated?"

Kaitlin gave Kelly her magnificent smile. "I've never been so happy as I am with Sierra."

Kelly leaned into Kaitlin's arms as they hugged each other tight.

The sudden, annoying rumble of a 130-horsepower Jet Ski filled Bradley Bay. Kaitlin squinted her eyes to watch the young teenager swerve erratically and irresponsibly across the bay as Kelly muttered, "Asshole!"

Kaitlin sat stiffly in her seat and watched him disappear around the bend. "Good riddance!" She barely took another breath as the rumbling maniac returned and did several 360-degree turns and barely managed to keep the Jet Ski from flipping dangerously.

The girls all jumped to their feet and rushed to the edge of the dock in a flurry of anger and anxiety. They watched him soar over the wake of a passing motorboat as Kaitlin turned to Logan and grabbed her shoulder.

"Logan, call the marine police and get somebody out here now to stop that kid before he kills somebody."

Logan rushed to the dock phone and dialed 911 as Sabrina stood beside Kaitlin. They watched him circle wildly back into Bradley Bay at sixty miles per hour.

"Get the guests out of the water now," Kaitlin screamed at the recreation staff, as she kept her eyes riveted on the Jet Ski.

Terror and panic filled Kaitlin's chest as she watched Sydney and Sierra pedal farther and farther away, knowing that they would never be able to hear her screams above the roar of that Jet Ski. Kaitlin started praying like she had never prayed in her life for the safety of everyone out on the water. Kaitlin couldn't stand the thought of Sierra and Sydney being defenseless out in the middle of the lake against that nut as she turned to Sabrina. "Get the motorboat started, Bri."

Kaitlin heard another approaching speedboat and looked out to see the marine police patrol roar into Bradley Bay. Kaitlin recognized Liz on board and saw her point at the Jet Skier. Her anxiety and dread mounted as she watched Sierra and Sydney sit idle in the center of the lake.

The two male and two female police officers aboard the patrol boat quickly spotted the crazed Jet Skier. They turned the boat sharply and headed toward him as he foolishly tried to bolt and outrun the cops. Kaitlin clutched her chest as she watched the kid suddenly jerk the Jet Ski wildly and head straight for Sierra and Sydney. He tried to swerve sharply to avoid the paddleboat and completely lost control of the powerful machine.

Time stood still as Kaitlin and the girls watched in horror as the kid jumped off the Jet Ski just as Sierra and Sydney attempted to jump clear of the paddleboat. Everyone on the dock gasped as they watched the powerless Jet Ski flip in grotesque, twisted, slow motion and careen into the paddleboat, exploding on impact.

Kaitlin's world stopped as her heart constricted in her chest and made breathing impossible. Logan quickly grabbed Kaitlin and Kelly and hauled them both into the awaiting motorboat.

Sabrina reached the splintered, burning wood within a minute as Kaitlin, Kelly, and Logan dove into the water and searched frantically for Sydney and Sierra.

Sierra felt oddly weightless as she floated aimlessly toward the fractured sunlight filtering through the lake's surface. She couldn't make sense of the painful burning in her chest as her eyes searched unseeingly in slow motion at the debris around her. She tried to push up to the sunlight, but her limbs felt like useless, heavy cement blocks. She saw an image silhouetted by the light that looked oddly like a hand stretched frantically toward her, begging her to hang on and reach for the hand in what seemed a distorted dream. Sierra's mind felt numbed as the burning in her chest threatened to erupt into flames. Sierra tried to focus on the hand that seemed to come closer and closer and weakly reached toward it; she felt her body suddenly jerked free of its cement restraints and plummeted to the ice-cold surface.

Her lungs erupted with searing pressure as Sierra gasped and struggled with unbelievable air hunger. Her arms limply grabbed the body of the silhouetted image as she gasped fiercely to fill her lungs with air.

A life jacket was snapped into place around her as Kaitlin grabbed her face and shook her firmly. "Sierra! Look at me, Sierra. Slow down your breathing, sweetheart. Look at me, Sierra, and breathe with me."

Sierra's head snapped forward as she focused on the familiar voice before her. She obediently mimicked each deep breath and felt a shadowy fog begin to free her brain from its terrifying grip.

She stared into the emerald eyes before her as reality and shock slapped her simultaneously. She suddenly gripped Kaitlin with every ounce of her waning energy as she looked at the burning rubble floating around them. "Oh my God, baby! I'm alive! I thought we were dead. I saw that Jet Ski fly toward us, and I never thought I'd see you again."

Sierra sobbed against Kaitlin's face as Kaitlin held her tight. "I'm here, my darling, and you're going to be fine."

Sierra jerked her head up and looked around her wildly. "Sydney! Where's Sydney?"

The police boat floated alongside them as Logan swam up to Kaitlin and Sierra and slipped a life jacket onto Kaitlin.

Kaitlin pointed up to the police boat. Sierra saw Sydney leaning over the railing. "I'm right here, Sierra. I'm okay. I just have a sore hip, but we're all ecstatic to see your beautiful face. We're so grateful that Katie finally found you. You scared us to death! This was hardly the time to turn into a mermaid, you crazy girl, you."

Sierra smiled weakly as she hung onto Logan and Kaitlin in total relief. Sierra focused on Kaitlin's concerned eyes and answered all of her questions as she tried to assess her injuries before she let anyone move her out of the water.

Liz and the male police officers pulled Sierra carefully out of the water and wrapped her in warm blankets before helping Kaitlin and Logan into the boat.

Kaitlin quickly shed her blanket to assess Sydney before turning her attention to the three-inch gash on Sierra's left shoulder. She yanked the first aid kit off the cabin wall and flipped the lid open. She reached for a pressure dressing and noticed a young teenager wrapped in a blanket, sitting coyly behind the police driver. Their eyes instantly met; Kaitlin sensed his immature aloofness and arrogance. Her anger seared her to the core as she lurched forward and grabbed the kid by the head and slammed him up against the wall. "You fucking idiot! You could have killed my family. Do you understand that, asshole? You could have killed the people I love."

She repeatedly slammed him back against the wall as Logan, Liz and the male police officers pried Kaitlin away from him. They dragged Kaitlin up against the opposite wall as Sierra reached for her face and screamed, "Let her go! Everyone just back off and let her go."

Kaitlin jerked away from Liz as Sierra securely pinned her up against the wall. "No, baby! Stop! He's not worth it. We're all okay. That's what matters right now. Not that irresponsible piece of shit that has no idea what could have happened out there."

Kaitlin felt her tears sting her cheeks as Liz stood beside Sierra and glared at Kaitlin. "Cool it, Dr. Bradley! Let the law take care of this punk, and you take care of your family. I don't want to see you pull any stupid shit like this again. You're just giving this kid ammunition to fight back, so back off and let us see to it that he gets appropriately punished. Slamming his head against the wall is not going to knock any sense into a teenager. You know better than that. Now let's get you two seated back there so we can head back to shore and get you guys out of these wet clothes."

Kaitlin glared at Liz as Sierra guided her back to their seat and wrapped them both in blankets. Kaitlin reached for the first aid kit once again and expertly dressed Sierra's shoulder laceration with shaking, cold fingers. She applied the last strip of tape as Sierra watched the huge tears fall onto her cheeks and pulled her into her arms.

"I'm okay, baby. I'm going to be okay."

Kaitlin held her tight and shed her terrified tears at what could have been. She took Sierra's face in her hands and looked intently into her eyes to make sure she hadn't missed anything. "How's your breathing, Sierra? Does your chest feel tight at all?"

"My breathing's fine, sweetheart. I'm just thrilled to be back in your arms again. A little soggier, but back nevertheless."

Kaitlin tucked the blanket tighter around Sierra and pulled her close in her arms. Kaitlin was engulfed with the realization of how much Sierra had come to mean to her and how close she had come to losing her.

After returning from having Sierra and Sydney checked out at the hospital, everyone had showered and changed into warm clothes. They stood close together in Kaitlin's kitchen and sipped on stiff drinks. They all shared their relief and terror as they watched Sierra sit very still on a kitchen stool while Kaitlin, once again, peeled back the small dressing on her left shoulder and assessed the small skin tear for any signs of bleeding.

Liz stood among them and recorded their statements. Kaitlin placed a kiss on Sierra's shoulder before applying a new dressing.

Sierra looked over at Kaitlin's handiwork and watched her dispose of the old dressing. Her huge blue-gray eyes met Kaitlin's as they shared a loving smile. "I think I deserve a kiss and a happy face sticker for being such a good girl, don't you think, Dr. Bradley?"

Kaitlin winked at her seductively. She gently took Sierra's ventolin puffer from her hands and set it down on the counter behind her before washing her hands at the sink.

Sydney leaned toward Sierra and kissed her quickly. "There you go. Feel better now?"

Sierra squished her face playfully at Sydney and blushed. "That was nice, Sydney, but it wasn't exactly the lips I was looking for."

Sydney rolled her eyes and leaned back against the counter. "That's the story of my life."

Kaitlin leaned slowly toward Sierra's soft lips and whispered, "I love you," as she kissed her with tender, aching passion. Kaitlin reached for her thick white sweatshirt and helped Sierra slip it over her white tank top.

Kelly stepped seductively before Sydney and rested her hands on her waist. "Your lips are exactly what I have always been looking for."

Sydney's face burst into a jubilant smile as she stuck her tongue out at Sierra and kissed Kelly with unbridled passion.

Everyone cheered her loving display as Liz smiled and closed her clipboard. "I think that's all I need from you ladies right now. I'll bring the final reports around for you guys to sign in a few days. If I have any more questions, I'll call you guys here. In the meantime, I promise to let you know what happens to the kid."

Kaitlin stepped toward Liz and touched her arm. "Thank you, Liz. We appreciate everything you've done." They hugged warmly as Sierra ceremoniously cleared her throat and caught Kaitlin's attention.

"Isn't there something else you wanted to say to Liz, baby?"

Kaitlin grimaced at Sierra and shyly turned back to Liz. "I'm really sorry for being such a bear on the boat. I don't usually lose my cool like that."

Liz smiled and gently squeezed Kaitlin's arm. "That's okay, Kate. I totally understood your reaction. The punk's lucky it wasn't Darcy he rammed with his Jet Ski, or I would have pulled out my gun and shot off his balls."

They all burst into laughter and applause as Liz gathered her clipboard. She reached for Sierra's hand and smiled. "I'm so grateful that you and Sydney are okay. You had us all pretty scared out there for a few minutes when we couldn't find you."

239

Sierra held her hand warmly. "Thank you for everything, Liz. We really do appreciate your kindness. When you bring those papers back, why don't you bring Darcy and join us for dinner?"

"I'd like that. Consider it a date."

They all watched Liz descend the deck steps and wave good-bye before she climbed into her police cruiser.

Kaitlin turned back to face the women she loved as she watched Sierra refresh everyone's drinks. Kaitlin thanked Sierra for the cold glass of beer and took a big sip. She handed the glass back to Sierra and turned to Sydney.

"Sydney, I'd like to have another look at your hip to make sure you're okay."

Sydney sipped on her rum and Coke and looked apprehensively at Kaitlin. "I'm okay, Katie. Really. You don't have to worry about me."

Kaitlin took the crystal tumbler from Sydney's hand and set it on the counter behind her. She stepped menacingly close to Sydney's leery eyes and demanded, "Drop your pants, Sydney. Now."

Kelly reached for the button on her Levis and helped Sydney slip out of her faded jeans, leaving her standing in her form-fitting, sensual pink Joe Boxers.

"Sure, Dr. Bradley. I've waited patiently for five years to hear you say that to me. Well, you're too damn late. I'm a married woman now, and I don't need to wait for you any longer."

Kaitlin kissed Sydney's flushed cheek. Kaitlin and Kelly squatted beside Sydney as everyone watched Kaitlin intently inspect the nasty purple and red bruise already swelling over Sydney's hip. Kaitlin palpated it gently as Sydney instantly jumped back from her touch. Kaitlin looked up into Sydney's grimacing face and frowned.

"I thought you said you were okay, Syd. That bruise is nasty. Does it hurt to walk?"

Sydney looked down at her hip and frowned. "Not really."

Kaitlin rose to her feet and stood behind Sydney. "Walk for me, Sydney. I want to make sure your hip is okay."

Sydney sighed and walked around the kitchen island as Sabrina, Logan, and Sierra tilted their heads playfully to watch her. Sierra smiled and watched Sydney sway as she walked. "Nice ass, Sydney."

Sydney jerked her head around and glared at the giggling girls. "I've waited for five years for you to notice that, Sierra Vaughn. You're just as slow as your lover."

Kelly leaned across the kitchen island. "At least they appreciate a gorgeous ass when they see one, and yours is exceptionally gorgeous, my love."

Sydney smiled and leaned across the island to meet Kelly's warm lips.

Kaitlin reached into the freezer and pulled out a bag of frozen raspberries. She reached for an elastic wrap and squatted beside Sydney while she was deeply distracted. She placed the frozen fruit against Sydney's bruise and instantly got her attention.

"Ouch! What the hell are you doing, Dr. Bradley? That hurts!"

Kaitlin completely ignored her evil stare as she began securing the bag of frozen berries to her thigh.

Sydney looked down at Kaitlin's handiwork and glared at her. "I've always dreamt of having something sweet attached to my hips, but this is ridiculous!"

They all burst into laughter as Gladys arrived with a steaming Crock-Pot full of mouthwatering chicken cacciatore.

CRBDCRBDCRBD

After the girls locked the door behind them, Kaitlin held Sierra close in her arms. They sat snuggled together amongst a heap of pillows on the living room floor as they stared into the soothing fire. Kaitlin leaned forward to kiss Sierra's bandaged shoulder as she caressed her dolphin pendant between her fingers.

Licorice displayed her compassion by curling up between Sierra's feet with her little black nose buried in her tail.

Kaitlin wove her fingers through Sierra's shiny hair and kissed her soft cheek as she watched the flames dance in her intense eyes. "Are you sure you're okay, darling?"

Tears swelled in Sierra's eyes as she stared transfixed into the fire. "I couldn't get myself up to the surface. I didn't even realize that it was your hand reaching toward me underwater."

Kaitlin held her tight and watched her tears spill over her thick eyelashes. "I know, darling. You were in shock and the water was freezing, so it was hard for you to swim to the surface."

Sierra turned in Kaitlin's arms and looked at her with terrified blue-gray eyes. "I could have drowned. You saved my life, baby. I saw your hand urgently reach for me and I tried so hard to reach you, but I didn't feel like I was moving at all till you grabbed my hand and pulled me out." Sierra dropped her face into Kaitlin's warm neck and sobbed painfully as Kaitlin caressed her back and soothed her.

"You were swimming toward me, sweetheart. It probably felt like you were moving through quicksand because you were so cold. You would have made it to the surface without me, but I'm so grateful that I was able to help you up faster." Kaitlin touched Sierra's gold dolphins and let them slip between her fingers. "Besides, your dolphins will always guide you back to me."

Sierra looked up into Kaitlin's shimmering eyes and touched her lips with her fingertips. She watched the tears well in her eyes as she kissed her soft cheek.

"I was terrified when I saw that Jet Ski slam into you guys. I would have done anything to find you in that water."

Sierra held Kaitlin's damp face in her hands and rested her forehead against hers. "I can't imagine how horrifying that would have been for you, to watch that happen from the dock."

They held each other tight and shed their painful tears as the fire warmed their souls. Sierra leaned her lips toward Kaitlin and kissed her with gentle passion. "You'll always be my hero, Kate. I owe you my life."

Kaitlin kissed Sierra's moist, slightly parted lips. "You've already given me your life and your love, my darling. I just wanted to make sure you were around for the next fifty years to share it with me."

Sierra caressed Kaitlin's cheek and leaned closer, kissing her with soothing passion. Sierra's fears melted into a sea of warmth and safety as Kaitlin tenderly responded to her kiss, taking her face in her hands and nipping gently at her lips, evoking a torrent of heat and need from deep within.

Sierra gasped as Kaitlin's tongue tenderly probed her, drawing on a well of arousal that only she had ever tapped. She reached toward Kaitlin's partially open blouse and grazed the palm of her hand across her erect nipple, reveling in the response that she craved.

Kaitlin gasped with pleasure and reached for Sierra's face. "You've been through a horrible experience, my darling. I don't expect us to make love. I'm happy just to hold you in my arms and know that you're safe."

Sierra rose to her knees and eased Kaitlin down among the cushions and easily loosened her blouse from her jeans. She planted a warm, wet kiss on her slender abdomen and eased herself over her clouded eyes. "We've been through a horrible experience, sweetheart, and I need to feel the beautiful things in my life. I need to feel your loving touch and know that nightmare is truly behind us." Sierra eased herself toward Kaitlin's waiting lips and kissed her with astounding urgency as Kaitlin glided her hands beneath Sierra's sweatshirt and caressed the silky skin of her lower back.

Sierra rose above Kaitlin and urgently guided her to her knees. They faced each other in heated passion as Kaitlin helped Sierra remove her sweatshirt and tank top. She eased Sierra out of her jeans as she sent their clothing flying in disarray around Licorice's sleeping form.

Sierra ached to touch her as she reached forward and glided her fingertips across Kaitlin's strong shoulders and down below each breast. She marveled at her beautiful body as her hands trailed over her hips and down along her parted thighs, never getting enough of the sight or feel of her.

Kaitlin moaned softly and slowly sat back against the couch and guided Sierra to straddle her lap. Kaitlin glided her hands slowly over each of Sierra's curves as she luxuriated in her soft, warm olive skin, touching her as if for the first time. Kaitlin's fingers trailed along the inside of Sierra's thighs and into her curly mound as she closed her eyes and inhaled deeply.

"God, I love your scent."

Sierra leaned toward Kaitlin and kissed her with aching need, taking the warmth and comfort she needed as she plundered the depths of her sweet mouth.

Kaitlin moaned against Sierra's sensuous lips as she carefully eased her fingers along the inside of her thighs and into her pool of wetness.

Sierra held her breath and released a gasping moan as she rocked her hips hard against Kaitlin's probing fingers. They ground rhythmically against each other as Kaitlin gently removed her fingers and glided higher to Sierra's most sensitive spot. Sierra arched her neck and groaned with ecstasy as she rocked with Kaitlin's gentle strokes.

Kaitlin rested one hand on Sierra's silky back and guided her closer as she took her erect nipple deeply into her mouth, taunting it with her wet tongue.

Sierra gripped Kaitlin's head tight against her breast as she felt an undeniable surge of passion build between her thighs. She rocked slower across Kaitlin's fingertip and felt an astonishing tingling sensation spread from her nipples to her belly. Sierra buried her face on Kaitlin's shoulder and moaned erotically, "Oh yes, baby, yes!"

Kaitlin felt a surge of wetness bathe her fingers as she caressed Sierra slower and slower and felt her wondrous shiver cascade across her entire body.

Sierra dug her fingertips into Kaitlin's shoulders and suddenly stopped moving as she screamed, "Oh God, baby! Yessss!" as her knees buckled and she collapsed into Kaitlin's loving arms.

Kaitlin eased Sierra down onto the pillows and lay beside her as she watched her breathing return to its gentle pace. Her fingertips glided across Sierra's left shoulder and traced the outline of her bandage. Sierra's smile glowed brightly as Kaitlin's fingertips found their way to her soft nipples and entwined with her dolphins.

Sierra slowly opened her heavy eyes and luxuriated in Kaitlin's beautiful smile. She swiftly rolled her onto her back and eased herself above her elegant body.

Kaitlin glided her hands onto Sierra's sexy ass and pulled her tight against her as Sierra traced the curve of her neck with her tongue. She flicked her earlobe playfully and whispered seductively in her ear, "Are you wet, baby?"

Kaitlin turned her face and looked into Sierra's ravishing eyes. She entwined her hand in Sierra's and guided it to her mouth. She took Sierra's fingertip and guided it into her mouth as she bathed it with her tongue. Sierra's eyes burst with seething eroticism as she watched Kaitlin's tongue play with her fingertip. "Wet like that?"

Sierra swallowed hard against her dry throat as she replied in a husky voice, "No, wetter."

Kaitlin slowly placed Sierra's hand on her own thigh. She closed her eyes and sighed as she felt Sierra's wet fingertip glide along the inside of her thigh teasingly. Sierra gently separated Kaitlin's thighs and burrowed into her dark mound before plunging deeply into her drenched pool of passion.

Kaitlin arched her neck and groaned with delirious pleasure as Sierra rhythmically entered her and moaned against her neck. "Oh God, baby. You are very, very wet!" Sierra swayed against her and felt her complete surrender to their rhythm as she was filled with an empowering love that moved her even more than their uninhibited passion.

Kaitlin grabbed Sierra's hips harder than she intended as she arched beneath her and screamed out her violent release. She held Sierra tight to her as she floated back down onto the pillows from her euphoric experience of soul-shattering release.

⚙ **14**

Gladys's log home is nestled at the top of a hill, among the gangly spruce and willow trees. She loved the location just a short ten-minute walk from Kaitlin's home and the main estate. On a clear day she could look out her kitchen window and see across the lake to the opposite shore line.

Her home was her pride and joy but nothing gave her the sense of peace and serenity like her rose garden. It was filled with roses of all colors and hybrids. Gladys tended her garden as if each flower were a work of art.

She crouched down and clipped another peach colored rose and placed it gingerly in her basket as if it was made of porcelain. Peach were Kaitlin's favorite. She gathered enough to fill the vases in the office and reception area. She slowly rose to her knees and put away her shears and garden gloves in the shed off her front deck. She gathered her basket and headed down the trail to the main estate.

Gladys placed a Waterford crystal vase filled to perfection with her beloved roses on the main reception desk as she saw Jennifer's mother, Anne, coming out of the library with a puzzled frown. "What's wrong, Anne?"

"I seem to have lost Jennifer, Gladys. Have you seen her lately?"

"No, not since lunch. That's not like her to not let you know where she's headed."

"No, it's not. After we had lunch I told her I was going to lie down for a nap and then start packing for our trip home. She said she felt like staying up and was going to go down to the lake and see what was happening around the dock. After my nap I searched everywhere down by the water and the recreation staff down there said they had not seen Jennifer since lunch either."

Anne stared out the front doors of the resort with a concerned frown.

Gladys reached out and touched her arm. "I'm sure she's fine, Anne. Jennifer knows this place as well as anyone. We'll find her. If she doesn't show up in an hour we'll organize a search party with bloodhounds and horses. When we find her we'll horsewhip her for worrying you like this."

Anne laughed half-heartedly as she turned to Gladys. "I normally wouldn't be so concerned, it's just that she was pretty down about our stay coming to an end. She just loves this place. I hate not knowing where she is when she's feeling so sad." Anne looked down at her watch and blew out a heavy sigh.

"Why don't you go upstairs and get packed while I take a walk up to The Summit and see if I can find our wayward wanderer. I'll take my cell phone and call you as soon as I find her."

"Would you mind terribly, Gladys? That's the only place I did not go looking for her. I really do need to get our stuff packed."

"I don't mind at all. You go ahead and I'm sure I'll find her in no time."

Anne squeezed Gladys's hands. "Thanks, Gladys. You're a doll. Please call me as soon as you find her so I can stop worrying."

"I will, Anne. You go on and I'll go find her."

Gladys stood fifty feet from the crest of The Summit. She slipped her cell phone back into the pocket of her daisy print dress after calling Anne and telling her she found Jennifer.

She made her way beside Jennifer's wheelchair on the viewing platform and looked out on the breathtaking view. Their eyes met briefly as Gladys saw the pain and sadness haze Jennifer's eyes. The tilt of Jennifer's chin and tension in her shoulders dared anyone to challenge her. "You're mothers worried about you. She didn't know where you wandered off to."

"I'm a big girl, Gladys. I can take care of myself around here without having to constantly burden my mother."

"If you're such a big girl then you can watch your mouth and show some respect for the people that love you and care about you."

Jennifer threw Gladys an icy stare before turning her eyes away. Minutes of stony silence passed as Gladys allowed Jennifer to stew in her anger.

"I'm sorry, Gladys. I didn't mean to be such a bitch. I'm just in a lousy mood. I live for the day we come up here and dread the day we have to leave. I never meant to worry my Mom. I didn't expect to sit here so long."

"We hate seeing you go, Jen. This place is never the same without you. And, apology accepted by the way. I hope your mother will be as forgiving as my kind heart."

Jennifer couldn't help but smile as she reached for Gladys's hand and felt warmed by her presence.

"You've dealt with so much pain and heartache in your short, precious life, Jennifer. You've picked yourself up from the ashes and built a life for yourself that far exceeded anyone's expectations. Whenever anyone would say a sympathetic word about your situation Kaitlin would say, 'don't pity that girl or she'll run you over with her wheelchair and squish you like a bug.'"

Jennifer laughed as her eyes misted with tears.

Gladys reached out and touched her pale cheek. "You carry yourself with quiet dignity and unflappable self confidence even though your legs won't. When you dare to indulge yourself in a retrospective moment you startle us into realizing that you are actually human after all."

Jennifer tilted her face into the palm of Gladys's hand. "You're really ruining my lousy mood, Gladys."

Gladys leaned forward and kissed her forehead. "Come on, let's head back and put your mothers mind at ease. And the whole way you can recite all the wonderful things you have to be grateful for in your life. Top of the list should be me of course."

Jennifer spun her chair around and headed off the viewing platform. "Actually, Gladys, top of my list would be my mother."

"I'm glad you realize that, girl. I think she would really like to hear that from you."

CR&OCR&OCR&O

Sierra stood at the base of the front deck and watched Logan referee a game of wheelchair volleyball. She could hear Sabrina try to convince Jennifer that shuffleboard is not just a game for eighty year olds on a cruise ship. Sierra turned as she heard Kelly's laughter and Sydney's encouraging cheers as they tossed a football around with several paraplegic guests.

Sierra climbed the front steps to the resort and walked into the main office in search of Kaitlin. She found Gladys adjusting her bifocals over an accounting ledger and hugged her tightly from behind.

Gladys squealed with delight and hugged Sierra close.

"Am I interrupting something important, Gladys?"

"Hardly, my darling girl. I was just balancing the accounts for this month. I hate numbers. Katie's so good with these columns of numbers but I thought I would give her a break for a change and get started on this months figures."

"Kaitlin really appreciates everything you do around here, Gladys. She loves you dearly and feels you play a major part in keeping her dream alive."

Gladys leaned back in her black executive leather chair and slowly removed her glasses. Sierra leaned her hip against the edge of Gladys's desk.

"I wasn't always so supportive, Sierra. In the beginning I thought Kaitlin and Quinn were taking a big risk in changing an already successful business. I thought they had enough to handle with Quinn's physical limitations and Mary's Alzheimer's disease. One day Kaitlin laid her dream out for me and explained what they hoped to achieve. They were determined and felt the

250

risks were worth it. They said they needed my help and blessing to make it happen. I couldn't argue with that. I would never hold Kaitlin back from accomplishing her dreams. These past three years we have achieved our goals beyond our wildest dreams. We have seen so many physically challenged adults leave here after two weeks, stronger and more emotionally secure. That's what it's all about."

Sierra squeezed Gladys's hand. "It's also about your love and undying support, Gladys. That's where you touch Kaitlin's heart the deepest."

"She's the greatest gift God ever gave me, Sierra. We certainly have had our share of issues to deal with but I'm so grateful that our relationship is as strong as it is."

"You are the reason why Kaitlin is such an incredible woman, Gladys." Sierra looked down at their joined hands and across at all of Kaitlin's photographs. "There's something I've been meaning to ask you, Gladys."

"What is it, Sierra?"

"How did you feel when you first found out that Kaitlin was a lesbian?"

Gladys watched the unease and apprehension erase her smile. There was a depth of sadness etched in Sierra's eyes that bore years of concern. Gladys knew to tread carefully as she wondered about the relationship between Sierra and her parents.

"I started to see the signs when Kate was very young, Sierra. She excelled in academics and sports and loved to spend time with the girls on her sports teams. She never had any interest in dating boys and only spent time with her girlfriends. Then she developed her first crush on a girl in high school and was so distraught by it that she came and talked to me about it. Even though I was aware of the subtle signs I was still very upset by what was happening. I knew that if Kaitlin chose to pursue this path that her life would be so much more difficult. I didn't want that for her. I wanted her to be happily married and have babies. Kaitlin told me that this was not a choice. It was her calling. It took me a while to accept that but then years later Katie met

Quinn and I came to see how happy they were. They even started talking about having babies when Quinn's accident changed their lives forever."

Gladys eased out of her chair and stood before Sierra. "The bottom line is that I love Katie with all my heart. She came to me when she was confused about her sexuality and together we spent years working through it. During that time we grew closer and wiser. Katie has always included me in every aspect of her life and for that I feel blessed. She always knew she could talk to me about anything and it would never affect my love for her."

Gladys took Sierra's chin in her hand and wished she could ease the emotional friction from those shining eyes. "I would bet your parents have an over abundance of love for you, Sierra, that would never change because your path has led you into the arms of another woman. Lucky for me, that woman happens to be my niece."

Sierra's melted into Gladys's hug. "Thanks for sharing your heart with me, Gladys."

"You're very welcome, my darling. Just remember that those that truly love you will always love you."

Sierra hugged Gladys tight and felt encompassed by her strength and love. Sierra looked over Gladys's shoulder, through the huge office bay window and saw Kaitlin walking into the woods behind the resort with a single red rose in her hand.

Gladys turned and followed Sierra's gaze.

"Where's Kate going, Gladys?"

Gladys leaned against the corner of her desk. She stared out among the beautiful spruce and fir trees and watched Kaitlin disappear down the trail. "Katie has always preferred to walk that path alone, but she said if you came looking for her that I could guide you in her direction."

Sierra looked puzzled and concerned as Gladys gently touched her bandaged shoulder. "Go to her, Sierra. She needs you now more than she cares to admit."

Sierra tilted her head as Gladys kissed her cheek. "Follow that path, Sierra, and it will lead you to a thorn in Katie's heart that only you can remove."

Sierra squeezed Gladys's hands and headed for the office door.

"Wait, Sierra." Gladys pulled out two peach roses from a vase on her desk and handed them to Sierra. "Take one for both of us. You'll understand when you get there."

C3&C3&C3&

Licorice bounded alongside Sierra as they followed the path till it ended at an elegant stone archway. The Gothic stones were emblazoned with brilliant colored climbing clematis flowers and clinging ivy. Sierra followed Licorice through the archway and stopped to admire the garden before her. It was like a scene from a children's fairy tale with a carpet of blooming wildflowers and purple lilac bushes embracing a flowing water fountain. Sierra stepped carefully around the bubbling fountain and looked up to see a canopy of crawling ivy. She followed Licorice beyond the lilac bushes and felt her breath catch in her throat. Kaitlin was sitting in an area of well-manicured grass sobbing quietly before four majestic marble headstones. Sierra moved closer and read the inscriptions. One belonged to Kaitlin's father, her grandfather and grandmother. She looked beyond Kaitlin and saw a marble statue of an angel with its arms spread wide perched protectively behind the final headstone. Sierra looked down to the glossy headstone and read the engraving:

Dr. Quinn Sarah Taylor
Your heart will beat forever in us.
1965–2000

Sierra's breath caught in her throat as she quietly set her roses down and eased herself in behind Kaitlin.

Kaitlin instantly jumped and twisted to see the intruder.

253

Sierra pulled her into her arms and held her close. "It's okay, baby. It's just me."

Kaitlin reached up to Sierra's beautiful face and melted into her loving arms. Sierra held her close and rocked her gently as they sat embraced in silence with Quinn's spirit in this ethereal secret garden.

Kaitlin wiped away her own tears and turned to face Quinn's headstone. She took a deep, emotional breath and whispered softly, "It was a year ago today that Quinn died, Sierra." Kaitlin struggled to escape the sobs racking her chest as Sierra held her tightly and allowed years of painful memories to flow from her heart. "I'm sorry, sweetheart," Sierra whispered as she handed Kaitlin a tissue from her pocket. "What have you been thinking as you sat here with Quinn?"

Kaitlin leaned back against Sierra and stared at Quinn's headstone. "I was thinking you would have liked her, Sierra. She was an exceptional woman. I never thought I would love like that again till you came into my life. Even though Quinn has been gone for a year now I still can't help but feel that I'm abandoning her by falling in love again. I vowed to protect her and make her life as meaningful as possible and it felt like we were finally getting there when her pneumonia took that all away. It took Quinn away when I wasn't ready to lose her. I know it's what Quinn wanted but it wasn't what I wanted. I wanted my old Quinn back. After she died I was so angry with her for giving up so easily and leaving me to deal with everything and my grief alone. Once I got past the anger and allowed myself to grieve I spent more time cherishing the good memories. I know that sounds stupid but it's hard to completely let go of someone that was such a big part of my life for so long. Regardless of how difficult things were for us at times. Everyone kept telling me in this past year that I needed to let go and get on with my life. Well, that's easier said than done. A year has passed and I don't miss Quinn any less or love her any less. Does that make sense to you, Sierra?"

"It sure does, babe. A year is not a long time when you are talking about grieving for someone that was such a big part of your life for so long. She was very special to you, Kate. I admire and respect that. I don't ever expect you to lose sight of what Quinn meant to you."

"I was not expecting to fall in love when you stormed onto that dock, Sierra, but it happened. It happened hard and fast. My head may not have been ready for you but that didn't stop my heart from pounding in my chest and cutting off the blood supply to my brain."

Sierra combed her fingers slowly through Kaitlin's hair and tucked a loose strand behind her ear. "I love that affect I have on you."

Kaitlin smiled as she entwined her fingers with Sierra's. "I love what we share, Sierra. Everything about you and us feels so right in my heart. That doesn't mean that I won't still have days where I'll grieve for Quinn and feel that nagging disappointment that I let her down in some way."

"I totally understand, Kate. All I ask is that you share those feelings with me and let me at least be there with you when you're down. I'll never replace Quinn and what you both shared. I can only be me and ask to have a chance to create our own life and memories."

Kaitlin cupped Sierra's chin in her hand and guided her face closer, brushing her lips softly. "That's a deal. That's more than any woman can ask for."

Sierra hugged Kaitlin tight and rocked her in her arms. "That's really touching that Quinn is buried here with your father and grandparents."

"They would have wanted it that way. They all loved Quinn like another daughter and one of her wishes was to be buried here with them in this private garden."

Sierra and Kaitlin stared at the bouquet of red roses adorning Quinn's gravesite as Kaitlin caressed the palm of Sierra's hand with her thumb. A peaceful silence enveloped them as the heady scent of lilac permeated their senses.

"I was sitting here telling Quinn about you before you arrived. She said she really enjoyed your lecture on butterflies and hummingbirds. She always loved to watch butterflies in flight."

Sierra feigned a playful mask of dread and leaned closer to whisper in Kaitlin's ear, "What else did she say about me?"

Kaitlin laughed softly at Sierra's playfulness as they both watched Licorice bounce onto Quinn's headstone and lurch off the other side in hot pursuit of an elusive bee. Kaitlin rested her forehead against Sierra's cheek and smiled. "She thinks you'll make an adequate girlfriend for me."

Sierra recoiled in horror and glared at Quinn's headstone. "Now you listen here, Dr. Quinn Sarah Taylor. I believe I make an awesome girlfriend for Kate, so there."

Two blackbirds squawked loudly in the canopy of ivy above and made a hasty departure. Kaitlin turned to Sierra and laughed at her spooked expression. "Quinn was only playing with you, Sierra. She totally agrees that you're an awesome girlfriend. She just asked that you lower your voice and not be so defensive," Kaitlin teased.

Sierra stuck her tongue out at Quinn's headstone as Kaitlin felt a light, peaceful feeling that she had never experienced in the garden before. Kaitlin smiled at Sierra and kissed her rosy cheek. "Don't worry, my darling, I only told her the good stuff about you, not the bad stuff."

Sierra leaned her face close to Kaitlin's and breathed a sigh of relief. "Wait a minute! What bad stuff?"

Kaitlin couldn't help but laugh at Sierra's playful charm as she tilted her chin up to her and kissed her softly. She stared deeply into her blue eyes and whispered softly, "I love you. Thank you for coming here."

Sierra brushed a stray strand of hair behind Kaitlin's ear. "What happened to your promise of no more surprises, Dr. Bradley? You certainly have a unique way of introducing me to the people you care about."

Kaitlin smiled sheepishly and leaned her forehead against Sierra's cheek. "I was going to tell you about the anniversary of Quinn's death and ask you to come up here with me, but you had been through so much with the Jet Ski accident yesterday that I didn't want to add any more painful memories."

Sierra held her tight and kissed her forehead. "I appreciate you always protecting me, Kate, but next time, ask. Until now you've been responsible for making the decisions for yourself and the ones you love, but it's not like that anymore, Kate. I will expect that from now on you will include me in any decisions that affects either one of us. Understood?"

Kaitlin stared deeply into Sierra's serious eyes and nodded her head obediently. "Understood."

Sierra reached up for Kaitlin's glowing face and gently shook her head. "I want you to share everything that goes on in this incredible mind with me, Kaitlin Bradley. Is that perfectly clear?"

Kaitlin reached up for Sierra's hands and playfully vibrated her voice. "Perfectly clearrrrrrr! Nothing is going to be clear if you don't stop shaking my brain, Sierra."

Sierra laughed and held Kaitlin's face in her hands. She tilted her face toward her and gently kissed her sensuous lips.

Kaitlin looked into Sierra's shimmering blue eyes and ran her thumb across her moist lower lip. "Okay, my tower of emotional strength. I'll try and remember that there is a bright mind and strong, independent will that now shares my life," Kaitlin said with an admiring smile.

Sierra brushed her lips against Kaitlin's, softly, slowly, passionately, till their tongues gently collided and forced a hedonistic gasp from Kaitlin's lips. Sierra leaned her forehead against Kaitlin's and looked shyly over her shoulder. "I hope you don't mind, Quinn, but I find this woman totally irresistible and absolutely delicious," Sierra said impishly.

Kaitlin reached up to caress Sierra's face. "Now that you have met my entire family, when do I get to meet yours?"

Sierra hesitated and looked intently into Kaitlin's eyes. "I'd really like you to meet my parents, Kate. I mentioned to you before that I'm an only child and my parents are both in their early seventies. I love my parents very dearly and they're going to love you to bits, but there is something you should know before you meet them."

Kaitlin watched a wave of sadness darken Sierra's eyes as she quickly looked away. "My parents don't know I'm gay."

Kaitlin was stunned as she guided Sierra's eyes back to her. "Why haven't you told them, my darling?"

Sierra sighed deeply and struggled to explain. "I don't know. They're older, Kate, and they always wanted me to get married and have kids. I knew at a young age that was never going to happen, but I never felt my parents would understand. I just couldn't break their hearts. They always saw Linda as my roommate, and I never felt the need to explain any further."

Kaitlin wiped away Sierra's tears and kissed her softly. "I understand, sweetheart."

Sierra leaned back from Kate and gripped her tighter. "No, you don't understand, Kate. With Linda I never felt the need for my parents to know because I never sensed a permanence in our relationship. With you it's totally different. For the first time in my life I feel complete. I have found the relationship that I always dreamed of. I want my parents to share my life and my love for you. I want them to know about us. I want them to know how much you mean to me."

Kaitlin kissed Sierra's teary face and hugged her tight. "If that's what you want, Sierra, then we will tell them together."

Sierra hugged Kaitlin tight and whispered against her ear, "I love you so much. Your footsteps will always be beside mine."

They held each other tight as Licorice bounced toward them. Suddenly, she dove into the tall grass and crouched low to the ground, then sprinted back behind the headstones after an imaginary prey.

They both laughed at her antics. Sierra brushed bits of grass off her sundress and looked up at Kaitlin with concern. "I had a really nice talk with Gladys before I came up here. I asked her how she felt about your lesbianism."

Kaitlin leaned back and watched the serious frown crease Sierra's forehead. "I bet that was a fascinating discussion."

Sierra picked up a blade of grass and ran it under her thumbnail. "It sure was. She only reinforced how much I've missed by not fully involving my parents in my life."

Kaitlin held Sierra close in her arms and kissed her temple. "We'll change that real soon. Okay, babe?"

"I'd like that, Kate. I'd really like that."

Sierra stayed cocooned in Kaitlin's arms for several minutes before she looked down at her watch. "I hate to end our time here, sweetheart, but Jennifer is heading home in an hour, and Sydney and Kelly said they would be leaving for Toronto this afternoon. And last but not least, the Rainbow Lodge should be dropping your mother off soon for our cookie extravaganza. If we don't beat her to the house, she's liable to think that Licorice is a plump raisin and toss her into the cookie batter."

Kaitlin looked horrified as she quickly jumped to her feet and helped Sierra up. Sierra rested her hand on Kaitlin's tummy. "Hang on one second, sweetheart. There's just one thing I have to do," Sierra said softly.

Kaitlin watched her bend to pick up the two peach roses and step forward to place them across Quinn's grave. Kaitlin watched her reach up and touch the angel's wings.

"One rose is from me, and one is from Gladys. Now, I don't want you to think that I'll be bringing you a rose every time, Quinn. I don't want to make Kate jealous, and when you can appreciate the fact that I'm more than just an adequate girlfriend for Kate, then, and only then, will I consider bringing you more treats."

Kaitlin shook her head and laughed at Sierra's endearing warmth as she watched her kneel down and brush her palm against the glossy marble. She reached forward and slowly traced the letters of Quinn's name and whispered, "Quinn, I hope that together we can keep Kaitlin safe and happy. I'd really like it if you would keep an eye on her from above and I'll watch over her down here. Just make sure that you keep your eyes on all of her and not just certain parts of her gorgeous body because I can tell you for a fact that I have a hard time keeping my eyes off her sexy ass."

Kaitlin reached for Sierra's hand. She brought the palm of her hand to her lips and kissed it tenderly. "I love you," Kaitlin whispered.

Sierra was moved by the intensity of her words as she took her in her arms and hugged her tight. "I love you more than words can say."

Kaitlin took Sierra's hand and entwined their fingers. They walked toward the flowering archway. The blackbirds returned and emitted their high-pitched squawk. Kaitlin stopped and looked up at the hovering birds. "I know, Quinn. I know. She really is something else." Kaitlin gave Sierra an impish smile as they both followed Licorice through the archway. "Sierra, Quinn said to tell you that you have a very sexy ass yourself."

Sierra stopped and looked back at the blackbirds sternly. "Cut that out, Quinn! This ass belongs to Kate and nobody else."

The birds squawked as if in reply as Kaitlin laughed at Sierra's shocked look. "Quinn said it never hurts to look."

They both burst into laughter and followed their little furry, four-legged tour guide down the path hand in hand, heart in heart.

೮೮೨೦೮೩೮೨೦೮೩೮೨೦

The girls all hugged and kissed Jennifer good-bye and helped her mother, Anne, to load their bags into the back of the van. Kaitlin slid the last bag in and turned to Anne. "Have a safe trip home. Please call us when you get there."

"I sure will, Kate. Thank you again for everything. It's always such a pleasure to come up here with Jen and be with you girls. You are all so great with her. You give me a much needed break from her physical care when we are here."

Kaitlin reached out and took Anne's hands in her own. "It's always our pleasure to have you both here, Anne. We love you both very much. You do such a fabulous job with Jen. She would not have done nearly as well since her accident if it wasn't for your love and support. It's a tough job caring for a quadriplegic daughter. It's nice you allow us to take over while you're here so you can get the rest you deserve."

"I love her very much, Kate. I'd do anything to keep her mind and spirits intact. She really enjoys being with you girls and she always finds some woman to flirt with. It's good for her spirits and makes her feel very alive, regardless of her limitations."

"You're great with her, Anne. She is very fortunate to have you."

"Well, you taught me a lot, Kate. You went through so much with Quinn and now you share that knowledge with the rest of us to help us live as normal lives as possible."

"Quinn wanted us to share our experience so we could make others lives easier, Anne. I'm just grateful that it has benefited Jennifer."

"You're a godsend, Kate. You really are." Anne took Kaitlin into her arms and hugged her tight.

Sierra knelt down beside Jennifer's electric wheelchair and gave her a warm smile. "I'm going to miss you, Jen."

Tears clouded Jennifer's eyes as she reached her arm forward and rested it on Sierra's shoulder. "I'm going to miss you, Sierra. I'm going to miss all you guys. It's always a soul-invigorating experience to come to Bradley Bay, and this time you made it very special."

Everyone stopped and watched the warmth between Sierra and Jennifer. Sierra reached up and wiped away Jennifer's tears. "Don't you know it's dangerous to cry in an electric wheelchair, Jen. You could get electrocuted," Sierra teased.

Sierra caressed Jennifer's face. "Are you okay, Jen?"

Jennifer smiled softly and looked into Sierra's eyes. "I'm fine, Sierra. I just want to thank you for treating me like one of the girls and believing in my abilities. You guys are a rare bunch that see what I can do before thinking about what I can't do." Jennifer gently touched the back of Sierra's head with her withered hand. "Thank you for letting me feel the grass and fly a kite. You allowed me to hold a butterfly in my hand when nobody believed I would be able to hold my own head up again. You're a special woman, Sierra, and I'll never forget you."

Tears welled in everyone's eyes as they watched Sierra turn her teary face and kiss Jennifer's arm. Jennifer smiled beautifully as she looked around at the women before her. "You are all very special and hold a special place in my heart."

Jennifer turned to Kaitlin and smiled. "Come here please, Katie."

Kaitlin squatted down on the other side of Jennifer's chair and wiped away her tears. "Nobody has to tell you to treasure every moment of every day that you share with Sierra."

"No, Jennifer, nobody has to tell me that. I learned that lesson a long time ago."

Jennifer reached for Kaitlin's hand and smiled into her emerald eyes. "You both share a very special love, Katie. Enjoy it, cherish it, and nurture it. I've never seen a woman give so much of herself to others as you do, Katie, and now you have been rewarded with a woman who wants to give completely to you. You've been blessed, Katie, and it's about damn time."

Kaitlin leaned forward and kissed Jennifer softly. "Get out of here before you have the entire place in tears," Kaitlin scolded.

Sabrina reached for the hydraulic controls and eased Jennifer's wheelchair onto the ramp.

Michael expertly wheeled himself around the front of the van and pulled up beside Sierra. "Hey, Ms. Knievel, have a safe trip home."

"What? One good-bye wasn't enough for you, fly boy? You would think you were going to miss me."

"Only in your dreams, Evel. Just make sure you email me when you get home. My day would not be complete without a catty comment from you."

"I sure will, Mike. Call me when you get home tomorrow and tell me how boring this place is without me."

Michael rolled his eyes and shook his head. "Dreamer. Get out of here so the rest of us can go about our day in peace."

Jennifer blew him a kiss and gave him her trademark smile that always warmed his heart. "I love you too, fly boy. Always have, always will. Talk to you tonight, Mike. Stay safe."

Michael gave her his devilish wink as Sabrina maneuvered the hydraulics and eased her wheelchair into the van.

"Hey, Mom, can I drive home?"

"Hey, Jennifer, can I ride around in your wheelchair?"

"Not on your life, Mom."

"Dido for the answer to you driving home, darling."

Jennifer waved at all the girls and shouted, "See you guys around Thanksgiving. Keep the home fires burning for me."

Sierra leaned back into Kaitlin's arms and basked in her tender touch. Jennifer looked back at Kaitlin and Sierra one final time. "Sierra, keep that woman smiling. Whatever you're doing to her, it certainly puts a beautiful smile on her face."

Kaitlin and Sierra exchanged a loving smile. Sabrina closed the van doors and signaled for Anne that she was ready to go. The van eased onto the gravel road and headed out of the Emerald City as everyone waved good-bye.

Sydney gently squeezed Kelly's hand and sighed. "I hate teary good-byes. So let's all just get this over with so Kelly and I can get on the road before we all turn into emotional messes."

Kaitlin put her arm around Kelly's shoulders. "How long can you stay in Toronto with Sydney before you have to be back at work?"

Kelly looked toward Sydney. "We'll have four days together before I have to be back. We have a lot of things to talk about in that time. Neither one of us wants to be away from each other, so considering we live three hours apart we need to make some decisions about our relationship and our jobs."

Kaitlin kissed the top of Kelly's blonde curls and hugged her tight. "It always seems like a million decisions in the beginning, but your love will guide you guys along the right path. Try not to let it consume your every waking moment. Do what Sierra and I did. Get in a bathtub with a bottle of wine, and you'll be amazed at what can be accomplished."

Everyone hugged and kissed Sydney and Kelly good-bye. Sydney guided Sierra into her arms and hugged her tight. "Will you be coming home next week?" Sydney said.

Sierra frowned and watched a cloud of sadness blanket Kaitlin's eyes. "Unfortunately I have to, Sydney. I already called the hospital and gave them my two weeks' notice. I have to go back to work those last two weeks of the schedule. It'll give me the chance to pack my things. If you and Kelly decide to stay in Toronto, you know you're welcome to move into my place."

Sydney hugged Sierra tight and kissed her cheek. "Thanks, Sierra. We'll certainly keep that in mind. Now, you take care of yourself and drive carefully back to Toronto. Call me when you get home." Sydney kissed Sierra softly, and then stepped into Kaitlin's arms.

"Good-bye, beautiful. Thanks for finally asking me to drop my pants."

Kaitlin burst into laughter and hugged Sydney tight. Sydney leaned back and pressed her forehead to Kaitlin's. "I love you both very much, Katie. In all the years I have known either one of you, I've never seen you so blissfully happy. I believe that Sierra has finally found the woman who deserves her."

Kaitlin leaned back and held Sydney's face in her hands. She looked into her chocolate brown eyes. "Sierra told me about your feelings for her. This can't be easy for you, Sydney. Thank you for accepting our relationship and giving us your blessing. That means a lot to Sierra and me. You mean a lot to Sierra and me."

Sydney closed her eyes and sighed. "I really am thrilled to see Sierra so nuts about you. I think I knew in my heart that the two of you would really hit it off when you finally had the chance to meet. I guess I just never imagined things would move so quickly. I wouldn't deny that I'm a teeny bit jealous, Kate. Five years ago I would have given anything to have Sierra fall for me the way she has fallen for you, but that just wasn't meant to be. Instead she has blessed me with her friendship, and I couldn't have asked for a greater gift from her. Well, I could have, but I guess she's just blind to my sexual goddess qualities, unlike Kelly, who sees me for the goddess that I am."

Kaitlin burst into laughter as she hugged Sydney close. "I'm so glad to see that Sierra's rejection of your lust has not damaged your ego in any way."

Sydney leaned back and grinned mischievously. "Please! It would take a harem of rejection before my ego was even dented."

Kelly stepped in beside Sydney and rested her hand on her waist. "We should get going, babe."

Kaitlin leaned forward and kissed Sydney's forehead. "You know there will always be a job here at the hospital for you, Sydney, if you feel the urge to leave the big, bad city behind."

Sydney stepped back and smiled at everyone. She felt Kelly's hand slip into hers as she gave her a loving smile. "I actually think I'm ready to leave the city behind if Kelly and this little town will have me."

Kelly squeezed Sydney's hand. "I will certainly have you, but I think we need to call a town meeting to see if this town can handle another deviant lesbian."

Sydney reached up to touch Kaitlin's smiling face. "Take care of Sierra, Katie, and continue to love each other completely."

Kaitlin held Sierra close. "I have dedicated the rest of my life to taking care of Sierra and loving her completely."

They all stood back and watched Sydney toss their bags into the back of her Chevy Blazer. Sydney unlocked the passenger door for Kelly and opened the door, as Kaitlin said, "Take good care of her hip for us, Kelly."

Kelly looked back at the girls with an impish grin. "I plan on taking very good care of both of her hips, Katie. Don't you worry."

Everyone watched Sydney slip into the driver's seat and drive away in a cloud of dust just as the van from the Rainbow Lodge arrived.

Kaitlin helped her mother out of the van and into everyone's loving hugs. Gladys hugged her sister tight as she noticed the lost, bewildered look in her eyes. "It's me, your sister Gladys."

"My sister? Oh, I'm sorry, I didn't know I had a sister."

Regardless of the number of times that Mary had forgotten their names and faces, Gladys never managed to escape the hurt she felt. Gladys watched her look at Kaitlin with the same vague, blank stare. Gladys reached for Kaitlin's hand and pulled her closer. "This is your daughter, Kaitlin."

Mary looked at her with disdain and disbelief. "My daughter. I'm sorry. You must be mistaken. I don't have a daughter."

Everyone looked shocked as Sierra reached for Mary's arm and tried to dispel the unease in the air. "Would you like to go inside and bake some cookies, Mary?"

Mary took Sierra's hand without hesitation and started climbing the stairs. "Oh, yes. We were going to make peanut butter cookies for Katie's lunch. And what is your name?"

Sierra stuck close to Mary as she guided her up the stairs. "My name is Sierra. I'm Katie's friend."

"Oh, how lovely. Do you go to school with Katie?"

"No, I don't go to school with Katie. I live with Katie. Katie is your daughter."

"Well of course she is, Sierra. I know that."

Mary stopped at the top of the stairs and turned back impatiently to Gladys. "Come on, Gladys. We have Christmas dinner to make for all these lovely ladies. Stop being such a tomboy and come inside and help Sierra and me bake peanut butter cookies for Katie," Mary said seriously.

Sierra smiled as she watched Kaitlin squish her face in disgust at the thought of peanut butter cookies.

Gladys shook her head as she turned to Kaitlin. "I can't believe her. One minute she doesn't even recognize us the next minute she's scolding us for not moving fast enough to her wishes."

"That's the mystery of Alzheimer's disease, Gladys. You never know when their memory is going to fade in or out. With or without the disease you know my mother was always a bossy little thing."

Kaitlin guided Gladys up the deck steps and into the sun-filled kitchen. Kaitlin stepped in behind Gladys and whispered playfully, "I believe she called you a tomboy. Now I know where I get it from."

Gladys turned and glared at Kaitlin as she swatted her behind. "Since when have you ever believed a word your mother has said?"

Sierra laughed at Gladys's indignant look and gently secured an apron around Mary. "Tell me, Gladys, did you give Kate a Barbie doll when she was a little girl?" Sierra asked.

Gladys looked puzzled and stood before Sierra. "Yes, I did. As a matter of fact I gave her two."

Kaitlin and Sierra squealed with delight and pointed at Gladys with accusing fingers. "Ah ha! So it's your fault, Gladys, that Kate is a lesbian."

Gladys rolled her eyes with disbelief as Sierra explained the naked Barbie doll story.

Gladys burst into laughter and glared at Kaitlin. "You always said you never put clothes on them because they wanted to feel free and feminine."

Sierra stood before Kaitlin's glowing eyes. "I've heard that line somewhere before."

CBEOCBEOCBEO

Kaitlin and Sierra sat cuddled on the back deck steps after returning Mary to the Rainbow Lodge. Licorice was perched on the railing above them licking her little paws after enjoying a meal of savory salmon. Kaitlin gently touched the new dressing on Sierra's left shoulder.

Sierra tilted her face up to Kaitlin's and shook her head. "I just about died when Mary dumped the jar of peppercorns in the cookie batter thinking they were chocolate chips."

Kaitlin glided her hands onto Sierra's tummy and held her tight. "I guess that's better than mistaking Licorice for a raisin." They both looked up and watched Licorice repeatedly clean her furry little face.

Sierra turned slightly in Kaitlin's arms and looked at her sternly. "I couldn't believe it when Mary insisted on sprinkling the cookie sheets with cinnamon. You just leaned over the cookie sheet and swirled your fingers through the mounds of cinnamon and told Mary it was your most favorite spice in the whole world and encouraged her to keep sprinkling." Kaitlin giggled sweetly and leaned her forehead against Sierra's. "And then you made me crazy with desire for you when you started licking your finger and Mary told you to be nice and share with me," Sierra said, in animated shock.

Kaitlin stared into Sierra's glistening eyes. "Oh sure, I made you crazy. How do you think I felt when Mary told me to share with you and you came right up to me and took my finger out of my mouth and put it in yours?"

Sierra giggled shyly and buried her face in Kaitlin's soft neck. "Cinnamon tastes so delicious on your fingers and on your lips," Sierra said seductively. Kaitlin turned her face and stared at Sierra's moist lips. Sierra raised her face and leaned toward Kaitlin's wanton eyes and claimed her lips with ardent, burning desire.

Sierra sighed and nestled deeper into Kaitlin's arms. Kaitlin ran her fingers through Sierra's shiny hair and held her tight. "Darling, would you say that this is coddling and pampering?"

Sierra smiled and turned to face Kaitlin. "I sure would."

Kaitlin leaned her lips against Sierra's cheek. "I thought that first night on the dock you said you would never want that from me."

Sierra stiffened and spun in Kaitlin's arms, swiftly pinning her down to the deck. "You were so mean that first night we met, Kaitlin Bradley."

Kaitlin laughed with guilt and reached up to hold Sierra's stern face. "I certainly got your attention though, didn't I, Sierra Vaughn?"

Sierra scowled menacingly and jerked Kaitlin's zipper down on her shorts in one swift movement. "Yeah, well, Dr. Bradley, I think I'd like to get your attention at this very moment."

Kaitlin raised her face closer to Sierra's sensuous lips and whispered, "What if I get splinters, my insatiable little cinnamon lover?"

Sierra grinned from ear to ear and reached into Kaitlin's Calvin Kleins. "I'll use my teeth to remove them," Sierra threatened.

They both burst into laughter and raced each other up the spiral staircase in a fit of flying clothes to dive under the covers and hungrily quench their burning desire for one another.

⚙ **15**

Kaitlin hurried down the resort steps, rushed toward Sierra's beaming smile, and took her into her arms. "Where have you been all afternoon, sweetheart? I was worried about you. Everyone I asked about you said you were planting a garden. Now what the heck have you been up to, my adventurous girl?"

Sierra's eyes danced with mystery and excitement as she guided Kaitlin's face closer and kissed her deeply. "I finished all my assigned tasks for the afternoon and then I went on a secret mission. Come with me please, Kate. There's something that Licorice and I want to show you."

Sierra entwined her hand into Kaitlin's and called to Licorice as she wordlessly guided them both into the woods behind the resort.

Kaitlin had to move faster to keep up with Sierra's exuberant steps, laughing at her youthful enthusiasm. Licorice bounded along the path ahead of them as Kaitlin turned to look at Sierra's ecstatic smile. "Are you going to give me a clue about your surprise, my precious darling, or is this more like a show and tell thing?"

Sierra squeezed Kaitlin's hand. "Definitely a show and tell thing. Licorice wouldn't want me to ruin our surprise by giving you any clues so we decided just to show you." Kaitlin obediently followed Sierra to the stone archway as Licorice dashed in before them and bounced up onto the fountain ledge. Sierra looked up at Kaitlin and guided her around the fountain and stopped her before Quinn's grave.

Kaitlin blinked back tears as she stood in total disbelief. Rows of marigolds and petunias bordered Quinn's grave with bunches of lilac branches draped across her headstone. A plate of sliced oranges sat beneath her name as a menagerie of monarch and thistle butterflies fluttered above the newly planted butterfly garden. Kaitlin stepped closer and watched a beautiful deep maroon and black butterfly with baby blue spots flutter atop Quinn's headstone.

Sierra was mesmerized by Kaitlin's reaction as she squeezed her hand and whispered softly, "That's a Mourning Cloak butterfly. I haven't seen one since I was a little girl. It seems so appropriate that it would come to visit us here with Quinn."

Kaitlin turned to Sierra with tender eyes. "It's so beautiful, sweetheart. Quinn would be so tickled to see all these butterflies floating around her."

Sierra leaned into Kaitlin's arms. "She already knows. She helped me plant the flowers. She admitted to not having much of a green thumb, but I put her and Licorice to work anyway."

Kaitlin laughed sweetly and held Sierra tight. "You're so incredible, my darling Sierra. This butterfly garden is so beautiful, and I can't believe all the gorgeous butterflies already here."

Sierra took Kaitlin by the hand. "Let me show you the front row seat I reserved for us to watch the show." Kaitlin turned around and saw a cozy blanket spread out with a picnic basket beneath a huge willow tree. Kaitlin was speechless as Sierra guided her to the inviting blanket. Sierra reached inside the picnic basket and jumped back with fright as Licorice jumped out and raced behind the willow tree. Sierra clutched at her heart as Kaitlin laughed softly.

Sierra glared at Licorice's little face peeking out from behind the tree trunk. "Licorice! Cut that out! You scared me to death."

Kaitlin carefully lifted the basket lid and peeked inside. "It looks safe in there now, my darling. No more surprises."

Sierra glared at Kaitlin and reached inside the basket. "It seems that both my girls love to surprise me."

Licorice cautiously sauntered into Kaitlin's lap. Kaitlin picked her up and whispered in her ear, "I think we're in trouble, Licorice. We'd better behave ourselves, or Sierra will not feed us any supper from her delicious smelling picnic basket."

Sierra pulled out a plastic container filled with cheese, crackers, fresh strawberries and green grapes. She picked out a plump, juicy strawberry and popped it into Kaitlin's mouth. "Getting you two to behave yourselves may be a lifelong venture for me," Sierra said, with an exasperated sigh. Kaitlin devoured the delicious fruit and pouted beautifully at Sierra. Sierra gave her a stern look and leaned toward her pouting lips. She barely brushed her lips against Kaitlin's and whispered, "A venture I'm thrilled to embark on."

Kaitlin released Licorice as she guided Sierra closer and kissed her with insatiable hunger.

Sierra hesitantly sat back beside Kaitlin and pulled out tuna croissant sandwiches, homemade chocolate chip cookies, and white linen napkins. Sierra spread their dinner before them and luxuriated in Kaitlin's company as they devoured their delicious meal. They sat back and watched the butterflies adorn Quinn's memory as they barely fluttered out of Licorice's reach.

Kaitlin and Sierra returned the picnic basket to their home and changed into warmer clothes before heading to the main office to give Sabrina and Logan a break for the evening.

Kaitlin followed Sierra into the office and saw Gladys rearranging the bouquet of peach roses on her desk. "Those are my most favorite color, Gladys."

Gladys wheeled around and squealed with delight as she hugged Kaitlin and Sierra tight.

"Did Sabrina and Logan take off already?" Kaitlin said.

"They sure did. Sabrina planned a romantic dinner for Logan at the Sheraton Hotel in town. I told her to rent a room for the night. You know our Sabrina. She looked at me like I was a genius and the only woman on the face of this earth to ever have such an idea." Gladys rolled her eyes as Kaitlin and Sierra smiled at their romanticism.

"Sabrina got right on the phone and called the Sheraton and made a reservation for the night. She had me keep Logan busy while she went home and packed them an overnight bag and hid it in the back of their Cherokee. She gave me the number to the hotel and their room number. Logan is in for a nice surprise tonight.

"Speaking of nice surprises, Sierra, how did your little mystery go?"

Sierra's eyes filled with excitement as she reached for Kaitlin's hand and told Gladys all about the success of Quinn's butterfly garden and Kaitlin's shocked reaction. She told her about Licorice's surprise attack and their romantic picnic.

Kaitlin's pager vibrated at her hip. She quickly snatched it off her belt and frowned. Sierra and Gladys watched her reach for the cordless phone on her desk.

"What's wrong, sweetheart?" Sierra said with alarm.

Kaitlin punched in several numbers and turned to Sierra and Gladys's concerned faces. "It's the Rainbow Lodge. What sort of mischief do you think my mother has gotten into now?" Gladys rolled her eyes while Sierra leaned closer to Kaitlin. "This is Dr. Kaitlin Bradley. I believe I was paged."

Sierra and Gladys listened intently for several minutes as Kaitlin leaned forward and buried her face in her hand.

"She did what? Jesus! I'll meet you guys in the emergency department. No, it's all right. Short of hiring someone to shadow her twenty-four hours a day, there's not much we can do to stop her creative thoughts, so please don't apologize. I appreciate you guys paging me right away. I'll be at the hospital in fifteen minutes." Kaitlin hung up the phone and dropped her face in her hands with groaning frustration.

Sierra reached for her head and caressed her hair. "What is it, babe? What happened to Mary?"

Kaitlin raised her face and shook her head in disbelief. "It appears that my mother saw a ladybug fly under her cast. She became terribly worried that the ladybug's suitor, Mister Bug, would miss her, so she tried to shoo her out with a spoon and completely wedged the spoon under her cast."

Sierra and Gladys failed miserably at concealing their laughter as Kaitlin glared at them both.

"The only way to get that damn spoon out and free this mystical ladybug is to cut Mary's cast off and reapply a new one. She's going to need another set of X-rays to make sure she didn't displace her fracture. She's refusing to have anyone touch her arm unless I'm there." Kaitlin ran her hands through her hair in frustration and exhaled a deep breath. "This is terrible, Gladys. Sierra and I were going to send you home early for a change and run things ourselves tonight. Now I have to leave and ask you and Sierra to keep an eye on things."

Gladys reached for Kaitlin's hand and smiled warmly. "Don't be silly, Katie. I'd be happy to stay here with Sierra. You go along and take care of my little sister for me."

Sierra reached for her troubled face. "Gladys and I will be fine, sweetheart. You take care of Mary. She needs you right now."

Kaitlin massaged her pulsating temples and sighed deeply. "That would mean a lot to me, darling, if you help Gladys. I'll go and take care of Mary and her newly adopted ladybug."

Sierra laughed softly. "Go take care of Mary for us, sweetheart, and I'll ask Gladys to tell me all about your childhood."

Kaitlin kissed Gladys's cheek. "I love you, and I'll be back as soon as I can."

Gladys hugged Kaitlin tight and kissed her face. "I love you too, Katie. Drive carefully and give your mother a hug for me."

Kaitlin scoffed and turned to Sierra. "I'd like to give my mother more than just a hug from all of us. I'm going to ground her from any ladybug watching for the next month." Kaitlin leaned toward Sierra and kissed her tenderly. "And you, young lady, I love with all my heart, and I promise to make this up to you."

Sierra ran her thumb along Kaitlin's moist lower lip and smiled seductively. "That's one promise I intend to make you keep, my sweet Kate."

Kaitlin smiled and kissed Sierra. She stepped back and waved as she rushed out the main entrance.

こうとうこうとうこうとう

After helping assist the quads and paraplegic guests into bed Sierra and Gladys settled into the front office with a tray of tea and shortbread cookies.

Gladys reached for Sierra's hand and smiled deeply. "I've never seen Katie so happy as she is around you, Sierra. You're very special to Katie and to all of us."

Sierra leaned forward to kiss Gladys's cheek. "I love her and all of you very much, Gladys. You are all my special family, and I'm ecstatic about being a part of Bradley Bay."

Gladys's took a cautious sip of her steaming tea. "You're the spark in Katie's eyes, Sierra. She's absolutely radiant from your love."

"I've never loved a woman like I love Kate. I look forward to nurturing that love for the rest of our lives."

Gladys looked at Sierra with a puzzled frown. "Sierra, do you really think those naked Barbie dolls had anything to do with Katie being a lesbian?"

Sierra burst into laughter as Gladys covered her mouth with her hand and giggled uncontrollably.

こうとうこうとうこうとう

Hours later the cordless phone on Kaitlin's desk startled the calm in the room. Sierra set the photo album down and reached for the phone. "Bradley Bay. This is Sierra, how may I help you?"

Kaitlin felt an incredible warmth cascade across her chest as she answered, "Hello there, my sexy, blue-eyed darling. What sort of services are they offering at Bradley Bay these days?"

Sierra held the phone close, wishing it were Kaitlin she was holding. "Hello, baby. For you, I'm running a special this evening that includes a bubble bath and a full body massage. However, that offer expires by midnight tonight."

"Well, then, I better hurry since I only have one hour till my special expires. And I hope that I am the only woman you're offering this special to, Ms. Vaughn?"

"The one and only woman is what you are to me, Dr. Bradley."

"What are you and Gladys doing, sweetheart?"

"Gladys retired to bed about thirty minutes ago. But first she told me some wonderful stories of your childhood. I particularly liked the one about you giving your little sixth-grade classmate, Mary Ellen Parker, a piece of peanut brittle as a token of your affection and watching as she bit into the sweet treat and broke her front tooth."

Kaitlin burst into laughter at her fond memories. "Ah, Mary Ellen Parker, my first love. She would always kiss me on the cheek when I helped her with her homework. That was one girl that I loved to tutor."

Sierra could hear Kaitlin remind her Mother to turn off her bathroom light. "What are you doing now, darling?" Kaitlin said.

Sierra readjusted herself in her chair. "The receptionist took over at the front desk at eight so Gladys and I went around and made a final check on everyone and tucked everyone in. We settled into the front office with tea and cookies and all of Gladys's photo albums." Sierra could hear Kaitlin groan with disbelief. "I've been sitting in your office chair flipping through the albums for the past hour. You were absolutely beautiful growing up, Kate. Didn't you ever have an awkward stage, or were you just born beautiful?"

"Your love for me has made you biased, my darling. Hang on one second Sierra while I help my Mother under her covers."

Sierra hugged the phone close. "How are you, sweetheart? How is Mary?"

"Mary is just fine. However, I don't think that the orthopedic staff will ever have such an entertaining experience of removing a cast as they did with Mary. She insisted that they be extremely careful with their cast cutter so as not to injure the precious ladybug. She was absolutely sure that Mister Bug was somewhere in the room watching all of them as they worked to free his little ladybug. She assured them that Mister Bug would not hesitate to sue if they injured his little mistress."

Sierra burst into unsuppressed laughter as Kaitlin felt her warmth deep in her soul.

"We finally managed to remove the cast and spoon that of course hid no ladybug, but Mary had everyone convinced that the ladybug flew off her finger and into the arms of her suitor. Her story was so animated and vivid that she had the entire staff mesmerized by her imagination. Mary certainly gave them a lesson on the imagination of an Alzheimer's patient.

"The X-rays showed that Mary's fracture is healing nicely and she didn't do anything to injure her arm any further, thank goodness. She's now safely in her bed and feels reassured that the ladybug has been returned safely to her suitor, Mister Bug."

Sierra laughed sweetly as Kaitlin felt embraced by her warmth. "She insists on reading me a bedtime story, so I hope she will drift off soon. I should be home within the hour. Why don't you climb into our bed, sweetheart, and I'll check with the front desk to make sure everything is okay when I get home?"

Sierra closed the photo album gently and set the book in her lap. "That sounds great, sweetheart. Please drive carefully coming home, and I want you to know that I love you very much."

"I love you too, my darling. See you soon." They both said good-bye as Sierra gathered all the albums and tucked them under her arm before turning out the lights.

ᲝᏳᎾᏳᏰᎾᏳᏰᎾᏳᏰᎾ

Kaitlin slipped out of her dress jacket and smiled as she saw Sierra huddled on top of their duvet dressed only in her white, terry cloth robe. P.J. was snuggled under her arm, and Licorice was nestled behind her bent knees.

She looked so fragile huddled like a child, but Kaitlin knew that beneath that array of chestnut hair was a keen mind and spectacular personality, both fueling a strength and determination that continually astounded her. Kaitlin walked softly to the edge of their bed, leaned into Sierra's warm cheek, and kissed her gently.

Sierra quickly awakened and turned her head. She squealed with pure joy and hugged Kaitlin tight. "Baby, you're home!"

Licorice yawned and stretched as she gave Kaitlin an evil look for disturbing her peaceful haven.

Kaitlin kissed Sierra's warm lips. "I'm finally home, and I'm so happy to see you. However, I see that you've found another woman to keep you company while I was away."

Sierra laughed against Kaitlin's cool cheek. She watched Licorice rise and stretch like a Slinky before she sauntered to the foot of the bed and curled up at Sierra's feet.

"That'll teach you for sending me to bed alone," Sierra uttered playfully.

They both laughed as Kaitlin touched Sierra's chin and guided her lips closer. Their lips met softly, tenderly as Sierra entwined her hands into Kaitlin's hair and kissed her with burning passion.

Sierra leaned her forehead against Kaitlin's and whispered against her moist lips, "How was your bedtime story?"

Kaitlin settled on the edge of their bed against Sierra's cuddly body. "It started off as Jack and the Beanstalk until Mary's vivid imagination took over, and then it turned into a Stephen King horror flick." Sierra laughed and entwined her fingers into Kaitlin's hand. "I told Mary to stop or I'd end up having nightmares tonight."

Sierra saw the smile on Kaitlin's face and the sadness brimming in her eyes. "I can't imagine how difficult this must be for you, Kate. You lost your mother to her career, then to her alcoholism and finally to Alzheimer's. It has to tear your heart out from time to time to deal with her in the capacity of a child."

Kaitlin stared down at their entwined hands. She brought Sierra's hand to her lips and kissed her knuckles. "Some days are worse than others. My relationship with my mother has always been distant and superficial. I often thought she kept in touch with me out of some sense of obligation rather than a maternal want or need. When my father died we actually became quite close for a while, which I think surprised us both. Then she started drinking heavily and I lost her again. I ran out of ways to help her. I ran out of energy to fight for her. But, I never ran out of love for her. Then when she was diagnosed with Alzheimer's she deteriorated so fast and become very childlike. For the first time in her life she needed me. I vowed to be there for her. As difficult as our relationship has been and as difficult as it is to see her like this, she is still my mother and I love her dearly."

Sierra leaned up on one elbow and touched Kaitlin's face. "You are an exceptional woman, Kaitlin Bradley. You're mother is blessed with a loving, devoted daughter."

"Well, I don't think she felt so blessed when I was telling them to cut the cast off and she was terrified that I had given them permission to cut off her arm."

They both laughed, as Sierra said, "Was everything okay when you checked in at the front desk?"

"Peaceful and calm."

Sierra stared into Kaitlin's emerald eyes and hooked her finger into her elegant yellow blouse. "Come here and kiss me, you gorgeous woman."

Kaitlin leaned slowly toward Sierra's lips and teased her with her tongue. Sierra gasped against Kaitlin's parted lips and leaned closer to kiss her with aching need. Sierra slowly released each button on Kaitlin's blouse as Kaitlin smiled against her sensuous lips.

"I'll just grab a quick shower. I promise to be back in your arms in ten minutes."

Sierra smiled seductively and kissed Kaitlin's nose. "Hurry back, my love, or I'll just have to start without you."

Kaitlin grinned mischievously and glided her tongue along Sierra's pouty lower lip. "That I would love to see," Kaitlin whispered hoarsely. She kissed her with a playful, toying kiss before heading into the bathroom.

Kaitlin returned to find Sierra's robe draped over their footboard and her naked, slender shoulders barely covered by the soft, pink duvet. She eased herself beneath the cool sheets and slipped into Sierra's outstretched arms. Kaitlin nuzzled into Sierra's silky neck and whispered in her deep sultry voice, "God, darling, you are so soft and warm."

Sierra caressed Kaitlin's cool skin and smelled the fresh scent of soap as she held her tight against her. "I missed you so much, babe. How am I going to survive without you when I have to go back to work for those two weeks?" Sierra said sadly.

Kaitlin raised herself up on one elbow. She looked into Sierra's moist eyes and glided her fingertips across her warm cheek. "I was wondering how I was going to be able to even breathe without you," Kaitlin whispered

Sierra reached up, tucked a damp strand of hair behind Kaitlin's ear, and caressed her face. "I was wondering, sweetheart, if you could take some time away from Bradley Bay and come join me in Toronto on my days off? I don't expect you to be there when I'm working, but I can't imagine spending a whole two weeks away from you."

A huge smile burst across Kaitlin's face. "I thought you'd never ask. I was so afraid that Licorice was going to be your choice of company in Toronto over me."

Sierra guided Kaitlin to lie on top of her. "You silly girl. How would I ever train Licorice to make me shiver like you do?" Sierra reached for Kaitlin's face and glided her fingertips across her chin. "You are my shining light, Kate, and there is no one who will ever take your place."

Kaitlin leaned over Sierra's waiting lips and kissed her with an urgent hunger. Kaitlin pressed herself intimately against Sierra and rocked gently as she smiled into her passionate eyes. "You're leaving me on Sunday and have to work Monday and Tuesday. Why don't I leave early Wednesday morning and you can introduce me to your big-city bed when I arrive?"

"That would be wonderful! My big-city bed can't wait to meet you."

Kaitlin whispered hoarsely against Sierra's waiting lips, "Consider it a date. Now tell me, my precious cinnamon girl, did you start anything without me?"

Sierra smiled coyly and touched her fingertip to Kaitlin's warm, wet tongue. "I sure did. Shall I show you?" Sierra offered with uninhibited sensuality.

Kaitlin's eyes blazed with desire as she seductively caressed Sierra's fingertip with her tongue. "I would love to see you touch yourself, Sierra. Please do that for me."

Sierra slowly withdrew her wet finger from between Kaitlin's lips. She eased her hand down between them and ran her wet finger over her own erect nipples as the desire in Kaitlin's eyes aroused an aching lust in her. Kaitlin eased herself to lie beside Sierra as Sierra returned her finger to Kaitlin's mouth and toyed with the tip of her tongue.

Kaitlin took Sierra's finger deeply into her mouth and groaned with aching need.

Sierra slowly separated her own thighs as she removed her wet finger and glided her hand over her flat belly. Her eyes never left Kaitlin's as she watched her arousal darken her eyes to a deep sea green.

Kaitlin watched in erotic amazement as Sierra slowly circled her own navel before trickling her fingers through her dark mound and into her velvety folds. Sierra's uninhibited passion ignited Kaitlin's arousal as it burned like liquid fire throughout her belly.

Sierra closed her eyes and basked in her own wetness as she felt Kaitlin's warm breath against the inside of her thigh. She slowly caressed herself as she felt Kaitlin guide her hand lower and deep within herself. Sierra moaned and rocked against her own fingers as a surge of ecstasy mushroomed in her groin. Sierra ached for Kaitlin's touch as she removed her fingers and felt Kaitlin's hand entwine around her wet fingers.

Sierra slowly opened her eyes as she felt Kaitlin's warm breath ease closer and her tongue replace the path of her own fingers. Sierra arched her back and groaned erotically as she rested her hands on Kaitlin's head and guided her tongue deeper. Sierra swayed and squirmed as her surge of ecstasy climbed higher and higher. She hungered to reach that pinnacle of rapture, begging Kaitlin with the gyration of her hips for more of her agonizing delight.

Kaitlin felt Sierra's dire need as she rolled her tongue lightly around and around, as she felt Sierra suddenly stop moving and her undeniable shiver of ecstasy rocked the bed.

Sierra gently grabbed Kaitlin's head and held her perfectly still as she arched her back and shouted, "Yes, baby, yes! Oh God, I'm coming!" A barrage of tiny gold lights erupted and faded before Sierra's closed eyes like the trail of a falling star.

Kaitlin luxuriated in Sierra's extraordinary release as she glided her fingers into her gripping center.

Minutes later, Kaitlin slowly removed her fingers and eased herself into Sierra's arms. She nuzzled against her warm neck as she basked in her euphoric smile.

"Wow! What an amazing trip! I'm sure I circled as high as the Polaris star."

Kaitlin kissed Sierra's flushed cheek. "Ummm. I certainly enjoyed your trip myself."

Sierra turned her face and tasted their intimacy on Kaitlin's heady lips.

Kaitlin eased herself onto her stomach and reached for a tissue on their bedside table to dry her damp chin.

Sierra pulled the covers back from her gorgeous body and eased herself onto Kaitlin's back. Kaitlin moaned softly and stretched her arms above her head as Sierra provocatively swayed against her bottom and whispered into her ear, "You have such a sexy ass, Dr. Bradley."

Kaitlin eagerly separated her thighs as Sierra ran her palms over her strong shoulders and down her arms till their fingers entwined. She gently swayed between Kaitlin's thighs and covered her shoulders and back in warm, wet kisses. Sierra kissed Kaitlin's flushed cheek and tickled her ear with her tongue. "Now, this is how a back rub should be given," Sierra whispered seductively.

Kaitlin groaned and arched higher against Sierra. She basked in the scintillating sensation of Sierra's breasts brushing against her back. "Please, Sierra. I want to feel you deep inside me."

Sierra prevented Kaitlin from rolling over as she pinned her back down onto the bed and basked in their playful laughter. Sierra entwined her fingers into Kaitlin's and whispered into her ear, "Don't move, missy. You're my prisoner of love." Sierra released her hands and glided her fingers down Kaitlin's warm back. Her fingers lightly traced the contours of her sexy ass and along the inside of her parted thighs. She gently bent Kaitlin's leg higher and felt her arch her bottom toward her. Sierra molded her hand over the silky smooth curves of Kaitlin's bottom and glided between her folds and deeply into her pool of wetness.

Kaitlin gasped in aching pleasure as she reached for a pillow and clutched it beneath her chest. She gently rocked her hips to the steady rhythm of Sierra's fingers as she felt a tingling surge that cascaded toward her chest. Kaitlin was surrounded by Sierra's heady scent and filled with a passion that astounded her.

Sierra knew how to drive her to that ragged peak and each time strove to guide her there differently and make her hang longer. She coaxed Kaitlin's sighs and moans with gentle thrusts till she knew Kaitlin needed more.

Sierra glided her fingers higher and found Kaitlin's engorged center, caressing her lightly in her own wetness.

Kaitlin buried her face in the pillow and groaned with tense pleasure as Sierra rested her forehead against Kaitlin's back and inhaled her womanly scent. She gently glided over Kaitlin's erect center as she felt her suddenly tense beneath her.

Kaitlin felt her imminent eruption of ecstasy as she gently swayed against Sierra's soft fingertip. A stairstep surge of heat washed over her as she felt the air rush from her lungs and heard a deep, resonant cry that sounded vaguely like her own voice.

Sierra gently eased herself to lie beside Kaitlin as she saw the tears squeeze from beneath her dark eyelashes. Sierra guided

Kaitlin into her arms and hugged her tight. She reached up and wiped away Kaitlin's tears as she whispered softly, "Are you okay, baby?"

Kaitlin nuzzled deeper into Sierra's chest. "I've never experienced such astounding lovemaking as I do with you, Sierra."

Sierra brushed a stray strand of hair away from Kaitlin's moist eyes. She leaned toward her face and kissed her damp cheek. "See, it's not so bad being married to a big-city girl, is it?"

Kaitlin took a deep breath and glided her hand over Sierra's warm breasts. "No, actually, this big-city girl makes quite an adequate girlfriend."

Sierra looked horrified as she grabbed for Kaitlin's hands and whipped her onto her back. She jumped to her knees and straddled Kaitlin's hips as she grabbed a pillow and began pummeling her into a fit of laughter.

Kaitlin begged for forgiveness and finally rolled Sierra onto her tummy and pinned her to the bed. Sierra giggled against the mattress as Kaitlin pinned her hands above her head and forced her thighs apart with her knee. Kaitlin rested intimately between Sierra's thighs and whispered menacingly against her ear, "Who's the prisoner of love now, my sweet Sierra?"

Sierra moaned with unadulterated ecstasy as she arched her hips and pressed her bottom firmly against Kaitlin's soft mound. "I've been your prisoner of love since the moment you branded those emerald green eyes into my soul."

Kaitlin released Sierra's hands as Sierra turned her face and looked into Kaitlin's loving eyes. Kaitlin guided Sierra onto her back and eased herself over her as their lips met in a breathtaking kiss of undying love.

ഌഇഌഇഌഇ

Kaitlin was jarred from a deep sleep as she felt Sierra thrash against her. She quickly reached for the bedside light and moved back to Sierra, who was covered in a fine sweat and moaning painfully.

"I can't reach you, baby! No, I can't see your hand. I can't breathe, baby! I can't see your hand. Help me, Kate! Help me!"

Kaitlin grabbed Sierra's shoulders and gently shook her and called her name till her eyes flew open in fright.

Sierra stared blankly at Kaitlin and struggled to fill her lungs with air.

"You're okay, darling. I'm here with you. Here, take my hand. Feel me beside you. You're not underwater anymore. You're safe here with me," Kaitlin said reassuringly.

Huge tears spilled onto Sierra's cheeks as she buried her face in Kaitlin's neck. "I'm so sorry, baby. I dreamt I was still underwater, and I couldn't see your hand anymore." Sierra sobbed against Kaitlin's cheek as Kaitlin held her tight in her arms and rocked her gently.

"You're okay, my darling. I have you, and I'm never going to let you go. You will always feel my hand in yours."

Sierra sniffed softly and kissed Kaitlin's face. "And I will always see your footsteps beside mine," Sierra whispered warmly.

They held each other tight as Kaitlin gently caressed Sierra's damp face. They talked into the wee hours of the morning till Sierra's traumatic memories ebbed from her soul and they slipped into a peaceful sleep cocooned in the safety of each other's arms.

CROCROCRO

Their precious days together flew by quickly. Every responsibility and chore became a joyful event for Kaitlin and Sierra as Sierra quickly learned the multitude of responsibilities involved in running Bradley Bay.

Kaitlin took Sierra away at every opportunity she had to show her the highlights of living in northern Ontario in an attempt to reinforce the wonderful reasons for her move to Bradley Bay.

Sierra filled Kaitlin's days with laughter and her nights with ecstasy, making her realize she already had a list of wonderful reasons to move without knowing anything about the town. Their relationship was blissful and unconditional except for their unspoken sadness. Neither one dared to share the pain they carried for the gut-wrenching moment when they would have to say good-bye.

CRUCRUCRU

Sierra's last night at Bradley Bay was filled with the festive music and roaring bonfire of her huge going away party. The outpouring of love overwhelmed Sierra as she walked among the crowd with Kaitlin.

Sierra and Kaitlin finally found a peaceful moment to be away from the jubilant, playful crowd and slipped down to the dock. They settled onto the cushioned bench where they had spoken for the first time a mere two weeks before.

Sierra watched Kaitlin intently lean forward and follow the path of the moonbeam across the lake. The wind gently played with her silky hair and blew it back from her saddened eyes. Her hands entwined slowly, repetitively, as Sierra watched the muscles tense in her jaw.

Kaitlin struggled to control the slight, emotional twitch of her pouty lower lip as she fought back the tears she has been battling for days.

The dock lights gleamed off her moist, emerald eyes as Sierra reached for her chin and guided her eyes to her. They stared into each other's eyes until Kaitlin had to force herself to look away. Sierra reached for her face one more time, only to have Kaitlin move her face away from her reach.

Sierra stared at her tense profile and ran her fingers into Kaitlin's hair. "Do you want to talk about it, babe, or should we continue to ignore our pain as we have done for the past several days?" Sierra said softly.

Kaitlin continued to stare at a fixed point across the lake, struggling to control her whirlwind of raw emotions. "I'd prefer to pretend our pain doesn't exist and just pretend that you're not leaving me tomorrow morning, if you don't mind. I know it sounds childish, Sierra, but I can't deal with this pain, and I can't deal with you leaving. I've been trying hard all week to prepare myself for this. I want to make this as easy as possible for you without you seeing how it's killing me inside."

Sierra jumped off the bench in a flurry of anger and knelt before Kaitlin. She took her teary face in her hands and stared into her distraught face. "Damn you, Kate! You're not the only one who's hurting here. How easy do you think this is for me to leave you? Do you think for one second that this is any easier for me than it is for you? I've tried for days to talk to you about what we're both feeling, and instead you shut me out and chose to deal with your pain alone. I've respected that, Kate, and given you your space, and I've been so afraid to tell you how I feel for fear of alienating you any further. Well, damn you, Kaitlin Bradley, because I need you! I need to reach out to you and tell you that I'm dying inside and I can't stand the pain of being without you. I need you to hold me in your arms and tell me that everything is going to be okay. That our time apart will be brief and that nothing is going to change between us. Instead you're scaring me, Kate. I feel like you're slipping away from me before I've even left."

Kaitlin sobbed as she reached for Sierra and pulled her into her arms. They held each other with an intense ferocity. Their tears mingled as they held each other like they never wanted to let go. Kaitlin melted into Sierra's arms and released her agonizing tears. "I'm so sorry, darling. I never meant to hurt you. I didn't want you to see how badly I was hurting."

Sierra reached for Kaitlin's face and held her close. "Then you have no idea what these emerald eyes say to me. You don't have to say a word, Kate, and I just look into your eyes and see it all. These beautiful eyes are my windows to your soul, and they share everything with me. Unlike you, who I am going to beat to a pulp one day till I can get you to stop trying to protect me and start sharing yourself completely with me."

Kaitlin reached forward and wiped away Sierra's tears, smiling weakly. "You know, there are laws out there that say beating your wife to a pulp is not allowed."

Sierra shook Kaitlin's head and pushed her back up against the bench. "I don't care about any damn wife protection laws out there. I'm going to have to find some way to get through your thick skull and show you that I feel everything you feel. I love everything you love, and I hurt every time you hurt. You once told me our hearts beat as one, Kate. When are you going to start believing that and start seeing that I'm here to share your love and your pain?"

Kaitlin slowly reached for Sierra's hands and held them still. "Darling, I won't be able to see anything in a minute if you don't stop bashing my brain against the inside of my skull."

Sierra struggled to control her burning anger as Kaitlin guided her to sit on the bench beside her.

Sierra crossed her arms across her chest and glared at Kaitlin. "I'm pissed at you!"

Kaitlin slid intimately close to Sierra and carefully wrapped her arm around her slender shoulders. "I can see that, Ms. Vaughn. I do believe you have been pissed at me on this dock once before."

Sierra tried to lean away from Kaitlin's comforting arm and shot daggers at her with her blue-gray eyes.

Kaitlin reached for Sierra and guided her closer. Sierra remained with her arms crossed as Kaitlin held her intimately against her. Kaitlin was awed by her fiery temper knowing that it only equaled her uninhibited passion. She was in for a roller coaster ride with this one and smiled at the prospect. She reached up and brushed a strand of hair away from Sierra's enraged eyes and let her finger linger across her soft cheek. Kaitlin was mesmerized as she trailed her finger across Sierra's soft lips and

288

watched the anger seep from her every pore with each gentle stroke.

Kaitlin felt Sierra take her finger into her mouth and shrieked with fright as Sierra clamped down playfully. Sierra pinned Kaitlin's finger between her teeth and stated, "Start talking, Dr. Bradley. I want you to tell me exactly how you feel before I feed your fingertip to the Loch Ness monster!"

Kaitlin grimaced with imaginary pain as she wiggled her finger free from Sierra's grip and held it gingerly. She stared at Sierra in total shock and shouted, "You bit me!"

Sierra leaned menacingly close to Kaitlin's glimmering eyes. "You deserve to be bitten, Kaitlin Bradley!" Sierra grabbed Kaitlin by the collar of her white cotton shirt and pulled her close. She slipped one hand from Kaitlin's collar and touched her heart. "This place belongs to me now, and I want the key. I want to be able to have a way of getting inside there whenever I see the need because you, Dr. Kaitlin Bradley, don't seem to understand how much I love you and how much I want to share your every thought and feeling."

Kaitlin stared into Sierra's emotional eyes and entwined her hands into her hair. She guided her face intimately close as she whispered against her lips, "I love you so much. I didn't want to make our final days together sad. I wanted us to enjoy every moment together and not be crying constantly over the fact that being without you is going to be one thousand times more painful than I already thought it would be."

Sierra leaned her forehead against Kaitlin's and closed her eyes. "I know, babe, but it hurts so much more when you shut me out and don't share your pain with me."

Kaitlin touched Sierra's chin and guided her moist eyes up to her. "I'm sorry, darling. I never meant to hurt you. I only want you to be happy. I didn't want you to think I was some small-town baby that couldn't handle the fact that her incredible big-city wife was leaving her behind for two weeks for her big-city bed and big-city job."

Sierra burst into laughter, then quickly covered her mouth as she saw the big tears well in Kaitlin's eyes. Sierra reached forward for Kaitlin's face and wiped away her tears. "You have no idea how much I love you, Kaitlin Bradley. Every damn thing about you melts my heart. Now come here and kiss me, my small-town baby."

Kaitlin hesitantly leaned closer to Sierra's moist lips and stopped. "Are you going to bite me again, my big-city girl?"

Sierra guided Kaitlin closer and grinned mischievously. "Why don't you bring your delicious small-town lips closer and see what happens."

Kaitlin's hand flew to her mouth, and she shook her head adamantly from side to side. Sierra laughed as she watched Kaitlin wisely fear for her safety.

Sierra slowly reached for Kaitlin's hand and guided the bitten finger to her lips and kissed it softly. "Better now?"

Kaitlin shook her head no with childlike innocence as Sierra smiled at her. Sierra slowly took Kaitlin's finger between her lips and watched her squeeze her eyes tight and hold her breath with impending doom. Sierra caressed her fingertip with her tongue and kissed it softly. Kaitlin slowly opened her passionate eyes and stared deeply into Sierra's radiant smile. "Better now?"

Kaitlin slowly nodded as Sierra leaned toward her soft lips and kissed her softly. Their lips met slowly, gently as Sierra probed Kaitlin with her tongue and encouraged her to come and play. Kaitlin was wisely hesitant as Sierra smiled against her moist lips. "Chicken," Sierra teased.

Kaitlin glided her hands along Sierra's back and slender hips. "I'm not sure if I've been forgiven, so till then I'm not sure that I'll get my tongue back intact."

They both laughed as Sabrina stepped onto the dock. "Hey, ladies. Liz, Darcy and the whole group of female police officers are leaving and they want to say good-bye to you, Sierra."

"Interruptions, interruptions," Sierra sighed as she rose to her feet and reached for Kaitlin's hand.

Kaitlin squeezed Sierra's soft hand. "You go ahead, Sierra. I'm not much in the mood for good-byes." Sierra looked at Kaitlin with concern. "Go ahead and leave me to deal with my pain alone. I'll just sit here and wallow in my small-town misery while I wait for you to come back and hold me in your arms and try to convince me that I'm going to survive the next two weeks without you," Kaitlin said tauntingly.

Sabrina looked puzzled as she watched Sierra lean closer to Kaitlin's demure pout. "I strongly suggest that you remain sitting, Dr. Bradley, before I dunk that thick skull of yours into this ice cold lake," Sierra threatened as she slowly stepped away from Kaitlin and slipped her hand into Sabrina's. "Bri, do you have that anchor handy?" Sierra asked menacingly.

Sabrina slowly started walking away with Sierra and turned back to give Kaitlin a worried look. "Uh-oh, Katie. Sounds like the Loch Ness monster is going to have you for an evening snack."

Kaitlin leaned back in the bench and stuck her tongue out at Sabrina and Sierra.

Sierra turned in time to see Kaitlin's playful rebuttal. "You, young lady, had better not dare move from that spot while I'm gone. I expect that you'll think long and hard about being sarcastic about our parting tomorrow," Sierra scowled, as she turned to Sabrina and started walking with her toward the resort.

Sabrina looked back at Kaitlin's squished face and laughed softly. "Bye, Katie. Don't forget to think long and hard."

Sierra gently smacked Sabrina's behind and glared at her. "Cut that out, Sabrina. Don't encourage her."

Sabrina looked back at Kaitlin's grinning smile and stuck her tongue out at her as Sierra pulled Sabrina forward and turned just enough to give Kaitlin a scolding smile.

Sierra returned to the dock thirty minutes later and felt instantly concerned when she couldn't find Kaitlin. She politely visited with the crowd gathered on the dock and eventually hugged and kissed everyone good-bye. She excused herself to find Kaitlin and allow them some precious time alone.

Sierra climbed the steps to their back deck and watched Kaitlin lean against the railing with a glass of wine in her hand. She stared transfixed out at the lake as the star-studded sky twinkled above her. A gentle glow from the deck lights reflected off her tears; Sierra ached to ease her pain. Sierra stared at the soft features of her beautiful face illuminated by the moon as if to imprint this picture in her mind. She slowly walked toward Kaitlin and leaned back against the railing beside her.

Kaitlin quickly straightened up and wiped at her tears as Sierra reached up to stop her hand.

"I've been looking for you, sweetheart. I was worried about you," Sierra said softly.

Kaitlin leaned her hip against the railing and looked down at their entwined hands as she set her glass of wine aside. "I know. I watched you look around for me out on the dock. I waited for you down there, but then several people started to gather. I didn't feel much like socializing, so I thought I would come up here and wait for you. Besides, I thought I would piss you off as much as possible so you wouldn't miss this crabby, cranky Wizard so much when you're away."

Sierra reached for Kaitlin's damp face and guided her before her. She stared into her moist, emotional, emerald eyes and whispered softly, "You're so damn adorable when you're bad, Dr. Bradley. Cut it out because you make it so hard for me to be mad at you." Sierra guided her into her arms and hugged her tight.

Kaitlin leaned back slightly and dug into the pocket of her slender, black Levis and pulled out an antique key. She turned it over several times in the palm of her hand before offering it to Sierra.

Sierra took the key and admired its uniqueness. "What's this key for, sweetheart?"

Kaitlin rested her hands on Sierra's waist. "That key is for you. It's the key to my heart."

Sierra looked up into Kaitlin's beautiful, moist eyes and hugged her tight.

Kaitlin sobbed against Sierra's cheek and struggled to speak. "I'm going to miss you so much, Sierra. It hurts so badly just thinking about you leaving tomorrow."

Sierra's tears coursed down her face as she caressed Kaitlin's hair and held her close. "I'm going to miss you so much, Kate. You're the shining light in my life, and my world will remain dim till we're reunited again."

Kaitlin hugged Sierra with all her might and glided her hands along her back. "Look what you have done to me, Sierra Vaughn. You've turned me into a small-town baby."

Sierra entwined her fingers into Kaitlin's thick hair. "You'll forever be my small-town baby."

Kaitlin laughed weakly through her tears as Sierra held her face in her hands. "I love you so much, Dr. Kaitlin Bradley. I'm so sorry for causing you this pain."

Kaitlin leaned her forehead against Sierra's and caught a painful sob in her throat. "Licorice and I don't want you to go. We're going to miss you so much."

Sierra caressed Kaitlin's back and held her tight against her as she allowed her tears to flow. "I hate the thought of leaving you, sweetheart. I will promise you that in two weeks' time we will be standing on this deck celebrating the beginning of our life together."

Kaitlin leaned back and gently ran her thumb along Sierra's chin. "That's one promise I expect you to keep, Sierra Vaughn. That's one party I promise to celebrate with you."

Sierra kissed Kaitlin softly and basked in her tender kisses and warm body. "I can't wait for you to arrive at my house on Wednesday, Dr. Bradley. That alone is cause for celebration."

Kaitlin sniffled and brushed away her tears. "Just promise me you won't start anything without me."

Sierra laughed against Kaitlin's lips and teased her with her tongue. "Only if you promise to kiss me after." Sierra kissed her passionately. She reached for Kaitlin's hands and held them between her own. "Come with me, Dr. Bradley. I have a gift for you."

Kaitlin obediently followed Sierra up to the loft bedroom and stopped suddenly before the elegant four-poster bed. She stared at the bedside table and slowly walked closer. She knelt before a beautiful, glass lighthouse model illuminated like a nightlight.

Sierra sat on the edge of the bed and watched Kaitlin glide her fingers over the luminescent figurine. "Its beautiful, darling. It's absolutely beautiful," Kaitlin gushed.

Sierra rested her hand on Kaitlin's shoulder. "While I'm away I don't want you to ever feel lost or alone. You once told me that looking at a lighthouse makes you feel safe and secure. That's how I want you to feel when I'm away. That lighthouse will always shine as bright as my love does for you."

Kaitlin turned to kneel between Sierra's legs and guided her into her arms. "You are forever in my heart, Sierra. No matter where you are." They held each other close as Kaitlin kissed Sierra softly. "Thank you, darling. I will always cherish that lighthouse from you." Kaitlin kissed her softly and turned to pull out a small gift box from their bedside table. She gently handed it to Sierra and watched her huge blue-gray eyes dance with excitement. "That's for you, my darling. Go ahead and open it."

Sierra tore the shiny red wrapping off and held a tiny, black velvet box in her hand. She slowly opened the squeaky lid and looked up at Kaitlin in shock. Kaitlin gently took the solid band of rubies and diamonds from the box and slipped it onto Sierra's ring finger. They both stared at its rare beauty and admired the perfect fit. Tears spilled onto Sierra's cheeks as she stared into Kaitlin's eyes. "When I saw that ring I was awestruck by its beauty and warmth as I was the first time I met you. You're the most loving woman I've ever met, Sierra. Your charm and personality continually astound me and I feel so blessed to be your wife."

Sierra wiped at her tears and looked from Kaitlin's shining eyes to her breathtaking ring. "Its absolutely beautiful, sweetheart. I would be honored to wear your ring and let the world know that I am your wife." Sierra reached for Kaitlin and kissed her deeply as they ached never to let each other go.

Kaitlin leaned back and smiled deeply as she watched Sierra admire her new ring. She reached forward and brushed away Sierra's remaining tears. "I have one other thing for you to take back to Toronto with you, my darling."

Sierra held her dolphin pendant between her fingers as she watched Kaitlin walk into the walk-in closet.

Kaitlin returned with a handheld telescope and once again knelt before Sierra and placed it in her hands. "It's the first telescope I bought. I thought you could take it home with you so when you looked up at the Toronto night sky you'd know we were looking up at the same stars and making the same wish."

Sierra's eyes filled with tears as she gently caressed the telescope. "Will I be able to see you with this telescope, baby?" Sierra asked wishfully.

Kaitlin leaned closer to Sierra. "You won't need that, darling. Just close your beautiful blue eyes, and you will always see me."

Sierra's sob caught in her chest as she leaned toward Kaitlin and kissed her softly. "Every night I will look for the Polaris star and when I find it I will always know you're near," Sierra said.

Kaitlin set Sierra's telescope aside. Sierra reached for her face and struggled to control her tears. "I love you so much, my sweet Kate. Now and always."

Kaitlin leaned closer to Sierra and gently caressed her back. "I love you, my sweet Sierra. Now and always."

They held each other tight and willed their pain away as Kaitlin whispered softly in Sierra's ear, "I wanted to get you some peanut brittle, but I was so afraid of breaking your front tooth."

They both burst into laughter as Kaitlin eased Sierra to her feet. They stood before each other, suspended in time, slowly removing each other's clothing as if for the first time.

Sierra gently glided her hands over Kaitlin's soft curves and committed this image of her to memory.

Kaitlin reached her hands toward Sierra and stared into her shimmering eyes. They slowly entwined their hands and let their fingers merge as one. Kaitlin slowly walked Sierra back to the edge of the bed and set her down across the duvet. She eased herself over her and felt her wetness against her thigh as they slowly, sensuously made love to each other for hours in hopes of making this night last forever.

ର⅋ଓର⅋ଓର⅋ଓ

The beautiful, sunny Sunday afternoon contradicted their moods as they all stood on Kaitlin's front deck shuffling their feet uncomfortably. Kaitlin's sadness seemed to emanate from her pores as she loaded one of Sierra's fluorescent orange suitcases into the back of her Honda Passport.

The air was heavy with tense emotions as Sierra stepped out the front door and held Licorice tight in her arms. Her tears coursed down her face as she nuzzled against Licorice's whiskers.

"You be a good girl, Licorice. I'm counting on you to take care of my girl for me. Make sure she eats right and gets lots of sleep and most importantly make sure she spoils you like I do." Everyone smiled through their tears as they watched Sierra kiss the top of Licorice's head and set her free to run after Kaitlin.

Sierra took a deep breath and looked at the loving, sad faces before her. She struggled to control the aching pain in her chest as she eagerly stepped into Gladys's outstretched arms.

Gladys hugged Sierra tight and kissed her damp cheek. "I'm not going to say good-bye, Sierra, because I know you're coming back to us. Two weeks seems like an eternity right now, but before you know it you will be back with us struggling to protect yourself from Sabrina and Logan and struggling to keep Katie in line."

Sierra sniffled against Gladys's cheek and took a deep breath. "Those are the kinds of struggles I live for, Gladys."

Gladys laughed softly and lost her own battle with her tears. She turned her face and kissed Sierra. "You're going to be sorely missed around here, Sierra. Hurry back so there can be some sense of normalcy around here."

Sierra kissed Gladys's cheek. "I will hurry back, Gladys. I can promise you that." Sierra reached up for Gladys's cherub cheeks and wiped away her tears. "I love you, Gladys. Please take care of yourself, and please take care of Kate for me as you have done so beautifully her entire life."

They hugged each other tight as Gladys whispered, "I love you too, Sierra. Please stay safe."

Sierra gently touched Gladys's face before she hesitantly stepped back and stood before Sabrina and Logan. She reached forward and touched both their beautiful, teary faces. "Good-bye, my wicked stepsisters."

Sabrina and Logan laughed as they pulled Sierra toward them and hugged her tight. Their tears all flowed as Sierra rested her head against theirs.

"Okay, you two, no more water follies while I'm gone. I'd hate to miss out on all the fun."

"We're going to miss you terribly, Sierra. The Loch Ness monster also told us to tell you that he's going to miss nibbling on your toes," Sabrina said.

Sierra squished her face playfully and kissed Sabrina and Logan good-bye. "Be good, girls, and please keep Kate safe for me."

Sabrina reached for Sierra's hand and squeezed it tight. They all looked toward Kaitlin, leaning against the cedar railing, lost in her emotional anguish.

Sabrina held Sierra close and smiled. "We will take care of her for you while you're gone. But you'd better hurry back because you know what a huge responsibility that is."

Sierra reached for Logan's hand and guided her close. "I love you, guys. I'm going to miss you both so much."

Sabrina and Logan smiled through their tears as they hugged Sierra close. Logan wiped at her own tears and squeezed Sierra's hand. "We love you too, Sierra. Take care of yourself and hurry back to us."

Sierra kissed them both one more time and slowly headed toward the steps and Kaitlin's devastated eyes.

Sierra stood before her, took her teary face in her hands, and guided her eyes up to her. Blistering heartache was streaming from Kaitlin's eyes as Sierra melted into her arms and held her tight.

Kaitlin's tears coursed down her cheeks as she leaned toward Sierra's soft lips. "I'm going to miss you so much, my darling. My life will be so empty till you come back to me."

Sierra reached up to hold Kaitlin's face and kissed her with tender passion. They both moaned with painful intensity. Sierra leaned back and brushed away Kaitlin's tears. Kaitlin reached forward and took Sierra's dolphin pendant between her fingers, resting her forehead against hers. Sierra smiled at Kaitlin's tender gesture as she kissed her damp cheek. "I'm going to miss you so much, baby. I love you tremendously, and I can't wait to feel your arms around me when you arrive on Wednesday."

Kaitlin smiled and kissed Sierra with aching need. Sierra hesitantly stepped back and took Kaitlin by the hand and guided her down the steps. She turned and looked back at the teary three musketeers and blew them each a kiss.

Kaitlin opened Sierra's driver door for her and guided her in. She closed the door firmly and watched Sierra start the engine and glide the window down. Tears spilled from Kaitlin's eyes as she leaned in the open window and kissed Sierra softly. She leaned her forehead against Sierra's and whispered against her sensuous lips, "Please drive carefully, darling, and please call me as soon as you get home."

Sierra kissed her softly and held her face in her hands. "I will, baby. I promise." Sierra held Kaitlin close and stared into her emotional eyes. "I left my journal under your pillow just in case you needed to be reminded of how much I love you. Turn to any page, and you will feel my love pour out for you."

Kaitlin sobbed against Sierra's hands and struggled to kiss her one more time. She hesitantly backed away from Sierra's window and bent down to scoop Licorice into her arms.

Sierra smiled through her tears and reached out to touch Licorice's paw. "Good-bye, Licorice. I love you."

Kaitlin waved Licorice's paw at Sierra as Licorice looked at her with a startled look. Sierra's tears blurred her vision as she watched Kaitlin stand in anguished silence.

Their tears fell in unison as Kaitlin tenderly blew Sierra a kiss. "I love you, my darling. I'll see you on Wednesday."

Sierra dropped her chin onto her chest and sobbed painfully. Kaitlin set Licorice down on the ground behind her and jerked the driver door open. Sierra flew into her arms. Kaitlin cocooned her in her arms with all the love in her heart as they struggled to control their anguish.

Kaitlin reached for Sierra's face and guided her eyes up to her as she wiped away her tears. "Look at me, sweetheart. I need you to be that tower of emotional strength for me so that you can drive home safely. Will you do that for me, Sierra?"

Sierra covered her mouth to stifle a sob as her ruby ring sparkled in the sunlight. "I would do anything for you, my love. Anything." Sierra kissed Kaitlin passionately and touched her face one final time before she forced herself to get back in her vehicle. Kaitlin gently closed her door and stepped back to join the girls.

Sierra hesitantly put her vehicle in drive and waved sweetly. "Good-bye, my baby. I love you. Now and always."

Kaitlin's sob echoed in her chest as she stood with the others and waved good-bye. They all watched the dust fly behind Sierra's departing wheels as Kaitlin released an anguished sob and whispered, "Good-bye, my darling. I love you. Now and always."

⚙ 16

Sierra sat before the computer in her patients glassed-in cubicle typing in his last set of vital signs. She added a note about the morphine she had given for pain and the phone call she placed to the Neurosurgeon, updating him on the lab results. She clicked save and looked up at her patient's cardiac monitor and scanned his current vital signs. She flipped through his medication sheets on her clipboard and double-checked when he was next due his antibiotics.

Sydney stepped into the room and scanned Sierra's patient with her experienced eye. "He finally looks stable, Sierra. You've been busting your buns in here for hours."

"He is doing better, Sydney. At least for the moment. The police finally contacted his parents and told them about his brainless police chase in the stolen vehicle. They should be here shortly. What possesses a sixteen year old to do something so stupid?"

"A dare. A bet. A couple of beers and a defiant teenage crowd. They all seem to spell danger these days."

"Well, he'll be lucky if he walks away from this without any permanent brain damage. The police said they found his body fifty feet from the car after it rolled three times."

"Geez, do his parents know any of this?"

"I doubt it. It will be up to us and the doctors to answer all of their questions. I'm just glad this shift will be over in a couple of hours. I can't wait to get home and talk to Kate. I can't wait till she gets to my place tomorrow. These past two days have crept by so slowly."

Sydney placed her hand on Sierra's shoulder. "And I was hoping that once you got home and away from that gorgeous outback woman you would realize what a horrible mistake you were making. You would finally come to your senses and realize that I am the only woman for you."

"And what do you think Kelly would say about that?"

"Kelly, who?"

Sierra playfully smacked Sydney's arms and folded her hands in her lap. She glanced back at her patient and his cardiac monitor. "Actually, Sydney, I have been doing a lot of thinking."

Sydney blinked with disbelief. "Don't tell me you're having second thoughts, Sierra."

"Honestly, Sydney, yes I was. I suddenly realized what I was changing and what I was giving up to move to Bradley Bay with Kaitlin. I got really scared when I realized I was giving up everything that was familiar and comfortable. Then I would pick up the phone and call Kate. The sound of her voice, the whisper of her breath, the strength of her faith in me all slammed my doubts and worries right into the nearest trashcan. When I am with her or talk to her everything is so clear and right. Everything makes sense. She makes me feel complete. My love for her is like no love I have ever felt or experienced before. That alone makes my decision to move in with her and be her partner worth the risks we are taking."

"Damn, and I thought I was seeing a glimmer of hope for me here."

Sierra laughed as she took Sydney's hand and squeezed tight. "What do you think, Sydney? Have I made the right decision?"

Sydney held Sierra's hand and brushed her thumb across her wrist. "No decision has ever been more right for you, Sierra. I promised myself if I couldn't have you then I would make sure you only had the best. You have the best, Sierra. You and Katie are made for each other. I wish you both many, many years of happiness together."

Sierra's eyes misted with happiness as the charge nurse stuck her head in the doorway. "Sierra, the family is in the waiting room."

"Thanks. I'll go out and talk to them before I bring them in." Sierra slipped from her chair and touched Sydney's arm. "Will you keep an eye on my patient for me, Sydney, while I talk to the family?"

"Of course, Sierra. You go ahead."

"Thanks, Syd. You're the best."

"Obviously not the best if you're planning on moving in with that outdoorsy, rugged woman of yours in two weeks."

Sierra smiled from the doorway and threw Sydney a sheepish grin. "The best is measured in many ways, Syd."

"Yeah, well, your measuring stick and mine are obviously very different."

Sierra waved as she headed through the automatic doors and down the hallway.

CRITORIO

Sierra slipped her key into the front door of her house and juggled her purse and lunch bag in the other hand. She entered her front hallway and flipped the lights on. She set her purse and lunch bag down on the captain's bench and turned to lock and bolt the door. She turned and tossed her keys onto the mahogany mirror table in the hallway when she felt the hair on the back of her neck stand on end. Her skin began to crawl as she instantly froze and listened to the scraping sound coming from her bedroom.

She instinctively moved two steps closer and heard a door creak. Sierra quickly scanned her home and began to breathe again as she saw that everything in her house was as she had left it. Her mind raced wildly as she suddenly realized that it must be Kaitlin. She must have decided to come down tonight instead of tomorrow to surprise her. Sierra instantly felt her skin prickle with excitement as she slowly tiptoed toward her bedroom. Her heart beat wildly in her chest as she pounced into her bedroom and flipped on the light switch. She turned to shout surprise, then saw the butt of a gun as it came crashing down against her skull.

302

Lights flashed before Sierra's eyes as she felt herself fall in slow motion and heard a distorted groan escape from her own lips. Her body fell like a lifeless rag doll as her head cracked against the corner of her dresser and bounced wildly into the cream carpet. Blood oozed from Sierra's head and mouth as she struggled to open her eyes. Her vision blurred and narrowed; all she saw was a pair of black sneakers run toward her front door.

Sierra felt like she was floating, yet her head pounded wildly as if it was about to explode. Her eyes betrayed her as her vision turned to black and her eyelids completed the darkness. A wave of cold enveloped Sierra's skin. She felt weightless and found herself floating toward a dark, cold abyss. A heaviness crept into her limbs and head as she sank deeper and deeper into the darkness. Sierra felt startled in her confusion as she saw a hand in the darkness reach toward her and call her name. The lights wouldn't stop flashing as Sierra struggled to reach for that hand. The voice was distorted and playing at the wrong speed, and Sierra could barely make out the words, "You're okay, darling! I'm here with you. Here, take my hand." Sierra reached and reached for that hand and could finally feel the fingertips as she saw her beautiful emerald eyes begging her to hold on. Sierra could not reach any further. She could not hold on any longer. She felt the fingertips slip away and found herself tumbling endlessly, deeper and deeper into the cold, dark hole as she barely whispered, "I can't reach you, baby! I can't see your hand. I'm sorry, baby. I love you."

⋙⋘⋙⋘⋙⋘

Kaitlin ran her hand through her hair in tense, despairing frustration. She paced her back deck like a caged lioness as she held the cordless phone to her ear muttering, "Come on, Sydney! Pick up the damn phone!"

Licorice watched her from her perch on the railing with an innate knowledge that something was very wrong.

"Sydney! Thank God you're home! This is Kate. I'm worried sick actually. Sierra should have called me by now. It's been almost two hours since she should have been home from work. I've left a hundred messages on her machine, and she still hasn't called me back. I didn't know if you guys got tied up at work and stayed late or if something happened to Sierra's Honda or if something has happened to her phone line or if ..."

"Wait, Katie! Just slow down. Let me set my groceries down on a chair here. Now, I'm sure there is a logical explanation for Sierra not calling you yet. We both left work at the same time and she was practically running out of the unit so she could get home to call you. We travel the same route home, and I never saw her vehicle along the road. I'm just getting in now because I stopped to get some groceries. Let me call Sierra and see if I can reach her, Katie."

Kaitlin massaged her pulsating temple. "I'd really appreciate that, Sydney. I'm about ready to lose my mind here."

"As soon as I do reach her I'll tell her you're a nervous wreck and she'd better dial your number as fast as her fingers will let her."

Kaitlin felt slightly relieved to know that Sydney would search for Sierra as she walked in disjointed circles. "Sydney, just find her for me, please! I have a sick feeling in my stomach, and I'm not going to be able to breathe till I hear from you and Sierra. Please, Sydney, find my Sierra now! This is so unlike her not to have called by now."

Sydney tossed her milk and eggs into the fridge as she felt a lead balloon settle in her chest. "All right, Katie. All right. I'm going to take my cell phone and call Sierra as I drive over to her place so I can give her royal shit for scaring us both to death. Now you do your best to stay calm, and I'll call you as soon as I get there." Sydney heard Kaitlin's gasping sob as she felt panic rising in her chest. "Katie, listen to me. We're going to find her. I'm on my way now, so I'll talk to you in about fifteen minutes. Try and keep yourself together and for God's sake get Sabrina and Logan to sit with you while you wait for my phone call;

otherwise you are definitely going to lose your mind. And Katie, please have Sabrina call Kelly at work and let her know where I'm going, so she doesn't worry when she can't reach me. I don't plan on terrifying my lover as Sierra has terrified you."

Kaitlin barely whispered into the phone, "Go, Sydney! Find my Sierra. Please!" They quickly said good-bye as Sydney grabbed her car keys and cell phone and raced out the door.

ⒸⓈⒸⓈⒸⓈ

Kaitlin paced relentlessly past Sabrina, Logan, and Gladys, oblivious to their calming words as she checked her watch for the hundredth time. Her muscles burned with tension, each of her senses feeding off raw adrenaline.

Thirty minutes had passed when the cordless phone finally rang. Kaitlin jerked the phone to her ear and heard sirens' wailing behind Sydney's terrified, sobbing voice.

"Oh God, Katie! It's awful! I got to Sierra's house and found her front door wide open. I ran in and screamed for Sierra and found her lying on her bedroom floor still dressed in her uniform. She was moaning and crying for you and lying in a puddle of her own blood from a deep gash in her head. I called 911 right away and the cops, and paramedics are here with her now. The cops think that Sierra must have walked in on a burglary attempt. Oh God, Katie! I'm so sorry. I can't believe this has happened to Sierra."

Kaitlin stood stone still as her face became deathly pale and her world spun completely out of control. Her heart beat wildly in her throat as she gripped the phone with white knuckles. She felt burning anger and nerve-shattering terror as she saw the terror in Quinn's eyes as she pulled her out of the pool. This time it was Sierra's eyes filled with terror.

Sabrina and Logan lurched for Kaitlin as they saw her sway and feared she was about to pass out.

Kaitlin felt the deck spin and buckle beneath her. Then suddenly Sierra's piercing screams in the background jolted her

305

back to reality. Kaitlin held the phone tighter and heard Sierra scream again and beg Kaitlin to help her. Kaitlin's mind instantly cleared as she focused on that gut-wrenching scream and knew where she needed to be. Sierra needed her, and she needed Sierra.

"Katie! Are you still there?"

Self-control possessed her as Kaitlin began pacing rapidly along the cedar railing, looking at the terrified faces before her. "I'm here, Sydney. I'm going to call my friend who does helicopter tours of this area and see if he can fly me into Toronto. I should hopefully be there in an hour, and I'll have Sabrina and Logan drive up right away."

"That's a great idea, Katie. The paramedics are just now loading Sierra onto the ambulance stretcher. God, she's so groggy and confused. I can't believe this is happening. I'm going to move into the living room to get out of their way."

Kaitlin could hear Sierra's sobs in the background as her gut clenched in a tight painful fist.

"Katie, when I first got here Sierra was barely conscious and mumbling a lot of incoherent words. But what I could understand was her continuously repeating your name and saying something about your hand. She couldn't reach your hand."

Kaitlin listened with a heightened sense of awareness as she heard a sob catch in Sydney's voice.

"She also kept saying she didn't want you to see her like this. She didn't want you to feel responsible for her."

Kaitlin's emotional anguish slammed against her chest as she felt the dread of her past crush her like a vise grip. Tears blurred her vision as she gripped the phone tighter. "Sydney, I'm on my way. Please stay with Sierra till I get there and, Sydney, thank you for finding Sierra. She's going to be okay. I will make sure of that. Please tell Sierra that I love her and that soon she will be able to reach for my hand."

"I'll tell her, Katie. Please hurry. We both need you."

They both quickly said good-bye as Kaitlin rapidly dialed the local airport.

෬෩෬෩෬෩

Kaitlin's feet barely touched the ground as she rushed through the emergency department's automatic doors. She was grateful Sierra had been taken to one of the cities best facilities where Kaitlin had spent two years doing her trauma residency. Kaitlin was met by the medical staff and quickly escorted to trauma room one. Kaitlin saw Sydney standing outside the glass room with tears streaming down her face as she heard Sierra scream her name. Kaitlin touched Sydney's damp cheek and rushed into the trauma room.

Sierra was flailing her arms and legs at the trauma team and violently shaking her head from side to side as they struggled to assess her properly. Her vital signs fluctuated erratically as Sierra pulled at her oxygen mask and tried to rip out her intravenous. The trauma team tried to calm her down as they grabbed her arms and legs and reached for the restraints to tie Sierra down.

Kaitlin quickly stepped to the head of Sierra's stretcher and saw the pure terror in her eyes. The staff continued to struggle with Sierra as they watched Kaitlin remove her oxygen mask and slowly take her face in her hands. Kaitlin leaned intimately close as she saw a spark of recognition in those beautiful blue-gray eyes.

Sierra instantly stopped screaming and fighting as she focused on Kaitlin's smile. Her vital signs slowly returned to normal, and her limbs fell limply at her side as her struggle seeped from her soul.

The entire staff stood back in awe as Kaitlin looked up at their amazed faces. "Please hold off on the restraints. I'll see if I can keep Sierra calm so you guys can do your job."

The trauma team leader stepped up beside Kaitlin and touched her shoulder. "It looks like you're doing a great job keeping her calm, Dr. Bradley. Talk to her, and let's see if she's aware of her surroundings."

307

Kaitlin turned back to Sierra and kissed her damp, blood-soaked face. "I'm here, my darling. Everything is going to be okay. You're safe here with me." Kaitlin slipped her hand into Sierra's and squeezed softly. "Here, take my hand. Feel me beside you. You're safe now. Nobody is ever going to hurt you again. I'm here, darling, and I'm never going to let your hand go, ever again."

The staff watched as tears trickled from Sierra's eyes and a flicker of a smile curled her lips. Her head throbbed uncontrollably as she painfully reached up to touch Kaitlin's face. "My baby. You're here. I love you, Kate. Now and always."

The two E.R. nurses, the respiratory therapist and the trauma doctor watched Sierra's hand fall limply to her side as she slipped into unconsciousness.

Kaitlin's tears fell onto Sierra's closed eyelids as she kissed her face and touched her bloody head dressing. "I love you, my Sierra. Now and always."

The staff gave Kaitlin a few minutes with Sierra. One of the E.R. nurses that Kaitlin had worked with guided her away from the stretcher. They allowed the trauma team to assess Sierra while awaiting the CAT scan of her head. She handed Kaitlin a gown, mask, and pair of gloves as she remarked on her amazing calming affect on Sierra. "For a girl that kept telling me she didn't want to see you, Dr. Bradley, and didn't want us to let you take care of her, she certainly changed her tune when you arrived."

Sierra's resistance shocked Kaitlin as she watched the E.R nurse reach into a tray and hand Kaitlin a small plastic bag.

"She even went so far as to have me take this off. She asked me to give it back to you and tell you to forget she ever walked into your life."

Kaitlin stared down at the tiny bag as the light reflected off the beautiful ruby and diamond ring and pierced directly through her heart.

↻ 17

Sierra felt oddly weightless as she felt herself float toward filtered rays of sunlight. Her eyes searched frantically, yet all she saw were tiny rays of light. She tried to move toward the light but felt cold and imprisoned in her own body. She tried to look around again and saw a shadowy movement obscure her rays of sunlight. Sierra squinted to see a hand come slowly toward her. She suddenly felt strangely calm and safe as the hand moved closer and a soft, familiar voice spoke very slowly. "You're okay, my darling. I'm here with you. Take my hand. Feel me beside you. You're not underwater anymore. You're safe here with me." Sierra reached out and felt her soft fingertips. She glided her hand into her palm and felt the hand close around hers and pull her toward the sunlight.

Sierra jerked onto her side and banged her bandaged head against the side rail. She winced in pain and reached for her head. Sierra felt the soft, cotton gauze beneath her hands and slowly opened her heavy eyelids. She blinked several times to moisten her dry eyes and saw P.J. snuggled against her chest. She smiled softly and kissed her fuzzy face. She could see a model train engine sitting on her over bed table. A subtle white light beamed from the train's headlight. Sierra sluggishly reached forward and touched the soft light with her fingertip and barely whispered, "Kate. You are my light."

Sierra heard a quick rustling of chairs and looked up to see the radiant smiles of her parents. "Mom! Dad!" She painfully hoisted herself up to a sitting position and hugged them both tight. Her tears flowed against her parents' faces as the cloud of confusion slowly lifted. Sierra leaned back slightly and looked around her hospital room as snippets of recall bombarded her brain. She reached up and touched the dressing on her head and stared back at the model train. Rapid flashbacks of her attack and

Sydney finding her on the floor pieced together in Sierra's mind like a puzzle. Sierra turned back to her parents with frightened eyes.

"Kaitlin! Where's Kate? I told everyone I wanted her to go away. I didn't want her to be responsible for me like this."

Sierra's mother smiled sweetly and brushed away Sierra's flowing tears. "Yes, my dear, you were very mean and hurtful to your lover."

Sierra's head throbbed wildly as she looked at her mother in shock. She looked into each parent's smiling eyes and repeated softly, "My lover."

Sierra's mother smiled with her blue-gray eyes and hugged Sierra close. "Kaitlin told us everything, sweetheart. We're not stupid, you know. We always knew about you and Linda, but we thought it would be more comfortable for you if you told us."

Sierra shook her throbbing head in disbelief. "And all these years I thought it would be easier for you guys if you asked me."

Sierra's father shook his head and smiled. "We always knew, Sierra. After all, we watched *Ellen,* you know."

They all laughed through their tears as Sierra hugged her parents' close. "I love you guys."

Sierra's father kissed her bruised cheek. "We love you too, pumpkin."

Sierra leaned back and searched the room behind her parents. Her eyes filled with sadness and despair as she turned back to her parents. "I said some awful things to try and make Kate stay away. I need to find her. I need to tell her how much I love her."

Tears streamed from Sierra's eyes as she felt a familiar warm kiss against her cheek. Kaitlin leaned in behind her and whispered into her ear, "Only if you promise to kiss me after."

Sierra spun her head around and erupted into joyful screams as she reached for Kaitlin and pulled her into her arms. They held each other with incredible intensity as they shed their tears of joy.

Sierra held Kaitlin's beaming face in her hands and whispered against her lips, "You came back!"

Kaitlin leaned her forehead against Sierra's. "I never left."

They both smiled as Kaitlin caressed Sierra's silk-covered back. "I had just stepped out of your room to call Gladys and update her on your condition. You've slipped in and out of consciousness for three days, and I never left your side. You must not have been listening when I said I would be at your side in sickness and in health. Till death do us part. Regardless of how mean you have been to me. But don't worry, my little Scorpio with the stinging tail, I will make sure you're thoroughly cleansed of your deplorable behavior by the time I'm done with you."

Sierra kissed the tip of Kaitlin's nose and smiled shyly. "Can't I just write out one-hundred lines?"

Kaitlin laughed deeply and held Sierra close in her arms. "Forget it! After some of the things I heard you said, I'm going to kick your sorry little ass from here to Timbuktu and back!"

Sierra quickly covered her bottom with her hand as Kaitlin kissed her blushing cheek.

Sierra's parent's laughed at their antics as they came to stand beside Kaitlin. Sierra's mother placed her hand on Kaitlin's back and smiled at Sierra. "Katie has been wonderful, Sierra. She has been doing all of your bed side care and overlooking every aspect of your medical treatment." Sierra's mother turned to Kaitlin with her smiling blue eyes. "Katie, we're going to get the girls. They'll be thrilled to see Sierra so awake." Sierra's parents kissed her on the way out and closed the door behind them.

Kaitlin glided her hands over Sierra's silky back and held her close in her arms. "Welcome back, my precious girl. I begged for one wish, and that wish has come back to me."

Sierra saw the tears well in Kaitlin's eyes as she leaned closer and kissed her with tender warmth. Sierra entwined her fingers into Kaitlin's flowing, shiny hair and stared into her exhausted eyes.

Kaitlin kissed the bruise on Sierra's cheek and let her lips linger against her pale cheek. "How are you feeling, my darling?"

Sierra furrowed her brow and reached for the bandage on her head. "I have a terrible headache, and my mind feels like I'm driving through a heavy fog." Sierra looked up into Kaitlin's worried eyes as more snippets of her attack clipped through her mind like a jumpy, old-fashioned movie. "I thought it was you in my bedroom, Kate. Never in a million years did I imagine someone had broken into my house and would hurt me. I have a jumbled memory of Sydney and the ambulance and wishing that you were there to help me. In my mind I kept trying to reach your hand, but it was always out of reach. Always beyond my grasp." A sob escaped from Sierra's throat as she leaned her forehead on Kaitlin's strong shoulder.

Kaitlin held Sierra securely and luxuriated in the feel of her slender frame cocooned in her arms once again. "I'm so sorry this happened to you, sweetheart. I can't imagine how terrifying it must have been for you. The police need to ask you some questions to see what you remember but that can wait till you're ready. The most important thing is that you are all right and you will never have to ask for me again because I'm never going to let you go. I'm going to protect you from harm for the rest of your life." Sierra hugged Kaitlin fiercely with trembling arms.

Sierra leaned back and wiped at her tears as Kaitlin tucked a stray strand of hair beneath her head dressing. "I'll get you something for your headache, sweetheart. I can't tell you how ecstatic I am to have you back."

Sierra guided Kaitlin into her arms and hugged her tight. Their warm tears mingled against their cheeks. Sierra looked over Kaitlin's shoulder and saw a reclining chair nestled beside her bed.

Kaitlin followed her gaze and lowered the side rail so Sierra could sit on the edge of the bed. "That's been my home for the past three days," Kaitlin said softly. "Here, let me disconnect your IV tubing before we lose that IV in your hand."

Sierra watched Kaitlin turn off her IV pump, cap the end of the tubing, and drape it over the IV pole. Sierra pulled Kaitlin toward her and hugged her tight. "I love you so much. Thank you for being here for me."

Kaitlin held her and caressed her back. "My past made you feel like you never wanted to be a burden, Sierra, and that's not fair to you. Our love is so deep that I know we will always be there for each other regardless of the nasty words that came from these sweet lips."

Sierra gently touched Kaitlin's chin and guided her closer as their lips met softly, slowly, tenderly, rediscovering the passion that had lain dormant for three days. Sierra ran her tongue slowly across Kaitlin's lower lip and whispered seductively, "You yanked me out of the closet to my parents and have been doing my bed side care, have you, my small-town girl?"

Kaitlin moaned softly and tenderly touched her tongue to Sierra's. "Ummm. I sure have. I particularly enjoyed doing my little outed lesbian's bed baths."

Sierra smiled playfully and looked into Kaitlin's loving eyes. "Thank you, baby. For everything, and for just being you and knowing how much I really needed you."

Kaitlin kissed Sierra's forehead. "You're very welcome, my darling."

Sierra looked down at Kaitlin's chest and saw a glimmer of gold resting against her midnight black turtleneck. She reached forward and gingerly trailed her finger over her dolphin pendant and ruby ring dangling together.

Kaitlin watched the tears well in Sierra's eyes. Kaitlin leaned back slightly and unclasped the necklace from around her neck. She slipped the ring off the chain and hooked the necklace carefully behind Sierra's neck.

Sierra looked down at her dolphins and smiled. She looked up at Kaitlin and saw her holding her ruby and diamond ring in the palm of her hand. Sierra's tears tumbled onto her cheeks as she slowly curled Kaitlin's fingers around her ring and whispered softly, "I'm not sure if I deserve that back."

Kaitlin leaned her face intimately close to Sierra's. "I'm not sure if you do either, but why don't I place it back on your finger on a trial basis. We will re-evaluate at the end of each and every day whether you deserve to wear my ring and be my wife."

Sierra looked up at Kaitlin with huge, shame-filled eyes. Kaitlin gave her a stern scowl as she tenderly slipped the ring back on Sierra's finger. They both marveled at its beauty and elegance. Kaitlin brought Sierra's hand to her lips and kissed it softly. She reached forward and touched Sierra's chin and guided her eyes up to her. "This ring belongs on this finger from this day forth, Ms. Vaughn. If you ever ask someone to give it back to me again and ask me to forget that you ever walked into my life, I will spank your gorgeous little ass and lock you in your fluorescent orange suitcase and ship you off to Timbuktu with no return address! Understood?"

Sierra's beautiful blue eyes danced with a renewed light as she nodded her head slowly and answered softly, "Understood."

Kaitlin growled playfully and nipped at Sierra's neck with her teeth as Sierra reached for her face and held her close.

Sierra reached for Kaitlin's soft hands and gingerly sat up on the edge of the bed. She looked down at her gold silk top and short set in wonder. She ran her hands over the luscious silk and looked up at Kaitlin. "This is beautiful. Is it mine?"

Kaitlin pulled a chair up to sit directly in front of Sierra. She took her hands and smiled. "It sure is. I bought you several different sets of p.j.'s to wear in the hospital. Now you know what kind of shopping adventure that would have been for me considering I've never seen you in any sleepwear."

Sierra smiled deeply and tried to adjust herself more comfortably. "What's pulling between my legs?"

Kaitlin and Sierra both looked down as Kaitlin picked up the catheter snaking out from Sierra's shorts. "Your catheter."

Sierra groaned in total disbelief. "My catheter! Oh God! You mean I was so out of it that I couldn't pee on my own! Who put it in?"

Kaitlin laughed at Sierra's discomfort and positioned the catheter more comfortably for her. "Sydney begged them in E.R.

to let her do it, but apparently some cute little blonde E.R. nurse insisted that it was her job."

Sierra groaned and dropped her head against Kaitlin's shoulder. "Oh, how embarrassing! Take it out, baby. Please take it out."

Kaitlin held Sierra tight and laughed. "Okay, my darling, I'll take it out. Don't worry."

Sierra leaned back and smiled into Kaitlin's loving eyes as she turned to see three smiling faces burst into her room with incredible exuberance. Sabrina, Logan, and Sydney all started screaming and cheering at the sight of Sierra's beautiful tear-brimmed eyes and magnificent smile. They all dashed for her outstretched arms and jostled to see who would hug her first. Kaitlin barely managed to escape the mayhem unscathed as she turned to see the tangled mass of arms hugging the life out of Sierra.

"Be careful, you guys! You're liable to give Sierra another concussion." Kaitlin stood in the doorway beside Sierra's parents and shook her head at the joyful celebration under way. Several of the intensive care nurses appeared in the doorway to join in the celebration as Sabrina and Logan sat on either side of Sierra.

A beautiful, elegant woman with hair of cascading ringlets placed her hand on Kaitlin's back. "What is all the ruckus in here? May I remind you ladies that this is an intensive care unit!"

The girls all looked impishly at Sierra as Kaitlin's eyes filled with tears. "Dr. Erica Beaumont, I would like you to meet my awakened Sierra." Kaitlin beamed Sierra an ecstatic smile and said, "Sierra, Erica and I went to med school together, and she is your neurosurgeon."

Sierra extended her arm and took Dr. Beaumont's hand. "It's nice to meet you, Dr. Beaumont."

Erica beamed with pure joy at seeing Sierra so awake as she watched her reach for her bandaged head. "It's a pleasure seeing you awake, Sierra. Call me Erica."

"Please don't tell me that I had to have surgery, Erica."

Erica sat before Sierra's shining eyes. "No, you didn't, Sierra. You were very lucky. You suffered a very serious concussion and a linear fracture of your parietal-temporal skull. You also had a nasty gash on your scalp that required fifteen stitches. I was tempted to insert a Richmond bolt to measure your intracranial pressure because of your fluctuating level of consciousness, but Kaitlin begged me to wait. She told me you're a tower of emotional and inner strength and to please give you a chance to come around without performing any invasive procedures. So we waited, and only because I have total faith in Kaitlin's intelligence and seemingly accurate knowledge of your willpower." Erica reached for Sierra's hands and held them tight. "You improved dramatically every day, Sierra, and I can't tell you how thrilled we all are to have you awaken from your deep sleep to reclaim your incredible family."

Sierra looked around the room with tear-filled eyes at all the women who had prayed and cried for her. She reached for Kaitlin's hand and squeezed it tight as they shared a smile.

Erica looked around the room at all the smiling faces and said, "Mr. and Mrs. Vaughn and lovely ladies, if you'll excuse us, I'd like to reassess Sleeping Beauty now that she has returned from never-never land."

Everyone began to leave as Kaitlin added, "I promised Sierra we would get her something for her headache and I'd remove her catheter that she feels she no longer needs tickling her thighs."

Sydney bounced before Sierra. "Oh, please let me take it out, Sierra. Please! They wouldn't let me put it in so the least you can do is let me take it out."

Sierra squished her face with embarrassment. Kaitlin took Sydney by the shoulders and shoved her toward the door. "Out, Sydney! Now!"

Erica smiled at the beautiful group of women gathered in the doorway. "Sydney, we need to find you a woman in the worst way," she said playfully.

Everyone echoed together, "She finally has one," and burst into laughter.

Sydney shoved her hands in her pockets and shuffled her feet shyly. "I do have a wonderful woman that I love dearly. However, I was wondering, Erica, where were you when I had my ad in the personal section of the lesbian find-a-mate pages?"

Erica shook her beautiful head of dark, flowing ringlets and smiled deeply. "Probably with the woman of my dreams that I've been with for the past five years."

Sydney sighed with playful frustration and took one step closer. "Oh, she wouldn't have figured it out if you had answered my ad a year ago. I promise."

Erica laughed softly and stepped intimately close to Sydney's playful eyes. "Sydney, Adrianna is a prosecuting attorney and has recently been appointed to the bench as a court judge. What do you think she can't figure out?"

Sydney took one terrified step back and gulped her next breath. Erica laughed at her fearful expression and leaned closer to kiss her cheek. "Sydney, I have no need for lesbian find-a-mate ads. I truly love the woman who shares my pillow."

Sydney raised her hand to her kissed cheek and grumbled beneath her breath as she walked toward Sabrina and Logan, "A judge! Huh! I still think I would have been much more stimulating."

Erica shook her head at Sydney. "Sydney, does your lover know you advertised for a woman to quench your lesbian lust?"

Sydney smiled shyly and leaned back against the wall. "She's actually the one who helped me write that ad a year ago!" Sydney's thoughts were filled with Kelly's bouncing blonde locks and crystal blue eyes. "If I had only known then that she is my forever girl and the only woman who can fulfill my lesbian lust, then I could have saved so much money on advertising and wasted dates!" Sydney blushed and smiled. Logan guided her out of the room and gently closed the door to allow Erica to perform her assessment of Sierra.

Sierra reached for Erica's hand and squeezed softly. "Sydney loves to get women going, Erica. She's really harmless under all that shocking verbiage of hers."

Erica smiled as she held Sierra's hand. "She's a hoot. I would love for Adrianna to meet her. Now that would be an interesting verbiage battle."

Kaitlin's laughter filled Sierra's soul. "That's the truth. I can't wait for Adrianna to meet Sierra and Sydney."

"I'd better prepare her well in advance for this meeting. Now let's get you comfortable so we can have a good look at you, Sierra."

Sierra lay back down on her bed, being careful to take her catheter with her. "I shudder to think of how much people have already seen of me."

Erica and Kaitlin laughed at her shyness. Erica had one of the nurses bring Sierra two plain Tylenol for her headache while Kaitlin removed her catheter. They then spent an hour doing a thorough neurological exam on Sierra.

Sierra gingerly returned from the bathroom with Kaitlin and found Erica sitting on the edge of her bed, writing in her chart. Kaitlin guided Sierra down beside Erica and checked the IV in her hand. Sierra playfully leaned her shoulder against Erica and started reading her note.

Erica signed her name and slipped the chart onto Sierra's lap. "Since your admission, Sierra, I gave your lover full access to your chart. I hope that was okay with you."

"Of course, Erica. I appreciate you giving Kate access to my chart."

Kaitlin reached for a nearby chair and sat before Sierra and Erica.

Sierra reached for her hand as she leafed through her chart. She read each of Erica's meticulously written notes and was amazed at the severity of her symptoms when she arrived in the E.R. She read the report of her CAT scans and several of the nurse's notes. She began to close the chart as she came across her admission form; it listed Kaitlin as her next of kin, with her parents listed beneath. Kaitlin must have given that information to the admissions clerk and nobody obviously questioned her.

Sierra felt overwhelmed with intense love as she looked up at Kaitlin with teary eyes and slowly closed her chart.

Erica saw the depth of love in Sierra's eyes and smiled. "Do you have any questions for me, Sierra?"

Sierra turned to face Erica and brushed away her own tears. "When can I go home with Kate, Erica?"

Erica placed her arm around Sierra's shoulders and hugged her close. "How about if you stay here another night, and I'll reassess you in the morning. If everything checks out okay, then you're free to return to the Emerald City with the woman who cherishes you immensely. I hear that everyone up there has been wishing and praying for your speedy recovery, and that's exactly what you delivered."

Sierra smiled and squeezed Erica's hand. "Thank you, Erica, for everything."

Erica took Sierra into her arms and hugged her tight. "You're very welcome, Sierra. Just don't scare us like that again."

Sierra dried her eyes and watched Erica rise and squeeze Kaitlin's hand.

"Thanks, Erica. For everything," Kaitlin said.

Erica bent down and kissed Kaitlin's forehead. "You're very welcome, Kate. I'm glad I could help."

Erica slipped from the room and gently closed the door behind her as Sierra carefully slipped between Kaitlin's legs. Kaitlin reached out for her and pulled her into her arms.

Sierra reached up and held Kaitlin's emotional face in her hands. "I'm so sorry, baby. I never meant to scare you like this, and I never wanted to hurt you." Kaitlin held Sierra tightly in her arms and sobbed uncontrollably as she drained the terror and despair that had clung to her heart for three long days.

⟳ **18**

Kaitlin helped Sierra slip into her brown corduroy slacks and saw the waist hang loosely against her. Kaitlin hooked her finger into the waist and tickled Sierra's belly button. "This will not do, Ms. Vaughn. Gladys is going to take one look at you and accuse me of keeping you in a concentration camp for the past four days."

They both laughed as Kaitlin watched Sierra slip into her cream turtleneck and tuck it into her slacks. "Just take me home, baby, and I promise to dispel Gladys's concentration camp accusations. I can't wait to get home and see Gladys and Licorice and tell them how yucky the hospital food is! Thank God you bought me much more edible food."

Kaitlin smiled as she clasped Sierra's necklace behind her neck and kissed her pale cheek. "Gladys and Licorice are dying to see you as well, my love." Kaitlin stared into Sierra's vibrant blue eyes and brushed her lips gently against hers. She slowly began to back away as Sierra reached for her face and guided her back with intense urgency. She leaned her lips toward Kaitlin's and kissed her softly. Kaitlin emitted a sensuous gasp that raced through Sierra's veins and ignited her aching passion. She stared into Kaitlin's shimmering, wanton eyes and kissed her with fiery passion.

The door to Sierra's room burst open, and Sabrina, Logan, and Sydney trampled through. Sydney stepped right up to their passionate kiss and dramatically cleared her throat. "Excuse me, but I do believe this woman is going to need more oxygen if you keep sucking on her face like that, Dr. Bradley."

Kaitlin never missed a beat as she reached out and shoved Sydney back onto Sierra's bed. Everyone burst into laughter. Kaitlin and Sierra hugged and kissed each of the girls.

Erica appeared in their doorway with a gorgeous woman dressed in a fitted, purple pinstriped skirt suit at her side. Sierra watched Kaitlin turn and smile deeply.

"Adrianna!" They hugged each other warmly as Kaitlin kissed Adrianna's forehead. "How lovely to see you!"

Adrianna smiled warmly into Kaitlin's bright eyes. "It's so wonderful to see you also, Katie. Talking to you on the phone over these past four days isn't the same. I've been dying to come and see you and your miraculous Sierra ever since Erica told me what happened."

Kaitlin turned and saw Sierra smiling beside her. She reached out and placed her hand warmly on Sierra's back and introduced her to Erica's partner, Adrianna.

They all watched Adrianna hug Sierra warmly. Sydney wormed her way inconspicuously behind Sabrina and Logan and whispered, "Uh-oh! Here comes the judge!" Sabrina and Logan giggled sweetly.

Adrianna held Sierra close. "Erica and I are thrilled that you've done so well, Sierra. Erica calls you her miracle patient. She was so distraught that someone else that Katie cared about was hurt so badly that she came home and cried the day you were brought in."

Everyone looked up at Erica and watched her blush sweetly. "Oh, I'm just a big suck for adorable, injured lesbians."

Everyone laughed softly at her tenderness.

Adrianna looked into Kaitlin's loving eyes. "Erica and I have prayed since the day Quinn died that someone special would come into Katie's life, and it looks like our prayers have been answered. However, this is not the way I would have chosen to be introduced to you, Sierra. A simple phone call from you, Katie, would have been wonderful."

Adrianna looked beyond Sierra's shoulder at the smiling faces behind her. Sierra followed her gaze and softly took her hand.

"I'm sorry, Adrianna. Have you met my wicked stepsisters?"

Sydney cringed inside as she huddled closer behind Sabrina and Logan.

"I have had the pleasure of meeting Sabrina and Logan." Adrianna stepped toward them and hugged them both tight. "Hello, ladies. It's so nice to see you both again. But certainly not under these circumstances."

"We certainly agree with you there, Adrianna. However, it's so nice to see you again," Sabrina said.

Adrianna peered over Sabrina's shoulder at the woman doing a poor job of hiding. "And this must be Sydney, whom I've heard so much about," Adrianna said cautiously.

Sydney took a deep breath and coyly walked around Sabrina to take Adrianna's soft hand.

"I understand you had an ad you wished for my lover to answer," Adrianna said accusingly.

Everyone burst into laughter at Sydney's distress and watched Adrianna guide her closer. "Yes, your Honor, as a matter of fact I did. However, that was a very long time ago and Dr. Beaumont has made it very clear that she is much too busy to fluff my pillow and yours."

Everyone burst into laughter at Sydney's gutsy response. Adrianna struggled to stifle her laughter as she tried to give Sydney a stern look. "Sydney, I'm flattered by your interest in my lover. However, I rule that you take your ad out in someone else's newspaper. Have I made myself perfectly clear?"

Everyone tried to silence their giggles as they watched Sydney slowly inch backwards. "Loud and clear, your Honor. I say we adjourn this court before you take out your gavel and use my head as your desk!"

Everyone's laughter vibrated in the room. Adrianna reached toward Sydney, took her hand, and pulled her closer to the circle of women.

Sydney smiled at Adrianna and turned to Erica. "Where did you find this woman, Dr. Beaumont? I want one just like her."

Everyone laughed as Erica and Adrianna shared a knowing smile. They both looked over at Kaitlin, who was holding Sierra close in her arms. "They met right here five years ago, Sydney. I was doing my E.R. residency at the time when Adrianna's mother was admitted with seizures and a frontal brain tumor. We had her admitted to Erica's service, and she was actually a patient in this room. Adrianna and her family unfortunately witnessed her mother having a grand mal seizure as Adrianna screamed at Erica to do something to stop the seizures. I heard they were at each other's throats like two crazed female cats," Kaitlin explained.

Everyone laughed softly. Adrianna leaned back into Erica's loving arms.

"Later that same day they both finally calmed down and talked, and the rest, shall we say, is herstory," Kaitlin said.

Sydney looked over at Erica indignantly. "Is that what I've been doing wrong all these years? I try to be kind to the women I meet. You scream at this woman when her mother is having a grand mal seizure and she falls in love with you!" Sydney barely stopped to catch her breath and pointed at Kaitlin and Sierra. "You two practically want to kill each other the first moment you meet, and look at you now!"

Sierra snuggled deeper into Kaitlin's arms and kissed her cheek.

"What is this world coming to? I've been in love with the same damn woman for three years, and it takes these knuckleheads all that time to finally let me know that Kelly feels the same way! Ugggggggh! Why can't women communicate like civilized human beings instead of playing all these crazy mind games? I give up. This is all enough to make a devoted lesbian like myself go straight." Sydney dropped into Kaitlin's reclining chair and buried her face in her hands.

Erica stepped toward Sydney and gently placed her hand on her head. "Don't tell your lover that, Sydney. She might just have to take her own ad out in the lesbian find-a-mate pages." They all laughed as Sydney threw Erica a scowling look.

Erica stepped toward Sierra and reached out to take her hands. "I'm so thrilled to see how well you've recovered, Sierra.

You've quickly become one of my star patients, and I look forward to seeing you and Katie in my office in two weeks. Let's schedule your appointment last in the day so you two, and anyone who comes with you, can join Adrianna and me for dinner."

Sierra's eyes filled with tears as she stepped closer to Erica. "That sounds wonderful, Erica. I want to thank you for everything, especially for allowing Kate to be involved in all of my medical decisions."

Erica squeezed Sierra's small hands. "Are you kidding? This woman was like a bull in a china shop ploughing through everyone till she got the people she wanted involved in your care. She asked for me specifically to be your neurosurgeon, and when they told her I was in a board meeting she practically ripped the door off the hinges and hauled my sorry ass out of there to come see you!"

Everyone laughed at Kaitlin's impassioned determination. They watched her shyly look down at Sierra's beaming smile.

"Erica's exaggerating slightly, darling. I didn't rip the door off its hinges. I merely nudged it open with my foot." Kaitlin beamed Sierra a glowing smile.

Erica smiled at the intense emotions between Kaitlin and Sierra and felt elated to see Kaitlin so in love again. She gently squeezed Sierra's hands and leaned closer to her sparkling eyes. "Take care of your beautiful head for me, Sierra. Kaitlin will remove your scalp stitches in another five days, and we'll see you in two weeks. Just promise me that you won't get run over by any more Jet Skis or run into your bedroom unless you're absolutely, positively sure that it's Kaitlin or another equally good looking lesbian rummaging around in there."

"Hey! What do you mean another equally good looking lesbian?" Kaitlin stated indignantly.

"Kate and I are going to build a house with glass walls, so I won't ever have to guess who's rummaging around our home again."

324

Sydney sat bolt upright in her chair. "Even your bedroom walls? Man, Kelly and I are moving in with you guys!"

Everyone burst into laughter and shook their heads. Erica guided Sierra into her arms and held her tight. She leaned back and kissed Sierra's forehead.

Kaitlin hugged Erica tight and thanked her for everything. "I think it's about time that you and Adrianna paid us a visit at Bradley Bay," Kaitlin said warmly.

Adrianna stepped in beside Erica and slipped her hand into hers. Erica gave her a smile and turned back to Kaitlin. "We would love that, Katie. Especially since my star patient will be residing there. Each time we have come up to visit, we always feel saddened by the memory of Quinn's death. We need to start creating some happy memories."

Kaitlin reached out and touched Erica's arm. "Since the day Sierra arrived on my doorstep, Bradley Bay has been filled with soap bubbles and flying kites, butterflies and water balloon fights. I promise you that your next visit will fill you with happy memories like the ones Sierra fills us with every day."

Sierra reached up and kissed Kaitlin softly.

Erica and Adrianna hugged everyone good-bye and wished them all a safe journey home.

The girls grabbed Sierra's packed bags and helium balloons with get well messages. "Your parents are parked beside our Jeep, Sierra. They're going to follow us to Bradley Bay," Sabrina said, as she headed for the door.

"Thanks, Bri. Tell them we'll be right down." Sierra entwined her fingers in Kaitlin's. "That was so nice of you to invite my parents to stay with us at Bradley Bay."

"Your parents are great, Sierra, and they love you deeply. I knew they would be really worried if they couldn't watch your progress themselves for the next little while so when I invited them they jumped at the opportunity. They plan to stay for a week but I hope they will stay longer. After all, your dream was to have your parents know about us and share our love. I thought this was the best way to get your dream started off on the right foot."

"You are incredible, Kaitlin Bradley." Sierra slipped into her arms and hugged her tight as she watched her look around the room that had held their lives in a precarious balance for three days. Sierra gently tugged on Kaitlin's hand and smiled deeply. "Let's go home, my love. I need to properly thank the Wizard for giving me the Lion's courage and the Scarecrow's straw head to protect my brain. I also want to thank her for giving you the Tin Man's heart to continue walking beside me every painful step of the way. You never let go of my hand, Kate, or faltered along the way regardless of the obstacles put before you."

Kaitlin guided Sierra into her arms and held her tight. "My lighthouse always showed me the way."

Sierra leaned closer and kissed Kaitlin softly, whispering against her moist lips, "Take me home, baby. We need to sit on our back deck and celebrate the beginning of our life together."

Kaitlin kissed her deeply and guided her into the awaiting wheelchair. Sydney spun the wheelchair around and made engine-revving noises before she dashed a giggling Sierra toward the elevator.

Kaitlin shook her head and laughed. She stopped in the doorway and looked back into Sierra's empty room one final time. She reached for the light switch and turned out the light, then left Sierra's room and all its painful memories for the final time.

☙ 19

One week after Sierra left the hospital Kaitlin threw her a huge welcome home party. All of their friends and Sierra's parents were there to shower Sierra and Kaitlin with their love and to welcome Sierra to her new address. Everyone banded together and plotted to bring Sierra gifts that she could use to help her survive in northern Ontario. She received everything from cans of bug spray to a book on how to treat snakebites.

Sabrina and Logan bought Sierra a pair of water wings and a floating lounge chair. Sydney and Kelly bought her a football helmet to protect her fragile skull and a copy of the book, *The Joy of Lesbian Sex.* Sydney stressed that the helmet and book were not intended to be used at the same time.

Gladys made Sierra a very touching, personal photo album filled with her precious pictures of Kaitlin's childhood. She put in several blank sheets and inserted a small note:

Dearest Sierra,

> *I have passed on to you my treasured memories of my life with Katie. Now I ask you to continue to fill these pages with her beautiful smile that radiates from your profound love.*

Sierra cried when she opened Gladys's gift and read her note. She told Gladys that this was the greatest gift she could have given her.

Sierra teased and badgered Kaitlin all evening long to try and find out what gift she had bought to help her survive in cottage country. Kaitlin tried to put her off and continuously changed the subject till she finally caved in to Sierra's insistent, playful prodding.

Kaitlin took Sierra's hand and guided her up the back deck steps as she stared totally transfixed at Sierra's shapely petite frame dressed in a raspberry, sleeveless, chunky-rib sweater and matching stretch pants. She looked ravishing and delectable. Kaitlin had to remind herself several times that they were surrounded by people as her hands itched to race beneath that chunky sweater.

Sierra took advantage of Kaitlin's distracted gaze as she cleverly scooped a glass of white wine from the buffet table. She was just about to bring it to her lips when Kaitlin stopped her in mid flight and eased the glass from Sierra's hand. Kaitlin set the wine glass back on the buffet table and guided Sierra into her arms. She floated her fingers over Sierra's scalp laceration and smiled at the look of total indignation narrowing those exotic teardrop, blue-gray eyes.

"Just one sip of wine, baby. That's all I ask for!"

Kaitlin playfully rolled her eyes as she listened to Sierra's whining argument. She held Sierra close and kissed her forehead. "Not while you're still on your medication, Sierra. Please be reasonable."

Sierra crossed her arms across her chest and buried her pouty face in Kaitlin's neck. "That's so unfair! Whose party is this anyway?"

Kaitlin tried so hard not to laugh as she held Sierra close. "It's your party, sweetheart, and I thought you were just bursting to find out what I bought you."

Sierra rested her hands intimately on Kaitlin's slender waist and glared at her with those shimmering eyes. "Now, you're changing the subject, baby."

Kaitlin entwined her hand in Sierra's and brought her hand to her lips, gently brushing her lips across her knuckles. She kissed the back of her hand and trailed her lips across her wrist, stirred by the bounding pace of Sierra's pulse.

Sierra sighed heavenly and rested her cheek against Kaitlin's. "What were we just arguing about, baby?"

Kaitlin kissed Sierra's closed eyelids and whispered, "You're such a pushover, my darling."

Sierra beamed Kaitlin her breathtaking smile as she tauntingly brushed her lips against hers. "I bet if you allowed me to have a glass of wine you could really have your way with me."

Kaitlin burst into her rich, deep laughter and took Sierra by the hand, guiding her to the sliding glass doors. "Nice try, Ms. Vaughn. But that still won't get you a drop of wine."

Sierra seductively brushed her body against Kaitlin's as she ran her hands over Kaitlin's camel, silk twill pants. Her eyes leisurely roamed across her v-neck, stretch silk top that hugged Kaitlin's breasts like a second skin. She hungered to have Kaitlin alone and peel that alluring top away and taunt those firm breasts to a rigid peak. She slid her hand across Kaitlin's slender belly and slinked in through the open door. "You're loss, Dr. Bradley."

Kaitlin dashed into the kitchen after her and sent Sierra into a fit of giggles as she held her tight from behind. She lingered her hand along Sierra's thigh and under her sweater, brushing her fingertips along the soft underside of Sierra's naked breast.

Sierra groaned deliriously as she arched back against Kaitlin, craving more of her sensuous touch.

Kaitlin darted her lips along the slender column of Sierra's neck and nibbled on her tiny earlobe. "We'll see if you need a glass of wine for me to have my way with you, my darling."

Sierra spun in Kaitlin's arms and ran her fingers into her thick, lush hair, holding her firmly in her hands. She stared at her full, moist lips and gleaming emerald green eyes. "I'm yours for the taking, Kate. Now and forever."

Kaitlin gripped Sierra's waist and guided her to sit on their kitchen island while she slipped between her thighs. She held Sierra's face in her hands and slid her thumbs across her cheeks. Their lips met slowly, softly till their aching need consumed them and their tongues ravaged and plunged, straining to fill a swirling need.

Kaitlin rested her forehead against Sierra's and struggled to catch her next breath. "I want you like I've never wanted another woman, Sierra. Please remind me to thank your parents for bringing you into this world for me."

Sierra kissed Kaitlin's cheek and leaned back slightly. "Where are those wayward wanderer's anyway? Do you think my parents are still playing bridge at Gladys's place? We haven't seen them in hours."

"I believe they are still at Gladys's. Apparently Gladys gathered quite a senior crowd and the last I heard it was a pretty rowdy game of bridge. Sabrina and Logan took them up the fixings for margaritas and they came back saying the geriatric crowd was totally out of control."

Sierra shook her head as she thought of all the wonderful times she had shared with her parents and Kaitlin over the past week. Memories that she would carry with her for a lifetime.

"Gladys said not to worry. She promises to keep your parents safe at her place. After hearing Sabrina and Logan's report it sounds like they may never leave Gladys's place."

Sierra laughed as she hugged Kaitlin tight. "At this rate my parents may never leave Bradley Bay."

"That wouldn't bother me in the least."

Sierra nestled tight into Kaitlin's embrace and felt the greatest peace and happiness she had ever experienced.

Kaitlin brushed her lips across Sierra's temple and kissed the tip of her tiny nose. "Ready for your gift, my darling?"

Sierra clapped her hands together with childlike glee as Kaitlin smiled at her endearing charm.

"All right, my precious darling. Let me give you a hint as to where you can find your gift."

Sierra bounced with unrestrained excitement as Kaitlin leaned forward and kissed her deeply. She leaned back slightly and whispered against Sierra's sensuous lips, "It is somewhere in this house where we have made love."

Sierra leaned back from Kaitlin and gave her an impatient pout. "That's no hint, baby. We've made love in every room of this house and on every piece of furniture."

Kaitlin laughed sheepishly and gently nipped at Sierra's pillowy, lower lip. "Well, then, I guess that's not a very helpful hint."

Sydney walked into the kitchen and reached into the fridge to grab a couple of beers, smiling at the passion displayed before her. She stepped up to the island and stood beside Kaitlin as she watched her consume Sierra's lips. Sydney smiled and took a sip of her cold beer.

"I hate to interrupt, ladies, but I'm dying to know. Sierra, did Katie give you her gift yet?"

Sierra turned to Sydney with smiling eyes. "No, Syd! She won't tell me where she hid it. I'm trying my best here to pry it out of her!"

Sydney burst into laughter and took another sip of beer. "Why don't I save you the time and energy. Katie said something about hiding it beneath her favorite spice."

Sierra squealed with absolute delight as she clapped her hands together and jumped off the island.

Kaitlin glared at Sydney and grabbed a bottle of beer away from her as they both watched Sierra dig into the kitchen cupboard. She reached for the jar of cinnamon and saw a white envelope perched against it. Sierra grabbed the cinnamon and envelope and pulled them both out of the cupboard. She looked at her name written beautifully across the envelope in Kaitlin's flowing penmanship and squealed with excitement. She bounced back up on the island and sat before Kaitlin. She handed Sydney the jar of cinnamon and tore open the envelope with the exuberance of a child on Christmas morning.

Sydney looked at the jar in her hand and frowned. "Cinnamon. Cinnamon is your favorite spice, Katie?"

Sierra and Kaitlin burst into laughter as Kaitlin leaned forward and kissed the tip of Sierra's nose. "It sure is, Sydney. It sure is."

Sydney looked at them both with a puzzled frown and set the cinnamon down. "I don't think I want to hear the story behind that one."

Sierra stared down at the gift in her hands in total shock. She finally looked up with teary eyes and stared into Kaitlin's loving face. "The Cayman Islands! Kate, you bought us tickets to the Cayman Islands!"

Kaitlin set down her beer and stepped intimately between Sierra's thighs. "Yes, my darling. I'm taking you for a two-week, sun-filled vacation to the Cayman Islands. I told you when you arrived here, Sierra, that this is the Emerald City, a place where wishes come true."

Tears rolled down Sierra's cheeks as she felt her words catch in her throat. She set the airline tickets down on the island and reached for Kaitlin's face. "I love you so much, baby. You are my wish come true."

Sydney smiled as she watched them unite in a deep, passionate kiss.

Sabrina and Logan strolled into the kitchen hand in hand. "We've been looking for you, Sierra. Looks like everything is ready," Sabrina said.

Sierra's face beamed with delight as she slipped off the island and entwined her fingers in Kaitlin's hand. She folded the airline tickets and slipped them into Kaitlin's pocket.

Kaitlin frowned and looked at Sabrina and Logan. "What's ready?"

Sierra took her hand and held it close to her chest. "I have a little surprise for you, sweetheart. Come down to the dock and I'll show you what they mean." Sierra turned to Sabrina and Logan. "Are my parents and Gladys on the dock?"

"They sure are. It's just starting to get dark and they can't wait a minute longer. They're the ones that told us to get a move on and get you guys down there. They're like a bunch of kids at an amusement park. They're just so thrilled to share this with everyone," Sabrina beamed.

Kaitlin looked from one woman to the next trying to decipher what was going on.

Sierra loved the baffled look on her face and couldn't wait to see her reaction. She gently tugged on Kaitlin's hand and guided her toward the sliding glass doors. "Let's go, baby. I have a wonderful surprise for you."

They all arrived on the dock to find all the guests crowded around holding an unlit candle. Kaitlin stood before Gladys and Sierra's parents and searched their ecstatic smiles. "All right, you guys. What's going on? Why is everyone standing around like this? The music's not that bad, is it?"

Gladys handed Kaitlin a tall white candle and squeezed her hand tight. "Be patient, sweetheart. Sierra has something she wants to give you."

Sierra stood before Kaitlin and lit her candle. She ignited her own candle from Kaitlin's and passed the flame onto Gladys. Kaitlin watched in awe, as each and every candle was lit one by one.

Sierra looked up into her radiant emerald green eyes and touched her arm. The flickering flame of their candles illuminated her vibrant face. The full moon above lit the dock with its lustrous beams as the stars blazed against the azure sky.

"You once told me, Kate, that your wish was to have the Lion's courage, the Scarecrows brain and the Tin Man's heart to keep your dream alive. Well, look around you, Kate. Tonight we all light a candle in support of your courage, intelligence and heart for what you have done here at Bradley Bay."

Kaitlin's vision blurred with tears as she looked down at her burning candle. Her chest swelled with emotion as she looked up at the woman who captivated her heart.

Sierra entwined her hand in Kaitlin's and looked around at all the guests. "On the count of three I would like everyone to blow out their candle and make a wish." Sierra stared into Kaitlin's shimmering eyes before she started her count. "One, two, three."

Everyone was pitched into darkness for mere seconds till a brilliant light blazed from the north shore of Bradley Bay. Everyone burst into wild applause and cheers as Kaitlin guided Sierra to the edge of the dock and squinted to capture the image of what she was seeing.

"A lighthouse. Sierra, it's a miniature lighthouse out there on the north rim."

Sierra squeezed her hand and beamed with joy. "That it is, my darling. It's the new Bradley Bay Lighthouse."

Kaitlin looked at Sierra in pure shock and delight as she pointed at the lighthouse and back at Sierra in dumbfounded shock. "How? When? Where in the world did you find a miniature lighthouse and how did you get it there without my knowledge?"

Sierra smiled victoriously as she leaned closer to Kaitlin. "Well, when one is shopping for a miniature lighthouse it helps to have parents in the real estate business. And it's not so miniature. That thing stands six feet tall."

Kaitlin looked over at Sierra's parents and felt engulfed by their love and excitement.

"The how and when is easy. There was no bridge game at Gladys's place tonight. The margaritas were taken over to the north rim where the recreation staff and the geriatric crowd were busy putting the lighthouse on its final resting place for us."

Kaitlin reached for Gladys's hand and held her close. "You were part of all this and you didn't tell me?"

"It's been so much fun to surprise you with Sierra's gift, Katie."

Kaitlin reached forward and kissed Gladys's cherub cheek before turning back to Sierra. "This is so incredible, sweetheart. I'm truly overwhelmed by all this."

"That lighthouse symbolizes everything that you and Bradley Bay stand for, Kate. It is a beacon of light and hope. People can look at that light and know that it will provide a safe harbor from life's difficulties. You said when you look at a lighthouse you feel safe and secure. I want you to feel that way

334

every day when we look at that lighthouse together. You once told me that your goal was to have quadriplegic and paraplegic adults come to Bradley Bay to discover their potential and not focus on what they'd lost. You want them to get back on the yellow brick road mentally and emotionally stronger in order to find their own way home. Well our lighthouse will now be here to help guide them, Kate. Just as you have done for three years."

The tears coursed down Kaitlin's cheeks as she guided Sierra into her arms and hugged her tight. "Thank you, sweetheart. That is the greatest gift I have ever received."

Kaitlin looked around at the crowd and back at Sierra. "If everyone is here with us then who turned the lighthouse on when we blew out the candles?"

"I did, Kate."

Everyone turned to watch an electric wheelchair hum its way around the back of the crowd and across the dock ramp.

"Jennifer."

Jennifer beamed her gorgeous smile at Kaitlin and stopped before her. She reached down on her lap and used both her arms to raise a remote box to Kaitlin. "Here is your remote timer for the lighthouse, Katie. Sierra called me at home and told me about her gift. She asked if I would come down and be the one to turn it on for you for the first time. I was honored. You and everyone at Bradley Bay are responsible for making my journey as smooth as it could be. The least I could do was light your way, Kate."

Kaitlin kneeled before Jennifer and gathered her tight in her arms. She kissed her softly and set her back in her chair. "Thank you, Jen. That was beautiful. That means so much to me that you are the one to turn on our lighthouse."

Jennifer leaned her forehead against Kaitlin's and kissed her cheek. "I think Sierra was just afraid that no one else could figure out the timer."

Everyone burst into laughter as Kaitlin touched Jennifer's face and rose to her feet.

335

"Sierra has something else she wants to give you, Katie." Jennifer reached in along her thigh and gripped a thin, flat package with her arms and handed it to Sierra.

"Thank you, Jen."

Sierra held the beautifully wrapped pink package in the palms of her hands and extended it to Kaitlin. "This is for you, baby."

Kaitlin leaned towards Sierra and touched her chin with the soft pad of her thumb. Their lips met slowly in a sensuous, burning kiss that equaled the heat of their passion. "You are truly incredible, Sierra Vaughn."

Kaitlin looked down at the gift and admired the beautiful pastel pink and purple wrapping paper and ribbons. She stared into Sierra's ecstatic eyes and watched her clap her hands with childlike glee.

"Open it, baby. It's from me to you."

Kaitlin slowly removed the wrapping paper and handed it to Gladys. In her hands she held a velvety, emerald green journal. Kaitlin ran her fingertip across the gold embossed letters on the cover and read softly:

Kaitlin and Sierra
Life at Bradley Bay

Kaitlin looked up at Sierra with teary eyes. Sierra brushed away her tears and said softly, "This is our journal, baby. You and I together are going to record all of our wonderful memories at Bradley Bay. I chose an emerald green journal because green signifies love, harmony, and balance. And those are three things that you bring into my life."

Kaitlin leaned her forehead against Sierra's and caressed their new journal. "It's beautiful, my darling. Absolutely beautiful. I would be honored to share our life in this journal."

Sierra kissed Kaitlin softly and whispered against her lips, "Look inside, baby."

Kaitlin wiped at her tears and slowly bent back the cover. Her breath caught in her throat and her heart beat wildly. She traced her finger along the silky green page divider and stopped at the knot securing a band of solid emeralds. She slowly released the knot and handed Sierra the ring.

Everyone strained forward to see as Sierra slipped the spectacular emerald band on Kaitlin's ring finger. "A symbol of my love for you, Dr. Kaitlin Bradley. You're my forever girl."

Kaitlin reached up and caressed Sierra's radiant face. "And you are my forever girl, Sierra Vaughn."

Their lips met slowly, tenderly, igniting the flaming passion that burned in their souls. Everyone broke into uproarious applause and cheers. The Bradley Bay Lighthouse circled its beam of light once again, casting the shoreline with its rays of hope.

Ana P. Corman

ABOUT THE AUTHOR

I spent the summer after I graduated from nursing school working in a resort. I remember walking along the edge of the lake and bravely dipping my toes into the ice-cold water. I watched the ripples extend outward from my reflection and wondered where those ripples would take me from that moment on. Seventeen years later I look back on the journey of those ripples that brought me to write my novel, *Bradley Bay*.

Since leaving the resort I spent six years working in a Neurosurgical Intensive Care Unit caring for spinal cord-injured adults. Those patients taught me the lessons of patience, hope and the strength of the human spirit. The essence of my story are those patients that profoundly touched my life.

I have been blessed to experience the beauty of love between women. It is that depth of understanding, passion and respect that I enjoy exploring through my stories.

I currently live in Arizona with my partner of ten years and our governing cat. I have also written the novel entitled, *Tender Heart* that was published by 1st Books Library in 2000.

Also available from 1st Books
Library books by

Ana P. Corman

Tender Heart

1st BOOKS LIBRARY
http://www.1stbooks.com

Sincere thanks to
Great Bear Log Homes
for graciously providing the cover photo.

www.greatbearloghomes.com

Printed in the United States
2701